A May Day Anthology

Highland Miracle
Christine Young

Defying the Odds
C.L. Kraemer

Love in Bloom
Rosemary Indra

No More Poodle Skirts
Genie Gabriel

Published by Rogue Phoenix Press
Copyright © 2013

ISBN: 978-1-62420-049-6

Cover Artist: Designs by Ms G

Printed in the United States of America

Highland Miracle
Christine Young

Chapter One

New York City 1895

"I dinnae ken what this contraption could be. I must be aff my heid," he said reverting back to the old language his great grandfather had spoken from time to time. Sean Michael Sterling walked around the tall red object he'd just come across in Central Park. His heart thundered with the realization this was an anomaly and for some reason...

"Is this a fire hydrant?" he murmured totally intrigued. Cautiously stepping closer, he rested a hand on the object of his fascination. The hackles on the back of his neck stood on end. The thing was smooth and touching it sent shivers up his spine. If this was a hydrant, it sure could hold a ton of water.

For some reason...his mind shifted and he thought time machine—Jules Verne—his favorite book.

He leaned in and smelled, nothing, just the scent of metal. He didn't recognize the odor. When he stepped back, he caught a hint of Daphne floating on the air. A slight breeze sifted through the meadow, filling his senses with new cut grass, wet dog, and something he couldn't quite identify.

Thoughts of pixie dust came to mind.

I am off my head.

A small dog ran around his heels, yipping and barking. "Crazy dog." Sean leaned down and rubbed the dog's ears. "You look like a bandit. Wonder where you came from? Go on, now. Where's your owner?"

The dog sat down, wagging his tale and stared at him. It seemed the animal was telling him he wasn't going anywhere. "Now, Bandit, you need to go find your owner. I'm not one to be taking you home with me. Don't think my landlord would appreciate a dog in the building."

Strangely he was the only one in the park, or at least this corner of it. The sound of carriages could be heard in the distance. He suddenly felt isolated and completely alone. The damn thing compelled him to know more, seeming to reach out to him and beckon. An eerie keening started in the back of his mind and grew. The impulse to explore overwhelmed him. Even as he looked at the machine, his mind cautioned him to stay away, but his curiosity sprouted to an uncanny level.

A little voice in the back of his head urged him forward. Damn, but he needed to go home. His stomach growled complaining of hours without food. His eyes burned from the fire he'd just been on and his body cried out for sleep. Rubbing his sooty hair, he muttered to himself.

But thoughts of what was inside this monster contraption intrigued him more than the demands of his body.

Walking around the monstrosity, he kept his hand on the metal all the while looking for an opening. What shocked him and what was more surprising was the fact that little Bandit found the opening for him.

Bandit sat down in front of what appeared to be a door and stared at him again. It seemed to Sean Bandit dared him to see what was inside. Well, he'd never been a man who could resist a straight on challenge.

Caution...

He inhaled a long and very deep breath. Closing his eyes he counted to ten. Even though the day was cool, sweat beaded on his forehead. He walked into fires, lifted burning timber, and he'd never really been afraid a day in his life.

This contrivance terrified him.

Nerves snapping, Sean pushed on the door. It slid sideways, revealing a dark abyss. He stepped back. Fear raced through him, caution cried out to him but he ignored all warnings.

Curiosity propelled him forward.

Bandit ran inside. "No," Sean cried out. "Dinnae....

Silence chilled him to the bone and a cold sweat broke out on his body. Birds chirped in nearby trees.

All seemed right with the world—except for this machine.

"Come here." He crouched down and called to Bandit. Bandit didn't budge. Instead the dog cocked his head to one side and seemed to be saying. *You come here.*

Sean wavered then stood his ground. Bandit seemed to like it in the machine.

And yet...

An extraordinary golden dust swirled around him, warming him like a golden rain.

~ * ~

"I do believe he's going to need a wee bit of nudging," Erin said to Adair. "This god-faerie business is harder than I thought it would be." She fluttered around Sean, hands on hips, seemingly exasperated with the man.

"More than a bit," Adair said in an understanding tone. In his mind Sean would need to be hog tied and thrown in to that monstrosity. Adair had never known time travel existed until he'd seen this. He wouldn't get into the machine unless he was hog tied. Yet he would have to, because he would have to travel with Sean.

Erin sighed, the noise a soft sound in the early morning breeze. She looked to the heavens as if help would come from above. "He will never find his true love, his soul mate if we can't get him inside. See, even Bandit can't lure him. I thought with that wee dog, we wouldn't have any problem."

"He's a stubborn man. A bit of faerie dust will not our difficulties unravel."

3

"I know..." Erin agreed completely. *"We have to get him to Scotland by the May Day celebration in the year of our Lord, 1621."*

"And we will. He will be on his way today." At least Adair hoped he could lure Sean inside before people started milling around the gadget. If that happened, he didn't want to see the results. Some stranger could be on his way and all of Erin's and his efforts would be in vain.

"So, Adair, do you have any ideas?" Erin asked as she tapped her little toe on the meadow grass.

"Not yet, but I'm thinking real hard." He was too, but there wasn't really anything they could do. A bit more faerie dust, another whisper in his ear then what? He surely didn't know. All he did know was their efforts had to get the desired results. If his intuition was right, they had about ten minutes left.

Erin fluttered around Sean's head, *"Go inside, go, you can you know,"* she whispered as Adair showered golden dust around Sean. *"You can do it. It's not hard and you will be forever and eternally happy."*

Sean stepped forward then back, rocking on his heels. He appeared to be on the brink. Both hands rested on either side of the door. A little push would get him through. Erin's words seemed to filter past the fear.

"Go inside," Adair said. *"Find your true love, seek your fate for it does not rest here in New York but in the highlands of Scotland."*

"You must trust in your god faeries. Trust, trust, trust..." she chanted softly into Sean's ear.

"For you a miracle will occur. Just step inside and take that final step toward true happiness," he told Sean. *"Please."*

~ * ~

Sean hit the side of his head. "I'm hearing things." *Meet my true love, a soul mate, find a miracle in the highlands...?*

Trust?

Who the devil am I supposed to be trusting? There isn't anyone around. I'm the sole person in Central Park. But he leaned forward, inching his way closer to the portal of the crazy machine. He'd be pure loco if he stepped inside but Bandit seemed fine. The dog had disappeared a couple of times into the darkness only to return again, sit down and bark at him.

I can do this.

He stood half in and half out, inhaled deeply then stepped inside. Behind him the door clanged shut. He jumped out of his skin at the realization he might be trapped.

The quiet was eerie then suddenly lights began to blink and something hummed. It was as if the machine had sprung to life. His nerves sizzled and terror crawled down his spine. He searched the room for the dog.

Bandit sat on a chair in front of a panel of buttons and blinking lights. It appeared the dog meant to drive this contraption. But drive it where?

Oh, to his one true love, to his soul mate and a miracle. Sean let out a loud roaring laugh.

Praying it wasn't too late, Sean turned to leave. But the door was shut tight, and he couldn't find another way out. Banging on the door did not make it open. He ran his hands up and down his arms in hopes of warding off the deathly chill seeming to take over his body as well his senses.

Bandit jumped from his perch and sauntered to the wall where he pulled down a handle and dog food poured into a bowl.

Well, at least the dog wouldn't starve.

"Please sit down and fasten your seat belt."

Sean jumped and looked around for the source of the voice. His heart raced as if it was going to run right out of his body.

"We are getting ready for take off. Please sit down and fasten your seat belt," the voice repeated.

A big red arrow pointed to a seat and there appeared to be a belt of sorts dangling from the chair. *Hell, what's a seatbelt?*

Feeling no real threat, Sean did as the voice commanded. He found the chair comfortable and the seatbelt acceptable. He wondered what it was for but soon found out as his body was savagely thrust back against the chair and air whizzed from his lungs. He hoped Bandit had found a comfortable place where he was safe. At the moment he couldn't check because he was pretty sure his eyelids were plastered to his eyeballs.

Suddenly, he gasped for air, realizing he'd been holding his breath. The ride was smoother now less intense. He felt as if he were floating in air. His stomach churned and dizziness engulfed him.

More golden dust floated around him. He was sure he heard a soft female voice telling him not to be afraid.

Motion stopped. He felt an eerie sense of deja vu, a feeling of coming home then a trembling in his legs he couldn't control.

Bandit jumped and barked then the door slid open. Sean swallowed the lump in his throat and wiped his sweaty palms on his jeans. For what seemed like an eternity, he stood, staring at the opening and the green grass. Had he gone anywhere?

"Okay, it's time to act like the brave firefighter you always thought you were. Go find out what's out there." He whistled through his teeth then inhaled a long deep breath for courage. A silent, swift prayer rattled in his brain.

Slowly, and he hoped cautiously, he strode to the open door and peered outside. Bandit dashed to freedom.

"Bandit! Come here." He didn't think that dog ever obeyed a command. "Bandit, you don't know what's out there." Central Park he hoped.

Sean strode a few yards from the machine and peered around him. He saw rolling hills, a river and the most breath taking scenery he'd ever encountered. When he looked to his left, a beautiful and very huge lake rested among the hills.

"This isn't Central Park, Bandit."

~ * ~

"Look, Tia," Reagan said as she pointed toward a nearby hill. "What is it?"

"A handsome stranger," Reagan giggled, instantly transfixed by the man. "Coming to dance around the May Pole?" Reagan looked a little more closely. "Oh, it's the Laird of Sterling Castle. Why is he on foot?"

"You are not thinking what I think," Tia said. "You dinnae know who he is. He looks like the laird but then he doesn't."

"How do I look?" Regan asked, ignoring Tia and smoothing her skirts then hoping she looked beautiful enough to snare this man. She wanted to sweep the laird off his feet. This might be her one and only chance.

She heard the celebration in the background. She watched as all eyes rose to meet the Laird's. Her brother William's eyes were startled then guarded and thoughtful. Tia's were intrigued. Some of the others gazes were wary and distrustful. They were a superstitious lot here in the Highlands. But even as she watched the people around her, she could not fully keep her attention from the Laird who had never attended this celebration before.

She felt a curious draw as she met his piercing gaze. She had only once before seen the man. He was an illusive creature, usually keeping inside the walls of his castle. Rumor had it the castle was haunted and the ghost was a woman who kept him from finding true love or happiness.

"Who do you think he is and where did he come from?" Tia asked peering intently at the man. "I really don't think it's the Laird. No one has spoken to the man in years. He is so reclusive. A few months ago people were saying he had died."

The man possessed a calm air as if he knew and recognized all the people in front of him. His dark gaze was mysterious, and when he stopped walking, he stood as still as a rock, striking and in clothes she had never seen anyone wear before. She had thought then, though, it would not have mattered what he wore.

Regan could not draw her eyes from his and felt her flesh grow warm. The way he stared at her was unnerving. Her heart thundered beneath her chest. It seemed as if she knew this man from some long ago time.

But that wasn't possible.

It was May Day. The very air was filled with such excitement, and now this man was here as if sent for her and her alone. In the meadow maids and youths already danced around the Maypole. A man with a bear had the animal dancing circles upon his hind feet, and a marionette show was in progress. A flutist played in honor of King James, a group of Highlanders played the bagpipes. Noise and confusion flourished. The day was bright, clear blue, and so very beautiful.

She saw a strange gold dusting swirling and dancing in air around her. Instantly, she felt compelled toward the stranger. For a moment she thought someone spoke to her, encouraging her onward.

Reagan was grateful she'd taken so much time with her clothes. Her hose were white silk, and her little leather slippers were blue decorated with glass stones. Next to her flesh she wore a soft silk shift and over it a binding corset and three different petticoats. The dress was blue brocade, with stomachers in velvet, low-cut bodices, and half sleeves with scores of blue lace. Her facemask was covered with feathers and plumes. Her golden hair was done in ringlets, tied through with blue satin ribbons. When she'd looked at herself in the mirror, she had been quite pleased with the results.

So lost in thought, she had lost track of the man.

Until he stood next to her.

"A...hi," he said. "I'm Sean Michael Sterling." He stared at her with dark dangerous brown eyes as he crossed his arms on his chest.

"I'm Reagan." She moistened suddenly dry lips and smoothed her skirts. "You're not from here."

"No..."

A man of few words. "Where?" she cocked her head sideways. She held her breath suddenly a bit terrified of his answer. So, he wasn't the laird of Sterling Castle.

"New York city."

"Ah..." She'd never heard of the place. But then she was sure there were lots of cities she'd never heard of.

Sean ran his hands through his hair, his brows creasing as if he worried about something. "You guys dressed up for something?"

"Yes," she said cautiously. "It's the May Day celebration. Many a lass will find a husband today."

"Really," he said. "You planning on finding one?"

"I wasn't." *Not until you.*

"How does that work—husband finding?" he asked, a smile lighting up his face.

Some goodwife handed them each a ribbon. "Come on," she said. They joined the revelers singing and dancing around the Maypole. He appeared a bit awkward, but he followed along in good sport. "The goodwife claimed they would all be fertile, and bear many children, like the seeds of the harvest.

"You know..." she said, wondering why he asked.

The dancing stopped. "Look they are going to crown the princess of the May. Tia will be among those who might be chosen."

"People still do that?"

Sean's hand was on her arm. They stepped back with the revelers to watch the ceremony. Her heart pounded, thundering beneath her breasts.

Tia mounted the dais. They watched as her brother made her princess of the May. It was a glorious picture. Pretty pageantry for the poor people. Her brother stood before his people, and they cheered him. He raised his hands—the magnanimous landlord—and the crowd fell silent. With a flourish he announced the dance of the May.

The musicians began to play. The beat was slow and methodical then increasing in its pace. Men and women moved into one another's arms. She was suddenly whisked into strong arms and swirled about with startling finesse. Stunned, she looked up into Sean's eyes. They began to circle and circle. Regan tried to speak, to tell him what was about to happen if they didn't let go and stop this foolishness.

She stared into Sean's eyes. She saw their heated darkness. She felt faint. They were whirling to the feverish beat with its pagan thunder of drums. She heard chanting in her ear. But it seemed as if the words said were encouraging her to keep dancing.

"Now!" her brother commanded and the music stopped.

She tried to pull away, to free herself. But for some reason Sean hung on to her. She felt the force of his arms around her, felt a moment of panic then a magical golden dust settled around them.

She turned around dazed. Looking into the depth of his eyes. "You have just agreed to wed me, you know."

~ * ~

Erin clapped her hands together. "We did it, Adair. We did it!"

"Don't be too hasty. He can still refuse."

"Oh, I don't think he will. Did you see the way he looked at her? He was smitten the moment he set eyes upon her. Oh, it might take a bit of convincing, but we have faerie dust enough." Erin removed her little bag from her back and looked inside. It was still more than half full, and she was sure Adair had more.

This was all the way she had pictured the scene. The two of them dancing around the Maypole then swirling to the music. She batted her wings and flew around the two of them, chanting a single phrase.

"You are soul mates." So many times she said the four words she was sure they would start to believe.

"Do you think he may want to return to his Central Park?" Adair asked.

"Oh my, he couldn't possibly," Erin said, knowing he just might want to do that. They would have to figure out someway to get rid of the time machine.

"He could take her with him."

"She wouldn't want to go. It is too fearful for a lass or a lad to move forward in time. Why they even have electricity and...

"Telephones." Adair finished.

"So much more. She wouldn't know what to do."

"You think he will do better in this time?" Adair asked.

"Yes," Erin said and she knew she spoke the truth. When she closed her eyes, she saw Sean as a great and powerful lord. He would rule the land with compassion and purpose.

Chapter Two

"I have done nothing of the sort!" Sean all but yelled at Reagan. He ran his hands through his hair then stared heavenward.

"Please, you would not let go of my arm. We are handfasted."

"I don't understand anything." He slowly turned in a circle, seeming to study all that surrounded him.

"You do not know who you are?" Reagan asked. She would swear on a stack of bibles he knew exactly who he was. He was the Laird of clan Sterling, ruling over his part of the highlands. Yet he wasn't. But no one would be able to say naught, because no one really knew the laird.

"Of course I know who I am."

She looked at him, cocking her head to one side, waiting. "And, that is..."

"I am Sean Michael Sterling from New York City." He spoke as if she should know who he was and where he came from.

"I've never heard of this New York. Is it on the other side of the channel?" She stepped away from him, trying to gauge his visible anger and seeming frustration.

"The other side of what channel? New York is bounded by two rivers, the East and the Hudson."

"I've never heard of those."

"Where do you think I am?" he ran his finger through his long thick hair, his eyes appearing clearly dangerous.

"You are on Sterling lands in Scotland." She spoke with authority. "You are the laird of this land, part of Scotland."

"How did I get here? This morning I was walking though Central Park on my way home from work."

"How absurd. You don't work. You are the laird. Your clan does your work for you. I'm thinking you have gone quite loony."

"All-fired!"

"What did you say?"

"Basically the world has turned upside down. I couldn't be in Scotland. The fire hydrant—the bizarre machine I stepped into. You know I was a fireman," he breathed in softly a whisper of a curse whispered from his lips.

"What's a fire hydrant?" *What's a fireman?*

"I'll take you—show you. It's just over that hill," Sean said just before he turned and strode back in the direction from where she had first seen him. "Come on." He looked over his shoulder and motioned her to follow.

Reagan stood flat-footed for several seconds before she picked up her skirts and darted after him.

What on earth had come over the man? New York City... She had to shake her head a couple of times. He lived in a castle and he didn't work as a fireman. Granted, when there was a fire, he would help put it out. But he was laird. He ruled over his clansmen. He had not come from some place she'd never heard of. He lived in Sterling Castle. Lord, but I'm trying to convince myself. *He is but he isn't.*

"Slow down. If you want me to see this fire hydrant, you've got to wait for me."

She thought she heard him chuckle. He turned around, walking backwards up the hill with half-grin on his face. She'd never seen the laird grin like that. Most of the time the man went around with a frown on his handsome face. There was something different about his face too. She'd figure it out.

Reagan found herself drawn to this man, and she'd never even given Laird Sterling a second glance. He'd been too withdrawn for her. She liked men who had a bit of a sense of humor. Not that she would ever be given the choice. But still...a girl could dream.

They rounded the top of a hill and looked down into the valley below. Sean had stopped and she bumped into him as she came to a grinding halt.

"What is it?" she asked, panting and inhaling deep droughts of air. His pace had been faster than she was used to, his long strides eating up the ground.

"Nothing," he said a low growl in his voice.

"Nothing?" she parroted.

"It's not there." He hit his head with the side of his hand. "It's gone. The damn time machine has vanished."

"What is gone? This fire hydrant? The time machine?"

"You didn't believe me and now I don't believe myself."

She blinked, thinking about her next few words. He didn't appear angry, just frustrated and maybe a bit confused. "Let me show you where you live." She wondered just how cautious she needed to be with him.

"I don't think you can do that."

"You must have had a blow to your head. In time your memory will come back."

"My memory is fine and nothing has hit me in the head." His exasperation was evident in his tone.

They turned and headed north, walking quickly back to her family's estate. Heading into the stables, she selected two horses and had the stable hand saddle them.

She mounted easily and waited for Sean to do the same. He stood as if frozen to the ground, staring at the horse. He pushed his hair back from his forehead then whistled softly.

"What's wrong?" she asked, "mount up and we'll be on our way."

"Don't know how. Never ridden a horse before. Give me my motorcycle and I'll show you how it's done."

Motorcycle?

Perhaps this journey would have been faster by horse.

A stable hand seemed to recognize Sean's distress and gave him a boost. As if born to it, he mounted with ease. She gave him a few instructions and they were suddenly on their way.

Reagan brooded and listened to the sounds of the forests as they rode through. She paid close attention to the path they took, fearing Sean was really telling her the truth when he said he had no memory of this place. Then suddenly she reined in, pausing to look upon Sterling Castle.

It was a wondrous sight. The castle sat high atop an embankment. They rode around to the front where a long path led to the portcullis.

Trying not to stare at Sean, she gave a gentle nudge to her horse and led the way.

"This is my castle?" he asked hesitantly. "I live here?"

"You are laird of all these lands."

"I must have a twin. I've never seen any of this before today."

"Let's go on. Once you're inside perhaps you will start to remember." She felt a pang of unease settle around her. She was of two varying minds. On one hand she hoped he would never remember who he had been, and on the other...

Well, suffice it to say, if he remembered, she'd be sent packing and she would forever be disgraced. Her stepbrother had threatened to find a husband for her. And she knew whomever he found, the man would be old and rich. And she would be expected in his bed whenever he pleased. At the thought she felt a moment's panic settle in the pit of her stomach.

~ * ~

"We are on the verge of success," Erin said happily, fluttering her wings around Reagan's head. She didn't want to use any more faerie dust, truly hoping the couple would find a way.

"It's not going to be easy for Sean once he figures out he isn't in Central Park," Adair went on to say.

"He's a believer in Jules Verne and all that stuff the man writes. One would think he could wrap his head around time travel." Erin flew on ahead, checking out shadows and possible problems the little couple might have. As long as Reagan thought he'd bumped his head and was

having a momentary bout of forgetfulness, he'd be ok. "Didn't the man write something about time travel?"

"Don't know that one." Adair caught up with Erin. "What's going to happen with the servants and the rest of the clan. They aren't identical, you know."

"No one liked the laird. They will happily over look any discrepancies," Erin said, hoping she sounded confident.

"You think so?"

"Oh, I don't know," she said with exasperation. "But we are going to have to save our dust for emergencies. And we must believe in the little couple."

"I do. I believe we have done the right thing. But there are so many variables, I can't figure out how to block the bad ones."

Erin let out a long heavy sigh. For a few moments she hovered over the gatekeeper. "Here's our first test."

Reagan and Sean stood in front of the man at the entrance. Reagan stepped through but the man put up his hand to stop Sean then just as quickly moved away, bowing as he waved the couple inside.

Adair rubbed his temples as if he didn't believe he saw correctly. When he looked at Erin, she gave him an "I told you so look."

She flew in a tiny loop, arcing her back to get around in the circle then flew to Adair. When she cocked her head to one side, she was welcomed with a huge grin from Adair.

"I do hope everyone has the same reaction. I'm sure by now they have heard of the happenings at the May Day celebration and are expecting the pair.

A loud scream penetrated the idyllic scene. But it came from the future. Of that Erin was sure.

~ * ~

We are here? Sean queried as he searched the area for something familiar even though he understood in the pit of his stomach, he would not find what he sought. Wondering what was happening to him, he

15

stepped back for a moment. She was beautiful, her eyes large and blue, her hair a shimmering curtain of gold. Things could be worse.

"Yes," Reagan said, cocking her head slightly as if she were trying to understand his thoughts.

He dismounted awkwardly then handed the reins to the stable hand. Running his hands through his hair, he turned in a three hundred sixty degree circle. Bewilderment and frustration ate at him. He liked a well-structured life, hated confusion.

"I own this?" he paused. "That's a lot to take in." He strode from the stable then into the castle. "It's just like the picture books. I never thought to find myself in a castle let alone own one. I don't believe any of this, you know." He turned to confront Reagan then decided not to say anything. He had the distinct feeling he might be better off keeping his thoughts to himself.

"Yes, everything here and the surrounding lands are yours. Come, I will show you around."

"How do you know this castle so well?"

"The Sterlings are friends to my family, well my father's family."

"But not you?" He felt as if he had known Reagan forever. A fierce need to protect her from whatever villainy abounded in this time surged through him and a strange possessiveness filled him.

"I am the bastard daughter. My father had an affair with an actress, my mother. She never told him about me until she was on her deathbed. He begrudgingly took me in, gave me food, shelter and clothing. In return I tried to stay out of his way and obey all of his wishes. Now he has passed on and I must keep away from his son who begrudges me all but the basics."

He stopped then turned to Reagan. "What are my duties? As laird of the castle and the surrounding lands, what is expected of me?"

"You rule over disputes, make sure your people are taken care of in times of need, open your castle to them if there are invaders..."

"Is that all?" he said, thinking he could do much more for his people. "What am I like? Do I love this land and my people? Am I evil and corrupt?"

Reagan shrugged small shoulders. "Really, none of those things. You rarely come out of your castle. In deed, your visit to the May Day celebration was a huge surprise."

"So, I'm a recluse."

"I suppose."

"So, this man is a twin in looks but not disposition."

"I don't understand. How can you have a twin if you are from somewhere else?"

"Because I am not the Sean Michael Sterling who owns this castle. But I would like to know where he is."

She gave him a look he couldn't' read.

"If you are not Lord Sterling who are you? Why do you have the same name and the same look?"

"I can't answer any of your questions though I wish I could. I am beginning to think I have traveled backwards in time. Sort of like the Jules Verne story and now I must figure out a way to live here."

"I dinna ken what you are speaking of. If I were you, I would keep all this about time travel to yourself. I wouldnae want anyone to think you were possessed or perhaps a witch. Here in the highlands we are a superstitious lot."

"Point well taken. Then I should pretend I am someone I am not at least until that someone returns. When that happens, I will be punished for pretending to be someone else. Hmm...it seems it is a tangled web we weave."

"You cannae be punished for pretending to be yourself." Her tone spoke of exasperation and frustration.

He wondered how he could pretend. He would have to start immediately, and he wasn't used to giving orders. In his life he obeyed the orders of his boss and in his home life he was by himself—a recluse too. Perhaps he had more in common with Laird Sterling than he would want to admit.

"Now that you are home, I must return to mine. I will have a great deal to answer for. I am not supposed to leave the estate without permission."

"Then I will see you home. I do not wish to see my future bride punished for helping me in my hour of distress."

"Thank you, but you don't have to. I'll understand..."

"What? There is no chivalry here?"

Reagan smiled at him, but he didn't feel as it the smile was soul deep. "For the right people," she told him. "If you are wealthy, privileged..."

"And who is that?" He felt a reaction he was unaccustomed to fill his body.

"The royals," she shrugged.

He wanted to wrap his arms around her and tell her everything would work out. *Everything happens for a reason.* But he couldn't ease her misgivings. He had too many of his own.

"He, William, will do what he thinks is right," Reagan went on to say.

"No, he won't." Sean's fists clenched, determination to keep this woman safe. He had never been political, but he'd been raised by a strong woman, a woman who taught him no one should be abused. There were things one could fight for in this life, and women's rights was one of them.

She tipped her head slightly to one side and her huge blue eyes filled with moisture. His heart nearly wrenched apart at the sight.

"You might be able to do something while you are there, but when you leave..."

She left the sentence unfinished. He didn't like where his thoughts took him. "You will come with me then. You said the May Day ceremony was good enough for us to be considered legally wed, although I plan to give you a proper wedding." *With the funds of another man...*

"You don't have to say that."

"Of course I do. You will teach me everything I need to know, and I will protect you with all that I am and all that I have."

Reagan's hand rose to her face to wipe a tear from her cheek. "You will not regret this, I promise you."

"Why do you speak of regret? We have entered into a bargain, which is mutually beneficial. There will be no misgivings." Perhaps in time we will fall in love, although he had to admit, at least to himself, he was more than half way there.

"Come, I must get you home so we can pack your belongings. I want you in Sterling Castle tonight."

"So soon?" she sounded breathless and the question hung in the air with a note of disbelief.

"Yes," Sean said with grim determination. He heard so much and yet too much. He didn't trust his actions if he found signs of abuse mental or physical.

By the time they reached Reagan's home, dusk had descended. A full moon rose above the hills, and a soft breeze seemed to whisper Reagan's name.

The hall shone brilliantly with lights, and when Reagan's brother heard them, he was in the stable just after they had dismounted.

Before Sean could do or say anything, William grabbed Reagan's wrist and drug her into the house and up the stairway. Sean dropped everything ,a protest on his lips but found he had to run to keep up with the pair.

"You have made a fool of our entire family and me. I will not have it. You will pay for your actions."

"Please." Sean heard her beg. He stood at the bottom of the stairs, unsure how to proceed. He could not risk giving away his identity but neither could he risk her safety. "I will leave. You dinnae have to keep me in your home."

Tia suddenly appeared and blocked his way. He could not get past her without bowling her down or physically picking her up and moving her.

William ignored Reagan and in minutes they reached his study. Sean watched from the bottom of the staircase as William threw her into the room, leaving the door open behind them.

"Tia, please get out of the way."

She shook her head. "This is between my brother and Reagan. You should not interfere."

"I have no choice. Reagan is my wife now." With that said, as gently as he could, he put his hands around Tia's waist and moved her far enough to the side to pass without incident.

Sean bolted up the stairs, planning to put an end to this whatever it was going to be before it happened. He watched from the end of the hallway as he raced to the study. Reagan struggled against William, but he was far stronger. He had thrown his desk chair into the center of the room and forced her down upon her knees. William had tied her hands to the back of the chair, having wrenched the satin ribbon from her hair. He'd wrenched the fabric from her back, leaving her bare. He held a riding crop, and he flourished it before her, slapping it against his palm.

"No," Sean roared. He knew she must be mortified by her position, for her torn garments hung from her and she was nearly naked from the waist up. Sean raced toward William.

William ignored Sean. "You see, my dear, the bastard children of my father do find certain benefits!" He stroked her bare back with the crop of the whip.

"Your Grace—" She screamed when he brought the whip down upon her naked back with a violent force that was shattering.

Sean was still too far a way. Helplessly, he watched her tense as if preparing for the next stroke of the whip.

"How many lashes, Reagan? How many do you think before you would obey me? You see, I fear that I could tear your flesh to ribbons, and still it would help little. Still I must try."

"William, you will not touch her again!" Sean commanded, grabbing for William's extended hand but falling short.

The lash fell again, and it seemed she could not help herself; she cried out with the agony of it.

"William, Stop!" Sean wrenched the crop from his hand. The need to beat William senseless surged to the forefront of his thoughts. He swung his fist, knocking William to the ground but refrained from continuing. He needed to see to Reagan.

"Damn you, Sterling, what right have you to stop me! My father brought me this chit to harbor, and she has defied me! It is my right to punish her as I see fit. She deserves this and more."

Sean wanted to give William a taste of the whip. He watched as Reagan tried to blink back tears. Her humiliation was complete. Her gown was completely awry, her breasts were bare, and his rage was overpowering. He would have to tread lightly.

"You will untie her this minute."

"By God, and all that is holy, Sean, we are friends, but this is my business now. She is betrothed to another, and she cannot run off whenever she pleases. Do not interfere!"

"I do have the right!" Sean's fists were clenched at his sides, and he struggled for control. He knelt down before Reagan and untied the ribbon that held her. She fell limply across the seat of the chair then to the floor. He walked around to her side, lifting her. She cried out from the cuts on her back and she cried out again trying to cover herself with the torn fabric. He stripped off his fireman's coat and wrapped it around her gently, taking care when she flinched as the fabric hit her back.

"Damn you, Sean Sterling!" William swore.

"It is my right, for I will marry her. Indeed by the terms of your own May Day celebration we are wed—handfasted."

"What?" William asked, seemingly astounded.

There were others in the room who heard Sean's proclamation. They all repeated William's exclamation.

"But that's ridiculous! Think of your position and title. You will have to have a special dispensation. You cannot marry this common—"

"Take care!" Sean warned. "It is my betrothed you speak of now!"

"Sean, you have lost your mind." It was Tia speaking. "Think of who you are and what you are, and think of your life and your life-style—"

"That is exactly what I am thinking of," Sean said curtly. He scooped Reagan into his arms then he whirled around to face William. "Where is her room? We need to pack her things. I would have her in Sterling Castle before dawn."

"This is madness, Sean," William called after him.

"I held her when the dance ended, did I not?"

~ * ~

"The poor wee lass," Adair said shaking with fury his hands clenched at his sides.

"It's a good thing we brought Sean to this place and time," Erin said. "I'd love for Sean to act on his feelings. They love each other already, don't you think?"

"It's what William deserves—someone to put him in his place." Adair had never felt so angry.

"Yes, and more but it's not going to happen tonight. Sean is too much a gentleman to do anything about William."

Adair watched the scene unfold and was heartily glad when he saw that Sean would not allow Reagan to remain the night. When he bundled her up and made William give them a carriage for the ride back to the castle, Adair knew all would be right with this pair. Now all they had to do was convince Alistair, his manservant, that Sean was Shaughnessy.

"Thank the heavens for small favors," Erin said as she fluttered her wings and sprinkled faerie dust on the pair. "For good luck," she said.

Chapter Three

"You do not have to carry me," Reagan said emphatically but with no affect on the man who seemed to have a mind and will of his own. Feeling protected felt good.

"You are hurt." His words were simple and straightforward.

"I must weigh as much as a whale, and these steps go on forever."

"You weigh nothing. I have carried grown men who are twice as heavy through burning buildings," Sean told her. "I don't think I will have any trouble with a tiny slip of a girl."

Reagan leaned her head against Sean's shoulder and gave up hope she would convince him to set her down. In truth, she wanted him to hold her. The gesture gave her a sense of home, one she'd never felt before.

The lashes on her back burned and stung, but they were not as bad as they could have been. William had done twice, no three times as much damage on several occasions when her stubborn nature had delivered her into trouble.

"Where is my..." Sean's voice trailed off as he seemed to realize he didn't know where he was going.

She didn't know where Lord Shaughnessy's solar was either, but she could guess. "Down the hall, second door on the left."

Sean nodded then picked up his pace. Only a few seconds passed before he kicked the door open and strode boldly into the spacious room. The solar contained a huge four-poster bed, a table and a couple of large chairs. Against the outside wall a brick fireplace was blazing, emitting a warmth that filled the room.

Reagan closed her eyes and wondered what heaven had brought her here and when would reality settle in and kick her out of this place.

The scent of cinnamon filled the air. Someone must have placed a potpourri in the room. Cinnamon was a scent that reminded her of her mother and a time that had been filled with love. Moisture threatened to fill her eyes. She sniffed and wiped the tear that loomed from her eyes.

"There you go," Sean said as he gently lowered her to the bed. "Stay put. I'll be back with soap and water."

As if his mind had been read, a servant appeared at the door. "M'Lord," he said. "I've brought warm water and soap. Didn't know if you'd want to bathe or see to the lady's wounds."

"How..."

The servant smiled. "I like to think I'm a fly on the wall. I keep my eyes and ears open. If there is anything else you need, please let me know. "I've arranged to have food and drink sent to your chambers."

"Thank you," Sean said. "I appreciate all you've done."

A few moments passed as the niceties were taken care. Then, "Let me see your back."

"I don't..." She moistened her lips and stared at him. "Please, I can take care of myself."

"We are wed." Once again his words were simple.

She tried to simulate the words. *Wed.* He could do whatever, and all he wanted was to look at her back, which did need tending to. Before, when William had lashed her, Tia's maid had taken care of her. Really, she could not reach her back.

"All right," she rolled onto her stomach.

He slid his coat from her back. She heard his rapid in take of breath. "I'll kill the son of a bitch," he whispered.

"No." She started to roll over then realized she wore only the shredded fabric from her dress. "You must not do anything."

"Lay still," he said as he turned his attention to the soft rag and warm soapy water. "This will sting."

She knew all too well how much it would hurt. She gritted her teeth together and tried to relax while she waited for this to end.

"I will try to work quickly," he told her. "But I want to make sure everything is cleaned from your wounds. Don't want infection to set in."

But it seemed to take an eternity. He was gentle and caring and every few seconds she heard a curse. He finished cleaning the cuts.

"It is done. Now, what will you wear?" he murmured. "I have no idea what is in the lord's chest and I'm not too sure if I should rummage through it."

"That will not be necessary."

His servant was back. Reagan didn't know how he had entered the laird's solar so quietly. It was in some respects a bit spooky.

"You have clothing?"

"I brought something she might be able to wear. Your mother was about her size. She had an extensive wardrobe. Your lady's clothing should be here tomorrow. But I have also taken it upon myself to arrange for a seamstress to be here on the morrow. I hope that is to your liking."

Sean cleared his throat. "Of course, thank you again."

The servant bowed then left the room.

"That is not necessary. My wardrobe—my clothes are suitable."

"For the lady of Sterling Castle?" Sean asked.

"Maybe not." She really wished he wasn't always right. And yet he never seemed to make a big deal about it. He wasn't even of this time yet he had an uncanny knowledge of how he should act.

"I will leave you then, to rest." Sean turned and strode from the room. The door shut silently behind him.

Reagan rose and took advantage of the hot bathwater that had been brought into the room. When she finished a long soak, Sean returned and covered the cuts with clean strips of cloth. When he left again, she dressed.

Standing by the window, she looked out over the grounds of Sterling Castle. She had never thought to be the lady of such a fine estate. Of course he could have the May Day fiasco annulled if he wished. But she sensed he would not.

Sean Michael Sterling was a caring man and a man of honor. He would protect her even though he didn't love her.

Could love grow from what they shared?

She laughed softly. Perhaps...

She could show him how he should act and what he should say. But probably more importantly, she could help him with what not to do or say. He had settled into this time as if he were born to it. They could compliment each other.

Perhaps he saw a future here and with her. She could only begin to hope. Before his untimely or perhaps timely arrival she'd had no prospects. Now her life had turned around.

She inhaled a long deep breath then let it out slowly. She would have to live up to her title. She'd not been groomed to be lady of the castle, but she'd watched Tia and had at times been a part of the lessons.

A coldness washed over her. The only reason she had been included from time to time was because William had intended to wed her to a wealthy merchant nearby. She shuddered then tried to rub the coldness from her body. He was not a nice man. He had already been married three times. Each of his wives had eventually died in an attempt to give him a son. Ironically, he had five daughters. It was rumored the women had been forced in the marriage bed. If not for Sean, she would have been the next victim.

Reagan turned from the window and walked to her marriage bed. Her solar was through an adjoining door. What did he want? Should she prepare herself for bed, or would he expect her to go to her room?

Sitting down on the huge bed, she ran her hands over the quilt. Silence seemed to hang heavily around her. Her heart thundering in her chest was the only sound she heard.

~ * ~

"Don't you just love it?" Erin fluttered nervously around the big bed. "Reagan has fallen in love. She may not know it yet, but she is in love with the rogue. He has charmed his way into her heart."

"Think so?" Adair asked rubbing his chin and following Erin with his eyes as she tumbled and danced. Faerie dust flew everywhere.

"I know so."

"And I think you are putting the cart in front of the horse," Adair said while he rubbed his chin.

"They will spend the night in this bed."

Adair flew to the adjoining suite. "The bed has been made up in here. Our Sean Michael is too much the gentleman to bed our lady until he has wooed her and knows where her heart lies."

"Hmmphf!" Erin said as she posed midair hands on her hips. She waggled a finger at Adair. "I just hate it when you are right. The last thing Sean is going to do is rush his fair lady."

"Of course I'm right," Adair said with a smug grin on his devilishly handsome face.

"You don't have to gloat about it. She is a wee thing and very sweet. I was just in a hurry for them to seal the deal. I don't want anything or anyone coming between them."

"We both know there are extenuating factors here."

"That's what our faerie dust is for—extenuating factors." Adair winked then smiled broadly.

~ * ~

The whiskey slipped down his throat, burning slightly. The view from the window was something he didn't think he would ever forget. Not that he would have a chance. He was pretty sure the time machine was not coming back to pick him up. The surety of his situation weighed heavily upon his soul.

In a land and a century he didn't understand, he knew he would have to do some quick thinking from time to time not to give himself away.

And Shaughnessy? What of the real laird of Castle Sterling? Was he headed for New York in 1895. He would be even hard pressed to understand the world he was headed for.

What should he do next? The one servant he'd had contact with seemed to know he wasn't the laird. And he didn't seem to care. Indeed there had been at least one occasion in the last couple of hours where the man, Alistair, seemed to be pleased he was the laird.

Alistair had seen to several small details since he'd ensconced himself in the library. The man had brought him food and showed him the liquor cabinet. He'd talked a bit about the history of the castle and several other things.

Briefly, he'd mentioned a mistress. Was he really keeping a woman? The thought made him a bit nauseous.

Feeling a headache coming on, he rubbed his temples, closing his eyes to help ease the pain. What he wouldn't give for some laudanum right now. If he didn't learn more about this life, he was dead meat. And the speech? He couldn't use phrases like that one. No one would understand him. Although he thought dead meat summed his situation up pretty clearly.

Alistair had shown him the books for the estate. Thank his lucky stars he could read and write. Indeed, he'd discovered several mistakes in the arithmetic and he saw places where he could save the estate money. The laird had been a bit of a wastrel.

Several entries made no sense to him. Money paid out to someone by the name of Cora McBride. Entries including ones to a dressmaker, a cook, a maid and the list continued to the tune of a small, fortune even for his time.

Cora McBride, he made a mental note to ask Alistair about her. Sipping his whiskey he rocked back on his heels then forward, leaning toward the windowpane. A carriage had rolled across the bridge and stopped in front of the castle's main door.

Not in the mood for company, he pulled the cord that would summon Alistair.

Sean heard the door swish open as well as the click of booted heels on the hardwood of the library floor. By the sound of the footsteps, this person was not Alistair.

He turned, feeling a bit amused that someone could or would dare walk into his private area unannounced.

A few minutes later he was less amused. A petite woman with golden curls stopped in front of him and slapped him across his face.

For a second he was speechless then he let out a loud guffaw of laughter.

Do I know her? I must. What did I do to this woman?

Knowing he had to keep his mouth shut until he had control of the situation, Sean cocked his head to one side and waited while he rubbed the mark on his cheek. "Did I deserve this?"

"Shaughnessy Sterling," the lady began. "I would have never believed my ears, but I heard the truth from so many people I had to come and hear it from your mouth."

"Cora..."

Her hands rested on her hips and her eyes blazed with fury. "You are a rogue of the worst sort. You could have told me."

"Told you what exactly?" he asked.

"Then it's not true?" She walked toward him until she was inches away, her pert little nose high in the air.

"What's not true?" He truly needed time to evaluate and plot the course of action.

"That you wed the bastard girl. The one pretending to be nobility. Her mother was a whore."

Sean wasn't sure that Cora wasn't exactly the same thing, a whore. But perhaps semantics were involved here. Perhaps a mistress was different than a whore. Hmm...

"I married Reagan at the May Day festival. It was a bit impulsive, but I don't have any regrets."

"Then you can still annul it?" Cora asked.

"Why should I? I'm fond of Reagan and intend to marry her in the church tomorrow."

"Oh!"

"As soon as possible, in fact."

"Are you feeling well?" Cora asked. "You are not sounding at all yourself. You know, once a rake always a rake."

Puzzled for a moment, he didn't know how to respond. "It's just time that's all. I'm thinking about an heir."

"What about me? I could certainly fulfill that role as well as anyone," she told him.

"Perhaps you could, dear. But I've made up my mind." He was suddenly impatient to see Cora vanish as quickly as she'd appeared. And he wanted to see Reagan, talk to her. He felt a strange kinship with her that he needed to explore in more depth.

"Can I keep the cottage? And the jewels and the..."

He waved a hand dismissing her questions. "Keep everything. I've no need for it, and I will continue to pay your bills until you find another protector. However, do not run them up and do not make a trip to the dressmaker without me. I will still want approval over all of your expenditures. Do I make myself clear?"

"Abundantly," she told him, a nasty looking smirk appearing on her tiny little face.

He nearly laughed but chocked it back. He didn't want to make any more an enemy of this woman than he already had. If anyone could make his life miserable, he had the decided feeling this woman would. She already suspected him of being different. Yet there was no way she could prove anything. Shaughnessy was gone, vanished into some unknown world in the time machine.

"Anything more?"

"No, but I promise you, you won't be pleased with your Reagan. She is a commoner and not suitable for the position of lady of Sterling Castle."

He cleared his throat. "I believe you made your feelings about the woman I love perfectly clear." Sean wanted to turn her around and give her a boost out the door. Even he knew this wasn't polite.

"Excuse me, Miss, your carriage and driver are waiting for you," Alistair appeared at the doorway in the nick of time.

"Yes," Sean said, "I believe we've discussed everything."

"Oh, not by any means," Cora said. "Rest assured, I'll be back."

~ * ~

"Ooohhh, don't you just want to strangle her?" Erin fluttered her wings and flew in wide circles around Cora McBride.

"No, I'd rather find the whisps and send her into the hillside never to return." Adair spoke of the tiny magical creatures that had always fascinated him.

"We could go talk to them. I'm sure they would do our bidding. After all there are several who owe us favors."

"True," Adair said thoughtfully. "But then someone might get suspicious. And of course Sean will be a suspect. We can't have any of that." Adair was thoughtful though. A plan was necessary, a must in this situation. If they weren't careful, people might think Sean had been cursed. He acted strange. Was different: his speech, his airs, his true caring nature. The real laird was not at all like Sean except in physical appearance.

"What are you thinking?" Erin asked, hands on hips as she settled on the top of a chair to watch Adair.

"I'm not sure. But perhaps we can put a scare into Cora that will keep her mouth shut and her body away from Sterling Castle."

Chapter Four

Reagan cried out, startled by the sound behind her. She had been so lost in thoughts about Sean and the wedding to come.

"M' Lady," the girl curtsied then said, "I'm Catherine Lee Douglas. The laird asked me to come here today. I've brought fashion plates and fabric as well. If we get started with the measurements and the choosing of the gowns, I can have one finished by tomorrow morning."

"I've never been allowed to pick my gowns." Reagan was surprised at Sean's leniency. Most times the man's opinion had priority. Her heart skipped a little beat as she thought.

"Well, he did say I was to keep the gowns modest but other than that, you have all of the input the style, the fabric as well as the color." Catherine motioned for her entourage to enter.

By the time they were finished, the solar was filled with stacks of fabric and Catherine had placed fashion plates on the armoire.

"Here you go." Catherine said, smiling when she motioned with her hands at everything they had assembled.

"These are beautiful," Reagan said. "I've never seen anything like this. Even Tia does not have such beautiful things."

"The laird told me to bring the best I have."

Reagan held up a royal blue fabric close to her face. "What do you think?"

"The color brings out your eyes. They look a gorgeous sapphire."

"Thank you." Reagan had never felt so cherished. The thought of pinching herself to make sure she wasn't dreaming rushed through her.

"We must get your measurements."

"Of course."

The two young women chatted happily while they worked. The dresses were chosen as well as the fabrics to compliment them. Hours swept by as if time stood still. By mid-afternoon, there were five dresses as well as a wedding dress chosen for Reagan.

Cook brought in tea and lemon cakes. Smelling them made Reagan's stomach growl.

"I'm famished," Reagan laughed.

"Me too," Catherine said as she played ladies maid and poured the tea.

"May I have one?" Sean asked, stepping into the solar and the women's domain. His grin stretched from ear to ear. "A lemon cake," he finished as he reached for one of the small cakes. "I might need more than one."

"Maybe," Reagan laughed. "Thank you so much for this wonderful day and for sending Catherine. She is quite the marvel."

"You are welcome." Sean snatched another pastry from the tray and stuffed it quickly into his mouth.

"However, I intend to pick out your night things. While I wanted your day dresses and ball gowns modest, I do think, I would love to have your night clothes...well," he paused. "For my eyes only."

Reagan felt heat sweep from her toes to her cheeks. She touched her face and knew she had turned crimson.

"You look beautiful when you blush," he told her. He tenderly drew a line down her cheek with one finger.

"I...I..." she stammered. Her heart raced alarmingly.

"Yes?" He questioned but he turned to Catherine. "When can you have the wedding dress completed? I would like to arrange the wedding as soon as we possibly can. Sleeping in separate rooms is going to become challenging."

He walked to the fashion plates and flipped through them, making little noises of approval as he looked at each one.

"I can have the wedding dress in a week, sooner if you allocate more funds for another seamstress."

"It's done."

It was done. She would be wed to Sean in less than a week. Her hands trembled when she brought her teacup to her lips. The hot liquid singed the inside of her mouth and tongue. Closing her eyes, she tried to imagine what it would be like sleeping beside Sean, making love to him.

Warmth radiated through her. Once again heat swept across her cheeks. She truly had no idea what making love entailed but she did so want to discover the truth.

"My blushing bride to be," Sean said with a smile on his lips. "Whatever are you thinking?"

Reagan shook her head and turned away. He was too close and she was letting him see too much. It would not do for him to know how much he affected her, how very much she cared.

"Catherine," Sean said, "are you finished?"

Catherine nodded and bobbed a curtsey. "Yes, M' Lord."

In a matter of minutes, the work area was clean and everything was out of the room.

Reagan stood in the center of her solar watching everyone dance around her, moving this here and there while Catherine wrote notes on a piece of parchment.

"I will have your first dress here tomorrow morning," Catherine said, curtsied then left.

Reagan turned to Sean. "Thank you," she said, her voice soft.

"Do you really want to marry me? You do know I am not the real Shaughnessy Sterling."

"I have guessed as much."

"Do you want to marry Sean Michael Sterling here, in Scotland, from the future?"

She nodded, her heart thundering in her chest. "I do."

He stepped forward then placed his finger beneath her chin. He lifted her chin until she looked into his eyes. They were clear and honest eyes. To Reagan it didn't seem as if he wanted any secrets between them.

"I can never go back. And I don't expect Shaughnessy to return. Therefore it will be up to you to teach me all I need to know."

She nodded.

"Are you sure you can do that?"

"I will not let anything happen. But you must follow my lead in all things. This is a superstitious time. Many have been accused of witchcraft. All it would take would be one person who held a grudge against either of us."

"Cora McBride?" he questioned.

"Yes, and the man I was betrothed to. We cannot give either of them a reason to cry foul."

Slowly, he lowered his lips to hers. The kiss was gentle; a daytime kiss with the promise of more. He pulled her close, his arms encompassing her, shielding her in warmth and protection. Golden beams of warmth filled her soul as well as her heart. She closed her eyes and allowed the kiss to linger. He traced the seam of her lips with his tongue.

She moaned softly, leaning into him. Then there was only space between them. She opened her eyes. He was still staring at her with a smile on his lips. His thumb brushed softly against her lips.

"You taste so sweet," he said softly.

She blinked and started to say something, but she stopped, the words catching in her throat, knowing she could not yet say what filled her heart.

"I have work to do and a certain gentleman to see. I believe he is owed some kind of compensation for what I took from him."

Reagan stepped back and nodded. "A wise decision."

~ * ~

"Was that a first kiss?" Erin asked. "And we didn't need to coax it. This is going to work. I know it."

"A first kiss and no faerie dust involved."

"I do believe these two will make the marriage work."

"Of course they will. They are soul mates after all," Erin said, feeling a bit indignant at the doubt in Adair's voice.

"What do you think Sean will give Becan Erskine?"

"Most likely he will find out what William promised the old man and give him double. It is the only way to silence the talk," Erin said, trying to figure out how they could fix this.

"And the talk has already begun. Becan has doubted his true character. Says Sean is an imposter and should be called out. But without Shaughnessy there is no way to prove anything is amiss."

"Superstitious people can be incited to do most anything." Erin sat on the corner of the desk, searching her mind. She didn't like what Adair was telling her.

"We do not need any trials by fire or water," Adair put in.

"Please..."

"Well, one never knows in these times."

Erin knew how right Adair could be. She'd heard the rumors circulating. It didn't bode well for the couple. Everything must be made right and it was up to them to do it. This was beyond the abilities of mere mortals.

~ * ~

"Sir, I do not think it would be wise of you to marry without the official reading of the marriage banns," Alistair said stiffly. "I hope I am not speaking out of turn."

Sean sipped the tea Alistair had brought to him and eyed the blueberry scones. The correctness of this marriage was important. But he did not want to wait. "It will take three Sundays for the banns to be read correctly. Am I right?"

"That is correct," Alistair said with a stiff grimace. "However, it will give the congregation the chance to object to your marriage, if they wish."

Sean tapped his fingers on his desk, annoyed with all the loopholes he seemed to be encountering. He had imagined the only obstacle was completing the wedding dress. It had been finished for several days now. "Do you think anyone will—object?" slow panic rippled through him.

"No, however," Alistair went on to say, "when I heard about the wedding dress, I took the liberty to inform the King. The two of you are friends and you would not want the objection of the Scottish King."

"Of course," Sean wasn't sure how much Alistair knew or guessed about his true identity.

"Sir, just to set your mind at ease, I saw Shaughnessy walk into that strange machine," he paused to take a breath then wipe his nose with a white handkerchief. "Then I watched it leave the ground and disappear into the sky. I do not believe he is coming back."

"I don't know what to say." Truly, Sean was baffled. He could not think of one reason Alistair would protect his identity.

"I know it is not your fault. It is the will o' wisps who led him there. I tried to stop the laird, but he wanted to see inside it, and there was the cutest little dog who seemed to lure him."

"Bandit," Sean mused.

"No, I dinnae think any bandits were involved."

"The dog, I named him that. He enticed me inside too." Vividly Sean remembered that day, how tired he'd been, how intrigued he was about the machine. Perhaps it had been fate and not Bandit.

"I don't mean any disrespect, but where did you come from?" Alistair asked.

Sean ran his hands through his hair, leaving it disheveled. "I came from the year 1895. I was a fire fighter in New York City. The damn fire hydrant was in the middle of Central Park."

"1895?"

"Yes," Sean said.

"Do you wish to go back?"

"I don't believe I have a choice. As you said the machine left with the real laird inside."

"Does the lady know?"

"Reagan is aware of some of the story." He had certainly landed in a fine mess. But he had a good feeling. Intuition had always served him well.

Alistair cleared his throat. "I need to tell you about the king. You will call him James. The two of you are friends. Once a year you meet at his lodge near Loch Rannoch and hunt. But let him talk first and don't offer any suggestions. You don't want to get caught up in a lie."

"So, I know nothing about this King. James VI."

"He became King of Scotland at the age of thirteen months, and he was the only son of Mary, Queen of Scots."

"I have heard of the Queen."

"Good, then you should know that he married Anne of Denmark."

"All right, Anne then. Am I friends with Queen Anne?"

"No, and she most likely will not follow her husband to your wedding."

"Anything else?" Sean asked a bit worried over this new development. Kings and queens were something he didn't understand and didn't have any idea how to proceed.

"He has an interest in the study of witchcraft. James considers it a type of theology. I believe you should be wary of him and not speak out of place or of things he would not understand."

Sean cleared his throat then gave a little laugh. No, he should probably not speak of electricity and motorcycles. He shouldn't say anything about trains and other machines.

"I will take the utmost care," he said.

For Sean the next hour involved lessons of protocol, topics about James that any friend would know. Patiently, Alistair explained the royal lineage to Sean as well his own family. The promise to continue the lessons everyday until Sean knew everything he needed.

"Sean?" Reagan poked her head around the corner. "I wanted to show you one of my new dresses." She stepped inside and twirled around in a tiny little circle. The dress billowing out around her ankles.

"It's very nice," Sean said as Reagan twirled in a circle in front of him. He liked her ankles very much and what he could see of her legs.

"Thank you," she said. "Could we go for a ride this afternoon. The sun is shinning and the sky is so blue. We could explore a little."

"I think that would be nice." He wanted to do all that he could for Reagan. He loved making her happy.

"Good, I'll put on my riding clothes. Maybe I can talk Cook into packing a picnic basket."

"I'm famished," he said, thoroughly enjoying her enthusiasm. Spending some time in the fresh spring air with his betrothed would be nice. He wanted to learn as much about her and Scotland as he could.

"We can discuss the wedding."

"It seems my earlier plans have all gone awry. I thought we would be wed by now. Alistair just informed me we have to read the marriage banns every Sunday in the parish churches for the next three weeks."

"If we want it done properly. " She agreed with him on a sigh.

"I believe properly is the only option."

~ * ~

"I object!" Becan Erskine stood in the little protestant church his hand fisted. "And I will object every time the banns are read. The girl is mine." He wiped a sweaty hand on his leg. He had bargained with her stepbrother. Everything was going well. He wanted Reagan and an heir.

The small group of parishioners gave a collective gasp at Becan's announcement. He waved his hand in the air one more time. His anger knew no bounds; he felt the rage rush to his cheeks.

"I will not allow this wedding to move forward." His beady little brown eyes scanned the room as if threatening to murder anyone who stood in his way.

The reverend cleared his throat. "You may sit down," he said quietly and with infinite patience.

Becan sat and with hands folded on his belly, waited throughout the sermon as well as the songs. When the service was over he left, intending to go to William's home and confront the earl.

"Becan?" a small hand touched his arm and he gazed into the most lovely brown eyes he'd ever seen. His heart did a jig inside his chest.

"Do I know you?" he asked, his voice quivering with the need to know more about this woman.

"No, but I think we have a common cause." She placed one hand on his arm and smiled seductively.

"And what would that be?" Becan asked, wondering what she was about and if they truly did have something in common.

"Neither of us wants to see Shaughnessy and Reagan married."

"That much is true."

"I heard you object. My heart swelled with pride you did it in such a manly fashion." She blinked and ran her hand up his arm.

"I am rather proud of myself."

She smiled at him again, and he once more felt a surge of heat sweep through him until he thought he might smolder.

"You are so sweet." She giggled then covered her mouth with her hand.

Becan placed his hand on hers. "Tell me, why is it you object to their marriage."

"I love Shaughnessy. I have no other reason. I have loved him for a very long time, and I always thought we would wed someday."

"I was betrothed to Reagan."

"Oh, my."

They walked for a few minutes. Neither one of them spoke. A myriad of thoughts swept through his mind. He thought perhaps he could use this woman for his purposes and perhaps she would gain something new.

"You haven't told me your name."

"My apologies. It is Cora—Cora McBride."

"Would you like to have a meal with me? We could discuss our strategy."

Chapter Five

"Where are we going?" Reagan asked as she pulled her hair back.

"There is a lake just east of here," Sean told her, a grin on his handsome face, the dimple in his chin showing.

A giddy happiness washed through her. For the first time since she'd moved to Sterling Castle, she felt at home. The last few weeks with Sean had been wonderful. Getting to know him had been eye opening. Every little thing about him fascinated her. Some of the stories he told about the future were truly unbelievable. She liked the ones about his motorcycle the best.

"You have been exploring?"

"I have. And I've taken everything you and Alistair have told me to heart. King James will be at our wedding. He should arrive tomorrow. Preparations for his stay were begun two weeks past, and I'm sure you and the king will be pleased."

A wave of apprehension shivered down her spine. "The king?" Neither of them had ever met a king before. There was so much at stake. Their very lives if the truth be told.

"I think I know what you are thinking."

"He could accuse you of witchcraft. Is there anyway we can convince him not to come?" Goose bumps rose on her arms and a horrible premonition rattled in her head.

"That would be a mistake."

"Perhaps," she said. "But it could be an even bigger one to have him meet you. What if he guesses you are not the real laird."

"I look just like Shaughnessy."

"But you dinnae act like him. You are much nicer. And there are certain things about you, things I cannae define."

Sean laughed. "I have to act mean then I'll convince the King I'm the real laird of the castle." He lifted one brow and smiled. "I cannot be worried about this and neither should you. We just have to take everything in stride so to speak."

"Yes," she said. "You should act indifferent and uncaring and that would most likely work."

Sean shook his head, a smile on his lips. "I will not change. The King may be a friend, but he does not see me all that much. And we will be busy. I'm sure James will not notice."

"How can you be so confident?"

He shrugged and helped her onto her little mare. "I have to be arrogant. Isn't that more like the man I'm supposed to pretend to be?"

"I don't like it," she said, as she took hold of the reins and waited for Sean to mount his horse.

"We can't change anything."

"You are ever more confident on your horse." She told him, wishing for everything to go smoothly.

"Again, I've no choice."

"You are a fast learner," she observed. "I will give you that, and if anyone can accomplish a miracle, I'm sure it is you."

"It seems everyone on this estate has been willing to help and overlook the fact that I'm not Shaughnessy. For the last few weeks, that fact has been a bit confusing. But I'm beginning to accept it."

"Anyone could turn on you. There is Cora and Becan and someone we might not have ever heard about."

"I think they like me better," he said then laughed again. "And once again we cannot afford to think up trouble before it even happens."

The day couldn't be more perfect. The sky was blue with a few lazy clouds drifting high above. The air smelled clean and fresh. They rode in silence for a while. Reagan could not help but dream up horrible scenarios. She was terrified of what could happen.

Cresting a hill, she saw the loch he'd been talking about. The water was a deep blue and ripples lapped the shoreline.

Sean nodded toward a spot near a tree. "Let's spread the blanket there. We can eat then take a walk."

"What did you have Cook pack?"

"Good question. We'll have to look inside. She said it was to be a surprise for me too."

Sean helped her down. His hands around her waist made her heart skip a beat. He'd been so wonderful. He'd kissed her a few times, but nothing demanding. She hoped perhaps today, he would... Well, she wasn't really sure what she hoped for. More of the same or much more.

Sean handed her the blanket. She spread it out, part in the sun and part in the shade. Basking in the sun felt so good.

He set the basket down then opened it. "Hmm... glasses and a bottle of wine." He pulled the items out one at a time.

"Are you hungry?" she asked.

"Famished," he smiled. "Let's see, we have chicken, cheese and bread."

He poured the wine and she pulled off a hunk of bread to hand to him. "Look, there are strawberries too."

Reagan thought on the twists and turns of her life. She had never expected to wed the laird of a castle, let alone Sterling Castle. Becan was to be her husband. And what would her future have been. Becan was well known for beating his wives.

Over the years, since her mother passed away and she ended up with William, she'd learned to avoid his beatings—until May Day. May Day when she'd watched Sean stroll nonchalantly over the hill toward the celebration. Instinctively, she'd known it wasn't Shaughnessy. She didn't know how though.

She felt the seductive glide of the back of Sean's hand across her cheek then down her neck to rest on her shoulder.

"Your thoughts?" he asked.

She inhaled a long deep breath then touched his hand. "I was thinking about the day I first saw you. And how much my life has changed."

"Funny, I was thinking about you and how you have changed."

"How so?"

"For one thing, you smile more and you seem more relaxed as if you don't have to look over your shoulder to make sure no one is going to hurt you."

"You're very perceptive."

"Are you happy?" He gave her a slice of cheese.

She ate it, chewing slowly and thinking about her answer. Was she happy? More so than ever before in her life.

"There you are." The voice came from behind them, shattering the pleasant afternoon and sending the easiness into shards of splintering glass.

She'd know that voice anywhere. Stiffening, she rose and dusted her hands off on her skirts. But Sean spoke before she could, seeming to take their earlier conversations to heart.

"Becan," Sean said, rising then extending his hand in greeting. "So nice to see you outside the church."

Fear slipped down Reagan's spine. She had never liked Becan and had dreaded the possible marriage to him. Now she was safe. Well, somewhat safe. She wasn't wed to Sean in the eyes of the church. In three days she would have Sean's protection.

"You won't get away with this," Becan said, his voice a low growl his jowls shaking with the anger that seemed to boil up from inside. His face was a mottled red and his hands were fisted at his sides.

"I'm sorry," Sean said politely. "Get away with what?" He crossed his arms in front of his chest with his stance wide.

"The girl is mine, Shaughnessy. You have no right to her. She was promised to me, and I mean to have her."

"You are mistaken."

He was so calm. But she sensed an undercurrent of anger, simmering deep inside. Yet all outward appearance spoke of confidence. And she was utterly glad Becan had addressed Sean as Shaughnessy.

"No, she has cast a spell upon you. She is a witch."

Reagan gasped for air. Being accused of witchcraft was an obvious ploy to get at Sean, but it could mean her death.

"I would not speak in such a manner again." His words were menacing, and Becan stepped back, clutching his throat as if someone was strangling him.

"Back off, but take care, sir. Reagan is no witch and if more rumors reach my ears, I will know where to find the real witch."

"Is that a threat?"

"Your words not mine." Sean told him, fury blazing from his entire being.

"I have proof."

"Liar. Show it now or forever hold your peace."

Becan sputtered, stepped forward then backed down. "I will show only the king when he arrives."

What could he possibly have that would prove her a witch?

"You have nothing. You only wait in hopes to find something. You will not. Perhaps you are the witch."

Reagan stepped forward a bit more courageous than she'd felt only moments earlier. "Yes, I would like to know what I have done to throw such horrible accusations my way."

"You are nothing but a jealous and weak man."

"She is a witch," Becan said before marching away.

~ * ~

"If you will excuse me," Sean placed a hand on Reagan's cheek. "I need to speak with Alistair."

"About me."

Sean could not bear the sad yet courageous smile Reagan gave him. He knew all too well what Becan's hate filled words could do to her to anyone. He wouldn't let that happen.

Hand in hand they walked from the stable to the castle. Her solar was filled with sunlight and that gave him the strength to proceed with what was prevalent in his mind.

"I'll see you at dinner?" he asked.

She nodded and he waited while she entered her room. This was not how he had planned for the day to end. No, his heart skipped a beat.

He had thought to have a little romance between them a kiss then he'd see where that would lead. He sensed she was a bit fearful of the wedding night.

Becan was an evil, small man. Yet, he had every right to feel anger at what had happened. William had promised him Reagan, and perhaps it should be William who righted this situation.

Never before had Sean thought of murder, but for the life of him other than finding another time machine to send Becan on his way to another time and place, he could think of nothing save Becan's untimely demise.

In his study, he poured himself a drink and sipped slowly, savoring the flavor yet still wondering what he would do. He could not leave Becan to his own devices. Because he would never let Reagan stand trial for witchcraft. No one came out the winner in those trials, save the accuser.

"Sir," Alistair said as he waited just inside the door.

Sean turned. "You have heard?"

"How did you know?" Alistair asked.

"Your grim face. What am I to do about this? I could kill him, but then I'd stand trial for murder. I'd rather that than the alternative." Every nerve in Sean's body tingled with raw terror for Reagan.

"I don't think you have to worry." Alistair approached Sean.

"You know something?" Lord, but he prayed Alistair had a solution to this problem.

"Yes, William has assured me that Becan will not pose any harm to Reagan. He says he owes you that much."

"Really," Sean said. "And how does he know Becan has threatened Reagan."

"He does not. He only knows what Becan has done at the church. He does not wish you any problems on your wedding day. As her stepbrother,. he feels that he has some obligations where Reagan is concerned."

A surge of adrenalin shot through him. For a moment his eyes closed. When he opened them, Alistair was nonchalantly flicking a piece of lint from his coat.

"I don't suppose you care to elaborate."

Alistair looked up. His thinness accentuated by his large nose and rounded bony shoulders. But his grin lit up his face. "No, I don't believe you should have knowledge. The surprise should be genuine. Besides, William does not plot Becan's murder. So you need not fear his demise."

"Perhaps you are already telling me too much."

He shook his head and with a grimace then said. "I never could keep a secret very well. So, I will take my leave and let you think about your wedding day."

"Thank you. Have you finished arrangements for the king?"

"I have taken care of everything. He does not have a large entourage, so it has been fairly easy. He will occupy the large guest solar in the east wing. There will be plenty of room for those who will accompany him."

"When he arrives, will you let me know. I should like to greet him." A flutter of apprehension swept through Sean. Good lord, a king; a few weeks ago he would have laughed. Now he was about to meet a real king, one he was supposed to know quite well.

Alistair bobbed then nodded. "He should be here any time. We received advanced word of his arrival about an hour ago."

"Efficiency should be your middle name. Thank you," Sean said feeling less apprehensive and a bit relieved Alistair could accomplish so much in so little time.

"You're welcome."

With that Alistair left.

Sean sat down behind his desk and leafed through the papers. He had already corrected several accounting mistakes made by the first laird. As he perused the information in front of him, he found legal documents and a wealth of intelligence necessary for him to pull off this identity theft.

The more he learned the easier it would be. Yet there were pitfalls. And he meant to avoid all of them. Becan's accusation now was the biggest problem at the moment.

The sun began to set and the sky was vivid with a myriad of colors. Oranges, pinks soft mauves filled the western sky. A sliver of a moon hung just above the horizon. Then trumpets blared. Sean laughed. Alistair would not have to let him know the king had arrived.

From the courtyard below, the sound of clanking swords, horse's hooves and a plethora of noises filtered in through his window. He heard someone shouting orders.

He wondered what the protocol was. Should he rush down to greet the king or wait here in the study for James' arrival? Out of his element, he wished Alistair would appear with a crystal ball and tell him what he should do.

As if Alistair could read his thoughts, he was in the doorway of the study. Sean stood, quickly knocking a pen off his desk.

"Sir," Alistair began. "King James pleads fatigue and asks if you will forgive his absence from the evening meal. He has ordered food brought to his solar and asks that I tell you he will see you in the morning."

Sean fell onto his chair. "Thank God," he mumbled. "I truly am not prepared to meet King James."

"You will do fine. Just as you have done in all of your endeavors. Just let James lead the conversation in whatever direction he wants. You have information on his likes and dislikes, the papers he has written and so forth."

"It is a lot to recall."

"Again, sir, I'm sure you will shine."

"Thank you, Alistair. I am relieved and I would like to have Reagan's dinner as well as my own brought here."

"As you wish," Alistair bobbed again then departed.

~ * ~

"Do you believe what William has done?" Adair asked. "He has set Becan up to disappear."

"With the whisps, even," Erin said laughing giddily. She was so pleased with this idea she wanted to shout out loud.

Christine Young

"Hush, there they are." The little bright lights lit a twisting path deep into the forest.

Becan followed, along with a friend. Becan seemed mesmerized by the light and unable to stop himself.

"Where do you think you are going, Becan?" the man asked. He'd stopped and was waiting for Becan to do the same.

"I have to see where this leads," Becan said.

"No, I won't go with you. It is foolishness."

"But they're so beautiful. Listen, can you hear that? They are calling to us," Becan walked toward one of the lights then bent over as if he meant to pick it up. The light lifted from the ground and swirled farther into the forest.

"They are not calling to me."

"Come on." Becan motioned for the man to follow, but his friend stood his ground and watched.

"Dinnae follow those lights. I'm warning you. Something or someone is up to no good."

Adair fluttered around Becan. This was horrible, yet it was the answer to their prayers. Both he and Erin had been at the loch when Becan had accused Reagan of witchcraft. Erin had been terrified of what could happen to their beautiful little couple. He had tried to reassure her but to no avail.

"I must," Becan said before disappearing into the darkness.

Chapter Six

"I never dreamed..." Reagan said. "The dress is so beautiful." Reagan had never seen anything so wonderful. The dress shimmered when sunbeams hit the crystals that covered it.

She held the dress in front of her and twirled around her solar, humming as she did so. Then she danced around the room one more time, stopping only to admire herself in a mirror.

"It is the most lovely dress I've ever created," Catherine said with a smile while she held her hands clasped in front of her. "He will only have eyes for you. And that is most definitely the way it should be."

"I cannot thank you enough." Reagan felt as if she were a royal princess as she held wedding dress. She couldn't imagine how wonderful she would feel with it on.

"Here let's put it on you and see what I have to do to make it a perfect fit." Catherine carefully held the dress up,

Reagan's maid helped her from her clothes. "Arms up and be careful not to wiggle too much," she said with a cheery voice.

Reagan lifted her arms and let her maid help her into the dress. The buttons were tiny pearls and seemed to take forever to fasten. Smoothing her hands down the front of her gown, she held her breath.

"'Tis beautiful," her maid said softly. "Now close your eyes and will bring you to the mirror." Catherine carefully guided Reagan to the glass.

"Open your eyes," her maid said softly.

"You have done a splendid job, Catherine," Reagan twisted and turned in front of her reflection.

"Aye, it is indeed beautiful, but we do need to take it in a bit at the waist."

"I wouldnae be able to breathe if you did," Reagan said as she walked to the mirror for a look. "No, it is perfection."

Catherine shook her head. "Not yet, but it will be. I will not allow you to go to your wedding in a dress that does not fit properly."

Reagan laughed softly. "In my world this fits. I would never expect to have someone take so much care."

"My work will speak for me and garner me new clients or not. Again, we will take it in around the waist and bust."

Catherine set to work and when she finished pinning it, "You can help Reagan from the dress, "she told Reagan's maid.

The maid slipped a robe around Reagans shoulders. Other servants brought in bath water and sweet smelling bath salts. The water in the tub steamed and cast off a wonderful perfume.

"Now, while I finish this, you will bathe and relax. Your maid can fix your hair afterwards. Close your eyes and try to breathe deeply of the intoxicating aroma." Catherine busied herself, getting all of the paraphernalia she needed to finish the gown.

A few hours later the dress was finished as well as her hair. Her maid had woven strings of crystal through her blue-black hair. "There, you have almost two hours until you are expected at the church." Catherine stepped back as if to admire her work. "You are magnificent."

"Reagan," With a flourish and unannounced, Tia stepped into the solar. Her smile lit the room. "I've brought the radiant bride some gifts."

Reagan was stunned at Tia's generosity. "Gifts?" she parroted. "That was not necessary." Reagan felt the slide of embarrassment sweep within.

Tia flashed Reagan a smile of friendship. "Yes, every bride needs a gift or two on her wedding day." She stepped forward hands outstretched. "I do come in peace and I hope to smooth things between us."

Catherine clapped her hands together and moved closer to see what Tia had brought.

"First, we have an embroidered handkerchief. I found it in father's trunk. I thought he might have some keepsake from your mother and sure enough, he did. See it has your mother's initials on it." Tia handed it to Reagan.

Overwhelmed, Reagan sat down a lone tear slipping down her cheek as she studied the small gift but one she would hold close to her heart. "That is so thoughtful," she said.

"Well don't get all teary eyed on me now. I have more and I don't want you walking down the aisle with red eyes. You should not appear as if you had been weeping."

"You don't need to give me more. This is all I need," Reagan said as she wiped moisture from her eyes.

"But I have two more gifts and you must accept them."

"You are too generous."

"This pendant is from me, and I would be honored if you wear it during the wedding."

"It's..." she was at a loss for words. The pendant was created in the form of a Celtic cross with a sapphire in the middle. "I cannot..."

"Of course you can," Tia said adamantly. "It is a loan. You must have something borrowed and I would be so very unhappy if you refused this small token."

Reagan swallowed hard pushing back the lump of tears forming again and wishing her mother and father could be at the wedding. "You have always been like a sister to me, but I never thought..."

"You are my sister. And you should believe I will always think of you that way."

Reagan rose and put her arms around Tia. They hugged and Tia found another handkerchief to wipe away the new tears. "Don't you cry again. I won't have it." Reagan told her.

Tia reached into the bag she'd brought with her. "I have one more gift. It is something father gave your mother. They could not wed but they loved each other more than life itself. I think that is what always made William so angry and why he treated you so badly."

"What is it?" Reagan could help her curiosity as well as her excitement. This had turned into such a glorious day. Not in all of her wildest imaginations could she have created this scenario.

"Be patient." Tia handed a small box to Reagan. A Celtic cross was carved on the lid.

Reagan inhaled a deep breath, somehow sensing this was a very special gift. As she opened it, she was stunned to see a ring lying on a bed of purple velvet. Picking up the silver rings, she studied the tiny circles.

"It's a fede ring," Tia said.

"A faith ring, It was my mother's?"

Tia nodded, "And see the inscription inside."

"Anam Cara...what does that mean?" Reagan asked.

"Soul friend," Tia said. "I talked to your soon to be new husband a few weeks ago and he wanted me to have similar rings made in gold. This one is an engagement ring. I know he should be giving this to you, but I had to give the goldsmith the original and today your beloved is occupied by the king."

"Oh..."

"Put it on. He says he hopes you can forgive him."

"There is nothing to forgive. It is beautiful." Reagan admired the ring, turning it then slipping it onto her finger.

"Here," Tia said. "Here is the wedding ring you will give the laird during the ceremony."

Reagan took the second box; the one with Sean's wedding ring inside. She thought she could never be happier. This was truly a blessed day and one she knew she would never forget.

"I don't know what to say." Reagan gazed at her friend, tears truly streaming down her cheeks. "I hadn't even thought of a ring."

"That's what friends are for," Tia said as she held out her arms and welcomed Reagan into them for a sisterly hug.

~ * ~

Tears streamed down Erin's cheeks. She wiped the moisture away with the back of her hand. "Just when I thought something would go wrong, Tia shows up with such wonderful gifts."

"I dinnae mean to put a damper on all of this, but the wedding isn't over and there is a wee problem called, Becan."

"The witch promised to keep him occupied until they are truly wed." Shivers of fear swept over Erin. But what would happen when he returned? He had proclaimed Reagan a witch. He could still do that.

"I know but there is always the human factor. Witches can only do so much. If Becan finds a way to leave her hut, she cannot hold him."

"We will be ready then with enough fairies dust to influence the King, Becan and all of the kings councilors."

"Reagan has a birthmark on her left shoulder."

"A witches curse," Erin muttered. She rose from the back of the chair where she'd been sitting and flew around the room. She began to shake fairy dust on Reagan until both Reagan and Erin sneezed.

The birthmark had disappeared. "We will stay close throughout the ceremony and the celebration afterwards."

"Yes, of course, nothing can go wrong."

~ * ~

"What are those lights?" James asked Sean.

"Lights? I don't see anything." Sean peered into the woods searching for what James described.

"They are dancing as if they beckon me. See," the king pointed in a direction deep into the woods. "They twist and turn then make an alluring pathway to follow."

Sean shifted then put his hand over his eyes trying to see more clearly these dancing lights the king spoke of. "For the life of me, I see nothing."

"Come, let's follow them."

"Would that be wise? I have a wedding in a few hours."

"Just a little ways. Perhaps we will also catch sight of a buck. Fresh venison would be welcome at your celebration feast, would it not?"

"Of course," Sean said, yet he felt little excitement at the prospect of shooting a deer even for meat. He'd never hunted and was proving himself a little inept. But James had insisted they go. Who was he to deny James a king's pleasure?

"Don't be such a lazy soul. I don't remember you not excited over the hunt," the king said, stroking his chin and staring at Sean.

"Forgive me, sire, but I have other things on my mind today." He could only think of the wedding and his soon to be bride. This much was true. All he thought about was the wedding night. He had waited weeks for his bride to come to him. Anticipation swept through him, his nerves a bit on edge. He inhaled a long deep breath of the forest air.

"They are gone, the lights," James said. "But look."

The king pointed in the direction of a tiny hut that was nestled into a hillside. One would miss it if they weren't looking directly at it. The cottage was well camouflaged. Vines covered the door and boulders stood in front of the windows.

"The lights have vanished, but they to have led us to a tiny hut. I don't believe it would be prudent for either of us to step inside."

"You are not curious?"

Suddenly the king's men surrounded the clearing. "Your men seem to think as I do," Sean said.

A strange keening noise filtered through the forest. A shiver surged along Sean's spine. He rubbed his arms where goose bumps formed.

"Best we go," James said, turning from the entrance with a long sigh. "I'm no longer very inquisitive."

James' men lined up behind them, creating a protective shield between his majesty and the hut. Sean had never believed in witches or magic, but the glen had an eerie feeling to it and he was more than happy to depart.

"I will see you at the wedding," Sean told the king as they walked through the portcullis, feeling as if a heavy weight had settled on his shoulders.

James nodded before dismounting and handing the reins to a groomsmen. "Two hours it is? Then you will no longer be a free man," James said with a chuckle.

Sean nodded. Once inside his solar, he sat down. The little hut and the strange sensations, he'd just witnessed would not leave his thoughts. A foreboding feeling of doom swept through him.

"Shaughnessy?" A tapping at his door broke his reverie.

"May I come in?" The door opened.

"Tia, for what purpose do I owe this visit." Sean grinned. Tia's expression was contagious.

"I have brought you something."

"A wedding gift?"

"Yes, but it's for Reagan. I brought her one also, a ring to give you when you say your vows."

Intrigued, Sean rose and walked to Tia. "What is it?"

"A gold ring. It was her father's."

"Shouldn't William have it?" Sean asked.

"No, her father gave it to her mother. They spoke vows to each other and exchanged the rings. But the marriage was never legal. Her father was already wed—an arranged marriage."

"Thank you." He truly felt awe at what was transpiring. "This is very thoughtful of you. I truly appreciate this."

Tia set the ring in Sean's open hand then curtsied. "I must go." She turned and hurried from the room.

Sean gazed at the ring for several seconds before placing it on his desk, overwhelmed by the act of kindness Tia showed and the love Reagan's father must have shared with her mother. He hoped and prayed he and Reagan would share the same kind of love.

"Your bath," servants filed in with steaming water.

The soak would ease his muscles and the steam might clear his head. He mulled over all that had transpired over the weeks he'd been in Scotland. He'd never believed in magic. Still didn't. His travel here, to this time in history, had nothing to do with magic. Science had brought him here. Perhaps someone in some later time had developed a time machine. And he was sure if he knew a bit more, science would account for the little lights James had seen. But he couldn't figure out why he didn't see them.

A picture of a crazy scientist with grayish white hair popped into his head and made him laugh. He could see the outrageous, amazingly intelligent man pouring over all of his inventions.

"Wacky scientist indeed," he mumbled. Sean settled into the tub and let the hot water wash over him. He closed his eyes for a few minutes of relaxation, slowing his breathing and trying to calm his heartbeat.

A few minutes later he washed then dressed and was ready for the upcoming nuptials.

"Laird, your carriage is ready," Alistair spoke from the doorway to Sean's solar then bowed. "May I say, you look very ready for this day. The kilt becomes you."

"And, I am ready."

"However, you do look a bit pale. Mayhap you are not quite so prepared for the wedding night to come."

"Nervous would be the appropriate word here," Sean said as he strode from the room and down the long stairs to the courtyard. "And I've waited, albeit patiently, for the wedding night. I am more than ready."

Alistair followed then opened the carriage door for Sean. "Good luck, sir. I will have the feast prepared."

"I am hoping I will not need luck good or otherwise."

"The king has gone ahead. His men line the roads, just as a precaution. Becan has been barred from the ceremony."

"Really?"

"Yes, but it seems no one has seen him. So he will not pose a threat." Alistair closed the door.

Sean watched as the carriage left the castle behind. True to his words, Sean caught sight of the king's men strategically placed along the road to the parish church where the nuptials were to take place.

People waited outside the church to see their laird wed. He laughed to himself, thinking of a standing room only event.

"Laird," one of the king's men opened the carriage door then ushered Sean around the church to a back door.

Inside music played and the pulpit was filled with beautiful flowers. Tia's doing, Sean mused.

Sean took his place beside the king who was his only groomsman. The congregation stood. Dressed in a beautiful blue dress adorned with pearls, Tia walked slowly down the aisle.

A few minutes later, Reagan appeared on the threshold. Tia assumed her place in the front of the church then Reagan escorted by William followed Tia.

The rest of the ceremony passed in a blur. Sean remembered saying, "I do." And he also recalled Reagan stuttering through her lines. The rings were exchanged sometime, but he couldn't recall when, then he was kissing Reagan. She felt so tiny in his arms, her lips so warm and tender. He suddenly wanted to scoop her up and toss her on his bed. Ah, but they had the celebratory feast to attend. He must be patient a little while longer.

Arm in arm they walked down the aisle and out of the church. People cheered and yelled out their names along with good wishes. Ribald jests followed that made him laugh. In any time men were the same when it came to bedding a woman. Some of the words were different but the meaning explicit.

"Kiss her, kiss her," the crowd yelled.

~ * ~

Adair sat on a tree branch and clapped his hands, applauding the scene below. His grin stretched from ear to ear.

In an excited rush, Erin flew up beside him. "We have done it. Do you think our work here is finished?"

"I pray it is." Adair tossed a bit of fairies dust toward the happy couple then another handful for good measure.

"No one has seen Becan. He has vanished. That cannot bode well for Sean. What if he is accused of kidnapping?"

"I believe if anything has happened, it will not be the laird who is accused. It will be Reagan. We must look out for her and protect her."

"Do you think the fairy dust will hide her birthmark?"

Adair nodded. "I do, but I am also praying it won't be necessary."

"I have a heavy heart about this. I dinnae believe it is over yet."

"We must remain vigilant."

Chapter Seven

"To the lovely bride and the handsome groom," James toasted the couple, holding his goblet high then turning to see the entire crowd of well-wishers.

"May they always live in happiness."

"Here, here!"

Reagan looked around the field. Decorations hung from every tree. Ribbons adorned a walkway. The food smelled heavenly. Cook must have gone to great lengths, for every food imaginable lined the tables. There was haggis and roasted boar. Scones and early strawberries sat on the tables. Mead, ale and pink champagne were among the drinks served. Everything smelled heavenly.

Sean draped his arm around her then leaned in close. "Are you having fun, my darling?" he asked before kissing her lightly on the cheek then leaning back to gaze on his lovely bride.

Heat swept through her at his easy touch and the way his eyes roamed over her. She wondered what this evening would bring. Would he make love to her as tenderly as he had treated her over the last month?

It would not be long before she discovered the answer to her questions.

"This day is wonderful—the happiest of my life." She set her hand on his chest as he leaned over for a casual kiss.

"Good, I want it to stay that way."

"Here's to your's and Shaughnessy's happiness." Tia stepped forward and hugged Reagan. "Are you enjoying the celebration?"

"Thank you. I hope you find someone to love," Reagan said. "Yes, you did so much for me. You didn't have to."

Tia popped a strawberry into her mouth. "I hope so too. To find my heart's true love would be divine. William is ever after me to settle down. He is forever trying to arrange a marriage. I will not agree to just anyone."

"You thought it would be Shaughnessy, didn't you?"

"Perhaps, but we no longer suit. And I would at least keep trying to find a true love. He used to be so preoccupied."

"Some people believe true love does not exist," Reagan said as she bit into a strawberry.

"But you think it does," Cora McBride stepped between Tia and Reagan. She spoke with a sneer. "You will not keep me from Shaughnessy. He has told me he will continue to see me and pay for my needs."

"You lie," Tia said.

Reagan felt as if the ground had just dropped away from her feet. Sean would not do such a thing. Pay for her maybe until she found another protector. But he would not sleep with her.

"Just wait, wedding bliss will not last forever. He will warm my bed as soon as he grows tired of your cold, boring one," Cora said before flouncing away.

"What does she mean by that?" Reagan asked as she watched Sean visit with their guests. She knew he would have to convince many of the guests he was Shaughnessy, the laird to the castle and these lands.

"Do not pay attention to Cora. She is evil and has only her interest at heart. I've heard she's taken up with Becan. But no one has seen that man in a couple of days. I can't believe he has not shown up here," Tia said.

"Be careful what you are thinking," Reagan said to her friend as all focus turned to a dirty and disheveled man stumbling into the clearing.

"She's a witch! A witch I tell you." Becan cried out as he pointed a finger at Reagan. "She lured me into a witches den—set will o'whisps to light the way. The path was evil." Spittle formed around his lips.

"He's crazed," James muttered. "Stop him."

James' men grabbed Becan.

Reagan shivered as goose bumps rose over her entire body. For a moment her breath stopped and her heartbeat seemed to cease. She backed away from the man, shaking her head, moisture gathering in her eyes.

"What is this?" Sean stepped forward then made his way to Reagan. He wrapped a protective arm around her. "You are cold."

"It is the voice of a man who has been cursed, and by her." Becan's hand trembled as he continued to point an accusing finger at Reagan. He scrubbed his face then pushed his hair from his eyes.

"Come now, calm down. Do you ken what you are saying? It is a terrible charge to point a finger at a woman and call her a witch." William stepped forward to take Becan's arm and lead him away.

For a moment it appeared Becan would follow William. Then he stopped and shook off William's hold. "She's a witch. Take her to the tower and examine her. You will find a witches mark on her."

"This is a wedding feast," James said, his voice thundering across the clearing. "Are you sure this is what you want to do? She was once betrothed to you. It seems perhaps this is revenge."

"She cursed me."

Reagan trembled, fear overcoming all the happiness she'd felt earlier. This was it. They would find the mark on her shoulder, torture her and burn her at the stake. "No..." she said, backing away from the people who were now gathering around her. "No..." The need to turn and run overwhelmed her, but Sean with a protective arm around her waist, kept her by his side.

James wiped his brow and with a long heavy sigh, "Take her to her solar. I will send a priest. Shaughnessy will go also. I do not want her defiled on her wedding day. If nothing is found, you will have a lot to answer for." He focused his gaze on Becan. "I will tolerate no foolishness because you are a cast off suitor."

Reagan flinched away from the men coming for her, pressing herself against Sean. Tears flowed down her cheeks as she looked at her husband. *Please help me...*

But she knew there was nothing her new husband could do to rectify this horrific situation. She stumbled and could barely walk. If not for the guards holding her, she would have wilted to the ground.

The walk to her solar seemed to fly by in a blur. The people at the celebration seemed horrified at the accusation, but just as Sean was powerless, so were they. Sean followed and when the door to her room banged shut the men holding her let her go. She dropped to the floor, her skirts spread around her. Her body trembled with the terror flowing within.

What seemed like hours passed before a priest entered. Sean stood and walked toward him. The man shook his head as if he knew what Sean was about to ask. "Take all of her clothes off. This will not take long. If there is a mark of Satan on her body, then she will go to trial. If there is not..."

"If there is not, I would like Becan to go to trial for false accusations."

Reagan cowered on the floor, her arms crossed in front of her.

"Now lass, this will go much easier if you remove your clothes yourself."

Reagan was horrified but she understood the truth of his words. There was no room for pride here. "All right," she whispered. "But I need help. I have a ladies maid usually. I cannot reach the buttons."

"I will help her," Sean said.

"Good, then I would like everyone save Shaughnessy to leave."

She waited while the guards obeyed the priest's wishes. Then, after her dress was unfastened, she slipped out of every piece of clothing until she stood before the man naked. He walked around her, lifting her hair so he could see her back and shoulders then examined her more intimately until she could not stop her shaking. She knew he would find the birthmark, but he did not. And she wondered at that.

The priest stepped back and folding his arms in front of his chest, he announced, "This woman is no witch. There is no mark of Satan upon her body. She has been falsely accused on her wedding day."

~ * ~

James stood in the middle of the wedding guests. His hands were raised high as he attempted to silence the crowd. The moment dragged on and James appeared impatient.

"Silence!"

"What is she? Is she a witch?"

"My priest has examined her from head to toe."

"And."

"She has been falsely accused. Bring her forth."

Sean walked stiffly with his bride on his arm. She was pale as death, and Sean feared for her safety even though she'd just been exonerated by the King of Scotland and England.

"How can you be sure?"

"I have no doubt," the king said. "Do not question my judgment. The man, Becon, was lost in the woods. No doubt his mind was a bit addled by the experience. We must forgive him and make sure he makes no more accusations. Now let us celebrated the marriage of the laird and his new bride."

"Here, here!" A tankard of ale was held high and cheers reverberated around the clearing.

Sean felt his knees go a bit weak. But he had to stay strong for Reagan. His arm encircled her waist and he drew her close. Then whispered, "This was not how I had wanted this day to proceed."

"At least it cannot get any worse," Reagan said as she leaned into Sean.

He felt the warmth of her body so close to his and longed to sweep her into his arms, carry her to his solar and make love to her. But he couldn't—not yet. First, his obligations as laird had to be seen to.

He strode to James, still keeping Reagan close. "Thank you," he said.

"If she'd had a mark there would have been naught I could do for you," James said. "No matter how much I wished it, she would have been tried and in these times most likely convicted."

"I understand," Sean said. But he didn't understand any of this. How on earth could a person just point a finger at someone and accuse them of witchcraft. The notion was absurd.

"Well, I think Shaughnessy is a witch." Cora McBride was pointing a shaking finger at Sean. "He is not the real Shaughnessy. Somehow this man has spirited him away and taken his place."

"Nonsense," James said, waving a hand in the air to silence the crowd. "No more of this. Haven't you all done enough to ruin this day? You were his mistress. Were you not?"

The crowd inhaled a collective deep breath. Mutterings of his mistress rippled throughout.

"He betrayed me," Cora said, stepping back as the wedding guests surged forward.

"Remove her," James said, controlling the situation. "This should be a day of joy."

Sean held his tankard high, and holding Reagan's hand, he spoke. "Thank you for sharing this day with me. We," he looked at Reagan then back to his clan, "will never forget what has happened here. Know that we love you and wish only for your happiness." He gave a nod to the musicians who began to play.

Reagan held her goblet high also and with a voice that grew with strength as she spoke, said, "Everyone, dance, enjoy this day for I intend to hold no grudges against anyone."

Sean whirled her into his arms, swinging her in circles, lifting her high as the crowd clapped and stamped their feet in apparent appreciation of the two. They danced until Sean was breathless and Reagan cried out, "Stop! I cannot dance a moment longer. I must breathe."

Sean leaned in close and whispered. "Laugh for them, put your fears and the accusations behind us."

Reagan looked at him and smiled. He tickled her and she squirmed in his arms, laughing.

But Sean would not easily put the accusations behind him. He feared for her safety and he knew he loved her more than life itself.

Finding a time and a place to tell his lovely bride of only a few hours was foremost in his thoughts.

In that short time she'd been through so much and here she was, laughing and dancing, performing for the crowd.

Just because Becan and Cora had been silenced by James, it didn't mean they would remain that way.

As if Becan had heard Sean's thoughts, he was beside him. "We are not done with this," he said, his voice a snarl.

"You're wrong," Sean said. "As laird I can have all of your lands taken from you. I can strip you of everything." His fists tightened. He had never felt such anger toward anyone than he did now.

"Shaughnessy, please let's turn our concerns to the other people. See, they wait for us," Reagan said.

"Be careful, Becan," Sean said.

Sean turned from the man he now loathed to address the crowd. "Eat, drink to your hearts content. I find I need time with my new bride." He pulled Reagan close and kissed her. Reagan's lips parted and he tasted the sweetness of her.

How had she so quickly become the center of his universe? How had she stolen his heart to the point where he did not regret leaving his past behind? She was his soul mate, his life, his new world.

From the moment he'd stepped from the time machine, he'd felt as if he'd come home. Now all he needed to do was to tell Reagan how he felt about this—his new life—and her. But he wanted privacy and he needed to make love to her. He wanted to show her how he felt. Words were important but...

Lord, but he wanted to show her.

"Shaughnessy?" She questioned, touching his arm. "You seem to be far away, a land no one else has been to?

He marveled at how she was always so able to call him Shaughnessy in the company of others. She would never give anything, none of his secrets away.

"You are wise beyond words," he said as he replaced a lock of her hair that had fallen across her cheek.

"No, but maybe perceptive," she laughed softly, the sound like silver bells on the wind.

"I would keep you happy forever if I could."

"Thank you," she said, looking at the ground then back to him. "I am nervous."

"About what?" He suddenly didn't know what to think.

"The night to come."

"Ah, I am a bit nervous too."

"Really? You dinnae mean that."

"Yes, I've never made love with someone I care so much for."

"So, I will not be your first."

He felt a bit of heat on his cheeks. He couldn't remember blushing before, but this time it felt right. "No, not my first but my last I pray."

She looked down again and he could not see her eyes. He wanted to reach inside her soul and understand what she thought.

"Do not be afraid."

~ * ~

They got off to a bit of a rocky start, but I think things are going well now," Adair said as he watched the happy couple.

"Our plans worked. Now for the bedding and children."

"Children," Adair *tapped a finger on his chin in thought. "Children. Perhaps they should wait a bit. Don't want more rumors to fly."*

"Theirs will be beautiful. I foresee two boys and a girl."

"I do hope the girl looks like Reagan," Adair *said thoughtfully. "His forehead is far too masculine for a girl."*

"Of course the girl will look like Reagan. I will sprinkle a bit of fairy dust on her when she is pregnant and make a few wishes. Nothing to it." Erin *fluttered around the couple as made their way up the solar steps.*

"We should leave them now."

"Privacy is what those two need."

Then the door clanged shut. The hallway was empty and a soft breeze flowed from a window.

Chapter Eight

A table near the fireplace was set with an assortment of food, strawberries, lemon cakes, scones, chicken and much more. Two glasses of champagne had been poured. The table looked wonderful. Reagan heard her stomach grumble.

"Alistair?" Reagan asked, weariness overcoming her she wanted nothing more than to forget the past couple of hours and eat. She was famished.

"He is wonderful. Isn't he?" Sean said gesturing toward the food. "It all smells so appetizing."

Sean pulled a chair out for Reagan. She sat down. The strawberry melted in her mouth it was so delicious.

"We should probably talk," Reagan said.

"About what?" Sean sat down across from her then leaned forward, forearms on the table.

"About you, me—us." Her nerves were a bit frayed, and she really didn't know what he thought. If he could love her and live with her for the rest of their lives, she would be the happiest person on earth.

He picked up her hands and held them, stroking the tops with his thumbs. "You know I'm not Shaughnessy and I came here from another place and time. I can't return."

She swallowed hard, "Are you a witch?"

He let go of her hands then roared with laughter. "Hardly. I think I would call myself a victim, although I do not regret in anyway my presence here."

"Tell me about the future, where you came from."

"There is a lot to tell," he smiled at her. "For example, instead of candles we have electricity."

She looked at him a bit puzzled. "What is electricity?"

"I can turn on a light with a flip of a switch."

A flip of a switch. She mulled that over in her mind for a moment. "I'm not sure I'm ready to learn more. It seems like wizardry to me."

"Perhaps it is a bit much." He broke off a piece of scone and handed her the other half. "I rode a motorbike not a horse. It was powered with gasoline not hay. The building in the city reached for the sky and we moved to the top in what is called an elevator."

"You are teasing me," she told him. "I dinnae ken what this gasoline is, elevators or electricity."

"New York City, Manhattan has hundreds of buildings. I lived in Manhattan in an apartment with twenty or so other people living in the same building. I rode my motorbike to work everyday." Sean paused a moment, thinking. "Except the day I found the time machine. I walked that day and I don't even know why."

"I see," she said but she really didn't understand anything he was telling her. They finished their meal in silence. When they were finished, he brought her to a soft fur rug in front of the fireplace.

The flames were dying so he added wood. Reds, yellows, and blues played across the fire. "I was a fireman then."

"What is that?" she asked watching him, praying he truly did not want to return to a different time.

He stroked her cheek then ran his finger lightly down her neck and across her collarbone. She shivered with expectation. He was so tender and sweet. Before Sean, all she'd know from men was violence.

"I put out fires." He ran his finger around her ear then picked up her hand. Turning it over, he kissed her palm then the tip of each finger. "In homes and buildings."

"Sounds dangerous." A golden heat, simmered inside. She felt as one with the flames in the fire.

"Perhaps, sometimes, I never thought..."

"You have started a fire in me," she told him as he kissed her other hand in the same fashion he had kissed the first. "But I don't want you to put it out."

He held her face between both hands then lightly kissed her forehead, both cheeks then her lips.

"I would make the fire blaze with love," he told her between kisses. "The fire grows within me too."

She grew bold and kissed him back. Touched his cheek with her finger. He held her hand to his face. "You must take care. I would not have this end before we started. I was on fire at the wedding, cooled during the accusations, but now..."

She smiled. "I do the same to you? I believe I like that."

He nodded. "I would not frighten you, only pleasure you." Once again he kissed her, this time running his tongue across her lips.

Instinctively, she opened for him, reveling in the feelings sweeping through her. She'd never been wed, had never felt the touch of a husband. She delighted in how right this felt.

"I want you," she murmured softly, wondering what it would be like for her husband to make love to her.

Suddenly, thoughts of Cora pushed to the forefront of her mind. She drew back. Looking into his eyes she saw his love for her, felt it. He did not think of anyone save her. Happiness was something she'd known so little of in her short life. Was this true happiness?

"Oh, my God, but I want you to, need you as I've never needed anyone or anything."

Reagan rested her head on his shoulder while she played with the fastening of his shirt. She wanted to run her hands over his chest, feel his muscles, delight in his warmth. She wasn't sure if it was proper.

"Can I touch you?" she whispered.

~ * ~

He groaned softly, knowing she could, but if she did, he wouldn't be able to take this as slowly as he wanted to.

"Not yet," he spoke softly. With great patience Sean's fingertips slid along the curve of Reagan's spine. Slowly he drew a path touching each vertebra as if learning every beautiful detail.

"You are the most gentle man I've ever known," she said, her breath whispering close to his ear.

Grinning, Sean switched attentions to her lips, carefully touching her. She made a startled sound as a fiery heat surged within, and every part of him hardened with incredible need.

She cried out softly.

"I won't hurt you," he told her, knowing if she were a virgin, he would cause pain.

"I trust you," she said, shaking her head and watching him with wide and innocent eyes. The scent of spring flowers wound around Reagan. His body hardened even more as he embraced her scent and the feel of her flesh against his.

"When I touch you, tell me if you like it and how it makes you feel," he murmured.

"All right. Is that how I can help you?"

"Umm," he said. "It's one thing but there will be others."

"When you touch me, I feel as if I'm going to melt, but then goose bumps rise all over me," Reagan said as she watched Sean. "I think the little daisies in the meadow must feel the same way when the sun appears after a spring rain."

Sean's breath caught in a silent rush as he fought for control. "You humble me, Reagan."

"Why..." she started to ask but Sean's tongue found her ear and was tracing it. He felt her shudder and lean into him, her fingers sliding through his hair.

"I couldn't have even begun to guess," she said.

"Reagan?"

"There are parts of me I had never thought about before, and they are so very sensitive." She inhaled a long deep breath and cat-like, stretched her back, unknowingly offering herself to him.

His hand tensed then slowly moved over her collarbone as sweat beaded on his upper lip. He nuzzled Reagan's earlobe before he caught it between his teeth. She inhaled a sharp breath then let it out in a shivery sigh.

"If you like, I can find more spots," he whispered. "Then you will tell me how I make you feel."

Reagan arched into him while her hands pushed her long dark hair above her head, baring herself more completely to his questing lips. With a smile, Sean accepted her offering. His tongue traced her ear once more, spiraling inward until she gasped. He continued the rhythmic strokes until her voice broke over his name. Slowly, he released her and lifted his head, smiling wolfishly.

"Don't stop."

Laughing, Sean shook his head. "Little she devil. Where do you want my kisses?"

"I don't know. You're the teacher."

"Ah, and you are the willing pupil always desiring to please the instructor."

"I am," she murmured.

"Good." Sean looked from her wide eyes to the curves of her body beneath her wedding dress. "I'm a very good teacher, and I will show you places where everything I do feels better than the place before."

"When you are finished, can I do the same to you?"

The confirmation of mischief and innocent passion in Reagan's voice made Sean laugh. His hands gentled while he ran his fingers through the length of her hair.

"You are my miracle, my highland miracle," he murmured. "And I do believe it is time to take this to the bedroom."

"I love you," she said as he swept her into his arms.

"My sweet highland miracle."

Defying the Odds
C.L. Kraemer

Chapter One

In a meadow east of Eugene, Oregon

Bram ambled up the roughly hewn stairs to the willow lounge chair located at the front of his home. He pulled the scrimshawed pipe from his pocket and filled the bowl with his favorite blend of black cherry tobacco. The paced routine of loading the ivory bowl with fragrant leaves and tamping them firmly into place was one of his favorite after dinner rituals. Withdrawing a matchstick from the inner pocket of his vest, he struck the sulfured end against a river rock he'd placed on the root of the towering oak that served as his home.

The fading evening sky showered the mountains in hues of gold and red. Pushing away the light, a blanket of dark blue velvet sprinkled with luminous star points soon prevailed. Bram puffed smoke rings at the darkening heavens.

"Evenin'." A scruffy black and tan terrier mix meandered up and, after circling three times, lay next to the chubby gnome.

"Evening, Silas. How's the family?"

"Well, thank you. Daisy announced we're expecting—again."

Bram chuckled into his beard. "Congratulations."

"Humph. I'll be glad when we're both too old to care. I came over to ask if there are any jobs in sight. I'll need to be working as much as I can now."

It seemed he got one batch of kids out of the house and another was on the way.

Silence stretched between the business partners. Bram pulled deep draughts on his pipe, blowing the smoke away from his friend. His eyes were drawn to the large block of light spilling from the picture window of the behemoth on the hill. The Saun clan, night elves whose callous actions nearly destroyed the fae population of the meadow and surrounding forests, owned the out of place monstrosity.

Bram squinted his eyes to focus his vision on the methodical movement that broke the beam of light. He could just make out a figure pacing rhythmically in front of the casement. Unable to ascertain which of the night elves was engaged in the determined striding, Bram was sure of only one thing…if the night elves were restless and unhappy, the rest of the valley was in trouble.

~ * ~

Gitty paced in front of the picture window, ignoring the expansive view of the green valley below. The thick carpet covering the hand selected hardwood floors muffled the angry stompings of her boots. At the end of each turn, she jabbed the air with her finger.

"Think you can take away my magic, do you?" She spun on the ball of her foot and stamped to the other side of the room. "We'll see about that!" Jab, jab.

Morgan, the younger of the two siblings, stretched his limbs languidly across the fine leather couch, watching the angry display being played out in the living room, a smirk residing on his lips.

"What has your knickers in a twist?" His leg, hanging over the arm of the couch, swung slowly back and forth.

Gitty broke her tirade for a moment. "I'm surprised yours aren't. How can you tolerate not having magic to use?"

"Because, dear sister, I don't *need* magic to get my way. I have my," he waved a hand up and down his body, "*obvious* attributes."

Gitty grimaced. "Please. Don't make me sick."

Pulling to an upright position, Morgan stretched his long legs in front of him, tucking his hands behind his head.

"You're just jealous."

"Hardly."

"Then what's your problem?"

"I don't fancy living my life in pubs among the scum of the valley sponging off the pity of strangers. My plans include owning all I see."

Morgan rose from the couch and faced his sister.

"Good luck with that. Even the Others are wise to your quest for power. I'm going out. See you later." He moseyed out of the living room and down the hall.

Gitty gritted her teeth. Morgan might be her brother, but he was useless when it came to thinking beyond his next good time.

She glared at the source of the fingers of light stretching over the meadow. The owner of the Lending Library was an Other the local fae had embraced with open arms. Even Uther, the one-time leader of the night elves and her uncle, had taken a personal interest in the older female.

"Must be losing his sanity."

She spotted a pinpoint of red light glowing in the far distance. As hard as she tried, she couldn't sense the origin of the light.

"I hate not having my magic!" She smacked the wall with her hand, immediately regretting the action. Bolts of pain shot up her arm.

"Damn it!"

Turning on her heel, she tramped out of the room.

Chapter Two

Linda Brown, Librarian to most of the fae, peered down the entry lane, the cinnamon coffee exploding on her tongue. Spring was evident by the riot of color lining the road. Mist settled gently on the new foliage stretching to greet the sun. She sighed, a contented sound followed by a slow-forming smile. Her keen hearing picked up the subtle flutter of tiny wings.

Chrissy, the resident wood nymph, languidly made her way to the edge of the chair and, back-winging furiously, settled on the arm.

"Librarian?"

"Yes?"

"Would you like a refill?"

"Thank you, no. I'm doing fine. Your new coffee drink is heavenly. I think we need to create a name for it. What about *Cinnamon Chrissy*?"

There was a quick flapping commotion as the little nymph moved to face the librarian. Her deep violet eyes were wide with excitement.

"Really?"

"You did suggest and create it."

The nymph flew a loop-de-loop.

"Whohoo!" She buzzed around, settling once again on the arm of the chair, humming a tune the librarian recognized as an ancient Celtic song of celebration.

"Librarian?"

"Hhmm?"

"What are we going to do about May Day?"

"I'm not sure. What do you normally do?"

"We have a celebration of several days with dancing and feasting."

"I'll let you handle the planning. Just tell me what you need, and I'll do my best to provide it."

Silence stretched between the unusual friends.

"Chrissy?"

"Uh-huh?"

"You okay?"

"Uh-hum. Just trying to figure where to start."

Librarian smiled. The nymph had come such a long way from their first meeting when she'd tumbled into the library, disoriented and trembling in fear. The coffee shop and restaurant portion of the library ran smoothly under her guidance. A faint rustle of wings interrupted the librarian's thoughts.

"I think I'll start setting things in motion. If you need me, I'll be in the kitchen." The tiny figure zipped through the door, disappearing into the building.

Linda opted to stay on the porch and enjoy the sweet smell of the valley as the spring showers commenced to lightly sprinkle the earth. Through the mist, she spied a figure hiking up her driveway. Something familiar about the gait tickled her memory; the stride so confident, head held high.

Night elf?

Heat rushed to her cheeks, coloring the fair complexion. Stirring from her chair, she stood and stretched her legs. Her view of the traveler was better from a standing angle. There was no doubt as to the identity of the lanky man who assuredly strode to her front porch.

"Beautiful day, Librarian. Don't you think?"

"Yes, it is." Her cheeks glowed a healthy pink. "How've you been, Uther?"

"Well, I have a great hunger and thirst. Have you bread and drink available?"

"Let me speak with Chrissy. Please..." she indicated one of the chairs near a table, "…rest your feet. I'll be back soon."

Uther allowed a smile to cross his lips. This lovely woman whom the fae community had taken to their ranks so loyally made his heart pound. Removing his cape, he lowered his tired frame into the offered seat and leaned back to admire the scenery. His eyes threatened to close and would have had Linda not brought him a glass of water and several slices of fresh made bread. He could smell the delight before she placed the plate in front of him.

"Oh, my. It has been some time since I sank my teeth into the likes of fresh bread."

"You can thank Chrissy. I don't know why that little wood nymph is so determined to learn all the human tasks there are to living, but it's been a blessing in disguise. She really does make the best bread in the valley."

Uther slathered butter on the still warm slice and bit into the concoction. His moan of appreciation tickled Linda's heart. Sensations long forgotten started to make her uncomfortable.

"Would you like to try one of her coffee drinks? They're really quite good."

He held up a finger and slumped against the chair. "How anything can be as heavenly as this bread I don't know, but I'll try one of her coffees."

Linda noted the relaxing of his shoulders and settling of his body.

Good. Maybe, he'll stay longer than a day or two. Wait! Where did that come from? She hurried to the kitchen, slowing as she neared the door. A gentle knock to alert the nymph to her presence was given.

"Yes, Librarian?"

"Could you make one of your Cinnamon Chrissy's for Uther?"

The little fae buzzed to face Linda. "Uther's here?" Her violet eyes danced with delight.

"Yes. He just arrived and is tired and hungry. I thought he could do with a tasty pick-me-up."

"Where's he staying?" Her wings shook with excitement.

"I…I hadn't asked him." Linda's brows knit together. "Why?"

"He used to stay with the Sauns when he came to visit. But he can't stay there now."

"Hhmm, you're right. I suspect the welcome mat wouldn't be set out for him."

"I'd offer my tree, but I don't think he'd fit." Chrissy tapped her finger on her chin, forehead crinkled in thought.

Linda burst into laughter.

"What?" Chrissy frowned.

Shaking her head, the librarian settled into a warm chuckle. "The picture of Uther trying to squeeze into your home just hit me as funny."

The little wood nymph tried hard to hold her serious look but was soon giggling.

"It would be funny, wouldn't it?"

Linda nodded. "What say we brew up some of your magical coffee for our night elf?"

Chrissy set to putting her talents to use, whipping up her cinnamon specialty. Linda carried the steaming mug to the front porch. Toeing open the screen, she headed toward the table Uther occupied.

Legs stretched in front of him, the night elf sat with his head against the building. His arms were folded and his platinum eyelashes rested on his tanned cheek. Linda stopped in her tracks and sucked in a deep breath.

He's magnificent; so long and muscular. She set the steaming coffee cup on the nearest table and retrieved his cape from the back of a nearby chair. Gently, she covered her sleeping visitor.

He stirred and blew out a deep sigh.

Linda froze. When Uther shifted and his breathing deepened, she backed away.

"What am I going to do? You can't sleep on the porch for the next couple days. There's a real possibility of the temperatures dipping." She muttered gazing at the form of the man whose looks made her heart pound. *Wait a minute!*

The cup of coffee trailed cinnamon scented steam into the library.

"Didn't he like my coffee?"

7

Linda recognized the hurt tone of the wood nymph. "He didn't even take a sip."

"What!"

"Hold on, Chrissy. I went out to give him the coffee and found him sleeping in his chair. Who knows how many days he's been traveling? I didn't see a vehicle or horse, so I can only assume he was walking. I'll bet he's just exhausted."

Chrissy winged to the window and peeked out at the slumbering night elf.

"Too true. Where's he going to stay?"

"When Donald, my husband, was alive we used to go camping in the Three Sisters Wilderness area. Somewhere in the shed out back I think I still have some down filled sleeping bags he brought home with him from his time in the service. I can air them out and provide some comfort from the elements for Uther. He'll be able to use the floor of the library after we close up at night."

Chrissy winged to face the librarian. "What if he says no?"

Linda shrugged her shoulders. "I don't know."

~ * ~

She wrapped her grey woolen sweater to her body and shivered. "Feels cool." The librarian hadn't been down the trail to the shed in several years. When her husband died, she couldn't face the memories stored in the eight by ten building. Placing her hand on the lock of the hasp, she pulled in a deep breath and turned the handle. Squealing unhappily, the warped door opened with difficulty.

Linda covered her nose to ward off the pungent smell of mildew. "Whew! I should've done this ages ago." She leaned in and grasped the thin string hanging from the socket of the bare bulb Donald had installed. The glare from the fifty-watt light momentarily blinded her. Recovering from the brightness of the light, Linda took a second look and groaned. Cobwebs blanketed everything in sight. She'd need to give the place a good cleaning before she'd be able to find anything.

Sighing in resignation, she turned out the light and closed the door. At the moment all she wanted to do was wash her hands in the stream and pull clean, crisp fresh air into her lungs. A hint of mildew clung inside her nostrils. Her throat tickled from the dust and everywhere she looked at her clothes she saw dirt. The path to the stream ran past the property line to the east of the shed. The proximity was too much for her to deny the pull and heeding her heart and not her head, she strolled through the woods admiring the spots of wild flowers exploding in spring color. Clear water tumbled wildly through the rocky riverbed. Linda stopped. By summer's end, this mad, rushing torrent would dwindle to a gentle, meandering brook.

She knelt down and dipped her hands in the closest pool. Chills exploded on her arms, and she fell against the mossy bank from the shock.

"Wow! I knew this was snow runoff, but I figured by the time it got here, the water would've warmed a bit." Linda furiously rubbed her hands together then stuck them under each arm for warmth. Rays of sunlight streamed through the forest canopy and speckled the riverbank, enticing her to lean back and close her eyes. A gentle breeze ruffled her hair. Muscles unaccustomed to relaxation betrayed her. For the first time in many years, Linda felt calm and at ease. Quieting her mind would prove more of a challenge; however, the roar of water exploding over rocks and rushing to the ocean soon gentled her overactive brain. As the rumble of water faded to background, Linda began to pick out the songs of robins and scoldings of bluejays nearby. Swishing grass tickled her arms and the new leaves on the overhead branches rustled. The scene was bucolic, but deep in the pit of her stomach, Linda felt a nagging. Something was off. She realized the birds had stopped singing. Opening her eyes, she looked around as she lay on her back. When she couldn't find the source of her uneasiness in the treetops, she propped on her elbow and reconnoitered the landscape around her.

The bank on the opposite side of the stream appeared barren of life. No swaying branches from the few bushes near the water. Linda's gaze moved south in the direction of town passing over a downed tree. She'd started to turn to her right when her brain registered what she'd just witnessed.

In front of the log, crouching low to the ground, sat an animal the size of a bobcat. This creature, however, was completely black with glowing yellow eyes. And worse yet, the animal had her in its sights. The eyes didn't blink. Linda looked away and turned back to find the creature crouching lower. She could swear the pupils had enlarged. The cat appeared ready to pounce.

Linda clamored up, turning to bolt back home as quickly as her legs would carry her. She ran square into a muscular chest. A piercing scream left her mouth as she fainted.

~ * ~

Uther swept the librarian into his arms before she could hit the ground. His heightened senses detected a presence across the stream. He narrowed his eyes and spied the black cat crouched on the bank. The malevolent eyes took him in, and Uther heard a low growl from the same general direction.

You are the traitor of your own kind.

The animal's thoughts jolted Uther. He kept a steady watch on the animal as it rose and slipped into the brush at the edge of the river.

"Ooohhhh." Linda was gaining consciousness. "Where am I?" She tried to focus on the nearest object. When she registered the fact she was in Uther's arms, her fair complexion disappeared beneath a rosy wave of color.

"Ple-please put me down. I can manage."

She wiggled in his grasp, causing him to let down one arm. Linda's feet dropped to the ground with a thump.

"What happened?" The worry in his eyes sent her to blushing anew.

"I went to the shed to find a cot and sleeping bag for you. I didn't realize just how long it had been since I'd been inside. When I emerged, I felt a desperate need to wash the dirt from my hands and, I guess, I sort of…"

Uther spared her the embarrassment she seemed to be experiencing.

10

"With the cat?"

"Oh, I was enjoying the beautiful day and realized I could no longer hear any birds. When I looked around that...that huge animal was glaring at me. I thought it was going to attack me. I'd gotten up to head back to the house when I bumped into you and, well, you know the rest."

He chuckled, a warm soothing sound bubbling from deep in his chest.

"I can't say I blame you. That creature is the biggest house cat I've ever seen."

Linda furrowed her brow. "Are you sure that's a house cat?"

Uther nodded. "I can be fairly certain it's not a wild cat. I've never seen a black bobcat in my life; not that there couldn't be any, but I've not seen them. What say we go back to the house? I'm fine sleeping on the floor. I've spent the last six months or so sleeping in places not as warm or as comforting as the floor of your home."

Linda felt the warmth of a blush touching her cheeks. *I'm too old to be blushing like a schoolgirl.* She tromped up the path toward the Lending Library.

Uther stifled the urge to chuckle. *She looks so determined.* This Other had captured his interest when the clans of the valley had gathered and stripped the night elves, Gitty and her brother Morgan, of their magic. She'd not backed down against the formidable pair. Knowledge circulating in the fae community spoke that she willingly opened her doors to any who needed assistance, asking for naught in return.

He opened his mind and issued a warning. *I'm not sure what you're up to, Lancelot, but if you or your master, Gitty, bring harm to this Other, I will string you up and use you for target practice.*

The air before him wavered slightly and he knew his message had been received.

Chapter Three

The lithe figure gave a flip of the tail and caught the current of rushing water to beyond the spot occupied by the large black creature. Finding her favorite lichen covered boulder, Trickle tucked behind the stone barrier and watched the action above her. The wicked, black cat was in the hunter mode and crouched to attack another victim. She ran a delicate webbed finger down the jagged white scar marring the beauty of her scales. The vitriolic beast had caught her off guard and nearly made her the object of a meal. Had it not been for— *His voice! He's close by.*

She poked her head from behind the rock and noted he held the female in his arms. Trickle allowed a wrinkle to mar her porcelain forehead. *Is she dead? Did that monster feline claim another victim?* Movement in the man's arms answered her query. Trickle watched the woman stomp off toward the building where her cousin worked.

Must be the one Chrissy calls The Librarian.

He stood on the bank of the river and she jumped when the sound waves carried his issued warning to all who could comprehend.

Lancelot. That is the name of my enemy. Swishing her tail, she moved to the center of the manic flow of water and peered at the bank where the cat had stood. *He's gone—good.*

~ * ~

Uther caught the flash of tail and undulation of golden hair.
"Trickle, my friend? Is that you?"

12

The tiny creature wiggled her way to his side of the river and peered up at him.

He held his hands in front of him as he spoke. "I've no net and I promise on my honor as a reformed Night Elf of the house of Saun, I intend you no harm."

The brown speckled green eyes regarded him suspiciously.

"If I had meant harm, would I not have kept you after the attack?"

He tried his best to give her an earnest look of honesty. He could only hope it would work.

The water fae slipped a delicate hand on a rock near the bank and pulled up, flipping around to sit in the best position to afford her a quick escape.

"How are you, night elf?" The words from the mermaid flowed eloquently over Uther's ears.

He smiled. The first rule to speaking with a merperson was to be armed against the bewitching tone of their voice. He murmured lowly. "Block."

The mermaid giggled. "Ah, but you are wary."

"Indeed, my watery friend, and still dry on the bank. How is your side?"

Trickle gently moved her hair, exposing the wicked white scar she bore from her attack. "It hasn't disappeared." She traced the route of the mark.

"Why don't you magic it away?"

"It's a reminder to me each time I pass my hand over the hard line to be more alert in my daily life. If you hadn't come along at the right time...well, I won't allow myself to become anyone's lunch."

Uther nodded. "A very wise move. Be careful. Lancelot appears to be hunting these woods, and I know he hates losing a good catch."

"I shall, night elf. *You* be careful. If my cousin Chrissy is right, you are next on the list of targets." She flipped water with her tail and spattered him. A giggle escaped.

Brushing off the droplets from his breeches, he rose from the bank.

"I will, little one, I will. Until next time." Uther watched the selkie dive under the turbulent rapids and disappear. Turning from the river, he made his way back to the Library.

~ * ~

He was aware there were selkies in some of the local rivers but hadn't seen one. On a hunch after the clan meeting where his niece and nephew had been stripped of their magical powers, Uther had followed them out of the building. He'd sent Linda the Librarian off to get him a piece of cake to occupy her while he slipped out the back door. Using his enhanced vision, he tracked the pair as they crashed through the woods to their home. They still believed their magic was viable and arrogantly issued spells to clear the pathway to walk. On many an occasion that evening, Uther was forced to cover his mouth so he wouldn't burst into laughter as the two night elves stumbled over bushes and tree stumps which didn't magic away.

When he'd decided the pair was well on their way to their home, he turned around and headed back. His senses were overwhelmed by fear. Following the path of the terror, he came upon a scene he would not soon forget.

Clutched in the paw of the massive animal Gitty Saun kept as a house pet, was a limp figure. One side appeared to be covered in scales while the other showed bare flesh and flowing yellow hair. Uther acted on instinct and blasted the animal with a magic command.

"DROP HER!"

The cat pulled in the paw, bobbling its prize and growling as the creature fell to the ground. It started to reclaim the booty when Uther threw a lightning bolt above the animal's head. Yowling in anger and fleeing as fast as the padded feet could move, the cat vanished into the dark night.

Uther dashed to the river's edge and was amazed to find a miniature mermaid bleeding profusely from a slash the length of her body. He knelt and lightly placed a finger on the open wound while uttering a healing spell. He had to repeat the spell twice before the slash closed completely.

Her body fit neatly into the palm of his hand and he was careful not to jar her as he carried her to the river. Water slowly filled his palm as he lowered her into her element. His heart pounded as he prayed this unique creature wasn't dead. Her eyes fluttered and she opened her mouth to scream.

"Ssshhh!!! We don't want that monster to know you survived."

Affirmation from the mermaid was all he needed, and Uther released her completely, watching her swim slowly on the river's top then, with a flip of her tail, slipping beneath the water.

He'd not seen her since that time. Spying the little selkie was a pleasant surprise. However, viewing the black monster, Lancelot, was not.

Uther groaned. He just knew Gitty and her brother Morgan were up to something, and the rest of the valley would be caught in the backlash.

Chapter Four

Large golden eyes observed from the foliage the interaction between the fair mermaid and the night elf.

So she survived. Not for long. I'll have that tasty treat before the next moon.

Employing all the lessons his mother had instilled in him, Lancelot moved through the underbrush with stealth. He needed to get home and communicate with his master, Gitty. Time was of the essence. It was imperative she be told Uther was in the valley again.

Breaking into a gallop, the sleek black cat sprinted through the forest. He stopped to reconnoiter the meadow when he reached the edge of the copse of trees. The air teased him with hints of mice nearby, but he couldn't stop to indulge his love of the hunt. The mice would be there in the early morning hours.

Tall grass whipped against his face as he raced up the hill. The sun cast golden shafts of light through the windows as he entered the house by means of his cat door. A quick stop at his water dish then he marched into the empty living area. The air hung in angry waves.

I'll check her room. He padded down the hall, skittering to avoid being kicked as Morgan burst from his room.

"Get out of the way, you wretched animal," he scowled at Lancelot.

Growling lowly, the black animal bared his fangs then continued on his mission. He flicked his ears when the door to outside slammed and slowed his pace as he neared his mistress' room. Cautiously, he surveyed the scene. Clothing was haphazardly strewn over the furniture, and the dressing table chair lay on its side. Lancelot eased his way into the space and hopped up on the overturned piece. He sniffed the air and twitched his ears forward and backward to catch the sounds of his lady, but his efforts were met with silence. Straining his neck and focusing his concentration, the wavering of air and clanging of steel crashed against his nerves. There could only be one place from where these sounds could emit.

He jumped off the chair and bolted to the basement gym. He must get to his mistress and make her aware of the enemy in the valley. The crashing of steel against steel muted his thundering paw steps.

"I HATE not having my magic!" Crash! The metallic clang echoed around the practice area. Grunting and thrusting with barely contained anger, Gitty attacked the dummy again. Crash!

Lancelot flattened his ears. The noise permeated his head and made his fur stand on end. Yowling, he tried to get her attention.

"I hate this." Crash! "I hate this." Crash! "I hate this!" Crash!

Sweat rolled down the sides of her face, and Gitty swiped at her forehead with the back of her free hand. Out of the corner of her eye, she spied Lancelot.

"What are you doing here?" Something about his presence rubbed her the wrong way. *What good are you if I can't use magic to talk with you?*

She ambled to the window and peered at the valley below. The sword clattered from her hand to the floor.

Lancelot cocked his head as she tried to choke back a sob. *Crying?*

"Yes. What's it to you?" Gitty barked.

Just haven't seen it before.

"Well it happens to everybody so—" She stopped and whipped around to face him.

"I can hear you."

Yes.

"Ho...how?"

Humph. You lost your magic, not your telepathy.

Gitty watched Lancelot roll his eyes. Then she started to chuckle.

Soon she was laughing and dancing around the gym floor.

"Whohoo! This is just the beginning! I'll get my magic back yet." She wrapped her arms around herself and began to hum.

There's a reason I wanted to talk to you.

Gitty looked at the black creature and smiled. "What?"

Uther is back.

The smile disappeared from her face. "Are you sure?"

Lancelot narrowed his eyes. *Of course. He threatened me.*

"He threatened you? Where is he? Why is he back?"

He shook his head. *I don't know why he is here, but he's staying with that Other in her lair. He threatened me when I was watching her by the river.*

"Really? Hmmm. This might work to our advantage. We'll let Morgan have his little play date tonight, but tomorrow, we need to come up with a plan to regain our rightful place in this valley—and get rid of Uther in the process."

She reached down and ran her hand over the fur on the back of Lancelot's body. "This turned out to be a *wonderful* day. Come on, big boy. Let's get you a treat."

~ * ~

Gitty stretched her legs to the mahogany coffee table. Lancelot had curled up at her side and napped by his mistress. Save for a haunting melody she quietly hummed, the room was silent. When the backdoor slammed, Gitty jumped and Lancelot raised his head and emitted a low growl.

Morgan stormed into the living room and started down the hall.

"Home a bit early, aren't you, little brother?" She glanced at the wall clock, noting the time was only a few hours later than his departure.

"Yeah, well, maybe I missed my loving family."

Gitty noted the acrid tone and sneer on his face.

"Pray tell what happened?"

"Don't feel like it."

"Fine, but don't come crying to me when Uther walks in to your favorite watering hole and sweeps the ladies off their feet." She stared at the retreating back and smiled when Uther's name stopped him in his tracks. She watched in fascination as he slowly turned her direction, noting the loss of color in his face.

"Uther?"

"Yes, dear brother, Uther. He's back in the valley and staying with the Other who's captured his eye." She watched the normally icy blue eyes of her brother darken to a cloudy grey.

Visibly shaking and gritting his teeth, Morgan measured his steps as he entered the living area. "He's the reason my nights have become so miserable."

The faint whisper of a smile touched Gitty's lips. "I thought you said you didn't need magic."

His brows knit together. "I say a lot of things. Doesn't always mean they're true."

She feigned surprise. "Really? Why, Morgan—I thought you to be a man of honesty and integrity."

"Save it. How can you know for sure Uther is back in the valley?"

"Lancelot told me."

He opened his mouth to answer then snapped it shut, rolling his eyes. "Sure. And the cow jumped over the moon. How can you talk with the monstrosity of a cat without your magic, sister?"

Lancelot raised his head to glare menacingly at the male night elf.

Morgan took a step backward.

Gitty inspected her nails. She allowed the ticking of the clock to fill the silence for five minutes before answering.

"I may have lost my magic but not my ability to use telepathy. And Lancelot saw Uther on the riverbank behind The Lending Library."

Morgan groped behind him to locate the chair. Once having found the leather seat, he dropped into the buttery cushions. "Uther…here in the valley again."

Gitty hid a smile. "Yes. A bitter fact we have to live with; however, dear brother, what would you sacrifice to have your magic back?"

Morgan snapped his head up and stared at his sister. "How?"

"That's the question to answer before the rising of the next sun. I think a pot of coffee with sugar and cream is in order. We need a foolproof way to implement this plan. And this time, *Uther* will pay with his life."

Chapter Five

Chrissy tumbled wings over toes backwards, throwing out her arm to grab the microwave handle. Wildly swinging from the chrome grip, she caught a flash of grey barrel past her, leaving a faint whisper of pine in the wake. Librarian's sun streaked haired danced in the wind caused by her rush through the kitchen. The crash of the door against the frame set the little wood nymph's teeth on edge. She winged into place on the kitchen counter and listened to footsteps skitter across the hardwood floors of the library's main room. A slammed door followed by silence ended the abrupt interruption to the tiny nymph's afternoon routine.

The small fae spread her delicate wings and loped across the main room to the closed door on the opposite wall. She hovered in front of the portal and keened her hearing to pick up sounds behind the barrier. Odd sounds of shuffling assailed her ears. She raised a tiny fist to knock on the door when Uther burst into the room.

"Linda! Linda! Where are you? Are you alright?" He searched the aisles of the bookshelves and opened the front door to check the porch. Spotting Chrissy, he moved toward her.

The fae whipped around and crossed her arms over her chest pinning her most fearsome glare on him.

"What have you done to her?" She cocked her head to one side.

Uther shrugged his shoulders. "Nothing."

"Really, Chrissy. He's done nothing."

The nymph zipped around to stare directly into the steel gray eyes of her Other friend.

"Then why were you making such funny noises in your room?" Violet eyes widened as the little fae cocked her head.

"It's, well, it's not Uther's fault. Just my own issues that have taken me off guard."

Chrissy shook her head. "What?"

Linda clutched a book in one hand. "Would you set the water to boiling? I feel the need for some tea."

"Sure. What kind, Librarian?"

"Chamomile. The calmness of the brew will help to set my mood. Uther? Would you care to join me on the porch? We need to talk."

He raised his brows at the fae and dipped his head in acquiescence to the librarian. "Of course, my Lady. After you."

He held the door open and followed Linda to the table and chairs on the porch.

When she bent to sit in the chair, an item fluttered from the book to the deck.

Uther leaned over and picked up a photograph. Pictured was a beautiful raven-haired maiden attired in a long satin wedding gown. A crown of tiny crème-colored roses perched atop a black mass of curls falling loosely about her face. Her delicate hand was slipped through the arm of a striking, fair-haired young man in Navy dress whites. Both young faces were glowing. His hand covered the small fingers resting in the crook of his arm. She smiled shyly at the camera. His eyes were tenderly locked on her face.

Uther handed the photo to Linda. "This is yours, I believe."

Linda snatched the photo. She felt heat crawling up her neck. "Darn it!"

He settled in the chair next to hers. "I'm sorry. Did I offend you?"

She pushed out a big breath. "No. It's why I wanted to speak with you." She turned to face him.

She held the memento in her hand and examined the two young people.

"This is a picture of me and my husband on our wedding day.

Donald had received permission to come home before he was shipped overseas to Vietnam, and we put together a rush wedding and reception. We had three days for a honeymoon, which we spent in Bend at a ski resort then he left for the war. For eleven months, I lived on pins and needles dreading every phone call, watching the road for the car that would bring the officials to my door to tell me he'd been killed. When he walked through the door of our home in Eugene two months early, I fainted. He picked me up and carried me to the couch.

"Your actions this afternoon took me back to that day so long ago.

"I've been embarrassed about my reactions to you when we're near each other. I'm too old to be blushing like a schoolgirl, yet every time you speak to me, I explode in waves of redness. I'm an old woman, Uther, and I don't have time to waste playing silly games. That's for very young people."

He looked into her steely gray eyes. "You are a beautiful woman, Linda."

"Was."

"*Are*. The bloom of youth isn't all a true man searches for in a woman; kindness, intelligence and courage are just as important. I listen to the tales of the woods and the fae who dwell there. Your acts of kindness are spoken of throughout the valley and into the mountain ranges as well. You've protected many of the lost fae and guided others who aren't sure where to go. You open your home and food stocks for all who would ask. What more could a man in his right mind ask?"

Her cheeks exploded with color. "Damn it."

Uther leaned toward her and ran his fingers down the soft skin of her cheeks. "It is a beautiful sight to see a woman who is still humble and appreciative of a compliment.

"As far as the game playing, I have entered into many a contest but don't toy with affections. When I gaze at you with caring in my heart, it's because I wish you to know how I feel. I, too, am too old to engage in the foolish deeds the young seem to feel necessary for their courting rituals.

"And, yes, my Lady, I intend to court you. I have but a few

decades more before my time to leave arrives. I intend to enjoy those years with a companion of my choosing."

Linda looked up to find teal eyes searching her face. She allowed herself to act without hesitation and placed her hand on his.

"I'd given up on the idea of finding a companion to spend my time with when you arrived for the counsel meeting, and I lost my heart. However, you left, and I was bereft; happiness was slipping through my fingers—again. Many a year has passed since my Donald lost his battle with cancer. Most Others believe you get one chance at a forever love. When you arrived, my heart told me once-in-a-lifetime was a fallacy. Sometimes, just sometimes, life pulls a fast one on you."

Linda ran a finger down Uther's hand, noting the musculature of his fingers.

"Courting is an old word and concept." She allowed a blush to color her cheeks. "But one I love. I like the idea of being wooed."

Uther raised a delicate white eyebrow. "Wooed? Whew! What a sexy word." The hint of a smile touched his lips. He gently lifted her hand to his mouth and placed a kiss on the back.

"I, too, have waited another lifetime to find a suitable companion. I was beginning to lose hope until the counsel meeting. Your reputation made you an interesting person. However, you are an Other and usually we don't get along. Your beauty intrigued me, but I believe what won me over was how you stood up to Gitty and Morgan. No one has laughed in Gitty's face and lived to tell the story. I knew then I had to get to know this Other who, first of all, believed and was able to see the wee folk and second, could stand her ground with a power hungry female Night Elf."

Linda had been staring at the floor as Uther spoke. He placed his fingers beneath her chin and lifted her eyes to meet his.

"So, yes, I plan to woo you and, if the gods favor me, make you my companion until the end of our lives." He leaned toward her.

"Librarian! Librarian!" Chrissy buzzed past Uther and hovered directly in front of Linda.

Pushing a wistful sigh from her lips, she replied. "What, Chrissy? What has you in such an uproar?"

24

"That wicked black cat is in the back yard prowling around."

Uther pushed up from the chair and bolted to the back yard. "He'd better not be."

Linda stood and stretched her legs. "Are you sure?"

Chrissy gave a delicate shrug of her tiny shoulders. "Well, the animal sure looked like that wicked creature." She caught the corner of her lip with her teeth as she brushed her light brown locks away from her face.

Uther returned with a smirk on his face. One hand was behind his back as he climbed the porch steps.

Linda gave a wary look his direction.

"This..." he brought his hand around to the front. In his palm snuggled a tiny black and white kitten, mewling noisily. "...is the wicked black cat."

Linda felt her heart melt. "Oh, my goodness. Somewhere a mother kitty is searching frantically for this little bundle." She held out a hand to Uther.

He placed the little cat in the center of Linda's hand and slipped his arm around her shoulders. "To the best of my ability, I searched her memories and discovered this little girl was born nearby, but her mother went out to hunt for dinner and never returned. This little thing wiggled her way to your backyard because, even in the world of animals, you're kindness is widely known." He ran his finger across the downy soft fur of the kitten.

Linda let a gentle smile light up her face. "Well, I guess I'll make sure she has a home. Did you get a name?"

Uther chuckled. "She says her mom calls her Piggy because she's always hungry. How do you propose to feed her?"

"You can't!" Exploded Chrissy.

"And why not?" Linda noted the crimson color of the nymph's face.

"That...thing will grow up and eat us."

"I don't think so."

"Fine. Then I'm leaving." Chrissy started to wing back to the kitchen.

Linda heard Uther mutter beneath his breath.

The little wood nymph stopped mid-air, her wings flapping furiously.

"UTHER! Let me go!"

"Not until you come back and apologize to Linda."

"I won't be eaten!"

He withdrew his arm from Linda's shoulder and walked to face the little fae. Crossing his arms, he set his face in a fierce scowl.

"Do you think the librarian or I would allow such a thing?"

Chrissy stopped trying to escape and slowed her wings to a hover. "And just what can you do to stop the animal from eating me?" She stuck her fist on a hip.

Linda stifled a giggle.

"Are you or are you not a wood nymph?" Uther slightly tilted his head as he asked the question.

Chrissy huffed. "Well, of course, I'm a wood nymph." She swept her hand up and down. "Duh! Tiny person with wings?"

"Yeah, I can see you and so can the librarian. Why can the librarian see you?"

The little nymph threw up her hands and rolled her eyes. "Because I'm not using magic to cloak myself."

Relaxing his expression, Uther stood back, allowing the statement to hang in the air, a slow easy smile replacing the scowl.

The thunderous frown Chrissy had mustered slipped away. "Oh, yeah. I can do magic."

"Um huh."

"So I can stay invisible as far as the creature is concerned."

"Yup."

"Oh. But…"

Uther reached out and placed his two fingers around the fae, breaking the spell. He carried her to Linda and stood with the fae facing the kitten. The tiny creature trembled in his grasp.

"This is an extremely young cat. Her memories are faint about her life lessons. You have the ability to perform magic and can be seen by the creature or not as you so choose. Imagine, if you will, training this creature to protect you."

Chrissy wiggled in his hand. "What? These are wild animals that hunt birds and small creatures to eat. I'm smaller than most birds. How could this beast be trained to protect me?"

Uther lowered her closer to the kitten. "Right now, this little one is desperate for love. She'll imprint on the person who gives her the most love. Pet her, go ahead."

The nymph cringed and opened her mouth to scream.

Uther shook his head. "You survived much worse in the woods. Try it. If the creature looks as if she'll try to eat you, I'll snatch you away and keep you safe."

Grudgingly, Chrissy reached out an arm and quickly slid her hand across the nearest section of fur. The tiny kitten began to purr.

"SEE! It's warning me to stop."

Linda smiled. "No. That's the sound they make when they are happy. It's called purring."

Chrissy glanced at the sleeping creature. She had to admit it was attractive, but so many years of fear couldn't be wiped away in five minutes.

"Okay. I'll give it a chance, but the first time it lunges at me, I'm setting its tail on fire."

Uther nodded. "Fair enough. Now I'll release you. Stay or go as you please." He opened his hand.

Chrissy shot him one last look of disgust and buzzed into the library.

"How are you going to keep it from eating her?"

Linda chuckled. "I believe after this one has had some nourishment, I'll sit down and let her know who's the boss around this establishment. We both know it isn't me. After a few weeks, I'm sure Chrissy will have Piglet dancing to her tune."

"Piglet?"

"Yeah. I like the sound of it better than Piggy. Shall we take this new member of my household inside and make a nest for her?"

Uther dipped his head. "After you, my lady."

Chapter Six

Morgan lolled his head to one side of the couch cushion. His eyes hurt from tracking Gitty's march back and forth across the living room floor.

"What is your problem, sister?" Yawning, he set his booted feet on the coffee table. "Unable to hatch a winning plan?"

"Some input on your part would be helpful." Gitty stood at the window and glared. The pair had been kicking ideas around most of the night and nothing had struck her as feasible.

Morgan dropped his head forward, his eyes glazed by lack of sleep. "Just kidnap the librarian. Tell Uther you'll kill her slowly unless he gets the clans together and gives back our magic. I'm tired and going to bed."

Dropping his legs to the floor from the coffee table, Morgan rose from the couch and trudged down the hallway to his room.

Gitty watched his retreating back and glowered. "Kidnap the librarian, indeed." She moved to the window to stare morosely at the valley below, Morgan's ridiculous suggestion ruminating in her mind. She hated to admit it, but the idea was beginning to have merit.

"Well, why not? The plan has viability. Two birds, one stone; Librarian is gone and Uther will be too once his lady love is out of the picture. But how?"

Gitty worried her bottom lip, lines forming above her brow as she turned over one plan of attack then another. Morgan's idea was a good one, but she was stumped on the execution. Lancelot wound his way around and through her legs.

Why not kidnap her while she sits on the riverbank?

"Riverbank, uh, what?"

I said why don't you kidnap her when she goes to sit by the river?

"That's a great idea if we can guarantee she'll be out there when we're ready to move ahead with our plan."

She will be.

"How can you be so sure?"

When you were pouting because you didn't have your magic, I started watching the library from the opposite bank for a chance to get even with those miserable little faeries. Every day when the light has started to dim, she sits by the river for a while.

"I don't pout."

What would you call stomping around the house muttering to yourself and ignoring the rest of the world?

Gitty graced the black animal with a cool stare.

"I was...thinking."

Same difference. You were acting irrationally—even for you. It's time you regained your rightful place in this valley. Sitting and...thinking...won't move the situation to where it needs to be.

"How can I guarantee the librarian will be there?"

A daily walk appears to be in your future. We're able to keep contact within the length of a meadow, but no further. If you stay back a couple of your long steps in the brush by the river, I can let you know if she's there.

"That's all well and good, but the moment she sees me she'll start screaming and our plan will be for naught."

Then we need to recruit Morgan to be part of the action. If he appears on our side of the river, she'll be so concerned with him she'll lose track of what's behind her. You can subdue her and we'll bring her to the shelter in the woods.

"Won't Uther be able to sense her?"

Not if we place enough sensory camouflage around the shelter. We can send a note to Uther with subtle references to a warehouse in town. Maybe he'll believe it, maybe not, but it'll buy time.

Gitty gazed in amazement at the black feline sitting at her feet wrapping his tail around her legs. "Where did you learn all this?" She could swear Lancelot was smiling.

I listen and learn from the best. He doffed his head to her then began to lick his front paw.

For the first time in many a week, Gitty smiled. "I do believe we have a plan of action that will work."

Standing up and gracefully stretching his legs, Lancelot moved to the warm spot in front of the heater vent. Circling three times, he finally lay on the floor and proceeded to go to sleep.

The she-night elf flipped off the lighting in the room and let her eyes roam over the landscape of the valley and surrounding mountains. She rolled her neck and dispelled the feeling of dread that had hung over her for the last few months.

"Retribution."

Gitty liked the way the word rolled off her tongue. She allowed a small smile to blossom and humming a Celtic war song, wandered down the hallway to her room. With any luck, tonight she would have the best night's sleep she'd had in longer than she cared to remember.

~ * ~

Morgan heard low humming and the soft swish of Gitty's house boots pass his door. The sound of silence followed a snick of the latch. An involuntary shudder passed through him. Whatever she and her wretched cat had cooked up would wreak havoc on the valley and further alienate him from the local inhabitants. Light from the scented candle on the nightstand next to his bed flickered across his chiseled features.

He leaned against the rosewood headboard and watched the changing shadows on the ceiling. There had been a time in the highlands back home when he and Gitty were inseparable. She'd been the only opponent to best him at the sword, and her skills at the Longbow were touted throughout the highlands by the bards. It wasn't until they came to this wretched country with its backward farmers and huntsmen did

Gitty's temperament morph.

The bonnie lass from Scotland who could drink, fight and cuss with the best of the boys became a shadow of her former self. When the love of her life, Glade, was killed in a battle between the fae and night elves, Gitty shut down completely, turning into the miserable elven being who currently lived in the room next to his.

As her attitude declined into sarcasm and scorn, she quit seeking his company for sword practice preferring to set up her own obstacle course and workout haven in the basement.

It didn't take Morgan long to come to the realization the way of life they'd been taught to live was fading into the past. He frequented the local pubs and, with his striking looks, developed a reputation as a ladies' man. After a fight or two with the farm boys, his position was secured in the community. That is until Gitty felt the need to tear apart the old oaks in the meadows.

"There was the dandy with the heavy Irish accent I dueled who lost, but I'm sure that had nothing to do with my getting kicked out of the pubs." Morgan checked the clock on the nightstand and blew out a breath. "Morning will arrive too soon."

He blew out the candle and crawled beneath his covers. His stomach was lurching with the anticipation of what scheme Gitty had hatched.

Chapter Seven

The clatter of metal against metal woke Uther from a lovely dream of a fair-haired maiden with cloud grey eyes who was lavishing a great deal of attention on him. He stretched his lanky form. Despite his statements about not needing anything but a blanket, Linda had scrounged a cot, his feet hung over the end, and several sheets and blankets to cover the canvas bed. Somewhere in the area behind her door, she'd located a pillow. The cover smelled of fresh spring days with a hint of warm spice. Sleep came easily within his warm cocoon between the aisles of the library.

The noise increased with the hour, and Uther gave up and crawled out of his bed. Rubbing his eyes, he pulled in a deep breath. The pungent smell of mountain coffee raked across his taste buds. He stumbled into the facilities and completed his morning routine.

Replacing the gentle warmth and sunshine of the previous day were light showers.

"Coffee?"

Uther had been staring out the front windows of the building and started when Chrissy spoke.

"Yes. I'd love a cup of black coffee."

She buzzed back to the kitchen and Uther heard the metallic clatter again. Curiosity got the better of him and he tiptoed to peek his head around the door. The little nymph was cooking by dancing in the air and on the tops of the pots and pans. The food on the stove was bubbling and hissing as she danced her magic to prepare breakfast.

"Oh!" She stopped when she spied Uther peeking in the

doorway. Pointing at the cup on the counter, she muttered. "Warm."

He watched the steam rise from the mug. "Thank you." Grabbing the mug, he strolled through the aisles to the front door and went out on the porch. There was coolness to the air punctuated with moisture, sending a shiver down Uther's back.

"Damp." The coffee cup rested on the rail of the porch as his gaze was pulled to the road. Raindrops splattered on the asphalt creating a patchwork of lights and darks, rivulets of water racing to the sides.

"Yes, but good for the garden."

Uther jumped. "I didn't hear you walk up." He could feel the warmth of her smile.

"You were so intent on something down the road I really didn't want to scare you. Guess I did anyway, didn't I?"

The abashed expression on Uther's face let Linda know she had guessed correctly. "What has you so serious this morning?"

He took a sip of the cooled coffee. "I can't explain it very clearly, but I have a very bad feeling the Sauns are planning something. We both know nothing good comes from that."

Linda nodded her agreement. The last time the Sauns had planned something, they came close to eliminating all the oak trees in the area. Chrissy had fled from the demolition of her ancient home and stumbled into Linda's home library. It was a meeting of destiny as the two were closer than ever.

Uther faced Linda. "Please promise me you'll be careful."

She took a breath to protest.

"I know of what I speak. As much as it pains me to admit it, my thinking was very close to theirs until I met a few Others who changed my mind." He leaned in and brushed a soft kiss across her lips.

Linda felt her knees wobble and she closed her eyes. His touch set her ablaze. Her stomach flipped. Parts of her body she thought long dead were reacting in ways she'd forgotten. White spots appeared before her closed eyes, and she realized her need to breathe.

Heat swarmed up her neck and across her cheeks. She pulled away. "Oh, my."

Uther picked up her hand and with his thumb rubbed across the soft skin on the top. "You, my lady, are special, not only to me, but to many others through out this valley. Should any harm befall you, I'm not sure anyone could stop the fae from declaring all out war on the Other inhabitants of the meadow."

"Baloney. The Others of this valley are ignorant of the magical population who live here. They choose not to see what's right in front of them. They couldn't be blamed if anything happened to me because we both know the anger comes from the hill above us."

"You speak the truth, my lady. Please give me your word you'll take care with your daily routines and should you wish to venture away from the house, you'll allow me to accompany you."

Linda frowned. "I think you worry too much. I'll be fine but just to make you happy, I'll get hold of you if I feel the urge to take a stroll in the woods. Will that make you happy?"

Uther smiled. "Yes. I know asking you not to go outside are fruitless, so this will give me some peace."

Before either of the two could speak again, a tiny figure buzzed out to face them.

"Enough talk. Breakfast is served."

The night elf and Other stared at the wood nymph hovering between them. Crossed arms and a ferocious scowl convinced them argument was futile. Uther offered his arm and Linda slipped her hand through the crook of his elbow, strolling inside to the café.

On a table covered in an ivory tainted linen cloth, sat a sumptuous feast; eggs and bacon were accompanied by toast and pancakes. Fresh butter and warmed syrup were placed near the pancakes. Real porcelain plates and silverware resting on linen napkins that matched the cloth finished the picture. Gracing the center of the table was a crystal-cut vase holding a single daffodil.

"Wow." Uther pulled out the chair for the Librarian.

"You can say that again." Linda pulled the napkin from beneath the silverware and placed it opened on her lap. "You've outdone yourself, Chrissy. This looks amazing and appetizing at the same time."

Linda observed the nymph's face color a deep pink.

"Thank you, Librarian. Now, no more talk—eat."

"Yes, ma'am." Uther winked at Linda as he reached for the eggs. "Don't have to ask me twice."

Linda watched him shovel several eggs onto his plate as he grabbed for the bacon. The hint of a smile dimpled her left cheek. *Haven't seen a man eat this well since before Donald got sick.*

"Don't tell me you're one of those Others who pretend not to eat until after the man has left." Uther snagged two slices of toast and with his knife slathered big globs of butter on each piece.

"Nope. Just didn't want to lose a finger or get my hand stabbed." She slid one egg and a couple pieces of bacon to her plate. Quickly snatching some toast she used her spoon to cover the top with homemade blackberry jam.

Silence filled the room as the food disappeared. When both plates were clean, Chrissy magicked her special coffee blend for them to top off their meal.

"I think you should tell Chrissy." Uther stretched his legs in front of him and took a sip of the cinnamon concoction.

"No. She worries enough without adding to it." Linda absently stirred the liquid.

"If you don't, I will. I want this land protected by as many entities as possible. I know how devious the Saun clan can be when they feel they've been wronged. Unfortunately, my lady, you stand in the center of their target right now."

"Fine. If you want to tell Chrissy, go ahead, but I won't put anything more on her."

Uther watched Linda gather their plates and stop at the kitchen door, knocking gently.

"Chrissy?"

"Yes, Librarian?"

"I need to get the dishes done and I believe Uther wants to speak with you."

The little nymph peeked around Linda's shoulder to the table. "Why?"

"I think you should ask him."

"Okay." She fluttered casually toward the table stopping just in front of Uther. Turning, she glanced at the librarian.

Linda made a shooing motion with her hand. She watched the tiny fae straighten her back and hover in front of the night elf.

Faced with such a show of courage, Uther cleared his throat in an attempt to keep from chuckling. "I would like to ask a favor of you."

"Why would I grant you...anything, night elf?"

Uther tipped his head in agreement. "Point taken. However, what if the favor had to do with the librarian?"

"Well, that's different." Chrissy rolled her eyes.

"As I thought. I fear for the safety of the librarian. I have an unsettling feeling the Sauns will attempt to harm the librarian in some way."

A wrinkle marred the forehead of the wood nymph. "Why would they do that?"

"They are aware I have...feelings for her. As they no longer have magic because of something I did and the Librarian supported, what better way to get back at me than by harming her?"

Uther watched the wings of the nymph tremble.

"They wouldn't DARE!"

"Ahh, but they would, and I'm afraid they will. That's why I need your help."

"What can I do?"

Uther watched the worry on the little face turn to fierce determination.

"Put the word out. If any of the wee ones see the night elves from the house on the hill acting...odd, even for them, please let me know. I'll do what I can to make sure the librarian is safe. Any help your people can offer will be greatly appreciated."

"I'll leave the rest to you. I need to find a permanent place to stay." He unfolded his frame from the chair.

"If the librarian is in danger as you state, would it not be better for you to stay and guard her?"

Uther watched a tiny eyebrow raise in question. *Linda is right. This little wood nymph is very quickly adapting to human ways.* "You're right. I just wanted to spare her from the gossip of having a single man living in her home."

Chrissy humphed. "As if our people ever worried about the rumors and gossip of the Others."

Uther had to agree. The fae community worried very little about the moral boundaries set by the Others. He dipped his head in acknowledgement at Chrissy and went about the task of clearing up his sleeping area. The doors would soon be open to the Lending Library, and the place would come alive with the flurry of tiny wings. The fae in the community used the building as a safe haven to gather and update each other on the activities within the local population.

From the corner of his eye, he spotted Chrissy streaking out the back door. *Wouldn't want to get in her way.* He could only hope she was carrying out the task he'd asked of her. His instincts set his nerves on edge and he was certain Gitty and Morgan would be planning some retaliation in the near future.

The silence from their household defied the nature of the two spoiled night elves and it worried Uther. Anything concerning the Saun clan concerned him. As a former active member, he knew the mindset of the family. They didn't tolerate defeat well and he found himself disquieted at the thoughts lingering in his mind.

"I can only hope the fae will band together again to protect the librarian."

Chapter Eight

Soft leather, moccasin-styled boots hugged the feet of Morgan muffling his footfalls down the hallway to the kitchen. His only thought this morning was of a rich hot cup of coffee. Aromatic whiffs of the potent bean drew him closer to the counter and his reward.

"Morgan!"

The tall night elf groaned. When his sister bellowed, he was usually in trouble. He set a mug from the cupboard on the counter and poured precious brown liquid inside.

"MORGAN!"

Throwing caution to the wind, he didn't answer but took a swig of the life giving fluid. Searing pain racked his throat, sending him into a coughing spasm.

"What?" he croaked.

Gitty's measured gait put him on guard. Her normal mode of travel was to barrel her way through, heedless of anything in her way. Most valley folk had learned to step back when they saw the statuesque blonde headed their direction.

"Good. We need to talk about the plan to get back our magic."

Blowing across the top of the cup, he lifted his eyes to stare at this sister. "What plan?"

"Again, I've had to come up with everything. So sit there and listen while I explain how we're going to accomplish our plan."

Our plan? He'd not submitted any input into the plan. How was it *our* plan? He could guarantee if anything went wrong he'd be the only one to pay.

Gitty filled a mug with coffee, adding sugar and milk to the dark brew. Beckoning her brother with a finger, she moved to the living room and sat on one end of the couch. Morgan followed her into the high-ceilinged room choosing to sit in the tufted leather chair near the fireplace.

"Your suggestion last night got me to thinking…"

"What suggestion?" Morgan furrowed his forehead.

"The suggestion about kidnapping the librarian."

"Wha? I, I, I didn't make any such suggestion."

Gitty watched the color drain from his face. She pushed an exasperated breath between her lips. *Constitution of a jellyfish.*

"Right before you skulked off to bed you said, 'Why don't we just kidnap her?' The more I thought about it the better I liked the idea."

"I was being sarcastic. I didn't really mean it." Morgan's hand shook as he lifted the mug to his lips.

"Of course you were being sarcastic. It's one of the things you do best. However, the idea took root. I think we have the means, without magic, to take back what's ours."

Morgan stared at his sister. She'd hatched some pretty wild ideas to get what she wanted before, but this was—insane! Without magic they risked being caught and taken to the Others jail…for life.

"Well, I think I can safely say you've lost your mind. I need more coffee." He pushed up from the chair and snatching his mug, disappeared into the kitchen.

Gitty ground her teeth but waited for him to return.

"What makes you think we can pull off taking the Librarian from under Uther's nose while all those miserable little fae people are meandering around her?" Morgan set his coffee on the side table and dropped into the chair.

Agitation drove her to stand. It took all her restraint not to start pacing.

"I have it on good authority the librarian goes to the river around the same time every day…and she goes alone; no fae, no Uther."

"Right. Who is this good authority?" A sneer began to form on Morgan's face.

"Lancelot."

"Ha! Now I know you've been into the liquor cabinet. We don't have our magic, so how can you communicate with your...pet?"

Because you both still have your telepathy. The aforementioned animal padded in and started rubbing against Gitty's legs.

I'm hungry.

Morgan sat, blinking his eyes in disbelief. "It's a trick. You've learned to throw your voice." He pointed a shaking finger at his sister.

Gitty shook her head. "I can't believe we have the same parents. You're an idiot, you know? Mental telepathy isn't magic. That's why we can still talk with Lancelot. I'm going to feed him then we'll continue this discussion." She strode to the other room.

Morgan heard the banging of silverware against the cat's bowl and clatter as the spoon was dropped into the sink.

Gitty strolled into the lounge and dropped to the couch.

"I think you need to take up a hobby."

"Do you now? And what would that be?" He cocked his head to one side and proceeded to cross his arms.

"Fishing." A sly smile tilted Gitty's lips.

"Okay. That's it. I hate fish. I hate fishing. I won't put squishy wiggly worms on a hook and throw it in the water to stand around for hours doing nothing. I can't stand the thought of cleaning them, and if you don't eat them, what's the point of fishing?" Morgan scowled at her.

"You won't actually be fishing."

"What?"

"You'll be observing the librarian and waiting for a good time to let me know when to grab her." She watched a puzzled expression replace the scowl. "You need to start appearing on the opposite bank of the Lending Library for the next week to ten days. Once you become a fixture, she'll give it no thought whatsoever. Observe the time she comes out and when she leaves. Once we have her pattern established, we can choose the optimum time to grab her and slip away."

"Yeah, but won't she recognize me?"

"Not if you wear fishing gear and a big hat to cover your face."

"Just where are we going to put her? This is the first place they'd look."

"Eons ago, after the war in the valley, I took the time to provide myself an escape from the insanity of this house. My cabin is five miles due north from this location."

She watched the wrinkle in Morgan's forehead reappear as he contemplated this information.

"How do we get there? The area you're talking about has no roads."

"That's right. The only way in or out is on horseback."

"Right. So we drag this Other, on horseback, to some cabin in the woods until…what? She dies of starvation? Or are we going into the business of murdering people?" Morgan pushed up from the chair to refill his mug. He wandered back to the chair and took up his position.

Gitty shook her head and sighed. "Again, I have to wonder how we can have the same lineage. No, we won't starve or murder her. That would defeat our reason for kidnapping her. We'll put her across one of our saddles carrying her to the cabin, which by the way is continually stocked with a month's worth of food and water. One never knows when the need will arise to take some 'alone' time."

"Just how are you going to take her without a ruckus?" Morgan lifted a brow in question.

"If you'd stop interrupting me, I'd be able to lay out this plan and fill in all the details."

He held up a hand and settled back in the chair. "Please…educate me."

"We don't have enough time for that. I'll just fill in the blanks so you can stop whining like a little girl. Each day you go to the riverbank to fish, Lancelot will accompany you until you've seen the librarian come out and go back into her library. After a week or so…"

Morgan groaned.

Gitty shot him a withering glance and he refrained from making further noises.

"As I was saying…when you've established a routine of fishing on the bank, the librarian should relax. During the second week, you'll need to ride your steed down the hill. I'll be out for an afternoon ride waiting for Lancelot to tell me when the time is right. I've devised a way to knock her out without leaving any physical marks. Once I've accomplished that feat, I'll throw her across my saddle, and from there we'll head to the cabin avoiding any contact with the locals.

"At the cabin, we can restrain her. I've located one of the old cameras that spit out pictures to use in making our demand. One shot of her tied up and gagged and we'll have Uther eating out of our hands. By my calculations, we should have our magic back by the end of the month."

Silence followed the detailed explanation. Gitty watched her brother mull over the plan.

"What's the issue? I've contemplated all the possibilities and worked out things so neither of us will get caught. What's taking you so long to agree?"

"Do I have to wear those stupid looking waders?"

"What?" Gitty jumped up from the couch to face her brother. "You're worried about how you'll look!" She stomped to the kitchen and slammed her cup on the counter.

"Complete idiot. The fates are against me. First, a total brainless wonder like Morgan as a blood brother then our father goes and marries a gnome. A gnome! And I'm saddled with that miniature female wanta-be-warrior, Tiamoon. What a joke. I should just liquidate the assets we have here and move back to Emerald Isles." Scrubbing the cup, she muttered between clinched teeth.

"Uh, Gitty?"

"What?" She turned to glower at her brother.

"I think your idea is really great. When do we start?"

She stared at him; a nervous smile attempted to blossom on his face. He shuffled from foot to foot and kept pushing his long hair behind his shoulder.

"Truth be told…I've been miserable without my magic. It seems I've overestimated my attraction to the Other women. Once they discover I have no income, they melt away. I'd love to have my magic back."

Gitty realized his reason was shallow, but whatever it took to have him work with her was fine. "We'll start tomorrow." She watched his shoulders drop as he relaxed.

"What time?"

"Lancelot says she takes a break around three in the afternoon. You'll need to be on the bank a little before. When you get there, pretend to be setting your line then monitor her actions. You might want to nod her direction so she isn't alarmed by your presence. Check the time she goes in then stay for thirty more minutes and pack up and leave.

"We'll continue this for the week, and about Wednesday of the following week, we'll make our move."

Morgan nodded and drifted off toward his room.

Gitty watched his lackadaisical shuffle and mentally kicked herself. *If we pull this off, I'm leaving this offensive valley and all the inhabitants behind.*

Chapter Nine

Chrissy zipped through the door Linda had specially made for her. She flew as fast as her wings would allow and arrived at the riverbank breathless. Slowing her speed, she surveyed the river, trying to recall the outcropping her cousin Trickle had described to her. About to give up, she caught the flash of flowing golden hair. She winged to the top of the water then hovered.

Trickle. The gold flash moved nearer her position. *Trickle, it's Chrissy.*

Rising from the water, the golden hair undulated down her back as the mermaid immerged from the depths of the river.

Cousin. What can I do for you?

Long ago the cousins had agreed to communicate nonverbally to keep eavesdroppers at a minimum.

Uther has asked me to convey to you the urgency of keeping an eye on the river.

The mermaid swished her tail and her eyes lulled seductively.

You mean the handsome, gentle night elf?

Chrissy huffed an impatient breath. *Yes, the same one. Could you keep you mind off your tail? Anyway, he's afraid his niece and nephew might try to harm the librarian.* She watched Trickle's eyes light up.

Nephew? Is he as handsome as Uther?

Come on, Trickle. Yes he's as handsome as Uther, but don't you... Chrissy stopped and stared at the flow of golden curls waving in the current of the stream.

That might just be the answer.

What? Trickle rolled a backward somersault coming up in the same place.

If you happen to see the very tall, very handsome Morgan, feel free to charm him the best you can. You might not be successful as he was once of the fae community but...who knows?

Trickle cocked her head and narrowed her eyes. *What do you mean* was *once of the fae community? Isn't he any longer?*

A smile touched the lips of Chrissy, exposing a small dimple in her right cheek. *He and his sister sought Thomas' gold and were willing to kill all the Ancient Ones in the forest to find the treasure.*

Trickle chuckled. *Everyone knows Thomas is a braggart and liar. Why would they believe him?*

He told them the treasure was around The Lending Library. When they arrived to dig up the fortune, the clan Chieftains were meeting, having banded together to find the culprit in the killing of the Ancients. So many fae had lost homes and been forced to move to Faetown, the elders were willing to put their differences aside until the mystery was solved.

Gitty and Morgan threatened to use their magic and, consequently, it was taken from them. They are as vulnerable as the Others.

Trickle fluttered her tail and giggled. *Ooo, a mortal for my very own. I've wanted to come out of the river, but only for a good reason. This might be fun. Maybe I'll just keep him.*

Chrissy started an ascent. *Have fun. Let me know if you see him.*

The little mermaid zipped around the river singing, *A man of my own, for my hearth and my home.*

Chrissy couldn't stop the blossoming smile. The night elves were in for a big surprise if they thought they could outwit the fae. *A big surprise.* She loped along the path to the Lending Library stopping every so often to admire the new growth of spring. This year the rain had fallen, just enough, to ensure spring and May Day would provide an explosion of color for the festivities. She spun around, lope-de-loping, before entering her door.

Time was quickly slipping away and she had so many things to do. With Trickle on the alert for the night elves from the back of the property, she needed to get the word out to the community to keep a watch on the nefarious two from the hill.

~ * ~

Uther had watched the lithe wood nymph zip from their conversation out the back door. A chuckle bubbled up from deep inside his chest and he marveled at the determination on the little one's face.

"I'd sure hate to be on the wrong side of that little fae." He stretched his arms above his head before standing and reaching for the ceiling. "Need to get some fresh air." Stepping out the front door, Uther meandered to the porch railing and surveyed the scenery. There was light chatter from the surrounding birds as new hatchlings tried their shaky wings in flight. A gentle breeze ruffled his long locks, and he pulled in a deep breath of the rain freshened air. The clouds last night had wept on the landscape but dissipated this morning, leaving a light layer of moisture over the budding earth. Everything felt…new. Uther smiled and straightened up. As he was about to turn and return inside, a movement on the driveway caught his attention. He stood watching in fascination as the black spot moved closer, revealing a small donkey cart pulled by some sort of wire-haired dog. In the driver seat, he recognized the being as a gnome.

Bram held the reins in his hand and let Silas take the lead. The two had been partners for all of Silas' life and could predict what the other was thinking a majority of the time. Silas, a terrier mix, was panting heavily as he slowed and positioned the cart in front of the Lending Library.

"Bram, my friend." He panted and folded his legs beneath him.

"Ahhh! Silas! Let me know before you do that." Bram grasped the front rail of the cart. "You nearly threw me over you."

"Sorry. I think you might want to, uh, cut back a bit on the mead. I do believe you have increased your girth." The terrier stood, leveling the cart.

"I think you, my friend, are too tired due to the Mrs.' condition.

However, I'll take your advice into consideration. We have business to conduct. We can discuss this after we have spoken with Chrissy."

The terrier waited for his passenger to disembark before lying on the ground. "I don't recall getting a message. When did you hear from her?"

"I received a message from the Sky Network. The bluebirds were busy gossiping as I cleaned the cart this morning. Sorry I didn't let you know." Bram realized Silas was fast asleep. He shrugged his shoulders and shuffled to the steps.

"Morning."

Bram snapped his head up and lost his balance, tumbling backward off the steps.

Uther scurried down the steps toward the gnome.

"Don't touch me! You've already scared the life out of me. Don't make it any worse." Bram scowled dangerously, lifting his gaze up to stare into cool, blue eyes sporting a twinkle set in a tanned complexion. Long silver hair fell forward around high cheekbones and an amused smile touched the stranger's face. Yet, Bram knew this face was...familiar.

"Uther?" The angry frown disappeared as the stranger extended a hand. "When did you get back?" Bram allowed himself to be assisted off the ground.

"I returned within the last few days. I've been feeling anxious about the librarian's safety. How have you been?"

Bram dusted the dirt from his breeches as he climbed the steps to the porch. "I've been just fine. Work has been a bit slow in coming, but it's the time of year when most everyone is hunkering down in their homes. And you, friend? How is life treating you?"

"Mostly I've been traveling the back roads, keeping tabs on the fae community."

"While I would love to sit and chat, I need to speak to Chrissy. Will you excuse me?"

Uther extended a hand. "Of course."

Bram reached up and shook the night elf's hand and dipped his head moving through the Lending Library's entrance. He stopped to get his bearings within the building and allow his eyes to adjust to the darker room. Humming directed him toward the kitchen.

Poking his head around the doorframe, Bram ventured a foot over the sill.

"Uhm, Chrissy?"

"AHHH!"

The clatter of dishes and silverware reverberated throughout the library.

"What the…Bram!" The flustered wood nymph fisted hands on hips and glared at the cart driver. "Watch where you're going! Look at the mess you made."

The gruff gnome furrowed his brows, the bushy slash marks of hair forming a dark sinister line above his eyes. "You're the one who called me. What do you need that is so important you'd use the Sky Network?"

Chrissy waved a delicate hand over the broken bits of dinnerware scattered upon the floor. Rising from their location, each piece found its corresponding mate and cleaved together, hovering above then lowering to the countertop.

Bram had to admit he admired the nymph's magic. Her temper, on the other hand…

"You saw Uther?"

"Aye."

"Did he fill you in on the reason for his visit?"

"I believe he mentioned something about the librarian."

"Good heavens, Bram, don't you ever get excited?" The little fae rustled her wings in agitation.

"What's the point? It's useless energy. What is it Silas and I can do for you, Chrissy?"

Pulling in a deep breath, the fae slowed the flutter of her wings to a hover before the gnome. "Uther believes the night elves, Gitty and Morgan Saun, will try to harm the librarian. He asked me to get the word out for the community to keep a watchful eye on them. If you see or hear anything that seems out of place for them, use the Sky Network to warn us as quickly as possible."

Bram lightly ran his fingers down his beard, trying to herd the coarse hairs into place. "I can make sure the word is spread. How will I be paid? I have a family and Silas' Mrs. just announced they're expecting—again."

"You're joking, right?"

"No ma'am. My services cost. You can try the Sky Network and see how well that works, but Silas and I are dependable."

Chrissy felt the urge to throttle the meadow fae with her bare hands but kept her irritation under control. "You, Silas and your families will be the guests of honor at the May Day celebration; all your food and drink will be furnished for you by the community. Fair enough?"

Bram rolled the idea around in his head. "Sounds good. I'll be shoving off. We've got lots of work to do and not much time. Miss Chrissy." He saluted the wood nymph and spun on the ball of his foot, marching through the rows of books to the porch.

Chrissy magicked the silverware to the sink where she worked with the water and dish soap to again wash the utensils clean. Gone was the contented humming replaced by muttering and banging of the forks and spoons. Once she'd cleaned everything, she ordered the items to put themselves away. She needed to take a break and rest her magic. Slipping from the kitchen, Chrissy winged her way to the windowsill and settled in the high heel shaped recliner the Librarian had given her. The sun streamed through the boughs of the tall pines warming the spot where her chair sat. Chrissy considered contacting the Mouse Network to ask the animals to keep watch for any unusual behavior on the part of the night elves. She'd be certain to set the plan in action…tomorrow. Before too long, the sound of gentle snoring filled the corner of the room.

~ * ~

Bram nudged Silas from his nap with the tip of his soft boots. "We have work to do."

The dog yawned and stretched his front legs. "Going far?"

"Yup. All around the valley."

"Big payday?"

"Not quite."

Silas had stood and was stretching his back legs. He stopped and turned to Bram. "We're not doing this for free, are we?"

"Nope. We'll be the guests of honor at the May Day celebration. Everything will be provided for all our families."

Silas used his back leg to scratch behind his left ear. Spring always made his skin dry and itchy. "Guess that'll do. We ready to go?"

Bram climbed into the cart and grabbed the reins. "Let's head out."

"Where to first?"

"We'll start going west then circle the valley. Should be back home in a couple days."

Silas tugged against the weight of the cart and Bram, getting his footing and setting a walking pace he could maintain for the long haul.

Bram saluted Uther and turned his attention to the road. He pulled out a pipe and lit the bowl with a quick flash of fire from his fingertip. *Chrissy isn't the only one who has magic.* He settled in his seat and pulled in the sweet taste of his black cherry tobacco. This job was going to test the flint of both he and his friend Silas. *We can do it.*

"Silas."

"Yes?"

"Stop when we come to the fae community of the lower meadows. I need to speak with the clan chieftain. It's important."

"You got it." Silas knew this was Bram's way of saying he was going to nap.

The easy pace set by Silas eased the tension Bram had felt at the Lending Library. He puffed on his pipe. Silas' nails click-clicked on the road, lulling Bram's eyelids toward his cheeks. He slid the pipe from between his teeth and knocked the smoldering tobacco into a tin can he carried for just this purpose. Once he secured the pipe inside his vest, he gave in to the urge to snooze. He could rely on Silas to wake him when they arrived at the fae community.

~ * ~

Uther watched with amusement as the odd pair disappeared down the driveway. He wasn't sure what had transpired, but glancing in the window he noted the little wood nymph lay out in what looked to be a reclining chair. Her tiny wings were tucked beneath her form. Eyes closed, her face glowed with serenity. She was indeed a beautiful creature.

Venturing into the library, Uther scanned the area, his stomach clenching when he couldn't locate Linda. His stride quickened as he moved from one aisle to another. Using his last resort, he knocked on the door he knew led to her private area. The response was a hollow unanswered sound. *Where is she?* A clock tolled from within her room alerting him to the time. Eleven times he heard the bells chime. *Where is she?* The slamming of a door sent him charging into the kitchen area, knocking Linda askew. He reached out and grabbed her arms as she started to fall backward.

"I—I'm so sorry."

She narrowed a look his direction. "What is *wrong* with you?"

"I said I was sorry. Worry clouded my thoughts when I couldn't find you."

"Why?" Linda put the overflowing basket on the counter, removing dirt-encrusted carrots from the top of the pile. She ran water from the faucet over the orange roots and used her hand to loosen the mud.

"I'm really serious about you being careful. I have a bad feeling you're in danger."

Linda continued to wash the fresh vegetables. "I've lived this long in my home with no problems, and I'll continue to live as I please. I'm not stopping my life because you have a *gut* feeling I *might* be in danger. Since Gitty and Morgan no longer have their magic, what can they do?"

Uther ground his teeth. "My lady, I hate to be a pain, but I know this family, and I know how devious they are when they feel threatened. Your involvement in taking away their magic is paramount in their thinking of you as an enemy. *Please* be more careful."

Placing the carrots in the sink, Linda turned to face Uther.

He noted her stormy eyes take on a softness, reflecting a light dove gray color.

"I've been on my own for so long, I've become quite adept at taking care of myself. It's…difficult for me to realize someone else might care if something happens to me." Linda stepped toward Uther and rose up on her tiptoes to place a kiss on his tanned cheek. She watched him slowly turn a ruddy pink and lower his eyes.

"Well, someone does care. Will you take care—for me?" He raised his gaze to her amazed expression.

The sincerity and—angst—held within made Linda's breath catch in her throat. "I—I'll try to remember." A tremulous smile touched her lips.

"That's all I can ask." He straightened and glanced at the basket of vegetables. "Need help?"

Linda glanced at the cornucopia of greens. "Nope. This is women's work. Now, scoot out of my kitchen." Giggling, she'd grabbed a dishtowel and snapped at him with it.

"Don't have to ask me twice." Uther hustled from the room and made his way to the porch.

His gaze fell on the back of the cart disappearing down the driveway. Birds merrily called to each other across the greening meadow and the sun peaked through the tiny sprouts of new growth on the pine trees lining the lane. Serenity appeared to be the weather of the day.

Uther felt a shudder travel his body. It was quiet—too quiet. Everything in him screamed of trouble brewing, and the cause had two names, Gitty and Morgan Saun.

Chapter Ten

Trickle lay on her back, slowly swishing her tail and watching the birds above the water arguing over placement of a nest.

"Silly beasts." She turned and swam to her cove. Wedged behind two rocks was a mirror she'd found on the side of the river. She gazed at her reflection, noting she was getting a bit thin and pale.

"Need to go top side for a day or two." The thought brought a smile to her face. She wiggled to the mirror and feeling along the backside, pulled an oblong piece of paper encased in plastic and a drying spell from behind the reflective glass. The paper had a picture in one corner and Trickle was amazed at how much it resembled her. She'd asked Chrissy to have the librarian tell her what it said, but her cousin had clucked her tongue in disgust, reading the black lines to Trickle. This piece of special paper was; what had Chrissy called it? Oh yeah, a driving license, whatever that was.

Trickle found the paper at the edge of the water and, on an impulse, dragged it back to her secret cove. She knew at some point it might come in handy. She was right. The last time she'd opted to go *above,* the paper had helped her to go where she wanted. She thought maybe there was magic in the paper because all the doors opened for her.

When she'd returned from her land adventure, she'd bargained a bit of simple magic for a small valise to store her human clothing. One of the few oak trees not bulldozed by the she night elf's company served as a storage and changing place, Trickle deposited the case deep in the hollow of the tree. She hoped it was still there. She'd have to ask Chrissy to help her come up with something to wear otherwise, and right now she wasn't willing to include her cousin in her plans.

~ * ~

"Really? I mean, really?" Morgan looked at the dark green, rubber wading boots, fishing hat and pole displayed on the couch. "You really expect me to wear these…hideous things? Not on your life. There's got to be another way."

Gitty was trying to keep from chuckling and not doing a good job of stopping herself. She burst into laughter.

"Oh my god, you should see your face. Ahh ha ha…" Rolling on the couch, clutching her abdomen, the she night elf was caught up in waves of hilarity. "I have to get a picture of this."

Morgan pulled up and straightened his back. "Then do it yourself." He turned and stomped to his room.

Gitty lay on the couch sniggering and trying to catch her breath. She'd better apologize to the drama king or they'd be back to square one and still have no magic. Sighing with exasperation, she moved from the couch and headed down the hallway to soothe her brother's ruffled ego.

She knocked on his bedroom door. "Come on, Morgan. Don't be such a baby. It's only for a week or two, no more. Just think…when you're done and we have the librarian, you'll get your magic back and everything will be the way it's supposed to be."

The door creaked open an inch. "I'm not wearing those hideous—whatevers."

Gitty backed away. "Fine. But take them, anyway. They'll be good props. Anyone passing by will think you're actually fishing."

He ventured out of his room, keeping a wary eye on his sister. "If this works and we get our magic back, I want a proper apology."

She turned on her heel and strode to the living room. "I'll write it in the sky with my broom."

Fitting. Once in the living area, Morgan stood in front of the picture window, ignoring the view of the valley below. He turned his back to the glorious sunshine and faced his sister on the couch.

"When is all of this to happen?"

"I'd like to ride to the area today and give it a look-over to see how much camouflage you'll need. Lancelot will lead the way. Once we've seen the stream and the foliage on the banks, we'll have a better idea exactly where you need to stand to get the best observation point. That alright with you?" Gitty cocked her head and hitched her right eyebrow.

"Fine. I'll change and get my horse ready. I'll be in the stables when you're ready to leave." Morgan marched out of the living room and back down the hallway.

Gitty blew a breath between her lips. "My brother, the drama king." Shaking her head, she got up from the couch and ambled to her room to change to her riding leathers. The weather was a bit cool so she grabbed her insulated jacket and quilted leather gauntlets. Her horse could do with a good brushing.

She was at the back door when Lancelot appeared. "Where've you been?"

Napping. It's what I do. Where are we going?

Gitty opened the door, letting the cat out first. "I thought we'd ride to the stream behind the Lending Library and you could direct us to the best spot to keep an eye on the Librarian. I'm going to brush my horse first, if you care to join me."

No thanks. I'll lay here in the sun until you're ready to leave.

"Suit yourself. I'll call you." She turned to the black creature only to find him sunning himself on the step of the back porch, his eyes tightly shut.

The brisk walk to the stables energized the night elf and she entered the barn with vigor. Her most recent acquisition was a mahogany brown stallion bursting with spirit. His haughty manner and rippling flanks caught her attention the moment she saw him running through the fields of a local farmer in the valley. Buying the animal involved a great deal of bartering on her part, and she knew the man overpriced the animal to discourage her. What he didn't know was once Gitty decided she wanted something, nothing could dissuade her from that goal.

Glade whinnied the moment he caught wind of her scent.

"Hello, my beauty. How are you today?"

The stallion threw back his head and pawed the ground in his stall.

"Ah, good to see you're anxious to get out and run. We're going on an adventure, but first I'll give you a good brushing so you sparkle in the sunlight. What do you think?"

The animal, seventeen hands at the shoulder, lowered his head, allowing Gitty to scratch behind his ears.

She stood on her tiptoes and whispered. "I miss you so much, Glade. If I had to do it over again, I'd let you catch me this time." Gently rubbing the horse's nose, she gazed into the dark brown eyes. "I know you're in there. I can feel it."

Brown eyes blinked at the night elf and the steed pushed his nose against her hand. Gitty grabbed the brush from the shelf. She put Glade on a lead and freed him from the stall, tying the lead to a center post. With determined slow strokes, she brushed him from the tip of his nose to the end of his tail. She felt the ripple of his muscled body and sensed the excitement building within him. It had been too long since the two rode from the grounds. They were about to resolve that problem.

Clip clopping of horse hoofs broke Gitty's rumination as Morgan and his horse headed toward the exit of the stables. She gave one last swipe to the mane of her steed and preceded to place the hand-tooled, black leather saddle on his back. Completing the task of readying her ride, she swung up and trotted out the stable door as she donned her riding gloves.

"Get that, would you, Morgan?"

He glared at her as he moved to close the entrance. "I'm not your personal servant, sister. If you want my help on the project, you'd best stop treating me as though I am."

"Fine." Gitty removed a glove from her right hand and, placing two fingers to her lips, whistled for Lancelot. She pulled Glade to a stop to replace her glove and wait for the third member of their troop to arrive.

Strolling up to the mounted elves, the black cat stretched his legs in front of him and yawned.

"You ready?" Gitty touched her heels to the stallion's flanks.

Yes.

Morgan snapped his head around to stare at the cat. "I can hear him!"

"Bravo. Now let's get going. I want to find this place and get this reconnaissance over. I have other things to do with my time before we set this in motion."

The odd party of large black cat and two night elves on horseback cantered out of the stable yard and down the hill toward the valley.

Chapter Eleven

Linda slipped out the back door and followed the trail from her garden to the bank of the stream. The sun was blessing her favorite spot, and she needed time alone to let her mind wander. Uther's intentions were pure, but he was being a bit of a pain about implementing them. After all, she was well over twenty-five and caring for herself was a daily ritual. She could spot danger the moment it appeared. As she sat and argued with herself, she succumbed to the warmth and peace of the moment. Linda laid back and closed her eyes—for *just* a moment.

~ * ~

Gitty let her body roll with the rhythm of Glade's easy gallop. The spring was in a teasing mood, providing sunshine and warmth to bath the valley. She allowed a moment of contentment to color her outlook—for a brief time. Her cat, Lancelot, sprinted through the tall grasses of the valley looking over his shoulder every so often to make sure she was still following.

His frantic gait slowed to a walk where upon he undulated behind a large bush.

"Lancelot." Gitty pushed an angry whisper between her teeth. "Where are you?"

Come on. Use your mind. I'm right behind the bush staring at the librarian across the stream. That is what we came for, right?

Gitty reined back on Glade's bit and dismounted in one smooth movement. Morgan brought up the rear, reining his horse to a walk before flipping his leg over the saddle horn and dropping to the ground.

"Shhh!" Gitty shot a nasty look Morgan's direction.

Straightening up, he tied his horse to a nearby bush. Morgan measured his gait as he inched toward the stream's edge. Rounding the mulberry, he spotted the form of the female the fae called Librarian. Bile rose in his throat. This being is the one who doomed him to a life of banality. Heat rose up his core and Morgan's vision blurred red around the edges. He took a determined step toward the stream.

Gitty watched her brother's slack features harden. His eyes locked on the human opposite their location. She'd never seen him so focused. When the color of his neck started to turn a deep pink, she knew Morgan had crossed the line of logical thinking. He was running on emotion alone and the consequences would be disastrous. She shot out a hand, grabbing the back of his duster to restrain him.

"WHA...!"

Tugging with all her strength, Gitty yanked him behind the bush and clapped a hand over his mouth.

"Ouch!" She snatched her hand to her chest. "Why did you bite me?"

His blue eyes were glacial. "You put your hand over my mouth. Why?"

"You were headed to the stream with blood in your eye. That's not the way I want this to go."

"I, what?" The surprise on his face was genuine.

"Little brother, I think it's time to go. I'll explain it as we head home."

Morgan leaned his head to look around the mulberry bush. The prone figure hadn't moved from the sunny spot. As he started to pull back, the glitter of gold flashed in his eyes.

Lancelot rushed the stream. *Mine, all mine!*

Lancelot! You can fish later. It's time to go home and finalize our plans. Gitty ground her teeth. If it wasn't her brother testing her limits, it was the single-minded cat.

Grumbling with each step, the black feline stomped his feet as he moved away from the stream. *I'll have that half fish yet.*

"Half fish?" Morgan untethered his horse and swung into the saddle. "What is the other half?"

It resembles one of those dreadful faeries.

"Really?"

Gitty turned and sneered to the lagging parties. "Get a move on. We don't want to be discovered because the two of you decided to have a leisurely conversation about fish. Move it!"

Hmm, half fish and half fae. Morgan's face brightened. *A mermaid.* He urged his horse on and was soon rolling the thought of mermaids around in his mind as he galloped toward the stables of home.

~ * ~

Trickle's scales itched. Something wasn't right, and she could sense an ominous force nearby. Swimming against the current near the rock-strewn bottom of the stream, she located a niche in the rocks by Librarian's favorite spot. Chrissy had entrusted her with the duty of keeping an eye on the human, and while she'd rather play in the currents, she had made a fae oath and was bound by the laws of the fae community to keep her word. She wiggled down behind a rock and clutched the lichen growing on the sheltered side. The nasty black animal skulked about the shoreline, concentrating on the area where Librarian usually sat. She crouched down. That's when *he* appeared.

His hair shimmered in the sunlight and his skin was pale—like hers. She wiggled to the top of the water and flashed her tail his direction. Maybe he'd look at her and she could whisper sweet words to him. She liked what she'd seen so far. As she was about to jump out of the water in joy, the form of the black cat materialized dangerously close. Gazing her direction, it moved with determination, stopping short of the river's edge. She felt the animal's disappointment as the dark figure slinked away.

Wiggling free of the rock confines, Trickle caught the current back to her home.

A talk with Chrissy is in store...and soon. She shivered with excitement. It had been quite a while since she'd walked on dry land. *I wonder if I'll remember how?*

Chapter Twelve

Bram and Silas trudged down the back road toward Bram's home. Silas had listened as Bram snorted and snored for the last two miles. Being just as tired as the gnome, the noise was grating on his tender ears.

"Bram. Bram. BRAM!" When yelling at his friend didn't work, Silas resorted to the old fashioned way of alerting and barked his high-pitched yap.

"Wha…what!" Bram yanked his head off his chest, whipping it from side to side. "Why did you bark?"

Silas plunked down. "Because we're at your house and yelling didn't work."

Bram stretched his arms above his head then rubbed his eyes. He lumbered from the cart and trudged to his front door.

"BRAM!"

"What, Silas?" Bram's voice took on a dangerous edge.

"Unhook me."

"Oh—yeah." He sloughed back to the cart.

The terrier rolled his eyes and huffed his impatience at his friend's negligence.

"My apologies, Silas. I can't remember when I've had so much mead and heard so many tales."

"I hope it was worth it because my pads are blistered. Think I'll go home and stay off my paws for a couple days." The terrier waited while Bram unhooked the harness and rubbed the chaffed spots on Silas' fur.

"Rest, my friend. We earned this payment."

Silas limped off and disappeared in the tall grass of the meadow. Bram watched him go.

"Funny, I've never seen his home." He shrugged his shoulders. "I'm sure he'll invite me one day. Now to a soft bed after a good meal." He pushed open the door to his home. Holding up his hand, he fended off a barrage of questions from his wife.

"Enough. I'll give you a detailed account of my journey after I've eaten and slept in my bed."

Igrayne narrowed her moss green eyes his direction. "Don't hush me. You take off for a week then stagger into my home reeking of mead and road dirt and tell me not to ask questions? If you want a home cooked meal, Mr., do it yourself."

Igrayne stomped into the bedroom, slamming the door behind her.

Bram blew out a deep, weary breath. It wasn't in his nature to argue, and he was bone tired. Tapping gently on the door, he acquiesced.

"I promise I will tell you all of the travails if you will honor me with a bowl of your marvelous stew, my love."

The door squeaked open an inch. "Really? All the things that happened?"

This time he held the hand to his chest. "I give my oath."

She pulled the door open and strode into the living room. "In that case, I'll warm the pot." She padded to the kitchen and lit the stove. Turning to ask Bram a question, she noted the empty room. She retraced her steps through the living area to the bedroom and found her husband planted in the middle of the bed on his stomach, snoring loudly.

"I guess I'll wait until the morrow for those details." She closed the door and turned off the stove. In the front room she picked up her embroidery to pass the time until he woke up or she fell asleep—whichever came first.

~ * ~

Uther was feeling a restless sensation wash over him. Being so long in one place was not in his nature. He gazed longingly down the lane, jumping when the gentle voice spoke in his right ear.

"You don't have to stay."

He turned toward the light smell of fresh meadow grass. "No, I don't but I wish to. I've many years on the roads wandering the land. It's time I settled and shed my nomad ways."

Linda moved to the railing of the porch on Uther's left side. "I think you'll be very unhappy and restless. You are very much the rolling stone, Uther."

He turned to look down on her. "Don't you want my company? I'll depart if you wish me to."

Time slowed as he watched her face mirror the thoughts roaming through her mind. First, she was terrified then hurt by his statement.

"I'm sorry. Did I offend you?"

"No."

He watched her face morph into a calm façade. Her stormy gray eyes took on a flinty hue and shuttered to the outside world.

"I simply meant once a man has traveled extensively, settling in a small community will kill his spirit. That's what happened to my Donald. Oh, they called it cancer, but he was never the same after we put down roots here. Eventually, the stagnation, as he called it, took his life."

Uther placed his hand on the small of her back, his fingers sensing the tightness through her chambray shirt. "I am truly sorry for your loss. Your Donald must have been quite a man to have captured your attention and love for so many years."

Linda felt her breath catch in her throat. Tears were pushing to escape her eyes. She pulled in a deep breath.

"He was very…special. I'm afraid I wasn't able to fulfill his dying wish to remarry. There just wasn't anyone I cared to spend time with," she turned eyes Uther's direction, "until now. I find myself hesitant to share my feelings. Being left alone and lonely is something I've already experienced and don't wish to do again."

Uther turned her to face him. "I *choose* to stay here. I made the decision long ago not to couple when I saw how miserable my brother,

Aethel, was. He married the daughter of the clan chief, a beautiful ethereal creature with flowing silver hair and ocean blue eyes. Unfortunately, she had the heart of an iceberg. It was almost a blessing when she died in childbirth with the second child, a son.

"He met the love of his life in the heat of battle. She was as opposite as his wife was like him; a gnome." Uther chuckled. "She was spunky, talented with a blade and took no foolishness from my brother. He was so smitten with her that…"

Uther hesitated knowing the information he was about to impart was privy to very few.

"…they produced a child."

Linda's eyes popped open. "Wow. The idea boggles the mind. The child must've been very—odd looking."

"No. I don't think he ever learned of the child. By the time his love was deep into the throws of pregnancy, Aethel was bound by his family's word to marry his night elf mate.

"So, you see, Linda," he tucked his finger beneath her chin to raise her face to his. "My family has a history of breaking the norm. When my eyes beheld you for the first time, I knew if I stayed I'd not ever leave."

She reached up and ran her hand down his face, hesitating lightly on his dimpled chin.

"Yet, here you stand." She rose up on her tiptoes, slipping her hand around his neck and pulling him to her. "Stop me anytime."

Uther groaned. "My lady, I would be a fool."

He lowered his head and allowed their lips to meld together. His heart pounded so hard he felt the pressure in his ears and realized other parts of his anatomy were responding in kind.

Linda pressed her body against Uther. She wasn't sure if the pounding she felt in her chest was her heart or his. He'd slipped his arms completely around her and drew her as close to him as possible. She sensed his passion against her stomach, momentarily confused by the pressure. *It's been too many years.* Sensations lost to time began to surge through her limbs, and she allowed them to overcome her.

The lovers pulled back to stare at each other.

"I never had this much emotion for another being. I fought it, believe me. That's why I left before. I couldn't face feeling the kind of loss Aethel did. I saw love tear him apart. Yet, I had to return when I heard my niece and nephew were being so vocal about the loss of their magic. I know them. When they start talking, it isn't too long before they put actions to their words. I…"

Linda pressed her finger to his lips. She stepped back and gently took his hand in hers, leading him inside the Lending Library to the door of her room.

She opened the entry and gave him a quizzical look. "Join me?"

Uther looked into the warmly decorated interior. A smile started to spread on his face.

"Yes."

The two passed the threshold into the Librarian's private sanctum. When the door closed, both knew the life they'd experienced before this day was about to change.

Chapter Thirteen

Trickle tugged at the piece of magically sealed paper. The time had come for her to get her feet on dry land. For the last three days, the handsome night elf Chrissy had called Morgan appeared on the bank in some very odd clothing. He threw line in the water, but there wasn't any bait or even a hook on the end. She watched him pace back and forth. Around the same time every day, he'd back away from the bank and disappear. She noted the librarian appear on the bank under the tree about the time the night elf would vanish.

Dragging the paper with her, Trickle cruised up stream several oak trees from the library before exiting the water. The oak roots created a cove on the bank where she could make the change from water creature to land creature. Maintaining her small size until she was done dressing, Trickle entered her land home beneath the oak. Beneath a tangle of moss covered roots sat a small dressing table fashioned by the fae workmen, a piece of mirror hung above. The two drawer sides held the slab of wood Trickle used to hold her brush and comb. She set the paper against the wall to dry as she looked beneath the cot for the valise and her clothing.

"Ahh, there you are." Pulling the brown case out, Trickle sat on the rug-covered floor and popped the latches. She ran her hands over the clothes inside before lifting out the top item. The simple, long-sleeved shirt was deep green with white mother-of-pearl buttons. The next item was a pair of fitted black jeans. She pulled the rest of the clothing from the valise and laid them across the small bed. Closing her eyes she murmured words learned during her childhood. The material wrinkled then straightened, all evidence of being locked away for several years gone.

Noting sunlight outside her tree, Trickle opted to take a nap until the sun left the sky for the day. Tonight was the beginning of her hunt for the night elf called, Morgan. The less magic she used to locate him the better. While the two cursed night elves may not have their own magic, she was sure they'd be able to spot the use of magic better than humans.

Grabbing a blanket of moss, Trickle covered her legs, drifting into a dreamless slumber.

Cold. So cold. Teeth chattering. Cold. Daring to open one eye, the merfae felt panic grip her throat. *Where am I? This doesn't look like my stream.* Feeling the panic creep up her spine, Trickle magicked a low yellow light orb sending it to the middle of the room. She clutched the moss blanket to her chin as she surveyed her surroundings. Slowly the terror subsided as she realized she was in the oak tree she called home when she walked. The cold continued to plague her so she conjured a heat orb to warm the room. The area outside the tree was dark and she heard crickets starting their nightly concert.

"Time to start my quest to find my night elf." Humming as she moved about, Trickle put together an outfit from her valise she felt would gather attention her direction. She brushed her golden locks one hundred strokes as her mother had instructed and fetched a cape of silken spider's web. A quick glance at the figure in the mirror and she headed toward the opening of her home. At the doorway, she turned to extinguish the light orb catching sight of the paper.

"Almost forgot." She returned to the dressing table to retrieve the item. She hurried to the door, closing then uttering a covering spell to camouflage the tree.

Trickle pulled in a deep breath as she stepped away from the base of the oak. Pulling a perfect pearl from her pocket, she held the smooth pebble in her hand and started to chant:

"Size is but an illusion,
Make this small form,

Become the human norm,
To create confusion,
And bring me the solution I seek."

The air wavered and a glow began at the base of the oak. A rainbow colored cloud plumed up and drifted across the stream. From the center of the light and color display stepped a tall, willowy blonde clad in figure flattering dark jeans. The tailored man's shirt was worn with the hem outside the jeans, collar opened at the neck and flipped up in the back. A black patent belt emphasized the tiny waist of the ethereal creature. The belt matched black, patent three-inch heels the blonde carried in one hand; the other hand carried a matching clutch bag carrying the driver's license she'd tended so carefully. As of this moment, Trickle was now Katherine Lee from Springfield, Oregon. She wasn't sure why this particular piece of paper was so magical, but in previous outings, it had opened all kinds of doors.

Trickle—Katherine closed her eyes and imagined the most likely location she would find her target. With a snap of her fingers, she disappeared.

Appearing at the side of the building, Katherine put on her shoes and flipped her hair behind her shoulder. A quick smoothing of the shirt, and she walked to the sidewalk and up the steps to the gathering place for humans and those who enjoyed their company. She opened the door and was hit with the pulsing of bass guitars thumping out a bottom line to a rock and roll song.

"This is for the fae and Librarian." There was a change since the last time she'd walked on two legs. This was one of their drinking places, but the air wasn't choking with cigarette smoke. She could actually breathe!

"I really need to get out more often."

"No kidding, babe. Let me buy you a drink."

Katherine shrank from the leering, weaving man leaning against the bar. She hurried past him and headed for a booth in the rear of the room. She slid into the leather bench seat facing the door. If the night elf showed, she'd have an eye on him first.

The hours ticked away with Katherine keeping a watchful eye on the door. Her sixth sense had never failed her before. *Why now?* As her patience wore thin and the bar emptied of patrons, she decided she'd made a huge mistake trusting her instincts. She grabbed the clutch and scooted to the end of the bench seat when the door opened and there he stood.

His hair took on the blue hue of the beer sign over the door.

Trickle, Katherine, noted his shoulders were slumped forward and he shuffled to the bar. According to her cousin Chrissy, this night elf was supposed to be so full of himself no one could bear to be near him. He'd left a trail of broken promises throughout the valley. The being she was looking at certainly didn't reek of confidence, quite the opposite. This might prove easier than she'd been lead to believe. A quick thought and she scented her skin with night musk. Plucking up her determination, Katherine stood and walked to the bar a couple chairs from the night elf. She caught sight of him in the mirror at the back of the bar. It was indeed the handsome face she'd been studying from beneath the surface of the stream.

She raised a hand to get the attention of the bartender. "Excuse me?"

The dark haired young man smiled and sauntered her direction. "Yeah, beautiful. What can I do for you?"

Trickle watched hazel eyes take stock of her. She started to speak and stopped. Enchanting someone was on her agenda but not this someone. She graced him with a smile.

"Yes. I've been waiting for a friend and," she shrugged her shoulders, "it looks as if I've been stood up. Can you tell me how to get transportation to Golden Meadows?"

"Wow. You're quite a way from there. It's too late for the buses to run and, truth be told, the cost to take a taxi is exorbitant. You'd be best to stay at one of the local motels and take the bus tomorrow."

Katherine did her best to look disappointed. "Okay. Can I get a cup of coffee and the phone book?" She glanced toward the morose figure occupying the bar stool to her left. The air around him wavered oppressively. His waist length silver hair was confined to a braid down his back. Pulling in a deep breath for courage, she turned to face him.

"Excuse me, but would you know of a nearby motel? I'm new to the area and it appears I've been stood up."

Listless blue eyes stared at her for a moment. Trickle saw the effect of her voice beginning to work on the night elf. The gray tint of his skin receded, and she noted vitality appear in his light orbs.

"What? I'm sorry. I didn't hear you." He motioned to the large black speakers overhead. "Too much noise. Could you repeat that?"

Got you. "Just wondering if you were familiar with the area."

The man turned to face her. Animation appeared in his actions and, relaxing his posture, he graced her with a brilliant smile.

Whew! He's good looking when he smiles.

"I'd love to help but I'm an infrequent visitor…"

Katherine caught the bartender rolling his eyes in her peripheral vision.

"…so I'm afraid my knowledge is limited. However, if you'd like a ride…I can offer to take you anywhere you'd like in my vehicle."

She graced him with a shy smile. "Thank you for the kind offer, but I make it a policy not to get in vehicles with strangers."

The fair-haired man feigned hurt, clutching his chest and swooning with his other hand to his forehead.

Katherine giggled. "You, sir, are a drama queen."

A flicker of…something dark passed over his face.

"Too true, my lady, but I'm fun to be with, and if you'll allow me but an hour to make your acquaintance, I can promise you an entertaining time."

She thought for a moment and checked the clock at the back of the bar.

"You have one hour to change my mind."

She had him. By the time the hour was up, he'd had her laughing and blushing. She made sure she departed at the time set—one hour later. Stepping around the corner of the building, Trickle removed her shoes and snapped her fingers, picturing the front door of her oak home.

She removed the door spell to enter her dry retreat. As she neared the cot, clothing fell to the ground where she'd peeled it off.

Tomorrow she'd magick the items from the floor and clean them. Right now, all she could think of was sleeping. She flopped on the cot.

"I've hooked him." *He wants to meet in a few days. I'll have to use all my tricks to reel him in. We'll just see who wins this fishing contest.*

Yawning, she closed her eyes. All scheming was shelved as the merfae tumbled to sleep.

Chapter Fourteen

Morgan stood in front of the window gazing on the valley below. A smile curled the corners of his mouth. He couldn't help it. The lady he'd met the night before at the pub made him feel the way he had before he'd lost his magic.

"What are you grinning at, you fool? You should be getting ready to go to the stream bank." Gitty stood next to him at the window. "Good heavens. You have on cologne. You'd better not be planning on leaving me in the lurch."

"I'm not, your highness. Don't get your panties in a bunch. I decided to shower and put on cologne. So what?"

"So, fishermen don't wear cologne." Gitty narrowed her eyes and leveled them his direction. "You've got a new girlfriend."

"What?"

"You have a new girlfriend. We can't deter from our plan. Dump her. When you have a girlfriend, you're absolutely useless."

Morgan faced Gitty. "I don't have a new girlfriend. I felt like cleaning up and putting on cologne. Why is it necessary for me to continue this charade of being a fisherman? We've established the librarian comes out every nice day around two-thirty pm. She takes a quick nap then heads back to the Library. How many more days do I have to waste my time?"

Morgan watched the color of Gitty's face slowly turn to crimson.

"Until I tell you to stop!" She punched his shoulder and stomped to the kitchen.

As Morgan sat rubbing his shoulder, his mind wandered to the previous evening. The mysterious blonde entranced him. In the hour he was given, he'd pulled out his best stories and tamed his boasting. For some reason, he really wanted this enigma to like him for himself.

"I think I succeeded, but she disappeared so fast I won't know for sure."

"Won't know what for sure?" Gitty carried a bottle of water in one hand and a glass container full of some white powder in the other.

"Nothing."

"Right. I've considered what you said, and I think you're on the mark."

Morgan jerked around.

"What?"

"Okay, little brother. I'm only going to repeat this once. You are right. Let's move forward. I've decided today is the day we'll complete our plan. You'll go to the stream as you have for the last few days with Lancelot at your side. When the librarian relaxes to take her nap, Lancelot will let me know and I'll subdue her. You'll need to have your horse ready to receive her. Bring mine as well, because I'll be taking us to a safe location to stash her."

Morgan gawked at her.

"Did you think this was a joke?" Gitty was in his face, eyes wide, teeth clenched.

He leaned back, putting distance between he and his angry sister. "N...no but I didn't think this would happen so soon." *I have unfinished business I wanted to complete tonight.*

"It is. Your impatience gave me the push I needed to move our situation closer to the resolution we want. It's time to act instead of waiting or talking."

Gitty shoved past him toward the back door. "Grab your stuff. We're leaving."

Morgan sloughed to the kitchen to rinse his cup.

"NOW!"

He trotted to his room and grabbed the fishing gear he used as camouflage.

"MORGAN!"

Good Lord, she's pushy. "ON MY WAY."

Double-timing his pace, Morgan snatched his sunglasses and bolted to the back door. The pair readied the horses and took off in a flurry of hoofs.

Silence punctuated the ride to the stream behind the Lending Library. Morgan set up in the spot he'd been all week with Lancelot hovered in the closest bushes swishing his tale back and forth. Morgan could feel Gitty's eyes burning a hole through his back. Sweat trickled down his back as the sun beat on his fishing vest. *Damn hot for spring.* Movement across the stream caught his attention.

The Librarian had a book in hand this time and settled in the sunspot verses the shade. She opened the text, turning to a specific page and started to read. Five minutes passed before the book teetered from her hands and rested on her legs. Morgan tensed. Things were about to get bad.

Lancelot let out a low growl. *Time?*

Morgan pulled the line from the water and made as if to button up his fishing. "Yes. She's sleeping."

The large cat trotted back to Gitty. An apparent conversation ensued between feline and night elf. Morgan heard the scuffle of hooves and turned to see Gitty walking her stallion away from the bank.

Maybe she's changed her mind.

Lancelot trotted up to Morgan. *Mistress says you are to follow her and be ready to follow her orders.*

"Great." Morgan set his fishing gear under a tree and mounted his steed. There was no turning back now.

Follow me.

He kept his eyes on the waving black tail pointing straight up in the air until they stood next to the slumbering Librarian. Gitty dismounted and pulled the water and white powder from her saddlebags.

"What are you doing?" Morgan whispered.

"Shut up and watch. This will guarantee cooperation and no damage to her."

Gitty scattered a bit of white powder on a washcloth she'd previously packed in the bag. She then sprinkled water droplets on the powder. White smoke start to spiral but quickly dissipated. She placed the cloth over the nose and mouth of the Librarian. In less than a minute, the form on the ground was limp. A fact Gitty proved by picking up and dropping the Librarian's arm to the ground.

"Get your butt over here and pick her up." Her voice was dangerous and low.

Morgan dismounted his horse and moved to the supine figure on the ground. He slid his hands beneath her shoulders and knees, lifting her from the grass. She was surprisingly light, barely one hundred pounds. His next stop was to slip her on his saddle before mounting up. The form leaned back against him and he noted the compactness of the woman.

Gitty swung up to her saddle and wretched the reins to the right.

"Follow me. Don't ask questions and don't lose me."

"I thought you were going to take her on your horse." Morgan's eyes narrowed at his sister.

"Things change. Just try to keep up and don't ask stupid questions."

Morgan nodded. When Gitty was this brusque, any deviation from what she said could bring dire consequences. The odd traveling companions galloped around the open meadows, keeping to the wooded areas away from prying eyes. Gitty stopped to let the horse drink from the upper section of the stream before plunging the riders into the forest on the opposite side of the valley.

For two hours they rode through wooded acreage. When the Librarian would start stirring, Gitty would repeat the process of putting the white powder on the washcloth, adding water then placing over the librarian's face.

Just when Morgan thought they must be getting near Eastern Oregon, Gitty slowed the pace of the ride.

"Stay here." She slipped off her horse and vanished into a dark copse of pines.

Morgan sat on the fidgeting horse that started pulling up tufts of stray grass nearby. Gitty emerged from the woods and waved him over.

"Don't go any further until I get my horse." She jogged to where she'd left her stallion and swung up to the saddle. "Follow me."

The pines closed around the small caravan as they moved deeper into the woods. Light beamed through the canopy of pine boughs. Five minutes into the ride, Morgan noted an area ahead where the forest thinned to expose a cabin. Gitty dismounted her horse and tied the reins at the porch railing. She motioned Morgan over. He nudged his mount forward.

Gitty lifted her hands. "Give her to me."

Morgan slid the sleeping form off the horse with ease.

"Tie up your horse then help me secure her."

Morgan did as he was bid, ducking his head under the doorway as he entered the shelter.

"When did you find this?"

Gitty dumped the limp form on a couch facing the stone fireplace. "I built it."

"What?"

She turned to find his eyebrows raised and shock on his face. "Don't look so surprised. I'm quite handy with a hammer and nails."

"I—I have no doubt. I just don't remember you being gone long enough to do this."

"Well, I was. Can we make sure she's securely fastened so we don't have to worry if we go outside?"

He moved to her side and assisted as she bound the Librarian's hands together at the wrists and feet at the ankles.

"You going to put something over her mouth?"

Gitty looked at the prone figure. "No. She can yell all she wants. No one will hear her. We're too far from civilization. I'm going to put a blanket on her so she doesn't get too cold."

"That's rather kind of you."

Gitty turned to him. "Not really. She's no good to us dead."

Morgan nodded his agreement.

His sister rummaged through the closet nearest the front door and brought out a battery powered camp lantern. "Use this until I get back. I'm going to locate dinner. Don't let her talk you into anything. Right?"

"Right."

Gitty shut the front door behind her. She'd planned this to the last detail but didn't want Morgan to know. He was the loose cannon in this formula. Who knows what he would blurt out given enough alcohol? She rode the quarter mile to the storage barn she'd constructed to house food supplies. Dismounting Glade, she pulled a set of keys from her vest pocket. Finding the appropriate key, she inserted it into the lock and turned. The lock opened easily and once removed, the door was easy to slide. Gitty stepped into the interior and stood still for a moment, adjusting her eyes to the darkened interior. Her breath caught in her throat as the light from the opened door featured an etched, wood portrait of Glade, the male night elf and love of her life, in a shadow box she'd created. She'd commissioned a member of his clan to create the likeness for her. Next to the portrait were his forest green, leather hauberk and broken blade. He was gone but not forgotten. Gitty's heart ached.

"Who knows my love? I may join you soon."

She went about the business of gathering supplies to feed three for a week. The food wasn't exotic but would keep them alive. After loading the supplies on her horse, she locked the door and headed back to the cabin.

Morgan walked around the large room. He was having a difficult time imagining his sister sawing wood, banging nails, installing windows or anything related to building. The sofa faced a stone fireplace complete with mantel. Framing the hearth was wood and stone shelving and two small windows, one on either side. The hardwood floor was a deep red brown in color and emitted a warm glow adding to the cozy feel of the room. To the right of the room, Gitty had installed a half wall that divided the sleeping area from the sitting area. Opposite the fireplace was a galley style kitchen with the fundamentals, nothing more. A bathroom had been built off the sleeping area. All in all, Morgan had to agree, this was an amazing retreat.

In his reverie Morgan failed to notice the librarian sit up. She groaned.

"Oh, my head. Where am I?"

He jumped. "What?"

"You! What have you done to me? HELP! HELP!" Linda tried to stand, only to fall forward and cut her lip.

"Great! See what you've done now?" Morgan grabbed the woman and hoisted her up, plopping her on the couch. "Sit still. You can yell as loud as you want. Hell, you can yell until you're hoarse but no one will hear."

Linda glared at him with blood running down her lips. "You're Morgan Saun, aren't you?"

"Lady, be quiet. It doesn't matter who I am. You can try to get away if you want but trust me, the effort will be futile. I'm getting a cloth and some Band-Aids to stop your lip from bleeding." He strode to the bathroom and opened the medicine cabinet door. An unopened box of the adhesives sat to the right. Grabbing a clean washcloth, he ran cool water over it and snatched the bandages from their spot in the cabinet.

Linda ran to the front door, both hands on the handle, trying her best to open the barrier. Her face dropped in surprise as the door opened and she stood facing Gitty.

"I should have known. You."

Gitty sneered at her. "Yeah. Me. You and your merry little band of fae friends ruined my life with your stunt of taking my magic. It's been nearly a year, and I think it's time I got back to being myself again. Don't you?" She pushed Linda back to the couch without consideration of her captive's stumbling. "I have no love lost for you, Librarian." Gitty leaned over to look at Linda's face. "What the hell happened here? Morgan!"

He bolted from the back of the cabin carrying bandages and a washcloth. "What?"

"What did you do? She's bleeding."

"Yes, I know. She tried to get up from the couch, tripped and fell." He sat next to Linda and placing his fingers either side of her head, turned her to face him. Linda fought to break free of his grasp.

He dropped his head to his chest. "Please. I really don't want to hurt you."

"Right. That's why you have me trussed up in some god forsaken hut in the middle of nowhere." Linda's eyes radiated hate his direction.

Gitty leaned down level with Linda. "Let me tell you something, Other. Morgan here is a lily livered coward who happens to be very adept with a blade. He's happiest carousing with you mortals in some pub, trying to impress the women. He probably wouldn't hurt you.

"Me, on the other hand, I have no love for the human population as a whole. As I'm going to live to be two hundred fifty years old or older, I'm more than willing to cut you to pieces to get my point across to the people I need to convince. I'm the one you need to fear."

Backing away, Gitty spoke to Morgan. "Fix her up. I'll put something together to eat in the meantime. I don't want her dead—yet." She turned a glare Linda's direction.

Linda shrunk back and looked at Morgan. He shrugged his shoulders.

"She means it. Now, please let me clean up your lip and put a bandage on it." He put the cloth to her face and very gently cleansed the blood from her lip. Once he dried the spot, a bandage was applied. Morgan checked his handiwork and rose from the couch.

Gitty was slamming pots and pans on the stove and grumbling. "I didn't sign on for this. All I wanted was a simple snatch and grab with a compliant body. Who the hell knew this *old* Other would have such— spunk? I don't need this."

Morgan waited until she quit ranting. "I have an idea."

Gitty whipped around with a large spoon in hand. "Great." She shook the spoon as she spoke. "This was your idea in the first place. What now? Let her go free?"

Morgan stepped backward with each shake of the spoon until he felt the couch back hit his thighs. He gingerly took the spoon from his sister. "Let's go outside. Turn off the stove and let's take a minute."

Gitty tossed a look Linda's direction. "What about her?"

"Use your sleeping potion."

She crossed to the counter and grabbed the cloth, sprinkling crystals and adding water. As she came at Linda, her captive tried to wiggle away. Winning the battle, Gitty had her prisoner unconscious within a few seconds.

"We may have to tie her to a chair. Let's go." She nodded toward the front porch.

When the brother and sister stepped on the precisely crafted boards of the front porch, they opted to leave the door open.

"Okay, what's your bright idea now?" Gitty placed the cloth over the porch railing and crossed her arms.

Morgan held up the washcloth smeared with blood. "What was going to be your next move? You're heading up this production."

She leaned against the support. "A note saying she's being held until the council convenes and agrees to reinstitute our magic—one hundred percent."

"How far do you think that will get you?" Morgan lifted a brow.

"As far as I need it. I don't think Uther will be happy about his lady love being held captive."

"True. But all he'll do is employ his magic to locate our whereabouts and come rescue her."

"So you have some idea that will inhibit this ability?"

Morgan smirked and held up the washcloth. "This."

Gitty huffed disbelief. "Get real. How's a bloody washcloth going to stop Uther from using his magic?"

"By seeing the bloody cloth, he'll know we're serious. There's enough blood to make him question how bad his lady is hurt. We can suggest if he tries anything, she'll be returned in pieces. How do you think he'll react to that?"

She stood looking at her brother. A smile slowly began to turn up the corners of her lips.

"I was beginning to wonder if our mother had been fooling around with the stable boy before you were born. That is a truly *wicked*, devious plan. I love it!" She unfolded her arms and headed for the cabin, humming a Celtic victory song.

Morgan smiled. Finally. His sister was actually appreciative of his plan. He'd have to remember this day; they came so seldom.

Entering the building, Morgan went to the kitchen to search for a storage bag. He dropped the bloodied cloth inside and sealed it. Rummaging in a small desk placed against the wall, he located paper and a pen. He sat at the two-person table and created the ransom note.

We have the Librarian. If you want her back alive and in one piece, send your reply via the Mouse Network to the family warehouse in Springfield for further instructions.

"Gitty, what do you think?"

She read the two-line note and nodded. "Excellent. For once, I can say I couldn't do better myself. How will we get it from the warehouse?"

Morgan chuckled. "That's the best thing about the Mouse Network."

Gitty raised an eyebrow. "What?"

"They have no loyalties. Given enough payment, they'll go anywhere to deliver a message. I've been working with one particular messenger who'll go pretty much where I ask."

"Well, well. Aren't you the devious one?" Gitty stood. "Can you contact your messenger and tell him to meet me at the house with the response?"

"WHAT?"

"Yes, little brother. You get to baby-sit the hostage."

"Great." Morgan grumbled.

"Just remember, when this is all over and you have your magic back, you'll thank me. I know if that—Other—tried anything with me, I'd have no problem eliminating her."

"Fine. But I have a…date in a couple days."

"If all goes well, you'll be able to charm her and get lucky with your magic." Gitty smirked. "I should be home in about an hour. Have your messenger meet me there in two hours."

"How am I supposed to do that since you have tied me to this house?"

Gitty glowered at him. "Get a messenger to find your messenger."

"How?"

"That's your problem not mine."

Morgan grumbled and watched his sister leave on her horse. "Open my big mouth and wind up babysitting. Some day..."

Chapter Fifteen

Uther checked her room. He walked the path to the stream and checked her favorite spot along the bank, finding her book opened to her favorite poem but no other sign of Linda. He trotted back to the Lending Library and hunted until he found Chrissy.

"Have you seen Linda?"

The tiny nymph smiled and looked at him, a twinkle in her eye. "Lost your lady love?"

Uther felt the blush crawl up his cheeks. "I'm serious. I've looked all over the property, and I can't find her. She's not in the garden or on the stream bank. I even looked in her room to be sure she wasn't napping. I'm worried. She didn't say anything to me about running an errand."

"Well, you know she's been alone for a long time. I don't think she would tell you if she was running an errand." The nymph cocked her head from side to side looking at her layout for the May Day festival. "Do you think I could put the gnomes next to the meadow fae?"

Uther looked at the seating chart. "Probably not. Why not put the mountain fae next to the gnomes? They get along better. I keep forgetting how independent Linda is. I mean, she doesn't always tell you if she's running an errand, does she?"

Chrissy had been erasing and rewriting when Uther's question struck her.

"Actually, she tells me where she's going every time she leaves." She turned to him, her brows knit together. "Uther? We need to do another search. It's not like her to take off unannounced."

May Day plans set aside, the odd pair decided to split the property in half and mounted a search. Uther took the building and front of the property; Chrissy opted to fly around the garden and stream. Her ulterior motive was to talk with Trickle and see if her cousin had any pertinent information.

Chrissy buzzed to the stream. *Trickle, you here?* Three tries yielded no results. Chrissy gave up trying to contact her cousin. It was obvious Trickle wasn't home. She checked with the birds and talked to the rabbits and no one had seen Trickle for a couple days. Chrissy hovered above the water and murmured. "Where are you, cousin?"

The garden proved as elusive as the stream; no sign of Trickle or the Librarian. Chrissy was feeling ineffectual and frustrated as she returned to the Library.

By the look on his face, Uther had met the same fate.

"Any luck, Uther?"

"No. I checked everywhere I could think of and no Linda. You?"

"Nothing. What are we to do? Call in the local police?"

"No. Other's police are very uncaring and will suggest she left of her own accord. I don't believe it. Do you?"

Chrissy shook her head. "No. She loves this place too much to just walk away. There's something going on."

Uther nodded his agreement. "Yes, and I can guess who's behind it. I'm afraid we'll have to wait until they make the next move."

Chrissy's wings quavered. "Uther, I'm afraid."

"I am too, my little friend, I am too."

The next morning Uther sat at a table near the kitchen, grasping a cup of Chrissy's Killer Coffee. His bloodshot eyes told the tale of his previous night. As he forced the dark brown liquid down his throat, a mouse wearing the maroon vest of the Mouse Network approached him.

"I'm looking for an Uther."

The night elf narrowed his eyes to focus on the messenger.

"You have found him."

"Please sir, a message for you is in the pocket upon my back. I'm to wait for a reply."

The mouse turned his body so Uther could retrieve the paper

tucked within the vest.

Chrissy winged in from the kitchen and hovered over Uther's left shoulder. She watched him withdraw a bag with a note taped to the front.

Uther pulled the paper from the bag and sucked in a deep breath when he spotted crimson blotches upon a white item inside. He unfolded the paper and read the cryptic message. Opening the baggie, he withdrew the contents; a washcloth covered in blood. Uther uttered an ancient curse.

Chrissy dropped to the table and reached out a tiny hand to touch the washcloth. "Please tell me this isn't the librarian, Uther."

"I can't, my little friend. The beings we're dealing with have no soul or conscious when it comes to the lives of others."

The nymph yanked her hand back and broke into sobs, winging her way to the kitchen.

Uther got up to locate pen and paper. When he found what he needed, he sat at the table and put together a carefully worded reply.

If you value your life, you'll not harm a hair on the Librarian's head. What do you want?

He tucked the reply in the vest of the mouse. "What is the cost?"
"None, sir. It has been prepaid."

He watched the gray creature scamper from the room and out the front door.

It took all his power not to follow the creature. He toyed with the idea of placing a magic tracker on the mouse but knew his adversaries while unable to *use* magic, would be able to spot the magic tracker.

"There has to be a way." Pacing the center aisle of the library, he examined his memory for other times when magic couldn't be used to track a foe. "Why can't I think of…hawks! If I can only remember the spell to call them." Uther stopped his motion and furrowed his brow. His hand rested on a book on the shelves. Eyes shut tightly to recall the proper incantation, he would get close to remembering then feel the thought slip away. He opened his eyes and turned to gaze at the spine of the book where he'd placed his hand. ***The Forgotten Spells of Merlin***. *Can it really be that easy?*

Retrieving the tome from its neighbors, Uther flipped to the page for aviary spells, sliding his finger down the page to the words used for summoning messenger birds. The moment he saw the ancient words, his sudden amnesia evaporated. *Of course.*

He replaced the work on the shelf, which he noted was filled with volumes on magical creatures and spells. Rolling the words around his head, he moved as quickly as his feet would allow to the lane in front of the Lending Library. The sky was dotted with rain clouds in various hues of gray, the sun peeking from behind them. He whispered the words to the chant twice, as recommended, and waited for results.

The air shirred with the languid flapping of powerful wings. Uther looked to the sky. His gaze was captured by the white and tan chest of an American Kestral floating on the thermals toward him. Once the creature leveled out, Uther watched as it flew at him back winging to rest comfortably on his shoulder.

Did you call for me, night elf?

Uther was surprised at the throaty, deep tone of the bird's voice. "I did."

How can I be of assistance?

"I need eyes and ears to find something I've lost."

Why not look yourself?

"Because I'm not quite sure where it is. I received a message from one of the Mouse Network representatives and need to see where the creature finally ends up. Are you familiar with them?"

Yes. We're forbidden to eat them. Waste of good food, if you ask me.

"This one left within the last fifteen minutes and is probably heading East."

Can you be sure?

"No, but I know the author of the original message and how devious her thinking is. If you don't find the messenger within the day, don't concern yourself with the hunt. Come back here and we'll agree on a price."

Fair enough. I'll return within twenty-five hours either way.

"Fly safely and don't get caught."

I'll watch my back.

Uther watched the kestral take flight on the spiral winds soaring toward the clouds.

I've done all I can—for the moment.

He watched Chrissy buzz around the Lending Library, putting together plans for May Day and envied her distraction. Waiting was the enemy here, and he knew if he didn't find something to occupy his mind and hands, he'd go crazy.

Chrissy whizzed past him.

"I'm going for a walk, if anyone is interested." Uther exited the building to the porch. The walls inside felt as though they were closing in on him. He pulled in a deep breath of the rain-tainted, spring air and made his way to the entry road. Maybe a walkabout would clear his mind and freshen his perspective. The driveway was lined with tulips and daffodils boldly opening their petals to greet the new season. He marveled at the serenity of the landscape. If he could just stand in the lane and inhale all the spring smells for the rest of his life, he'd be a happy man. At this time, his world was about to implode and he felt powerless to find a simple solution.

A reverberation in the distance caught his attention. Uther stopped and concentrated. He realized the noise was moving toward him at a fast pace. *It's coming this way but not to the Lending Library.* He zeroed in to the direction of the sound. Narrowing his eyes, he trained them to a road situated next to the farmer's field a quarter mile to the east. The tap tapping from afar morphed into thundering hoof beats. Uther beaded in on the figure of a familiar form racing a finely muscled black horse across the valley. The she elf sat ramrod straight on the stallion's back, her white hair billowing behind her as the animal galloped to their destination.

Gitty. Where are you going in such a hurry? He tried to touch her mind but met a blank barrier. *So, you're either blocking me or have lost your ability to telepath.*

The hurried horse and rider continued their journey up the road to the mansion on the hill.

Uther closed his eyes and mentally searched the area for the other night elf. His mind touched many creatures busily preparing for summer but couldn't sense Morgan. *That's odd.* Since the two night elf siblings had been deprived of their magic, word was if you spotted Gitty, Morgan was close by. *She's in a hurry and he's nowhere to be found. Unfortunately, I believe my fear has been realized. The Saun family is, once again, right in the middle of trouble.*

~ * ~

Linda smelled food. Her stomach grumbled. She couldn't remember the last time she'd eaten. Slowly, she opened her eyes and panicked. Nothing looked familiar. Where was she? She tried to bring her hands up to rub her eyes but couldn't budge them. Her throat constricted as she tried to swallow. Out of the corner of her eye she caught a quick flash of white and involuntarily emitted a low groan.

Where am I? What's happening and why is my head pounding?

"Where...?"

The question hung in the air. Linda realized her voice was nothing more than a whisper. She tried to get her legs to move but met resistance. Frustration hampered her actions. She cleared her throat with difficulty.

"Where am I?" That seemed to catch the attention of the other body in the room.

"Let me tell you where you aren't...at home."

Morgan appeared within her range of vision and she groaned out loud.

"I was hoping this was just a bad dream."

The night elf sneered. "Lady, when you play with the big boys, you suffer big boy consequences. If you're new *friend* values your life at all, you'll be going home."

"I don't know what you're talking about."

"Right. We'll play that game if you insist."

Linda tried to sit upright. "Please. Can you help me to sit up?"

Morgan's brow furrowed. "If I have to..." He moved to the bed and righted the librarian.

"May I sit on the couch?"

Morgan rolled his eyes. "Look, lady, I've got an important function to attend and babysitting you is not what I planned. I'll put you on the couch if you promise not to try to escape. I'm not as heartless as my...partner but I'll have no hesitation to duct tape you to the bed."

"I promise I won't try to escape. I'd put up my hand but..." Linda shrugged. "...at the moment my hands are unavailable."

Morgan slipped his hands beneath her shoulders and knees. He lifted her from the bed and within two steps had her upright on the couch. "There. Now be quiet."

"Thank you." Linda closed her eyes and slowed her breathing. She knew if she were to have her wits about her, she needed to try and eliminate the pain in her head as much as she could.

"Here." Morgan placed a bowl filled with macaroni and cheese next to her. "I'm going to undo your hands, but if you try anything, well, I'll have to take measures."

"I'm too hungry to do anything but eat."

"Good." Morgan stepped behind the couch and untied the ropes binding her hands.

Linda rubbed her wrists to push blood to her fingers. When the tingling and pain started, she knew she wouldn't lose any digits. Grasping the bowl in her fingers, she noted the lack of utensils.

"I need something to eat with."

"Fine."

She could hear him moving around the kitchen and jumped when a spoon was shoved in her face.

"Remember, I have no compunction about knocking you out."

"So noted."

Linda dug into the pasta, reveling in the taste of cheese and macaroni. *Never thought mac and cheese would taste so good.* She took in the layout of the cabin over the top of the bowl: *bathroom behind the bed in the right corner of the building, fireplace in front of the couch, kitchen behind and, most importantly, door to freedom on the left.* For the moment, compliance was the best course of action, but there would come a time in the near future where she *would* escape. When she did, this night elf better watch out. Her Donald had taught her a few self-defense moves from his time in the service. He'd always worried about them being so far from town. She hadn't practiced in a while, but the body had memory that would come in handy.

Morgan watched her devour the food. When she finished, he took the bowl and spoon to the sink. "I'll feed her but I'm not about to do woman's work."

Linda tucked her upper lip between her teeth to keep from smiling. This he night elf was in a foul mood, and she wasn't yet ready to push him to the brink.

"How long are you keeping me here?"

Morgan knelt in front of the hearth trying to figure out how to start a fire. He jumped when she spoke.

"As long as it takes to get what we need."

"I see."

"No, you don't. You've never had magic, and wouldn't have a clue how much it adds to being alive. Not having my magic has been...pure hell." He rose from his knees and stomped out to the porch.

I've hit a nerve. This time Linda let a smile touch her lips. *I have ammunition now. Bad move, night elf.*

Chapter Sixteen

Trickle—Katherine—stretched her arms above her head. She smiled as she crawled out of bed. The he night elf, Morgan, really wasn't that bad. To top it off, he was very good looking. It had been quite a while since she'd indulged herself with a mate. The human ones, while easy to enchant, had such frail bodies. They aged so quickly and couldn't hold up their part of the deal. She'd hated to do it, but the last one she had, she wiped his memory and left him at a hospital. Sad. He was an especially nice man who doted on her. Oh, well.

This he night elf could live quite a bit longer. Katherine loved that idea.

"I'm hungry." The one thing she hated about this form was the need to constantly feed it. She couldn't afford to waste the time doing the shopping thing so she'd magic the body into thinking it was full.

"I'm going back tonight to see if he's there. I've made up my mind I want this man for myself. I know Chrissy won't object because he'll do anything I ask—when I enchant him."

She hummed as she tidied up her land home. She'd need to present a picture of domestic perfection to her object of desire before weaving the spell to make him hers forever. Tonight was going to be the most exciting time she'd had in quite a while.

~ * ~

Chrissy hummed around the Library, adding touches here, moving furniture there. She was expecting a large turnout for the May

Day celebration and all had to be in order. When she'd sent Bram and Silas out to warn the locals about the night elves, she'd sent invitations to the May Day celebration with the Sky Network. Surprisingly, they'd returned with responses from nearly all the clans in the valley and the forests. If everyone showed, the local Others were sure to notice.

"Tough. We were here first. They'll just need to adjust." She flew through the coffee shop and out the door to the porch. Uther had taken up camp on the wooden appendage and was currently snoozing in one of the chairs. She hated to wake him, but while he slept, a carrier from the Mouse Network had arrived with another message for him.

"Uther?"

She was greeted with a grunt.

"Uther. UTHER!"

"What!" He jumped upright from his reclining position.

The wood nymph hovered before his eyes clutching a large white envelope. "Please take this. It's getting heavy."

He reached for the envelope, the white paper container dropping to the deck when the nymph could no longer hold on.

Uther leaned down and picked up the packet. His name was scrawled across the front in a familiar hand. He placed it in his lap and stared at the paper.

"Aren't you going to open it?" Chrissy winged to his leg and landed. She reached out a finger and touched the packet. "Do you think it's poison?"

Uther sighed. "No, little one. I don't think it's poison, but I believe it carries bad news."

She crossed her arms and tapped a tiny foot on his leg. "Uther. I've seen you face a field of opponents and charge in with no regard for your own life. How can one piece of paper cause you such hesitation?"

"Because on the battlefield, I only had to concern myself with the safety of my troops and myself. Most of my men I'd known from childhood and knew of their bravery and selflessness. This, I know, concerns someone I..." He gazed at the tiny creature before him showing more courage than he felt. "...I love for the first time in my life. I never knew how much she would affect my feelings. What if they've killed her, Chrissy? How could I go on?"

Chrissy unfolded her arms and winged to his face. She laid a small hand on his cheek.

"You'll go on because you know Librarian wouldn't have it any other way. She is nothing if not brave. After all, she did stand up to Morgan and Gitty."

"Which is why we're in this bind now."

"Open the envelope, Uther."

Fingers quavering, he tore open the sealed packet. Inside was a fine linen slip of paper, which he retrieved and unfolded.

Chrissy watched his face turn crimson as he read. She winged away from the chair and waited. Uther crumpled the paper and threw it on the wooden deck.

"I knew it! I knew they'd never sit quietly and accept what they'd done to themselves."

He stomped from the porch. Chrissy watched him disappear around the side of the house. She magicked the crumpled paper and read the contents.

We have one demand:

Call all the clans together and reinstate our magic—in whole.

If you don't comply in the next 48 hours, we'll start sending the librarian back to you: one piece at a time. Send your reply via the Mouse Network to the family warehouse in Springfield.

G & M

Chrissy buzzed to the side of the house to see if she could spot Uther. He sat in the librarian's favorite spot on the stream bank. She raced to his side.

"Uther?" She kept arm's length away in case he was too angry to think.

"Yes?"

"What are we to do?"

"I don't know, Chrissy. I can't afford to have Linda killed because she stood up to those two, yet giving them back their magic would bring nothing but trouble to the valley and the clans. Gitty would make life hell on all who crossed her."

Chrissy moved closer to him and settled on a stump near him. "She acts as though she is the gift to this valley. I've never seen anyone so self-involved. Well, maybe Morgan, but considering he's her brother, it's to be expected."

The two sat morosely for a moment. Chrissy watched pain flash across his face then noted a change of his body. He sat up straight and his eyes lit up.

"That's it!" Uther turned to the nymph. "You, my dear, are a genius."

"Okay, but what did I say that makes me a genius?"

"Vanity."

"Yeah. The two of them have it by the boatloads."

He turned and gazed at her. "Are you willing to help me free Librarian?"

She humphed. "How could you doubt that?"

"I'll need you to lend some of your magic to me."

"Done. What are you going to do?"

"Give Gitty something to think about. Morgan seems to have adjusted to life in the Others' world but Gitty fancies herself above all of us. Are you ready?"

Chrissy nodded and moved opposite him.

He sat straight up and closed his eyes. Chrissy hovered and closed her eyes.

"Please put all of your concentration on my incantation.

Gitty,

Every minute as a prisoner she spends,
Brings you one moment closer to your end,
The vigor and vitality you so crave will soon disappear

Replaced by the horror of old age and death you fear.

Your life source will find its way
To one whose life you would betray
Be forewarned
The change begins this very day.

As he'd been taught, Uther uttered the spell three times, lying back on the soft grass when the chant was ended.

"There's your answer, Gitty Saun. I hope you enjoy it."

Chrissy fluttered to the ground next to him. "Whew! That should knock her socks off."

"I hope so."

"Is there any way to reverse it?" Chrissy saw him smile.

"Yes. But the cost of reversing the spell is to accept what she wants changed. I seriously doubt she'll understand the simplicity of it. No, I think we're going to see a change in the she-night elf and a change in our own Librarian."

Chrissy seemed revived. She flew in front of Uther and winged loop-de-loops. "Yeah. We get to see what Librarian looked like when she was young." She stopped and looked directly at him. "Will it last?"

Uther sat up on his elbows. "As long as she lives which, now with Gitty's life source, will be quite a bit longer than she expected."

"I have things I need to get done for May Day. Do you want me to make you something to eat?"

"No. You've done more than enough for me today. Thank you." Uther watched the wood nymph fly off toward the Lending Library. He plucked a long piece of grass and stuck it between his teeth. The spell would either put an end to this foolishness or backfire to cause a war no one could win.

He desperately hoped the former would happen. Very shortly, time would tell.

Chapter Seventeen

Gitty stood beneath the warm flow of water and allowed the tension to be swept away with the dirt. She'd sent the second letter laying out their demands. By this time next week, she'd be back in control of her life and have the magic that was rightfully hers.

Turning the water off, she stepped to the rug and buffed her body with the towel until she glowed pink.

"I think my first move will be to bulldoze that miserable hovel, the Lending Library. Then I'll ban Uther from ever coming back to these parts and, in a generous display of compassion, allow the renegade fae the ability to go back to the homeland. Let's see how well they manage on the Emerald Isles."

She chuckled and retired to her room to change into her comfortable jeans and a sweatshirt. Warm slippers on her feet completed her outfit and she meandered to the living room. She was restless but didn't want to read, so she pulled out her Tarot cards and decided to give herself a reading. If she were correct, all signs would point to success. Gitty shuffled the deck and placed the first card on the coffee table.

"What? This can't be!"

~ * ~

Morgan combed his hair for the final time. Looking in the mirror, he smiled at the reflection. "Showtime. Tonight, I'll win—without magic." He winked and entered the living area of the cabin.

The librarian was settled on the couch, watching his preparation with interest.

"Date?"

He glared at her. "None of your business. However because I'm going out, you get to stay on the bed." He picked her up and carried her to the cot, securing her ropes to the head rail and foot rail of the bed.

"What if I have to use the bathroom?"

He turned to her. "Hold it or wet your bed. I don't care. I've been here for the last forty-eight hours, and I have something important to do. I told Gitty I was attending to business tonight and I will. I'll leave the light on for you, but otherwise…you are on your own. See you tomorrow."

He headed for the door.

"HEY! You can't just leave me here."

The corner of Morgan's left lip raised slightly. "Yes I can and I am. Deal with it." He started out the door and turned back. "You can yell as loud as you like. There's no one around for miles. Goodnight."

The door slammed, leaving Linda alone. *This is not good. What the heck am I supposed to do?* She figured if nothing else, she'd just sleep. Lately, her energy levels seemed to be dropping. *Must be age.* She tried closing her eyes, but they kept popping open. *What is wrong with me?*

In frustration she tugged at her bindings. She felt them give. *What?* She tugged again and felt the rope move. Normally, she would have been short of breath and feeling the need for a nap, but at this moment, Linda felt strength in her arms she'd not experienced in years.

The night elves perception of her as a weak Other was working to her advantage at the moment. Morgan had tied the ropes with a great deal of slack, expecting her neither to fight nor to be able to yank them loose.

Excitement fueled her. She jerked the ropes and popped to a sitting position. The bindings on her wrists had been tied with no thought of them being undone. Linda slipped her hands through the loops and massaged her chaffed, raw appendages. She needed to hurry, however. If either Morgan or Gitty returned and found her out of her bindings, they'd tie her so tight she could lose a limb.

The ropes on her feet proved more of a challenge, but Linda's energy seemed to be endless. She looked at her fingers in awe. The last few years had proved to be a lesson in frustration, with rheumatory arthritis invading her hands and knees and making everyday tasks impossible. She felt no pain whatsoever.

"I'm not sure what's going on but I'll take it." Linda swung her legs over the edge of the bed. Her feet tingled. She was forced to sit and twist her feet around until the circulation returned. Testing a foot on the floor, she was relieved to find her appendages functional and able to propel her away from the cabin.

Linda scavenged the drawers in the small cottage. She found some energy bars and a flashlight. She tucked the bars into her pockets and flicked the switch of the flashlight, blinking when she got light. In a drawer in the kitchen, she located extra batteries she cached in another pocket.

The librarian padded to the entrance and opened the front door slowly. Twilight blanketed the forest, giving the trees and surrounding plants an eerie glow. She slipped her body out and closed the door behind her. In front of the cabin was a single lane, disappearing into the canopy of trees. Linda bolted down the stairs and began to run. She might not have much energy, but she was going to use what she had to expedite her escape. But how to get back to the Lending Library?

"Moss grows on the north side of the tree." All those years in Girl Scouts had given her a bit of forest knowledge. When the lane ended in another road, Linda felt desperation creeping in to her mind.

"No. I'll not give up so soon." She stopped and pulled in a deep breath. When she opened her eyes, she noted horse prints headed in one direction. She looked to the sky and mouthed "Thank you" before proceeding to follow the tracks.

Three hours passed before the forest thinned and the Librarian began to recognize landmarks. She was amazed at her stamina and reasoned it must be the fear of being caught again. The meadow opened up, and she could make out a few lights on buildings close to her home. Now was the time she needed to be especially careful. Just another half mile or so and she'd be in her own home. Linda stopped and pulled in a deep breath.

"It's now or never." She bolted across the meadow, keeping her eyes on the lights of the Lending Library. She stumbled on to the driveway and began to cry. Nearing the porch, she saw a figure in the chair and hesitated. Did she continue forward or try to camouflage her arrival by going around back?

"I'm too tired to circumvent coming in the front. To heck with it." Linda pulled herself tall and walked to the porch, taking the steps confidently. She turned to face the figure on her deck.

Uther had kept an eye on the movement he'd noticed in the meadow. Someone was crossing the fields rather late at night. He trained his eye on the lone figure moving intently in his direction. When the figure started up the driveway, Uther tried his best to identify the person but was having a difficult time. The figure hesitated just out of the range of the porch light. It moved up the stairs and turned to face him, shoulders squared.

"LINDA!" Uther jumped from his chair.

Linda thought she would faint from relief. She'd recognized the long, white hair and angular limbs as that of a night elf, but her recent experience had wiped away any recollection of the night elf who cared deeply for her.

"Oh my god, Uther." Linda pushed out an exhausted breath. "I'm so glad it's you." She stood stiffly, checking the face coming toward her. "It is you, isn't it?"

He wrapped his arms around her and pulled her to his body. He buried his face in her hair and pulled in the essence that was Linda. "Yes, my lady, it is I. And I'm relieved, delighted and a million other things to see you."

Linda wrapped her arms around him and immersed herself in his strength. For the moment, all was well.

Chapter Eighteen

Morgan arrived at the pub and took his usual seat. He looked around but couldn't locate Katherine. His stomach dropped. "She's not here." He nodded at the bartender. "The usual, please."

The man pulled a glass from the cooler and filled it with draft beer. "Three dollars, Mr. Saun." Morgan reached for his wallet.

"I've got this. Please get me a blended Pina Colada. Thank you."

Morgan started and twisted to stare into the blue green eyes of Katherine.

"Did you think I wasn't coming?" She graced him with a shy smile.

"I, uh, I wasn't sure." He gave her a lopsided grin.

Katherine let him hang for a moment. "I couldn't wait to come back so I took a little—longer—to get ready. I hope you don't mind?" She twirled around.

Morgan took in the vision. "Not at all."

"Good. Now, where were we when we parted ways?" She looked directly into his eyes as she spoke.

Morgan saw her mouth move, but all he could hear was the sound of the ocean. *This is the most beautiful woman in the world. I don't ever want to leave her.*

Trickle watched his eyes glaze over. *You're mine now...forever.*

~ * ~

Gitty waited impatiently for her brother to show. "Where is that

101

idiot?"

She moved to rise from the couch and caught her breath as pain shot through her hands and knees. *What the hell is happening?* Sucking in a deep breath, she pushed off the divan.

Must be because I haven't done enough riding lately.

A quick trip to the bathroom to get an aspirin would take care of the pain issue. Gitty made her way down the hall, halting to catch her breath every ten or so steps. *This is ridiculous.*

She flipped on the light and opened the medicine cabinet. The aspirin bottle proved to be a challenge to open. Her fingers didn't seem to want to work the way they should. When she finally got two tablets out, she turned on the cold water and filled the glass. Tossing the pills down her throat, she washed them away with a big gulp of water and closed the door to the medicine cabinet. That's when she realized something was horribly wrong.

The face staring back at her was…showing signs of age. Skin sagged at the neck and chin line. The surface of the face was dry and gray looking. There were tiny lines around the eyes and mouth and in her platinum hair were—gray—hairs.

Gitty stepped back and opened her mouth. A blood-curdling scream rent the air. The last thing she remembered was some old woman looking at her from her bathroom mirror.

~ * ~

Linda stepped inside the door and pulled in a deep breath. The smell of her books always settled her nerves.

"Are you hungry, my lady?" Uther gently swept her hand into his.

She turned to him, marveling at the adoration shining from his eyes. "I'm so hungry I could eat a complete cow tonight. I guess it was all that running."

Uther's eyebrows raised and his eyes popped open. "You ran here?"

Linda nodded. "Yeah, and it's really weird because I'm not tired at all. I know it's going to irritate Chrissy, but I want to fix my own dinner. How about you, Uther? You hungry?"

She thought his smile looked a bit odd.

"No, my lady. Just out of curiosity, have you looked in a mirror lately?"

"Uh, no. I was too busy running for my life. I must look a fright."

He chuckled. "No. I'll let you see what I'm talking about."

Linda barreled to the kitchen and found the room empty. "Good. No interlopers in my kitchen." She pulled pots and pans from various cupboards and rummaged in the refrigerator. Not finding much food with girth, Linda opted for an omelet. When she'd mixed the ingredients and put them on two plates, she carried the food to the dining table inside the Library.

Uther had taken a chair and waited until she quit fussing to try and carry on a conversation. He touched her hand and looked up into the steel blue eyes. "Stop fussing. Sit and enjoy the meal. We need to have a serious discussion but not over this marvelous omelet."

She felt the color rise to her cheeks. "As you wish, sir."

Silence filled the room as the two indulged their taste buds in the veggie omelet. When Uther had finished, he dabbed his mouth with a napkin, placing it over the plate.

"I received a ransom note from Morgan and Gitty yesterday threatening to send you back in pieces if I didn't gather the clans and return their magic."

Linda coughed into her napkin. "What? Are you serious?"

"Very."

"I hope you didn't do anything foolish, because I couldn't live with it if you gave up something for me."

Uther's sly smile put Linda on guard.

"No, I didn't do anything foolish; well, not too foolish. I remembered an incantation my mother taught me to use on vain people who needed to be gently reminded to stop their self centered ways."

Linda leaned back in her chair and crossed her arms. "What did you do, Uther?"

He squirmed in his chair. "Put a reverse aging spell on her."

"That doesn't sound too bad. Why are you being so evasive?"

"Linda? Go look in the mirror." He nudged her with his foot. "Go."

Linda was looking for the opportunity to wash up from her dusty day walk. She entered her bathroom and put the washcloth in the sink to dampen. Then she looked in the mirror and passed out.

~ * ~

Uther had suspected the shock might be too much, so he'd quietly followed her and was there to catch her when she dropped.

"Who, how, what?"

He put his finger to her lips. "I put a spell on Gitty; for each minute she held you captive, she would age and you would, well, unage. I'm guessing you're about thirty-five right now."

Linda's hand went first to her hair. "It's black again. I'd forgotten how dark it was." She then ran her fingers around her eyes and mouth. "The lines are gone."

She pushed off the floor and grasped the sink, looking at the face of the person she'd been thirty years earlier. "Oh my. I'm not sure what I think. I'd gotten used to the old face."

"Do you want me to change it back?"

"Oh, hell no." Linda lifted her blouse to view the young, taut stomach she'd forgotten she once possessed. "I think I like this." Her eyes twinkled a deep blue.

"We need to talk, my lady." Uther took her hand and led her to the porch where they sat in chairs next to each other.

"What's so important?" Linda stuck her hands in front of her to admire the taut skin and lack of age spots.

"I want you to be my life companion."

Linda dropped her hands and faced Uther. "Are you serious?"

"More serious than I've been about anything in my life."

"When?"

"How about we have the clan chieftains approve it at the May

Day celebration?"

She took a moment and examined her nails. "I wasn't sure I wanted to ever spend time with anyone after Donald, but..." she looked at Uther. "...you're not anyone; you're special. Yes. I'd love to spend my forever with you."

Uther leaned over and captured her lips under his. His heart pounded in his chest and he felt a stirring in his loins. *Later.*

Chapter Nineteen

May Day

The yard was a patchwork explosion of flowers celebrating the spring. A pole had been erected in the front yard for the young fae to participate in the ringing of the Maypole. Chrissy winged her way back and forth directing the activities and sporting a new outfit for the occasion.

Linda gazed at the profusion of colors highlighting her library.

"I never thought I'd see the day when all of the clans would, again, come together in my home and celebrate."

Uther snugged her close to his side. "They have a special place in their hearts for you, my lady. You accomplished that which no Other has done. Come to think of it, no fae has been able to get all these ruffians to agree."

Linda smiled as she laid her head against his muscled chest. "Who would believe I could be so lucky twice in my life?"

Uther placed a gentle kiss on the top of her head. "It's I who is the lucky one to find you."

The fae children ran and winged their way through the Lending Library and on to the deck; the pounding of little feet reminding the grownups of a simpler time.

Bram and Silas sat in the chairs designated for them as co-heads of the May Day celebration. They were attended by their children and watched their wives talk about babies and childcare issues. Bram's wife was the local midwife who would be attending Silas' Mrs.

When the sun reached its zenith in the sky, each chieftain solemnly marched to the center of the front yard near the Maypole. They stood, waiting for the din of the crowd to lessen. When their presence didn't sufficiently lower the clatter, Kayne, the current clan chieftain of the meadow fae, put his two front fingers in his mouth and whistled. The shrill explosion stopped all the noise in the meadow.

"Thank you." He dipped his head in appreciation. "We have gathered today to join in the celebration of new life. For many of us..." he winked at Ailidh, heavy with child. "...this year brings bundles of joy. For others, the end of a threat we've all dreaded has been achieved. It's for this reason we are happy to join with our friend and ally, Uther, night elf, and Linda, Librarian and Other.

"At this time, they've chosen to join their houses together. A mighty spell has brought Linda into our folds and she now bonds with the fae. Will Uther and Linda please join us up front?"

Linda, her long, dark hair braided down the center of her back wearing a tan floor length dress with flowing lace sleeves and Uther, dressed in his finest tan leather pants and jerkin held hands as they walked to the center of the yard to face the chieftains.

Kayne flashed a grin at the pair and cleared his throat.

"Are all the clans represented?"

A roar of "AYE!" rang through the air.

"Does any here denounce or disagree with this pairing?"

"NAY!"

"Then let it be known that Linda, the librarian and Uther, the night elf, shall be joined together until the breath is gone from one or both of them."

The crowd erupted in raucous cheering and Uther bent to his lady, lifting her from her feet and kissing her.

The musicians struck up a wedding jig and the newly twined couple danced until they were breathless.

Bram leaned over to Silas. "What happened to the other night elves?"

Silas raised his head from his paws. "Rumor has it the male got himself tangled up with a merfae and is residing in the stream out back.

As far as the she night elf…seems she hasn't left her hilltop home since the librarian was found. Some say she's withered away to dust. Long as she stays away from me, I don't care."

Bram tapped his pipe against the chair. "I agree."

A comfortable silence descended between the friends.

Joining cake cut and devoured, presents given and the newly attached couple on their way to some time alone, Chrissy finally settled in her lounge chair and fanned herself with a leaf.

"Who would have thought we'd ever see the pairing of a night elf and an Other? Guess our librarian was always about defying the odds."

Love in Bloom
Rosemary Indra

Prologue

Mattie Harrison sat up in bed when two golden lights floated down beside her. The shimmering lights from her fairies caused excitement to bubble within Mattie in anticipation of their visit. For as long as she could remember, the two fairies were her constant companions. Tonight she had something important to ask them.

Cara sat cross-legged on Mattie's pillow. Kendra adjusted her green dress several times before she too sat down. Mattie looked down at her small friends then crossed her legs in front of her mimicking the way they sat.

Every so often Kendra's wings fluttered. Mattie knew she preferred playing than sitting still but tonight Mattie needed someone to talk to. Like always, Cara listened quietly as Mattie described her day and her plans for tomorrow.

When the fairies stood, their transparent wings flapped as they started to take flight. "Can you stay a little longer?" Mattie asked quickly.

Cara gracefully bowed her head and moved closer to the little girl. "What's troubling you tonight lass?"

A smile touched Mattie's lips at the sound of the fairy's soft voice. Cara had brown hair similar to her own. She always had suggestions and Mattie felt calm after talking to her.

They'd visit every evening when she went to bed to say goodnight. Mattie had asked her father for a nightlight not because she was afraid of the dark but so she could see the fairies easier without scaring them with the bright overhead light.

"My dad is very lonely." Mattie knew what she wanted but all of a sudden she didn't know what to say. She looked at her friends. "Can you help me find a wife for him?"

"Mattie it's bedtime. Quiet down," her father's voice carried down the hallway. "Tell your friends to go home."

Cara tapped her index finger against her lips and looked thoughtful.

"He doesn't believe in fairies," Kendra whispered. "That might be hard. He doesn't have faith in us."

"We haven't even started and you're already negative." Cara put her hands on her hips then glanced at Mattie, "You have to remember a non-believer doesn't like interference."

Feeling disheartened Mattie's lower lip started to tremble. She'd given this a lot of thought. After much consideration, Mattie knew she'd needed help to find a wife for her dad.

"We'll see what we can do." Kendra looked at Mattie her expression softened. "We'll help you."

Both fairies nodded. Now she'd have assistance in her quest. Satisfied, Mattie relaxed against her pillows.

When her father opened her bedroom door, light from the hallway flooded in casting elongated shadows across the room. The fairies instant disappearance didn't trouble Mattie. She knew as soon as her dad left the room they would return.

Her father stood beside her bed looking down at her. With dark circles under his eyes he appeared worried and concerned. He leaned down and pulled the blankets up to her chin.

"Dad, everything will work out." Mattie kissed his cheek. "Night."

"Goodnight sweetie. No more talking. You need some sleep. We're going to see grandma tomorrow."

After her father left the room, Mattie sat up in bed. She glanced at her friends who once again sat beside her on the pillow. Mattie raised her hands and wiggled her fingers in front of her. "Do you have any fairy dust to sprinkle on him?"

Chapter One

A gentle spring breeze kissed Shelia Roberts cheek the moment she stepped out her front door. She hurried across her concrete driveway to the stepping-stones which lead to her neighbor's porch.

Shelia inhaled the fragrance of the bouquet she held and smiled. The May Day basket reminded her of her school days. Every May First she walked to their neighbor's to deliver her flowers. The Harrison family had lived next to the Roberts' since the homes were built in this subdivision, now an older section of Forest Ridge.

There were times her mom accused Shelia of spending more time at the Harrison house than her own home. She'd treasured the time she had spent with her best friend. Derek Harrison. While growing up they were inseparable playing baseball or hiking in the field behind their homes.

Shelia shook her head to dissolve the playful memories which raced through her mind. She felt giddy and quickened her step. After placing the roses on the front step she rang the doorbell.

In previous years she was able to race back to her own porch before Martha opened her door. She turned and started down the steps. Hearing the door open, Shelia knew she was caught. For the first time, Martha was faster than her. The older woman must have been waiting at the door. Conceding defeat, Shelia threw up her hands, "You beat me." She turned to see the woman she called her second mom.

Only Martha wasn't standing in the doorway. The sparkle in the familiar blue eyes was the same as her childhood friend but the face which studied her was that of a man's not the boy she remembered.

Shelia swallowed quickly at the sight of him. "Derek," her voice a breathless whisper.

She knew the moment Derek recognized her as a smile erased the seriousness on his face.

Derek crossed his arms in front of his chest drawing her attention to his muscular build. He had a day's growth of dark stubble on his face, which added to his rugged sex appeal. His black hair was styled short and she felt the urge to run her fingers through it. Merely studying his features had Shelia's heart racing uncontrollably in her chest.

The last time she saw Derek was Christmas four years ago. He'd come home to visit his family and she was spending the holidays with her parents. The length of time between their visits didn't matter. They'd start talking as if they just saw each other yesterday.

His left brow rose and he appeared shocked to see her. Shelia suppressed a smile when she noticed his brow split in two from the scar she'd caused. The first summer they met, Derek said she couldn't play baseball as she wasn't able to throw the ball far enough. Frustrated, Shelia pitched a fastball to where he stood at first base. The ball cut his forehead causing a doctor's visit and five stitches. After that, Derek reluctantly allowed her to participate in their baseball games at the other boys' insistence.

"Shelia?" His voice sounded as surprised as she felt. "What do you mean 'I beat you'?" Derek's gaze held hers and he silently waited for her explanation.

She moved closer to the doorway. "I thought your mom answered the door." A blush warmed her cheeks when she had to explain her childish game further. With a desire to reach out and touch his chest, Shelia laced her fingers together. "It's May Day."

His eyes still showed no sign of remembrance. A little girl about five years old walked up and stood beside him. She looked at Shelia with the same vivid blue eyes as Derek's and there was no denying she was his daughter. The girl rubbed her eyes with the back of her hand. Her dark hair was pulled back in a single ponytail.

"Dad, who's she?" the girl asked.

Derek placed his arm around the girl's shoulders. "This is Shelia. She came to see grandma."

They'd known each other forever and his failure to mention they were old friends cut deep. Shelia couldn't take her eyes off Derek or form a coherent thought in her head.

"Maybe she can't talk," the girl said.

A slow sensual smile formed on his mouth. Despite the fact he found humor in the statement, Shelia had to suppress a need to stroke the stubble on his cheek. "No Mattie, Gabby was never at a loss for words." Shelia found it heartwarming that Derek remembered the childhood name he gave her.

His daughter elbowed Derek in the side then pointed to the basket of flowers; Shelia had placed on the porch. "She delivered flowers."

Finally finding her voice, Shelia said, "Those are for Martha."

When he looked up with a blank expression, she added, "You give flowers on May Day." Every year Shelia bought Martha flowers and she couldn't believe Derek didn't remember their tradition.

"Grandma was talking about May Day and flowers."

Derek shook his head. "Must be a girl thing."

His daughter shrugged her shoulders then turned and skipped in the opposite direction as she called for her grandmother.

"How are you Shelia?" Derek wore jeans and the blue work shirt he had on was unbuttoned with a white T-shirt underneath. There was a rugged sex appeal about Derek; she felt he'd be a great model for designer clothing. His full smile revealed his teeth and she remembered when they wore braces at the same time. She always had to remind him to put the rubber bands on the metal fasteners. She missed their easy going friendship and the way they watched over each other.

Folding her arms in front of her, Shelia hoped the slight physical barrier would prevent Derek from getting under her skin again. When she was younger, Shelia had the biggest crush on him and dreamed they'd find their way to a lasting relationship. "Good. I'm doing good. I didn't know you were here."

"Mom decided to update her kitchen so I'm helping her."

His daughter returned and stood beside Derek, her gaze never left Shelia's face. She tugged on her father's pant leg. "Dad, invite her in."

Lifting his shoulders, Derek stepped to the side and motioned her inside. "Come in, I'm sure mom would like to see the flower lady. She's in the kitchen."

The girl disappeared again and Shelia heard her running through the house.

Shelia pointed toward the street as if to emphasize her point. "I'm on my way to work." His arched brows challenged her to refuse.

Bending down, Shelia retrieved the flowers from the step then crossed the threshold. She'd been to their house so often Shelia felt comfortable in the old style ranch house. Following the sound of their voices, Shelia walked to the kitchen.

The aroma of coffee and freshly made pancakes filled the room. The hub of the Harrison's household, their kitchen was always full of good food and people. The older woman sat at the table with her granddaughter standing beside her. When she saw Shelia a smile formed on her lined face. Martha stood up and reached out her arms to Shelia.

The older woman now had salt and pepper hair but her blue eyes were sharp. Shelia knew she still wouldn't be able to get away with anything without the other woman knowing.

"Hi, Martha. Happy May Day," Shelia gave the older woman a hug then she handed Martha the bouquet of flowers.

"Thank you, Shelia. The roses are lovely. I wondered if you'd remember." Martha retrieved a large glass vase from under the kitchen sink. "You're such a dear."

"I enjoy bringing you flowers. I was always out of sight before you opened the door. And thought you'd never guess I gave you the flowers. Until today. Today was the only day I was caught."

With a quick glance at Derek she wondered if he was as glad to see her as she was in meeting him again. They had always been friends. When he came home from college Shelia longed for him to see her as a woman and not the little girl next door. It took a long time before she accepted he was no longer part of her life.

"Dad, you broke her record." The little girl pushed on her father's arm.

Derek shrugged. "I didn't know I wasn't supposed to answer the door."

"Records are made to be broken," Shelia said. Like hearts.

"Shelia would you like to come over for dinner tonight. It will be our last meal in the old kitchen. Derek is doing some remodeling for me. New cabinets and appliances, the works." Martha beamed with happiness and pride.

Martha had told her, Derek was a skilled craftsman and made beautiful cabinets but she hadn't seen any of his work yet. Not wanting to interrupt a family get together, she hesitated. Shelia could handle seeing Derek for a few minutes but an entire evening would be too cozy.

"I don't think…"

"It'll be like old times." Martha reached out and put her hand on Shelia's arm but looked at her son when she said, "Won't that be fun, Derek?"

His steady gaze held Shelia's. A lengthy silence penetrated the room. Did he recall the hours they played together in the vacant field? She watched him without wavering and wondered if he remembered the stolen kisses before he left for college. He ignited a heated passion within her an unfulfilled desire. All her memories rushed back warming her cheeks.

Derek studied her face but didn't reply. Finding his hesitation awkward, Shelia said, "Martha, maybe tonight isn't a good idea. We can make it another time."

"Nonsense. This is the last time the kitchen will look like this. Derek has promised a modern, hip looking work space."

"Hip mom. I think you're dating yourself."

Shelia watched the muscles in his arm flex as he raked his hand through his hair. Strong, firm muscles. For a moment, Shelia longed to feel his arms around her again.

"What do you think?" His daughter was crouched beside a kitchen chair talking to herself. Her small hands cupped together, she appeared to shelter something within her palms.

"Mattie, tell your friends to go home. We're here to visit grandma," Derek said.

The girl stood up and moved to his mother's side. "I just asked them a question."

Unsure what they were taking about Shelia looked from father to daughter. She found Mattie closely watching her then the girl quickly looked at her dad. A smile transformed her small features revealing cute dimples in her cheeks.

"I better get going. I'll see you later Martha. Mattie it was nice to meet you." Shelia bent down to shake the girl's hand.

"The fairies like you." The girl whispered but Shelia was sure everyone in the room heard her. "Especially this." Mattie reached up and gently touched the feathers in Shelia's hair.

She nodded with understanding. "Maybe you could introduce me to your friends sometime," Shelia said.

Mattie brushed her finger down the feathers again. "Okay."

"Time for school, Mattie. Get your sweater." Derek reached his hand out to his daughter. "Shelia, nice seeing you again." Without a backward glance, Derek and his daughter walked out the side door.

Shelia sighed, she didn't realize how wistful it sounded until Martha said, "Things are different now."

"No Martha. Derek has never been interested in me." She lifted her shoulder with indifference. "Nothing has changed."

Martha didn't acknowledge her comment but continued talking as if Shelia hadn't said anything. "I'm so glad you stopped by this morning."

"So am I." Shelia hugged Martha. "I enjoy seeing you."

"Thank you for the lovely flowers." The older woman walked beside Shelia to the door then added, "Dinner's at six."

Chapter Two

Derek couldn't get Shelia off his mind. He hadn't seen her in several years. Her willowy tomboy figure now had the curves of a woman. She looked good. Damn good. A beautiful desirable woman who he couldn't stop thinking about.

Her blue eyes sparkled when she recognized him, making him feel light hearted for the first time in a long time. He liked the way her short hairstyle framed her delicate features. Her face had also matured with high cheekbones and succulent lips. When had she'd become such a beautiful woman?

After dropping Mattie at the pre-school, Derek returned to his mom's. He whistled as he walked through the side door to her kitchen.

His mom was still sitting at the table nursing her cup of coffee. "You're in a good mood," she said when he walked toward her.

He shook his head. "Don't get any ideas, Mom." From the moment, Derek stepped in his mother's house, he noticed her sly smile. Every time she looked at him her face beamed with happiness.

"I don't know what you're talking about." She sipped her coffee then placed the mug in front of her.

"Yes, you do. You introduce me to every single woman you know. And now Shelia? Come on, Mom, she's not my type. I'm not going to fall for any matchmaking. Especially when it comes to Shelia."

Shelia's eyes still had a special sparkle when she smiled. He thought of how her short blond hair accented her face drawing attention to her blue eyes. The fact Shelia wasn't self-conscious to get down and

10

speak to his daughter won her a lot of points. When she squatted down, he couldn't help but notice the way her scrubs hugged her derriere.

"She hasn't grown up. Why does she wear a feather in her hair?" He knew his comment was lame but he wanted to emphasize to his mom there was no connection between him and Shelia.

Derek wasn't interested in a relationship with Shelia and he'd already spent too much time thinking about her. He didn't give her time to answer; instead Derek asked her another question. "What do you want in this corner mom?" Although he was curious about Shelia, Derek was relieved their conversation returned to the kitchen remodeling.

He'd already married a flighty woman and look where it got him. Divorced and a single parent of a five year old girl. His relationship with Kathleen was a lesson he would not repeat. Not with Shelia or any other woman. He had no interest in the institution of marriage or a lasting relationship.

"Shelia has a good reason for wearing the feathers in her hair or bells on her shoes. She even has a cute elf pin she wears. If you'd get to know her you'd understand." His mother walked beside him and patted his shoulder. "Talk to her."

"All I need is another person who believes in the little people." Derek had no desire to get to know Shelia again but he wasn't about to discuss his reasoning with his mother. Some times the less said about his personal life to his only living parent the better. Martha was a romantic at heart a believer of soul mates and happier ever after. Whenever he said there was no such thing she'd say he hadn't married the right woman.

Shelia had been his best friend. They'd been inseparable. He never experienced a more compatible relationship with another woman. Not even his ex-wife.

Two dark blue feathers had hung from the back of her hair and brushed her shoulders giving her a mysterious appearance. A free-spirit. She'd always gone against convention, even when she was younger. Shelia played with him more than other girls in the neighborhood.

Throughout the day his thoughts drifted to Shelia's expressive smile. He could visualize the feather brushing her shoulder and slender neck. The daydream left him wanting to caress her soft skin and kiss the column of her neck where her pulse beat.

Now he'd have to spend the evening with her without touching her. When the doorbell rang, Derek jerked back, startled his thoughts had become so realistic.

"Derek, could you get that?" his mother asked from the kitchen.

He felt edgy as he walked toward the door. However, once he'd opened the door and glimpsed Shelia's smile he relaxed. For the first time in a long while, Derek was content with his life and he knew it had something to do with the woman in front of him. She'd always had a calming effect on him.

When she'd hit him with the baseball, splitting his eyebrow, Shelia's soft voice and quick thinking helped him to stay calm and rational.

Now she wore a black blouse with a scoop neckline and a pair of jeans. He saw the feathers against her neck and smiled.

Irritated with himself his words were sharper then he intended. "Come in."

"With that tone of voice I don't know if I want to." He opened the door farther for her and stepped back.

"How long have you been back?" He asked, somewhat surprised she was living with her parents again. Shelia's independent nature always conflicted with her mother's domineering personality.

"I've been renting the house from mom and dad for the last three months."

His brow lifted, silently questioning her.

"They moved to Portland for better job opportunities. I've actually returned to Forest Ridge two years ago. I'm surprised we haven't seen each other before now."

There was constant chatter between his mother and Mattie from the kitchen. Within a short time, his daughter hurried into the room. Giving an elaborate bow she said, "Dinner's ready."

Derek placed his hand on the small of Shelia's back and followed her through the archway. He noticed his mother had made an extra effort with a tablecloth, napkins and the roses Shelia gave her nestled in a cut-glass vase in the middle of the table.

His mother had insisted they eat at the small breakfast nook since he would be removing the built-in table the next day. His legs felt cramped in the confined space. Stretching his right leg Derek inadvertently bumped Shelia's knee.

"Sorry." He sat up straighter. "I don't remember this nook being so small," he commented. He felt Sheila's leg slowly caress his. If he didn't know better he'd say her movement was intentional. With a quick glance at her he was surprised to see she looked nonchalant. In a deep conversation with his mother about gravy recipes she didn't even look in his direction.

Shelia always had long blond hair. The braid which usually hung down her back was gone. Her hair was now short and hugged her face. The tresses were still wavy with an obvious will of their own. Shelia leaned forward and squeezed his daughter's hand. A simple gesture he found endearing.

When she turned her gaze was fixed on him. The sexy shine of her lips drew his attention. He wanted to taste her inviting lips. Wondering if her mouth felt as soft as it used too, he leaned toward her then caught himself before making a total fool of himself. In a way of explaining his action he picked up the serving dish in front of Shelia and asked his daughter, "Mattie would you like some more." He held up a spoonful of green beans.

She glanced down at her plate. He followed her gaze and realized she hadn't touched the vegetables on her dish. "No dad I still have some."

Derek returned the bowl to the table then sipped his coffee trying to clear his head. He just needed to make it through this dinner. There was no reason to see Shelia after tonight.

"Martha, are you looking forward to the remodeling?" Shelia asked.

"Yes. This kitchen served its purpose but it's time to revitalize." His mother looked pointedly at him and Derek was positive her comment was strictly for his benefit and had nothing to do with her kitchen remodel.

When the meal was finally over, Derek was relieved he could get up and stretch without rubbing against Shelia's slender leg. Their contact had him hungry for more.

"Martha that was a lovely dinner." Shelia started picking up the plates. "You worked so hard I'll do the dishes."

"Young lady, you're a guest tonight. Derek, take Shelia into the living room and make sure she relaxes. She's had a long day."

His brow furrowed with what he'd hoped was a stern expression.

"Thank you dear. Mattie and I are going to work on the dishes. Come on dear, I'll get your favorite apron." Without a backward glance his mother ushered his daughter to the kitchen sink.

"But grandma—" Mattie started to complain.

There was an answering reply from his mother but he couldn't hear what she'd said. His mom turned toward them, "I forgot to mention, I found some old photo albums the two of you might find interesting. They're on the coffee table."

Following the light lavender scent of Shelia's perfume, Derek walked behind her. She sat on the couch once they entered the living room. Her slender legs were crossed at the ankle giving Shelia a very feminine pose.

Feeling restless, Derek walked to the opposite corner of the room. The farther the distance between them the less likely he'd act on his fantasy with his childhood friend. "You know what she's doing don't you?"

Shelia picked up a photo album and opened the scrapbook on her lap. "Your mother is playing matchmaker." She laughed. The soft humorous sound chipped away at the wall he'd built around his heart the last four years. "Why so serious Derek? We both know what Martha's trying to do. So don't fall for her trap. She's tried to set me up with her favorite clerk at the grocery store and her doctor. So why not you too? At least I have something in common with you." She winked.

Derek didn't see any humor in the situation. "Did you go out with them?"

A smile formed on her lips. "Jealous?"

"Curious," he snapped.

"I met one. Martha had her friend and grandson over for dessert one Sunday afternoon."

"And?"

She shrugged. "I'm not into blind dates."

He watched Shelia study the photographs of their childhood. The memories brought a smile to her lips. As long as Derek could remember, her mother worked and his mom was Shelia's babysitter.

"I didn't realize your mom had so many pictures of us. Look at this one." Shelia pointed to a photo in the center of the page.

Her laughter drew him to her side. When he sat beside her, Shelia moved the album to rest on his lap. Some of the images were pale but they bought vivid recollections to mind. His gaze studied her face more than the photographs. Shelia's expression was serious for a moment before her smile returned. They had a lot of happy times together. At first she'd been a nuisance tagging along with him and his friends. Then Shelia had become an integral part of his life. Overall his childhood would have been dull without her. She added a generous amount of fun and laughter.

"Do you remember this day?" her voice now tickled his ear.

The tomboy had two braids and wore an oversized T-shirt. The girl reflected in the image looked nothing like the beautiful woman beside him. With the desire to feel her softness Derek quickly looked at her. This was Shelia. He was crazy to allow his thoughts to run wild. She'd always been like a sister to him. There was never an attraction between them. He shook his head to the lie he was telling himself.

"How can you forget the time we played in the mud pit in the vacant lot? My mom was so mad I had to do the family wash for a week. I had mud caked everywhere." She reached up and brushed a strand of hair away from her face then tucked the blond curls behind her ear. Her amusement sparkled in her eyes.

Shelia's innocent comment gave him visions of her he hadn't had since he was a teenager. Their walk down memory lane needed to end.

He didn't want feelings for Shelia and Derek knew if their relationship continued it wouldn't be long before their friendship turned intimate.

"Mattie and I are going home in a few minutes. So I'll walk you over to your house now." His voice sounded hash and he regretted the pain which flashed in her eyes.

"Ouch. Don't bother. I'm capable of finding the way back." Shelia stood up. She glanced at their photo one more time before setting the album on the coffee table. "I don't know what I said back then or for that matter what is wrong now. Don't worry while you're working on Martha's kitchen I'll stay out of your way."

He felt like a heel. "Shelia I didn't—"

When she turned toward him, her fisted hands were on her hips. The stance so familiar he wanted to laugh but knew she wouldn't appreciate the humor. "Yes you did. I don't understand why you'd deliberately try to hurt me." Shelia walked out of the room with her chin held high. He always admired her spunky attitude. With her determination she never allowed anything to hold her down.

Shelia smiled when she saw Mattie standing on a chair in front of the kitchen sink with her grandmother standing beside her. "Martha, thank you for dinner."

"Don't you want to stay for dessert?" The older woman frowned then looked at her son as if he knew something Shelia hadn't mentioned.

"Not tonight. Thanks anyway." She leaned down then kissed the older woman's cheek. "Derek doesn't want to play," she whispered as she had so many times as a child.

Chapter Three

Martha grasped Shelia's hand between hers; dishwater still glistened on her skin. "I'm sorry dear. You know how he is."

Shelia nodded. She blinked quickly before the unexpected tears fell.

"I'm in the room." He moved closer to where they stood by the kitchen sink. "We have a long day—" His voice trailed off.

"No excuses, dear." His mother gave him a sharp disapproving look.

"I'm not twelve," Derek said.

Martha turned to face him. "You're acting like it, son."

"Dad, you didn't even try. The fairies said—"

"It's okay Mattie." Her grandmother placed her arm around the girl's shoulder and hugged her.

Shelia moved to stand beside his daughter. "It was nice meeting you, Mattie. I'll have to see your fairies another time." She unclipped the assortment of feathers and leather from her hair and fastened the clip to the collar of Mattie's blouse.

The girl's eyes lit up. "Thank you."

Shelia patted her shoulder. "You're welcome."

"I'm not sure why at this point, but I'm walking Shelia home." Derek opened the kitchen door for her and allowed her to precede him out to the side yard.

Shelia breathed deep the cool evening air as a breeze ruffled around them. It was a fresh spring evening, a perfect time for lovers. Countless times he'd walked her home but tonight felt different.

Intimate. She needed to break the silence between them and end the fantasy racing through her mind. Like always she wanted to mend the rift between them. She delighted in the fact they walked down the driveway and not the stepping stones between the houses. The extra steps gave her a little more time with Derek.

"Your daughter is sweet. She looks a lot like you."

"Thank you. She's the best thing that's happened to me."

Shelia knew he was divorced but wondered what had happened to his marriage. "Where's her mother?"

Derek remained silent for so long. She wondered if the question was too personal since their reunion had started off rather shaky.

"Kathleen had always been a little flighty. I thought after Mattie was born she'd settle down. I guess not all women are meant to be mothers." He slowed his pace and Shelia followed suit feeling Derek had wanted to talk. "Shortly after the baby was born, she started going to parties. When I'd get home from work I never knew who to expect to be with the baby. Usually she was with a babysitter and her mother was no where to be seen. I hired a woman to be there for Mattie when I was at work. Then I knew someone was taking care of her."

"That's sad. Does she see Mattie now?"

"She floats by once in a while. But since the divorce her visits are less frequent. At first the short visits were hard on Mattie but now she doesn't seem to care. Her mother is a stranger to her."

Touched by the sadness of their situation Shelia reached out for Derek's hand. Intertwining her fingers with his she realized how much she'd missed him. "Poor girl."

"We moved back to Forest Ridge." Derek lifted his shoulders then started walking again.

"Your mom & Mattie seem really close. She was cute helping Martha with the dishes."

"Yeah. Mom's been great with her."

They neared her front door and Shelia wished they had another mile to walk. Hearing someone whistle, she looked across the street and caught a glimpse of someone, wearing dark clothes and a dark knitted cap, walking in the opposite direction. The man appeared overly dressed, wearing a heavy trench coat, for such an unusually warm spring evening.

"Mattie's the reason I decided not to remarry. She needs stability in her life." He quickly let go of her hand as if he finally realized she was touching him.

For some unknown reason she felt disappointed by his comment. "In a way I see your point. But I also think you're doing her an injustice."

Derek shook his head. "It tore her apart every time Kathleen left her."

"Of course that was her mother. I imagine all children of divorce couples go through the same thing."

"Mom has been after me to get remarried. She makes it sound so easy as if I'm buying a loaf of bread." For a second Derek paused and when he started talking again his voice sounded crisp. "I have no desire to remarry."

The determination was set solid in his words and Shelia knew there would be no changing his view on the situation. She felt the same way about marriage yet a pain of disappointment hit her, when Derek spoke his thoughts out loud. They stopped in front of her house. She didn't want to go inside and he didn't show any sign of leaving. Content with his company she sat on the top concrete step of the porch. The breeze picked up and Shelia zipped up her hoodie to block the wind.

Mr. Whiskers, her black and white cat rubbed his face against her leg. He glanced up at her and meowed. Asking for more attention, he circled her leg. Shelia petted his soft fur a moment before he jumped off the porch and pranced down the sidewalk.

"And what about you?" He leaned against the porch post. "Have you thought of remarrying?"

"I like my life as it is." Shelia didn't mention the loneliness she struggled with or the fact she didn't like eating alone. She looked down at her hands, where they rested on her lap. "I still miss James…"

"How long has it been?" For the first time all evening Derek's voice was soft with sympathy.

"He's been gone a year. There are times it feels like yesterday." With her husband in active service she'd spent a lot of time on her own. Now there would be infinite solitary nights.

"I'm sorry. I'd say I know how you feel but my ex-wife still pops into our lives once in a while."

"Poor Mattie." She felt sorry for his daughter no wonder she had imaginary friends to comfort her. "That explains the fairies."

"They've helped her through this. Her doctor said its normal. Most kids have make-believe companions at some time. I worry about Mattie and often wonder if the divorce or her mother's neglect is too much for her to handle." Derek paused and Shelia waited for him to gather his thoughts. "Her fairies trouble me."

Shelia wrapped her arms in front of her. "They're friends who keep her company."

"I know but they have names and she describes them in great detail. Down to their personalities Cara is very positive the other tends to be offish and doesn't like humans as much."

Shelia laughed. "Mattie has an excellent imagination. She reminds me of a friend of mine."

His gaze met hers and she noticed humor lift the corners of his lips. The transformation of his features jolted her with a sensual awareness. "She has invisible playmates? How old is she?"

"You could call them imaginary." When his brows rose in question Shelia smiled. "She's not crazy. Miranda is a writer. She's told me she can see characters and scenes in her mind like a movie before she puts them to paper. And her characters talk to her."

"But Mattie's not a writer. She's just learning the alphabet." He sighed and straightened.

"You don't need to know your letters to have a vivid imagination."

Derek rubbed the back of his neck with his palm. "I play along with her and ask how her friends are or tell her they need to go home so she can sleep." His gaze looked troubled when he looked at her this time. She noticed the concern for his child harden his features, the stress of a single parent.

She stood up and moved closer to him. "What happened to the Derek I knew? He had a great imagination. Don't you remember when we were spies on a secret mission in the vacant lot?" Placing her palm against his cheek, she directed his gaze to hers.

"That Derek is gone." He shook his head. "Besides that's not the same."

"Of course it is. The only difference is you had me to play with and Mattie is by herself. Maybe you need to get in touch with the little boy within you." She reached out and poked her index finger in his chest. He looked down to where her fingers now rested on his shirt and drew back ever so slightly.

She had always touched him in the form of a pat or a hug. Now he appeared uncomfortable by her nearness. At one time they were inseparable. This Derek she hardly recognized.

After some consideration Derek nodded, "I see what you mean. Mattie's face lit up when you gave her those feathers. Mom said there's a specific reason you wear feathers in your hair."

"I'm a nurse in the oncology unit at the hospital. I don't always wear feathers sometimes I wear colorful socks. At Christmas I had bells on my shoes." In order to keep her hands to herself, Shelia fidgeted with the zipper tab of her sweatshirt. "I like to give my patients something to smile about. I'll do almost anything to distract them even if it's only for a minute."

"That's considerate." Derek reached out for her hand this time. "You're very creative."

Making light of his comment she lifted one shoulder. "Thanks."

His smile caused her stomach to do flip flops. Wondering if his lips would create as much passion as they had before he left for college she studied his mouth. Had her extreme desire been the anticipation of an inexperienced young girl? How would she respond to his kisses now?

A flame fueled within her. If she had learned one thing from their earlier relationship she'd gained the knowledge not to wait for Derek to make the first move or she could be waiting indefinitely.

When she leaned toward him, his eyes darkened. As a girl she wouldn't have recognized the desire which was reflected in his eyes but now she saw passion simmering in their depths. Maybe she wasn't the only one who felt the current spark between them.

With the palms of her hands she caressed his chest then linked her fingers behind his neck. He groaned deep in his throat.

"I haven't seen you in a long time and you're already driving me nuts," his voice sounded husky.

His breath was warm against her cheek. A flutter of excitement rushed through her. When she finally looked up at him, Shelia found his dark eyes studying her. The light exploring touch of his lips had her wanting more.

Derek stepped back, breaking her clasped fingers. "Thanks for a nice evening. You're still as stubborn as ever." He leaned forward and kissed her forehead. "Goodnight Shelia." then he turned and walked down the sidewalk.

Disappointed, her hands fell to her sides. She watched him turn and walk down the steps. All her childhood conflict churned within her. "I'm not a child," Shelia called out to him.

As Derek started walking toward his mother's house, he looked over his shoulder. His smile melted her heart. "I know."

Chapter Four

True to her word Shelia stayed clear of Martha's for several days. Whenever she was outside or driving by her gaze would automatically search for a glimpse of Derek. After a long day at work, Shelia drove home parking her Ford Focus in her driveway. Disappointed, she didn't see Derek's truck at Martha's. After gathering her purse and water bottle from the passenger seat, she started to open the driver door. Shelia smiled as she watched Mattie running across the stepping stones toward her driveway. After getting out of the car, Shelia met the girl in front of the garage door. "Hi Mattie how are you?"

"Good. Grandma would like to see you." Excited the girl reached out her arms for a hug.

"Okay, let's see what Grandma wants."

Mattie grasped her hand then swung their joined arms back and forth as they walked to the familiar house next door. Martha stood at the opened doorway. "I wanted to show you what Derek has accomplished." The older woman motioned for Shelia and Mattie to precede her.

Upon entering the kitchen the room smelled of fresh sawdust and coffee. The new knotty pine cabinets, edged with a darker color wood looked pristine. Derek had changed the design of the room by removing some of the upper units and adding a pantry in the corner.

"Oh, they're lovely." Shelia walked forward caressing the wooden cabinet door with her palm. The wood felt cool and smooth. She glanced around the room. Approximately half the cabinets had been replaced. In a few days, Derek had most of his work completed. When he finished this project he'd once again be out of her life. Shelia knew she'd miss seeing Derek and Mattie.

"You don't like them?" his deep voice sounded behind her.

She'd been so intent on studying his work Shelia didn't hear Derek come in. Turning around, she smiled when she saw him. A light dusting of sawdust was sprinkled in his hair. There were stain marks on the forest green T-shirt he wore and a frayed hole in his jeans. He looked rugged and sexy and his appearance had her heart racing.

"You do wonderful work, Derek. I like the way you've changed the layout of the room." Shelia tried to concentrate on his work and less on his physical attributes. She motioned to where he'd removed a section of upper cabinets which opened the room making the space appear larger.

"Mattie, let's finish the book we were reading," Martha reached out for her granddaughter's hand then lead her into the living room.

"I have some work I want to finish before I quit tonight." When Derek pushed a cabinet against the wall his biceps tightened against his T-shirt. Shelia wondered what it would feel like with Derek's arms around her. Now as a woman she knew the pleasures a man could give her.

"How can I help you?" She asked trying to distract herself from her desire for Derek.

"I planned to give these cabinets a final sanding." Picking up a sanding block and a piece of sandpaper, she fumbled with the supplies. Thinking of Derek she couldn't focus on the task at hand. He stepped closer distracting her all the more. Removing the sandpaper from her hands, he brushed his fingers against hers. His touch electrified her senses. Derek placed a sanding block covered with sandpaper in her palm. Covering her hand with his, he moved the sanding block up and down against the cabinet door.

"Sand with the grain." He stood directly behind her. She could feel the heat from his body against her back. Taking a deep breath she tried to still her clamoring nerves only to inhale the smell of sawdust mingled with Derek's scent.

Longing for his embrace Shelia leaned back pressing her body to his. "Why don't you use an electric sander?"

Derek's voice warmed her ear and his fingers tightened around hers. "I use electrical equipment but whenever possible I prefer hand tools. It's a great way to relieve stress." He whispered in her ear, "I like to feel the wood under my hands."

She longed to feel the roughness of his hand against her body and the passion he could awaken.

His firm grip held her hand even after their movement stilled then Derek removed the sanding block. Turning her hand over, he stroked the palm with a calloused finger. "You have such tiny fingers. You never grew up."

Infuriated she whirled around to face him. Now his face was mere inches from hers. Before she could express her frustration she noticed the passion flare in his eyes again.

"You've always been hard to get out of my mind. You were then and you are now," he said against her lips.

His lips felt soft and warm on hers. Leaning closer, Shelia pressed her lips to his. With a groan she opened her mouth to his, allowing his tongue to caress her lower lip before penetrating her mouth. The taste of his kiss was intoxicating. Desire heated her body and weakened her senses.

Shelia laced her hands around his neck, snuggling to the warmth of his body. Excitement and passion surged through her. Feelings she thought she'd never experience again rushed through her.

With his lips enticing her mouth Shelia felt renewed. Content within his embrace she didn't want to move.

Derek pulled back first. With his hands on her hips he studied Shelia's face. His eyes widened as he searched her features, he appeared as surprised as she was by their sudden passion.

"Daddy." When Mattie walked into the room, Derek quickly dropped his hands and stepped back.

"I've grown up, Derek," Shelia whispered.

She wasn't sure Derek heard her until he said, "Definitely." Humor rumbled in his one word reply.

~ * ~

The next morning, Derek dropped Mattie off at school then hurried across town to his mother's house hoping to see Shelia before she headed to work. When he turned down the street there was no car in Shelia's driveway. He'd missed her. What would he say if he saw her? I want your body. I want to have wild sex with you. Derek shook his head and jumped out of his truck. She'd think he was a sex-starved idiot.

When he rounded his pickup he noticed a tall, dark hair woman walking toward him.

"Derek, hi. I thought that was you," said Catherine Lee. Her and her family had lived across from his mom for the last five years. They had kept a watchful eye on his mom before he returned to Forest Ridge.

Derek reached out and firmly shook her hand. "Hi, Catherine. How are you and your family?"

"Good. All three of the girls are in school now." Her smile sparkled in her eyes from the pride of her family.

"Doesn't seem like their old enough. Your youngest must be around Mattie's age."

"Yes. Martha said there's only a month difference in their birthdays. You can send Mattie over to play with the girls any time. They love company."

"Thanks. She'd like that."

Catherine tucked a lock of her brown hair behind her ear. "I stopped by to tell your mom, my car was broken into last night."

"I'm sorry to hear that." Derek crossed his arms in front of his chest and listened intently. "Did they take anything?"

"My GPS and some CD's. I forgot to bring the unit in the house. The police said over the weekend two cars down the next block were also vandalized." She pointed diagonally to the north. "A cell phone and money were taken. You just don't know about people now days."

"That's too close to home." He nodded in agreement. "I'll be sure to tell my mom."

"Good. Also remind her not to leave anything valuable in her car."

"I'll do that Catherine. Thanks for the warning."

After she turned to walk back across the street, he closed the tailgate of his truck. Derek was halfway to his mother's door, when he heard an approaching car. Expecting to see his assistant Derek turned around to see Shelia's blue Ford Focus parked in her driveway. He walked toward her car.

He needed to hear the sound of her voice and feel her lips against his. "Do you have a minute?" Derek called out to her as she got out of her car. In anticipation, he quickened his pace.

"Sure." He couldn't help but notice the slight hesitation in her voice. With her shoulders slumped her pace was slow as she walked toward him.

Shelia didn't smile her normal greeting and her eyes were red and puffy. "Honey, are you alright?" he asked.

She gave a quick nod then more slowly she shook her head from side to side. "No, I've been at the hospital all night." Looking down, she sniffled slightly. When she glanced up he noticed tears glistening in her eyes.

"Shelia?" He placed his hand on her shoulder. "What's wrong?"

"One of my favorite patients passed this morning." Tears trickled down her cheeks unchecked. "The family asked me to stay after my shift to be with them."

Ignoring his desire for her, Derek wrapped his arms around her shoulders and held Shelia close. Silently he pulled her into his embrace. She rested her head against his shoulders, while Derek stroked her hair. He softly said words of encouragement much as he'd do to Mattie when she was upset.

She placed her hands around his waist and leaned into him. When her tears lessened she stepped back and looked at him. "Thanks."

"Do you have to go back to work today?" He watched as she slowly moved her head back and forth. Derek struggled to ignore the floral scent of her hair and the feel of her soft body within his arms. A

27

tingling sensation started in his groin and he questioned the logic of holding her.

"No I traded my day off," she whispered.

Silently they walked to her front door. The ranch house was the same style as his mother's but he noticed Shelia had decorated the entrance with a small metal table and two chairs. Along the edge, several containers of pansies colored the porch.

He followed her through the front door. Knowing Shelia needed to talk, Derek led her to the living. After they sat on the couch he silently waited for her to start talking. Her gaze never met his as she laced and unlaced her fingers. When he placed his hand on her back and rubbed her shoulders, she explained, "My patient was courageous and brave throughout her treatment. It's hard to see them go." A sigh shuddered through her. "She turned eleven last month."

Thoughts of Mattie circled around him; from her fussy mood in the mornings to her smiling face when she talked about her fairies. His hand stilled. He didn't know what he'd do if he lost her.

"Knowing you, you probably hadn't eaten since lunch yesterday." His voice quivered slightly as he thought of losing Mattie. She was his life.

"Something like that." She paused for a moment. Her large blue eyes reflected her sadness. "We were busy."

"You get ready for bed and I'll make breakfast for you."

By the way Shelia raised her chin, he knew she was about to object. "You need to eat before going to bed." He turned her toward the stairs and patted her butt.

Derek hurried to the kitchen trying not to think of her body pressed against his or the fact she was upstairs changing her clothes and possibly nude at this moment. Focusing on what he was doing Derek soon had breakfast cooking on the stove.

He opened the cabinet and set two mugs on the countertop then added tea bags and hot water from the teakettle. When his family went camping, Shelia tagged along. Not a coffee drinker she always had to have her cup of tea. Derek put the lid on the canister then returned it to the cabinet.

Grating a generous amount of cheese on the eggs, he folded the mixture over on itself. Setting the food on the table, Derek stepped back. He was proud of himself. By keeping busy he'd redirected his thoughts blocking out imagines of how sexy Shelia looked when he saw her standing beside her car. A slight breeze had ruffled her curly hair and molded the smock against her breast.

Shelia entered the kitchen wearing a thin cotton robe underneath he glimpsed a pink pajama top and shorts, leaving her long shapely legs exposed. Her attire was not at all sexy but the thought of her being ready for bed fueled his desire. His body responded so quickly to her as if he was still an adolescent.

"I fixed you an omelet."

Folding his arms around her, he held Shelia close. Derek wanted to protect her from the outside world. Independent and feisty, Shelia had never cried in front of him. He was touched she'd lowered her defenses allowing him to see her vulnerable. He linked his hand with hers. "I'm sorry I wish I could..." Her fingers were soft and warm within his. "Could help." Mattie's problems were solved with a bag of ice or a Band-Aid. Derek didn't know how to ease Shelia's pain. Running his fingers through Shelia's hair seemed to calm her as the tears tapered off.

"Thank you." Her lips quivered and he knew she was close to tears again.

Placing his hands on her hips, Derek pulled her close. With her hips pressed against him, he groaned. Her eyes were large and darkened with sadness. He lowered his head and captured her lips with his for a quick kiss. A clear image of her body beneath his stopped him short. This relationship was moving too fast or was it. They'd known each other all their lives.

On impulse he offered, "Would you like to have dinner with Mattie and me tonight?"

Chapter Five

Set in the newer section of town, Derek's two-story home had a welcoming feel. Natural cedar siding contrasted with large windows surrounded with dark green wood trim. As Shelia stepped up on the porch, the front door opened.

"Hi Mattie. Nice to see you." Shelia reached out and shook the girl's hand.

Mattie wore a lavender princess dress with a large dishtowel tied around her waist for a makeshift apron. "Dad said I could open the door." After Shelia walked inside the girl closed the door behind her. The entryway had hardwood flooring and a large staircase to the left leading to the second floor.

Mattie's dark hair and eyes looked so much like her dad's. A zigzag part separated her two braids a sign of Derek's dedication to his daughter. Her hostess led her through the living room where they were met halfway by Derek.

He wore a long sleeve button up shirt and khaki pants. His nearness started her heart racing. The smile on his face bought an instant curve to Shelia's lips. "Derek." She hadn't intended for her voice to sound so breathless and sexy.

"I'm glad you came." Derek leaned forward and kissed her cheek.

Another sisterly gesture, she sighed at his stubborn nature. Shelia started to cross her arms in front of her when she remembered the present she held. "This is for you." She handed Mattie a pink gift bag with sparkling stars on the sides. Seeing Derek's raised brows she said, "It's polite to give the hostess a gift."

The little girl starred at the bag a fraction of a second before removing the tissue paper. Mattie's eyes lit up when she pulled the fabric purse out of the bag.

"I thought of you when I saw this." Shelia pointed to the fairies. Brightly colored fairies with multicolored wings appeared to dance on the purse. "There's lots of room to carry your fairies in."

Mattie held up the purse in front of her father then clutched it to her chest. "Thank you, thank you." When Mattie wrapped her arms around Shelia, a surge of pleasure tightened her throat. "I have to show the fairies." She raced through the room without a backward glance.

"Mattie makes a charming hostess."

"Yes. She's five going on twenty. Sometimes I think she needs to be more of a kid."

Derek reached out for Shelia's hand and closed the space between them. "You're very thoughtful," he said against her lips. "I've been thinking of you all day." The kiss was light and teasing when their lips first touched.

As soon as Sheila wrapped her arm around him her hunger and need for Derek intensified. She returned his kiss matching the passion and longing he'd shown her. Feeling alive again, she leaned into his body. Within his embrace Shelia knew she'd found the lifeline she'd been missing.

Derek backed up but held onto her fingers. "I'm glad you're here." His gaze didn't leave hers as if there was more he wanted to say. An odor of smoke and burnt food floated in the room. "Damn I forgot the dinner." He raced into the kitchen.

"Can I help you?" she asked his retreating back.

"No. Make yourself at home," he called back.

Shelia slowly walked through Derek's living room. One wall graced a floor to ceiling stone fireplace and on the opposite wall were two large windows. She paused for a moment and looked at the view. The backyard gave Mattie ample area to play. In the far distance Shelia glimpsed the blue Columbia River with its steep cliffs.

She followed Derek into the open kitchen. Gorgeous two-tone wooden cabinets filled three walls with a work island in the middle. "Wow. This is fabulous. You have a beautiful home." Shelia waved her hand in front of her face. "Smells delicious."

"I was a little distracted," Derek muttered.

Placing her hands on the countertop she leaned toward Derek. Referring to their kiss, Shelia playfully asked, "Does that happen often?"

"Dad burns dinner all the time." Mattie bounced into the room and stood beside her.

"He does." Shelia laughed.

"No I don't." He placed the saucepan in the sink and added water to the burnt food. "And that's a 'no' to both of you." When he turned around his eyes were still dark with passion.

Returning his attention to their dinner he placed the large frying pan on the stove. Once the oil heated Derek added chicken to the pan causing the meat to sizzle.

"We made cookies for you. He didn't burn them." Mattie tilted her head and looked up at her. "Can I show you my room now?"

"That's a good idea then dad can concentrate on dinner." Shelia gave Derek a sly smiled then turned and reached for Mattie's hand. "To your room."

"She cleaned in there this afternoon because you'd be here for dinner tonight." Derek's voice followed them down the hall.

"I'm honored." Shelia followed Mattie up the wooden staircase. On the walls were photographs of Mattie as a baby and as toddler wearing a cute white and blue sundress. She enjoyed looking at the group of candid shots of Mattie and Derek laughing and playing. The center picture had Derek sitting with his daughter standing behind him with her arms wrapped around his neck. Their closeness tugged at Shelia's heart.

"This is my dad's room." Mattie pointed to a partially opened door on the left. As they walked by Shelia glanced inside. The room was simply furnished, neat and orderly. Shelia wondered if he too had cleaned his room for her visit. Despite the urge to linger, Shelia continued on to Mattie's room.

"Here's my room." The girl twirled around with her arms out stretched.

Walking into the bedroom, Shelia was amazed at how tidy the child's room was. A twin bed was to the left of the door with a pink princess comforter. On the opposite wall was a large oak bookcase. Dolls of all shape and sizes sat on the shelves. Books filled the lower two shelves.

"You have a beautiful room." She walked toward the dolls. Many of them looked as if they'd never been played with, their hair as smooth as if they'd just been taken out of a box. Shelia remembered Derek's earlier comment that he wished Mattie would be more of a little girl and less of a little adult.

"Thank you." Mattie sat on her bed.

When Shelia sat beside the girl, she noticed the hair clip with feathers she'd given her, on the nightstand beside the bed.

She was touched Mattie treasured the gift. "You kept the feathers?"

"Of course." Mattie patted the fabric bag which hung from her shoulder. "The fairies say you're very nice. They especially like the purse. Now I can take them anywhere."

"Do the fairies come here?" With a wave Shelia gestured to the room in general.

"Most of the time. But I can see them whenever I like. They help me all the time. Right now they're working on something special." Mattie jumped off the bed and hurried over to the bookcase. Picking up a cloth doll, she bought it over to Shelia. "This is my favorite doll. Grandma made her for me."

Shelia finger combed the doll's yarn hair then pulled the strands back to make a pony tail fastening her hair back with the clip of feathers. "She's lovely. She reminds me of a doll I had when I was little. We went everywhere together."

"Her name's Marmar. She's been with me since I was little."

"Oh that must be a long time." Shelia did her best to suppress the laughter bubbling within her. The face on the cloth was faded it was an obviously well-loved doll. "I can tell you really love her."

Mattie nodded her head. "She's as old as the fairies. Cara and Kendra came to help me look after my dad."

"You've done a great job watching over him. Knowing your dad I'm sure it's been a lot of work." Shelia smiled. "He looks really good." Shelia sucked in her lower lip to hide the humor of the little girl taking care of her father.

The girl shrugged her shoulders. "It's a tough job, but someone has to help him."

Shelia placed the doll on Mattie's pillow. "The fairies are good friends to help you with your dad."

"Right now I've asked them to help me with something special."

When they returned to the kitchen, Shelia helped set the table. While Mattie chatted non-stop about her fairies and friends at pre-school. Derek had a quiet patience with his daughter patting the top of her head when she walked by and nodding an agreement about her fairies. It wasn't long before Shelia was wrapped in the warmth of their family.

"Dad, Shelia said you look good."

Shelia's mouth dropped open. He watched her intently, "Well I think she's beautiful."

She felt warm from the inside out and wondered if he was only making small talk with his daughter or if there were feelings behind his compliment.

"That's a good start," Mattie said but Shelia didn't register the meaning behind the girl's words.

Shortly after dinner, Mattie disappeared to her room. Shelia placed the dishes with leftover food on the counter near the refrigerator. Then she gathered the dirty plates and set them in the sink. For a moment they worked in compatible silence. Derek rinsed the plates then handed them to her and she placed them in the dishwasher.

"Thank you. For dinner…" She paused for a moment and drew a deep breath. Remembering the solid shoulder she cried on Shelia added, "And for this morning. Every time I turned around today you were there for me."

He glanced her way and nodded, "Anytime."

Passing a bowl to her, Derek held on to the porcelain dish after she reached for it. "So you think I'm good looking?" his words were laced with humor.

Knowing a verbal exchange with Derek needed all her attention Shelia set down the bowl and stepped closer to him. "That's not what I meant. I…"

Amusement sparkled in his eyes. "Oh you think I'm ugly."

"Do you and Mattie always change the meaning of what people say?" She intended to shake her finger at him but placed her palm on his chest instead.

"Only when we like to see you squirm." Standing in front of her, he touched the highest point of her cheek. "You have a red spot here and here. Your blush is very becoming."

Derek's finger lingered a moment against her skin. She wanted to feel his touch on her body. Placing his hands on her hips he pulled Shelia closer pressing her against him. Her body fit his. Would an affair with Derek heal the hole in her heart?

She circled her arms around his waist. His lips touched hers with the lightest of touches. Derek's hands moved up her back holding her close.

When his tongue brushed the base of her neck where her pulse beat erratically, she sighed. Closing her eyes, Shelia gave into the passion which heated her body.

"Wow." Derek stepped back breaking the intimate moment. She opened her eyes and watched him pull his hand through his hair. "I can't keep my hands off you." He shook his head appearing surprised he voiced his thoughts aloud.

Old feelings of love emerged strong and more mature than before along with the memory of hurt and betrayal. "I thought we were good friends. Are you going to pull away now as you did then?" Taking a deep breath she stilled her clamoring nerves. She thought of the countless times she'd cried herself to sleep because her best friend no longer wanted anything to do with her. "We were inseparable then suddenly you wanted nothing to do with me."

"You were always my best friend." Derek rubbed his knuckle down her cheek. "When I was in high school I noticed the difference in our ages. I turned seventeen and you were just thirteen. Our needs were different at that time. I saw myself as an adult and you were still a child."

Shelia glanced up, unable to hide the sadness from her features. "I felt you deserted me."

"I didn't mean to hurt you." Derek cupped her face in his hands then kissed her cheek. Laughter rumbled in his chest. "Our age difference isn't an obstacle now."

"Dad," Mattie called from the living room.

She stepped back even farther. Feeling his daughter was doing a little matchmaking of her own, Shelia didn't want the girl to read too much into their simple embrace.

"Mattie, it's time for bed." Derek met her at the archway between the kitchen and living room.

Shelia moved to stand behind him and whispered, "I should leave."

"Dad hasn't read yet." She turned her gaze to Shelia. "You have to stay for a story," she pleaded. Her voice was threaded with a note of desperation. Maybe for the child's sake it would be best not to see Derek anymore. He had no intention to remarry. Mattie appeared to have different plans for her dad. Shelia didn't want Mattie or herself to hope for something that would never happen.

Shelia nodded. She silently stood inside Mattie's bedroom door and listened to Derek read a storybook to his daughter. A scene she was sure played out most nights. The closeness that father and daughter shared tugged at her heart.

She and James wanted to have a family. He'd promised her one last tour then they'd settle down in one place. They often talked about what their home and family would be like.

A lump formed in her throat for the family evening she'd shared with them. After Derek finished the last page of the book, Shelia stepped out of the room. Her breathing quickened as she walked through the house. A tightness formed in her chest. She clearly heard Derek's goodnight to Mattie and knew she had to hurry. She retraced her steps and found her purse where she'd left it on the living room couch. Digging through the contents she found her car keys.

With her hand on the doorknob, Derek's deep voice stopped her. "Leaving without saying good-bye?"

"It's not fair to Mattie." Shelia turned and faced him. "She wants a family…" Shelia whispered the last word.

"I decide what is right for Mattie." He studied her face then stepped toward her. "What's wrong?"

Her shoulders slumped. "I watched you read to Mattie. You're lucky you have a family. James and I talked of having children..." her voice trailed off.

"I'm sorry Shelia." When he reached out for her hand, Shelia hesitated. She wanted more than a few kisses and a passionate embrace. Could she settle for an intimate relationship, even though she knew Derek would never be willing to start over. She placed her hand in his as he lead her into the living room at least she'd have one evening with him.

Chapter Six

Mattie sat up in bed and watched as Cara and Kendra sat down on her comforter. Their wings fluttered softly. Both of them looked serious and Mattie thought they appeared skittish and would leave any second.

She narrowed her gaze on them. "How is it going? Do you think Shelia's the one?"

"I'm not sure," Cara's voice sounded strained.

"You don't think they'll get married?" Sadness filled her heart.

Kendra reached forward patting Mattie's hand. "Humans are unpredictable."

Mattie sighed. "That doesn't sound good."

"It's too early to tell." Cara reassured her and Kendra nodded her agreement. "Give them more time."

"I thought they'd know right away. I saw them hugging tonight." Mattie said, hoping that was a good sign.

"That's a good start," the fairies confirmed.

After she'd fallen asleep Cara and Kendra flew to the living room to check on Shelia and Derek's progress. The couple sat on the couch too far apart as far as Cara was concerned. "Are you sure that was the right fairy dust you sprinkled on them?" Cara asked her friend. "I don't see any starry eyes or hear any words of love."

"Shh. I know the dust was fine." Kendra paced back and forth then sat down. "I'm never wrong when I use fairy dust. I think they are stubborn and don't want to admit they're in love."

Kendra sat on the edge of the table beside Cara. "Humans." She lifted her legs and crossed them in front of her. Then with elbows on her knees Kendra rested her head in her hands. "Can you think of anything else?"

Cara shook her head. "No."

"Mattie will be very disappointed."

~ * ~

With thoughts of Derek on her mind, Shelia hadn't slept well and she was glad to have the day off. With a cup of coffee in her hand she walked through the house. Stopping in the living room, she thought of the time she spent with Derek.

She stared out the large paned window as a midnight blue Jeep stopped in front of the house. A young man opened the driver door and got out. He glanced once at her house then walked up the driveway. The jeans and polo shirt he wore were pretty nondescript but the extremely short military haircut spoke volumes. She'd recognize a solider even without a uniform. Shelia had seen hundreds of men with similar shaved heads while James was in the National Guard. She watched his purposeful steps to the front door.

For a fraction of a second Shelia froze after he rang the bell. Memories of hearing James had died came flooding back. She already knew her husband was gone the stranger waiting at the door couldn't bring her anymore sadness. Her legs felt heavy as she walked to answer the bell. Sunlight streamed into the room when she opened the door.

"Mrs. Shelia Roberts?" the man asked.

She nodded quickly. "Yes." Her voice sounded so quiet Shelia wondered if she spoke the word aloud.

"I'm Lieutenant J. T. Reynolds. I served with your husband James in Afghanistan."

Hearing her husband's name she snapped out of the surreal feeling. "Won't you come in, Lieutenant Reynolds?"

"Thank you, Ma'am. Just call me J. T. everyone does."

His eyes sparkled with kindness and Shelia felt at ease in his company. "Would you like something to drink?"

"No thank you. I'm fine." He glanced at the ceiling and Shelia had a gut feeling he was anything but fine.

"Won't you sit down?" She motioned toward the couch.

When J. T. sat in the large overstuffed chair he gave a heavy sigh. "I've never done this before. First I want to tell you, James was one of the best men I've ever known."

Emotions gathered and tightened the back of her throat. Although she felt a sense of comfort from J. T. she wasn't sure if she wanted him to continue. "Thank you."

"James always talked about you." J. T. rubbed the back of his neck. "Talking about our families helped to keep the loneliness at bay. The night before…"

He didn't have to finish the sentence she knew what he meant. J. T. had been with James his last night maybe even the last minutes of his life. Suddenly she wanted to hear everything he had to say. "Yes, I understand."

"Like always, he was talking about his family. About you. James handed me this..." He pulled something out of his pocket. "He asked that I make sure you get this if something happened. Shelia starred at the small envelope in his outstretched hand.

"J. T. I've already received 'The letter.'" She didn't have to explain further they both knew the routine of the required good-bye letter all service personal needed to write in case of an emergency.

"James said this was different. He knew I wouldn't be stateside for some time. James felt that would be perfect timing. It's as if he knew. Some do." His deep voice gave her comfort. J. T. handed her the small white envelope, the last thing James wrote before his death. His final words to her.

She sighed and didn't realize tears flowed down her cheeks until J. T. sat beside her and offered her a pristine white handkerchief.

"Thank you." She placed her hand on his arm. "For everything."

She held the lightweight envelope in her hand. Her name was printed in small block letters, typical of James' handwriting. Setting the letter aside, Shelia reached for the proffered cloth and wiped the moisture from her face.

"Where are you from, J. T.?"

"I was raised in California. But I've been in the service for so long I don't rightly feel I have a home anymore." He gave her a lopsided smile.

"You really went out of your way to deliver this." She glanced to her right where she'd set the letter on the corner of the coffee table. "You went above and beyond the call of duty."

"Honestly I have some business here in Forest Ridge. I think that's why James asked me to be his courier. But I would have made the trip regardless of the distance because I made a promise to him." He patted the top of her hand. "I hope I gave some comfort."

"Oh you have. I'm glad he was among friends."

"I think I know how you feel. Not only did I lose my friend James but a month ago I lost my brother."

"I'm so sorry." Shelia reached out and placed her hand over his. "Is that why you're here?"

"Yes ma'am. I just found out and wasn't able to come home for his funeral. So now I'm here to look after his family."

When J. T. quickly stood, Shelia noticed his eyes blinked quickly and knew his emotions were also close to the surface. His handshake was firm and comforting. "I wish you all the best."

"Nice meeting you J. T. Good luck with your family." By the time he left, Shelia understood why James entrusted J. T. with his letter. Her husband had touched more lives than she would ever know.

She avoided the living room for some time knowing the envelope rested on the coffee table where she'd left it. There were numerous chores which were more pressing, she'd told herself. Finally running out of excuses she sat on the couch and starred at the envelope. Momentarily she starred at James' handwriting then slowly she slipped her finger under the sealed flap. James' simple penned strokes brought new tears to her eyes.

Shelia,

My dearest love. I'm sorry you're receiving this letter. This is your last letter from me.

I imagine this has been a hard year for you, full of adjustments and changes. I'm sorry I wasn't able to be there for you.

I'm guessing you've been grieving for almost a year. It's time you move on.

There is no way I can write in a few pages the love and joy you've brought to my life. My only regret is our life together was so short.

You're a compassionate woman, so full of life and love for others. Because you're so caring I know this time has been hard on you. I need you to promise me you'll carry on. Find love again, marry and have the family which we were only able to talk about. You're too special a person to be on your own.

I can see you shaking your head no.

Shelia laughed as James had known her all too well.

Keep your heart open and love will find you. Who knows maybe this time you'll find someone who doesn't leave his dirty clothes on the floor.

You have my blessings.

Love,

James

A tear flowed down Shelia's cheek. When she first received word of James' death she'd prayed it was a mistake. There had been times when she expected to turn around and see him walking through the door. This new letter echoed the finality of his life. Their life together consisted of a marriage certificate and a few photographs.

He'd been correct in his assumption. She'd finally opened her heart again only Derek had no intention in sharing his life with her.

~ * ~

Derek drove west on Hwy. 84 to the hardware store at the edge of town. He barely noticed the sailboats with their colorful canvas sails which dotted the rich blue water of the majestic Columbia River.

He'd made the mistake of letting Shelia into his life again. Even now he couldn't imagine his life without her.

"Dad the fairies reminded me we're out of milk. Can we stop at the store?"

"After the hardware store." Not only did he have a five year old telling him what to do now there were two fairies bossing him around. When will this end, he chuckled to himself.

Once he picked up his supplies Mattie reminded him again about food. As they walked through the store entrance his precocious daughter asked "is this where Shelia shops?"

"Don't know." He struggled keeping his thoughts of Shelia at bay without everyone mentioning her name.

"Where's the shopping carts, Dad?" Mattie tugged on his pant leg. Derek reached down and took her hand. "We're only picking up a couple of things, we don't need one."

Now at the back of the store laden down with items, Derek looked around for an empty shopping cart or store basket to no avail. "How about soup for lunch?"

"What's this one dad?" She lifted a can from the rack and held the label facing him.

Derek shook his head. "Cream of asparagus. I don't think you'd like that."

"Why? I like cream of and I like asparagus." Her smile was his undoing.

"Okay, we'll have your soup for lunch." Remembering Shelia's subtle suggestion, 'maybe she needs to play more often'. Derek said, "Let's go to the park before we go home." He ruffled his daughter's hair and knew by the smile on her face he'd made the right decision.

Behind him a familiar voice said, "Are you finding everything you need?"

Reading the ingredients on the package of chili mix, Derek didn't notice Shelia walk down the aisle. The softness of her face warmed his heart. The thought of soup and lunch were forgotten.

"What are you doing here?" After the words were out he realized how stupid he sounded.

"I find it a good idea to eat. Don't you?" Her laughter was contagious. Derek stared at her lips wondering if he could kiss her without Mattie seeing them. He walked forward placing his arm around Shelia and kissed her cheek. "God it's good to see you."

One of the cans he held dropped and rolled across the floor. His daughter hustled after the wayward soup. Mattie skipped back to them with the can of soup in her hand.

"Why don't you share my cart? I'm almost finished." Shelia offered moving her groceries to one side.

"Thank you." Derek lowered their food into the shopping cart then reached out for the can Mattie handed him.

"How are you Mattie?" Shelia reached down and shook his daughter's hand.

Derek liked how Shelia went out of her way to include Mattie. Other women had befriended his daughter in hopes of getting closer to him. Watching Shelia interact with Mattie he knew her feelings were sincere.

"We're going to the park." She nodded once then said. "Come with us please." Mattie tugged on her hand. Derek could see a moment of hesitation on Shelia's face as she looked down at Mattie. "Please come to the park with us?" she pleaded again. Mattie turned slightly and looked into her fairy purse. "How was that?" she whispered.

Recognizing she was talking to her fairies, Shelia answered for them. "Mattie, your request was great. I'd love to go to the park." Shelia met his gaze. "I guess I should have asked if that was okay with your dad."

"That's fine. We're going to play." He winked at Shelia to remind her she'd suggested Mattie needed to play more often.

~ * ~

White cotton ball clouds dotted the sharp blue sky as they ate the impromptu lunch. After Mattie finished eating she raced to the play equipment in front of them.

Shelia closed up the box of fish shaped crackers. "How is your work at Martha's going?"

"Good. We're almost finished." Derek reached across the table and held her hand. "Shelia I want to continue seeing you. Not because you live next to mom or someone's matchmaking. I care for you."

His face was serious. She could tell he choose his words carefully. No declaration of love or ever after. 'I care for you' was more than she thought he'd ever say. Words tightened her throat as Shelia almost blurted she loved him and she'd settle for a one sided relationship.

Mattie called out from the top of the jungle gym. "Hi dad. Hi Shelia." Her arms frantically waved to draw their attention.

They both laughed at her drama action and the seriousness of their conversation dissipated. Derek released Shelia's hand to wave at his daughter.

When he turned back to her, he said, "I talked to Catherine Lee the other day she said her car and several others in the neighborhood were broken into."

Shelia didn't know if she should be relieved or sad that he'd changed the subject so quickly. She stopped closing the food container and looked at Derek. "On our block?"

He gave a quick nod. "I suggest you put your car in the garage at night."

Shelia grimaced. "I would if I could but mom has furniture and boxes stored there." Her parents never threw anything away. Several times Shelia asked her mom about the unused stuff in the garage and Kay Roberts reply was always the same. 'She wanted to keep everything.' "I never leave anything of value in the vehicle so it doesn't matter."

Suddenly she remembered a man she saw wearing a large coat. "The night you walked me home did you see the man walking in the opposite direction?"

"What man?" Derek quickly turned to look at her.

On the spot she was totally lost for a description. "He was whistling."

"Shelia a lot of people whistle. That doesn't prove he's the one."

She leaned closer as she warmed up to her idea. "He wore a large coat. Like a trench coat. It was warm that evening. Too hot for a heavy jacket."

Derek's brows rose and the split in the left side became more noticeable. "Maybe."

"You have to admit that sounds suspicious." Thinking of the possibilities, Shelia twisted a section of her hair between her thumb and index finger.

"What are you thinking? I don't like the look in your eyes." His penetrating gaze locked on hers. "You're planning something I'm not going to like."

"I just thought I'd set a trap for him. Leave something in my car as a way of attracting him." Warming up to the idea she couldn't suppress the excitement in her voice.

"No." Derek shook his head. "Leave the investigation to the police. That's their job. Besides something like that could be dangerous. And I'm not going to help you."

Shelia placed her hand on his arm for reassurance. "I never said you needed to help me."

"You always said that yet you'd pulled me into every scheme you came up with."

Seeing the laughter in his eyes, she replied, "You had as much fun as I did."

"Dad would you push me," Mattie called from where she now sat on the swing wildly kicking her feet in the air.

Before Derek could answer, Shelia stood up. "I'll help you." She moved behind the girl. "It's been a long time since I've done this." She reached out and grasped both chains of the swing and pulled the girl backwards. When Mattie squealed in delight Shelia released the swing sending the girl forward. She pushed Mattie until the girl called out she was high enough.

Shelia flopped onto the swing beside her. "I forgot how much energy playing can take."

Derek moved to edge of the play equipment and leaned against a support pole.

"Dad you should push Shelia. She's not going very fast." Mattie glanced her way with a broad smile on her face. "I'll race you," the girl challenged as she started to swing higher.

"No that's okay." Shelia shot back. Before she finished the sentence Derek walked behind her. Grasping both chains, he pulled the swing back. Shelia squirmed on the rubber seat. "I don't need help."

"What's the matter Shelia? Are you afraid to go too high?" His words were warm against her ear before he released the swing.

Shelia wasn't afraid of the height but the sensation of Derek's hands caused each time he pushed against her back. Carefree and giddy, laughter bubbled up within her.

On their way back to their cars, after they'd played the afternoon away, Shelia hugged Mattie. "Thank you. I haven't had this much fun in a long time."

Derek held her hand as they crossed the grass field to the parking lot. "I've missed you Shelia."

Chapter Seven

Sitting in the darkened mudroom Derek wondered how Shelia had talked him into something so foolish. After all these years she was able to get him to participate in her escapades. He'd had no intention of helping her. Then she gave him her slow, sexy smile which was his undoing.

While she was busy fixing refreshments he'd moved the antique wooden bench, which usually served as a place to remove muddy shoes closer to the window. He slid the glass pane open in order to hear anyone in the driveway.

When his cell phone rang he reached into his pocket to answer the call. Mattie's smiling picture greeted him when he opened the phone. "Yes Mattie." He listened to her request then replied, "Yes I'm with Shelia. And no you can't stay up past your bedtime. Grandma knows what time you should be in bed. Good night, Mattie." Derek turned the phone off before he slipped it into his pocket.

Shelia returned to the room with two steaming mugs and placed them on the table beside him. "Here I made us some hot chocolate."

The small entryway had a large window facing her driveway only a faint glow from the streetlight filtered into the room. Even in the dimly lit area he knew every move Shelia made. He could feel her around him. Her fingers lightly brushed his arm sending a current of electricity and excitement through him. His groin awakened to ideas he hadn't experienced in a long time. She'd always gotten under his skin but now there was the sexual awareness. The need for her pulsed through his veins, as sure as the air he breathed.

"Why do you think someone would break into your car?"

"I stuffed an old purse with newspaper and place it on the passenger seat. Then I set my GPS charging unit on top of the bag. When he looks into the car the bait will be too tempting to pass up," her voice held an air of confidence.

He knew they wouldn't catch anyone but their private investigation gave him some time alone with Shelia.

Their amateur investigator scenario turned intimate when Shelia sat beside him. Darkness surrounded them reminding him of waiting for a movie to started at the drive-in. Feeling crowded on the bench; he placed his arm behind her. A mistake he realized too late.

When she leaned against his shoulder, Derek laid his cheek on her head. Inhaling the fresh scent of her hair he sighed. Content he could stay here forever. Trying to break the closeness he asked humorously, "What no popcorn?"

"I could make some if you like." She turned to face him, her lips were close to his.

He hungered for their sweetness. With his arm on her shoulder he leaned into her. His mouth claimed hers with an intense longing and the need for her passionate response. Reaching under her sweater he caressed the softness of her skin.

He wanted Shelia. Without analyzing the depth of his need Derek kissed her again. A primal demand burned within him, so deep he knew a few kisses wouldn't quench.

When Shelia wrapped her arms around his neck, he groaned. Her parted lips were a silent invitation to deepen their kiss. Abruptly, she pulled back from their embrace before he wanted their encounter to end. "Derek, I think I heard something."

All Derek heard was the rapid beat of his heart and his blood racing through his veins. He tried to listen to the outside world but his senses were focused on the woman beside him and what he wanted to do with her.

Then in the stillness he heard a faint whistle. He recognized the tune but couldn't remember the title of the old television show. They stood up in unison and quickly moved to the outside door. Shelia placed her hand on his arm. "Wait till he gets closer. We have no proof at this point," she whispered.

With his hand on the doorknob he stilled his movements. The man was not in sight but the whistling became louder. Looking out the window, Derek could see a silhouette of a man standing at the edge of her driveway. Shelia lightly brushed her fingers on Derek's back, leaning toward him.

The figure stood still, he didn't advance to her car nor move farther up the street. Shelia caressed Derek's cheek then her fingers traveled down his neck. Intent on asking Shelia to stop caressing him, he turned slightly. His arm brushed her breast. Heated with the desire to make love to her, Derek pulled on the neckline of his shirt.

In order to escape the intimacy which surrounded them, Derek opened the door and rushed outside. Before he made love to her on the hard wooden bench, he needed to put some space between him and Shelia.

The cool evening breeze felt good against Derek's heated body. "Can I help you?" Derek walked closer to the man at the edge of the sidewalk.

The man jerked his head up apparently surprised by Derek's comment. "No. I'm just walking my dog and waiting for him to catch up." At that moment a large golden lab lumbered up to them. The older man wore a heavy trench coat just as Shelia had described.

Derek studied the man in the dim light. He appeared to be in his late sixties. Clean cut and well-dressed Derek didn't think he fit the bill of someone who'd break into cars.

"George and I go walking every night. For the most part he stays up with me. When he doesn't, I whistle to signal it's time to catch up and we start walking again." The man reached down and patted the dog's head. "We've been together for a long time."

Shelia walked out to stand beside Derek. "Good evening for a walk."

The older man nodded. "That's for sure. Not a cloud in the sky."

He wore a heavy trench coat just as Shelia had described. Unsure if he should believe him, Derek studied the older man's face. "Warm out tonight."

"That's a matter of opinion. My wife and I moved over from the islands last month." He pulled his lapels closer together. "To me your weather is cold. I wear long underwear most of the time and I'm still freezing. Wish we never left Hawaii." His voice deepened with regret.

At a loss for words, Derek felt sorry for the older man. "Hope you acclimatize soon."

"Thank you. You and your wife have a good evening," he said as he walked down the street with his dog beside him.

Derek didn't bother to correct the man. For the first time in years the thought of marriage sounded intriguing. He liked the thought of Shelia as his wife but he knew they'd never get married. "Poor guy."

"Here I thought he was the thief." She turned to face Derek, "He wore such a large coat, I was certain he was the one we were looking for. You're right I should leave the detective work to the police." Her sheepish smile made him laugh.

"You've always had a mind of your own. That's one of the things I like about you." Slipping his arm around her shoulder Derek gave her a quick squeeze before releasing her.

Derek enjoyed Shelia's company and wanted to see her more often. Hell, who was he kidding? His groin tingled with the thought of making love to her. For years he swore he'd never say he loved another woman. Linking the word love with Shelia felt oddly comforting and right. She'd not only warmed his heart, she'd reached into him and touched his soul.

Her palm caressed his cheek breaking into his thoughts. "I'm sorry I disturbed your evening."

Derek gave her a quick kiss. "I'm not."

Standing in the middle of her driveway, Shelia realized she didn't want Derek to leave. She knew he couldn't spend the night but if only they had a little more time. "Please stay." Shelia's voice was husky and she wondered if Derek noticed the longing in her words.

He raised one brow.

"I'm sorry." She brushed her finger across the scare she'd made all those years ago. "It does add to your sex appeal, gives you that rugged bad boy look."

Derek laughed deep in this throat. "Right."

Shelia grasped his hand and led him back into the house. Still holding hands he closed and locked the door behind them. Standing in the darkened room, she listened to their uneven breathing. She wasn't sure who moved first or if they reacted at the same time. Within Derek's embrace Shelia knew she was where she wanted to be. Needed to be.

His lips devoured hers. Shelia's hunger grew from a need for fulfillment. A yearning to possess the man she loved. Before she changed her mind she quickly reached up and unbuttoned his shirt.

"Not here," he whispered against her lips. "Your room." He pulled on her lower lip. The kiss which followed held a promise of a romantic evening.

Afraid if she released Derek's hand he'd disappear, Shelia weaved their way through the house. Excitement raced through her. She couldn't wait to feel Derek's nude body against hers. Heated passion warmed her body as she hurried.

She'd planned to have a romantic scene with candles and soft music. The strategy was quickly forgotten when the need to ravage Derek became her main focus.

As usual Mr. Whiskers was curled in a ball on her pillow. Shelia picked up the cat and carried him out of the room, closing the door behind him.

When she turned around Derek was beside her. His eyes flared with passion when he looked at her. His movements were slow and measured as he removed her sweater then unbuttoned her blouse. She saw the gleam of hunger in his eyes when he said, "You're lovely."

Passion surged as she stripped off his jacket and shirt. She needed to feel his skin beneath her fingers.

Derek didn't say any words of love. His kisses and touch told her he loved her as much as she cared for him. He sealed his lips to hers in a pledge.

Shelia slipped her hands under the waistband of his pants. His muscles were firm and taunt. After removing her blouse his movements quickened. Lowering both of the bra straps at the same time he left a trail of heated kisses across the swell of her breast. In one quick move Derek unhooked her bra and the lacy garment fell to the floor unnoticed.

His hands traveled up from her waist to the sides of her breast. His rough hands kneed her tender skin. When his thumbs captured Shelia's nipples she moaned deep in her throat. With his thumb and forefinger Derek tweaked the buds until they pebbled in his hands.

"I need you." Giving up on taking their union slowly she frantically pushed his jeans down over his taut thighs until the course fabric pooled at his feet.

Seeing the colorful boxers, she smiled. "Boxers. So you like them loose." In one swift movement his underwear followed the jeans. When he struggled to step out of the pant legs she lightly pushed him back on the bed and finished stripping off his clothes.

Shelia reached for her own zipper. Before she could undo the fastener Derek sat up and stilled her hands. "No you don't. I want the pleasure."

Sitting on the bed he pulled her closer. His tongue circled a nipple then greedily suckled causing the nubbin to stand erect. While Derek massaging her derriere, Shelia ran her hands through his hair keeping his head at her breast. When he released the nipple his mouth sought hers for a hard demanding kiss.

Her need was so intense she sat on top of him. The warmth from his erection heated her womanhood as she rocked back and forth against him.

"Derek I can't—" her passion filled voice trailed off.

"Honey, we're not finished." He rolled her onto the bed. He held Shelia's hands above her head for a moment then his palms stroked down to her breast. Flames of desire heated her body and a need for fulfillment pulsated at her core.

His hands traveled down the length of her body then tugged at the hair which covered her mound. As his finger slid inside her, she arched against his hand in a rapid rhythm. Parting her legs, Derek moved below her. When she started to moan his tongue teased her folds unmercifully. The warmth of his mouth touched her core and she bucked in excitement and pleasure.

She reached down and caressed his muscular shoulders then combed her fingers into his hair pushing his mouth harder into her softness.

"Derek. Derek," she moaned. Shelia arched and bucked against him as her pleasure erupted.

He moved over her, his manhood erect with desire, entering her with slow steady thrust. "I'm sorry honey I can't wait any longer." His movement quickened and pulsated within her with an erotic beat. Their breathing rapid, Shelia wrapped her legs around him and arched as they reached their pinnacle together.

The pleasure was so intense Shelia didn't want to move. Gradually she relaxed and lowered her legs then Derek laid down beside her.

Snuggling against him, she rested her head on Derek's chest. His heartbeat blended with hers. Their steady beat echoed in her thoughts, 'I love you.' She didn't intend to say the words aloud they flowed out with pure happiness.

The moment the words were out Derek's body stilled beside her. There was no verbal reply from him. Not even a 'What did you say?'

In the uncomfortable silence which followed the welcoming intimacy earlier in the evening was shattered into microscopic pieces never to be put back together.

Her declaration of love was heartfelt. Not a simple 'I love you' because we had great sex. The secret she'd always held in her heart was finally revealed. She should be happy but his sudden departure was proof Derek was anything but pleased.

Chapter Eight

With a sleepless night behind her, Shelia's muscles ached as she walked into the nurses' station the next morning. She'd always desired a more intimate relationship with Derek. Never in her wildest dreams did she think their union would be so perfect. And so devastating. He was on her mind throughout the night.

Shelia tossed her purse on the counter and slumped in to the nearest chair.

"What's wrong?" Miranda asked. "You look as if you haven't slept in a week, maybe two."

"Long night."

"I can see that. I hope you had a good time." Miranda turned her chair to face her. Since Miranda met and fell in love with her husband, her friend regularly suggested Shelia should start dating again.

When Shelia nodded then shook her head no, Miranda asked, "Guy trouble?"

Shelia rested her elbows on the desk then placed her head in her hands. "Guy trouble is an understatement." Her words were muffled against her arm. After taking a deep breath Shelia raised her head and turned toward her friend. "He's someone I've known forever. His mother and daughter have been playing matchmaker."

"He has a girl?"

"She's so cute and smart. I've liked her and her fairies from the start."

Miranda raised one slender brow. "You know girlfriend you're not making any sense."

"Oh, Miranda. I blew it last night. I said I love you after we had great sex," she whispered in case anyone was within hearing distance. "But it wasn't I love you because we had sex. Even though we did. I know that's how he interrupted it because he didn't move, didn't say a word." Shelia's words rushed out. She'd hoped by telling her friend she could sort through her tangled feelings. Only she gained no comfort from sharing.

"I finally opened my heart up and it has to be to a guy who runs from any words of love."

"I'm sorry honey." Miranda walked over and placed a hand on her shoulder.

Shelia was relieved when a patient light flashed and she could focus on the care of others and push her personal feelings aside.

However, Derek's impersonal kiss on the check before he left was the most frustrating part of the evening. A simple kiss. She'd never forget the departing image of Derek and his final goodbye.

~ * ~

After work Shelia stopped at the hardware store and purchased some bulbs and flower seeds. Digging in the soil was the best therapy for her. Thoughts of Derek and her fretful night were on her mind all day. The warm weather provided the perfect opportunity for her to work in the flowerbeds in her backyard. Planting spring bulbs gave her something to focus on other than Derek.

The moment the words 'I love you' slipped from her lips, Shelia could feel him pull away from her. Both physically and mentally. He left so abruptly. She hadn't seen or heard from him since he left last night. What a fool she'd been. Why did she think making love would have changed anything between them.

With the tiny hand shovel she rapidly dug into the soft soil. Once there were several holes dug, she opened the bag of gladiolas bulbs. After placing a bulb in each spot she covered them with dirt and compost.

Shelia stood up once the planting was finished. Scanning the backyard, she wished there were three times as many bulbs to plant. The stillness unnerved her. Derek and Mattie had become a major part of her life and now they were gone. He'd said from the start he wasn't interested in a lasting relationship. Derek was afraid of commitment and her words of love drove him away.

Frustrated, Shelia stripped off her gloves and tossed them into the white five-gallon bucket beside her. Then she picked up the small shovel and likewise set it in the pail of yard tools. With all the supplies secured she returned the bucket to the garden shed.

Rubbing her hands together, Shelia quickened her pace to the house. A shower to remove the dirt was in order.

The doorbell rang when she was halfway to the bathroom. She hurried to the front door to stop the continuous chime. Swinging the door open, Shelia froze.

Derek and Mattie stood on the porch both holding a bouquet of flowers. Bewildered, Shelia starred at them.

"Dad, she's not talking again. Maybe she's allergic to flowers," Mattie said.

Derek shook his head. "She's not allergic to flowers. Good morning, Shelia." He said as his gaze never wavered from her face. "Can we come in?"

"Sure." She stepped aside then closed the door once they were in the living room.

Derek sat beside Shelia and Mattie on the couch. "We'd like to talk to you."

"Do I give her the flowers now?" Mattie held the bouquet out then pulled the flowers against her chest.

Placing his hand on his daughter's back, Derek silenced her question. "Shelia, we've known each other most of our lives. You had always been my best friend. Even when you hit me with the baseball I knew you were someone to be reckoned with. Someone I'd never be able to forget."

Mattie leaned toward her father and whispered, "You were going to kneel."

With her prompting Derek got down on one knee then Mattie mimicked her father.

"Shelia, will you marry us?" Derek asked then handed her his flowers.

"Me too. Would you marry me too?" Mattie asked. "Dad forgot to say we love you."

Emotion tightened the back of Shelia's throat. Her gaze fixed on Derek's. "You left yesterday when I said I love you. You didn't say…anything."

"I'm sorry." He stood up then sat beside her again. His fingers gently stroked her cheek.

"This doesn't look very good," Mattie whispered to her fairies in her purse. She stood in front of Shelia. Her eyes looked large and edged with worry.

He reached out for Shelia's hand. "I needed to talk to Mattie before I said anything to you. Before I told you I love you." Holding out his hand for Mattie's, he pulled her on his lap. "Mattie and I are a package deal. I had to make sure she was alright with this change in our lives." He ruffled his daughter's hair then returned his gaze to Shelia.

"And what did Mattie say?" Shelia studied Mattie's face.

Her eyes sparkled. "Yes, yes!" With the flowers still in her hand, Mattie raised her hands.

Shelia wrapped her arms around Mattie, "I love you, too. I'd love to be part of your family."

Derek pulled Shelia and his daughter into a hug. Content with her new family, Shelia closed her eyes and sighed.

A light shown from Mattie's purse then two fairies flew out. They looked down at Mattie and her family and smiled.

"I told you this was an easy case," Kendra straightened her skirt.

Cara placed her hands on her hips and her wings fluttered faster. "You told me… Never mind." She waved her hand in the air. Glancing fondly at Mattie, Cara's eyes misted.

"We did it." Kendra quickly turned away. "I'm going to miss her."

Cara blinked to keep the tears from falling. "I'll miss her too. We've been with Mattie for a long time. She's my favorite child but she doesn't need us any longer."

"I'm sure our new case will be interesting," Kendra tried to reassure her. Together the two fairies flew away unnoticed.

No More Poodle Skirts
Genie Gabriel

Chapter One

Life seemed much simpler when all a girl had to worry about was keeping her bobby socks and the pompom on her poodle skirt a brilliant white. Daphne Madison wiggled and gyrated into panty hose that seemed determined to twist around her like a boa constrictor squeezing its prey.

A modern woman was expected to have it all—a husband, a family, a career—with never a wrinkle in her face or her confidence.

Daphne zipped up her dress and drew a shaky breath as she stared at herself in the mirror. The form-fitting pink dress wasn't as comfortable as her skirts, and the high heels shoved her feet down into the pointy toes.

I can do this, Daphne reassured herself. She hadn't even been born in the fifties, but it seemed like such an innocent time. If she could pretend to live in that time, surely she could live in the current millennium.

Something doesn't seem just right, she thought, as she fastened a strand of pearls around her neck. However, she refused to wear the short skirts she had seen on television programs. The pencil thin skirt that ended just above her knees was as daring as she would go.

She slid her arms into the pink jacket that matched her dress and considered herself once again. Something still seemed amiss. She settled a pink pillbox hat borrowed from her sister on top of her smooth blond hair. *Better.*

White gloves restored her confidence even more.

With another deep breath, Daphne swept down the stairs to garner the reaction of her family. She knew her adult son, Ryan, would be of little help but to offer a gourmet breakfast gleaned from the latest cooking show on TV. A meal Daphne knew her jittery nerves wouldn't tolerate.

Her sister wouldn't be stirring yet, but Linda would be organizing the house for the day. She was the mother of Daphne's daughter's husband. Did that make her and Daphne sisters-in-law? No, that wasn't quite right, and thinking about it made her brain hurt.

She gave her head a slight shake. It didn't really matter. Linda was quite practical and had motivated Daphne out of her fantasy life. She would know if Daphne was dressed appropriately for her job interview.

"So what do you think?" Daphne turned slowly as she entered the kitchen.

Her son glanced up from the television long enough to mumble a good morning. Linda considered her thoughtfully. "Very elegant. Where's your interview?"

"The bank is hiring for a teller."

"Ah." Linda nodded. "Perhaps take off the hat and gloves…"

Panic niggled in Daphne's stomach. The two accessories that had restored at least a smidgen of her self-confidence.

Linda smiled when she noticed Daphne's obvious distress. "Well, maybe just take off the gloves to shake hands with the interview committee."

Daphne swallowed. Perhaps she could manage that.

"Are you going to eat breakfast before you go?" Linda asked.

"I-I really couldn't." Daphne laid a hand over her belly. "Already full of butterflies."

Linda's smile grew wider. "You're beautiful and smart, Daphne. I'm sure you'll knock 'em dead."

Horror mixed with the butterflies in Daphne's stomach at the thought of her interview committee keeling over dead when she stepped into the room.

"It's just an expression." Linda patted Daphne's hand. "Try to relax and let them see how much of an asset you would be to their bank."

With a shaky nod, Daphne faced the long, long journey down the hallway and through the front door, out into a world she really wasn't sure she wanted to live in.

~ * ~

Madelaine Ainsworth shook out a fresh white, button-down shirt from the closet she shared with her husband of almost thirty years and slipped it on over a T-shirt and a pair of suspendered overalls, size sixteen tall.

Today she was starting a new art project: a mural on the outside wall of the newly constructed homeless shelter on the outskirts of Watermark, Oregon. In spite of objections of the mayor and city council, Father Jacobs and a group of Watermark's citizens had transformed a tangle of blackberry bushes into a haven for the men, women and children who found themselves with only a bridge or a tattered tent for shelter.

By the time May Day rolled around and her project was completed, the shirt would share the colors of the mural. Maddie settled a raffia straw hat over her silver-gray curls and tucked two of her favorite paintbrushes in the band.

Then she stepped lightly down the stone staircase of their modern-day castle to Horace's basement workshop. Long plank tables crisscrossed the cavernous room, covered with metal tubing, engines, wire, and lights—a stockpile of mechanical creations in various stages of completion.

A bespectacled man with silvery hair standing in startled spikes around a balding pate stared at what appeared to be a fire hydrant. Then it shimmered and disappeared.

Maddie blinked. "Horace, is it safe?"

Brilliant though her husband was, sometimes his inventions didn't work quite as planned the first few tries.

Horace lifted his head at the sound of her voice, and Maddie's heart melted a bit, as it always did when she looked at her husband. No matter their age, she still remembered Horace as he was the day she met him. Standing alone at a college fraternity party, shifting from foot to foot and glancing around the room, the only sober and clean-shaven person among a houseful of determined college partiers.

"I'm going to start the mural at the homeless shelter," Maddie said. "Don't forget to eat lunch."

Horace smiled broader and waved a wrench at her as she blew a kiss and turned to go back up the stairs. She saw a flash of red out of the corner of her eye and, once more, the fire hydrant sat in front of Horace.

With a shrug, Maddie continued up the stairs. She would ask Horace what project he was working on when she got home for dinner tonight.

As she reached the top of the stairs, the aroma of apples and cinnamon enticed her in a detour to the kitchen. Her nephew, Ryan, was taking a pan of muffins out of the oven.

"Would you taste these for me, Aunt Mads? I'm not sure there's enough honey in them."

How could she refuse? After a number of bumps in his love life, her nephew had become addicted to cooking shows, much to the delight of the rest of the family.

"The honey seems perfect, but perhaps a bit too much apple brandy," Maddie glanced at the half empty brandy bottle on the counter as she swallowed a bite of muffin.

"It wasn't a full bottle before I started. I think Mother and her date last night might have sampled it."

"Well, I'm glad Daphne is dating again. Your father passed on a long time ago. She needs some fun in her life. Did she go to her job interview this morning?"

"She might have been a bit overdressed. Wore pearls, gloves and a hat."

Maddie frowned. "Employers don't seem to appreciate elegance any more. Well, I'm off to the shelter. Probably won't be back before dinner. Would you make sure your uncle Horace has lunch? You know how he forgets everything else when he's working on a project. And thanks for breakfast—it's muffi-licious."

In the garages, Maddie considered the array of classic vehicles she not only collected, but drove on a regular basis. Pretty much one from each decade since cars had been manufactured, including the late forties Woody station wagon she decided to drive this morning. She spread a plastic tarp in the back and loaded her painting supplies.

The new homeless shelter was only a short distance from Maddie's castle. Of course, in a town as small as Watermark, nothing was very far away.

Father Jacobs was playing basketball with several of the men staying at the shelter when Maddie arrived. In a sweaty T-shirt and game shorts, he looked as lean and muscular as a man half his age. However, the deep lines bracketing his broad smile revealed harsher choices earlier in his life, and his eyes sometimes reflected a hard-won wisdom.

For the most part, Maddie let him keep the secrets of his past. Heaven knew she didn't want her earlier exploits dissected and examined for any whiff of wrongdoing. She was a firm believer in accepting people for their current actions and not judging mistakes made earlier in their lives.

The priest pulled on a sweatshirt, then joined Maddie in surveying the wall where the mural would be painted.

"By the way, some of the families staying at the shelter want to help with the mural. Their way of contributing and saying thanks for all you do here."

No! Claustrophobia coursed through Maddie's veins and pooled in her belly. She didn't want "help." Didn't want someone else messing with her design and leaving sloppy strokes for her to clean up. She wanted this mural to be perfect. To show the mayor and the snooty city council a person didn't need a blue-blood pedigree to be important. "I prefer to work alone, Father."

A slight frown flitted across Father Jacobs' brow before his usual

5

benign smile settled into place. "I'm sure we can work out an arrangement everyone will be happy with."

"Father Jacobs! Father Jacobs!" Half a dozen children swarmed around the priest. "Is it time to start painting?"

Stair-stepped in ages from four to ten—plus one sullen teenager—their eager faces shone up at the priest.

Father Jacobs looked at Maddie with a question in his eyes. She could say no and destroy the enthusiasm of the children. The good father was counting on her soft heart the win this battle and they both knew it.

With a curt nod of her head, Maddie agreed.

The priest's smile widened. "I want you all to meet Madelaine Ainsworth, our artist and your new instructor. Miss Maddie will be showing you the process involved in painting a mural."

Maddie forced a smile as the children shifted their attention to her.

"Well." Maddie cleared her throat and reminded herself to be nice. "Thank you all for offering to help. How many of you have painted a picture?"

Hands went up as the children nodded their heads and said "I have, I have."

"That's good. You have the basics. However, painting a mural outside has some different steps because we want this to last a long time. So we have to prepare the wall before we paint it and we'll put a special sealer on it when we're finished. We'll also do the actual painting differently than you've done when you painted a picture."

After a slight pause, she said, "Today, we're going to clean the wall."

Disappointment showed in most of the children's faces.

"Don't we get to paint?" One of them asked.

"We have to make sure the wall is really clean and then let it dry before we can start to paint," Maddie said.

Father Jacobs dragged two hoses with nozzles around to the side of the shelter. He also brought several stiff-bristled brooms and buckets to fill with soapy water.

"I'll hose from one side and—what's your name, young man?"

Maddie addressed the teenager.

"Devon."

"And Devon will start on the other side. Once we've sprayed the wall, the rest of you can start scrubbing." Maddie passed out the brooms, but didn't have enough for everyone.

"I want to help too." A little red-haired boy scowled.

"How about if you help me with the hose?" Maddie said.

" 'kay." His grin returned in an instant.

"What's your name—"

The little boy clamped down on the sprayer handle.

Suddenly drenched with icy cold water, Maddie's mouth flopped open and closed like the fish she had caught accidentally on her one and only fishing trip. The poor creature flopped around on the ground and gasped for water so terribly that Maddie threw it back in the lake. Like she was now gasping for breath, too stunned by the cold water to even demand the child turn it off.

Like waves rolling toward the beach, smothered giggles rippled through the children.

"The water should be sprayed on the wall, not a person." As Father Jacobs spoke, the water stopped, as miraculous as the parting of the Red Sea, to Maddie's way of thinking.

Maddie drew in a deep breath. "Thank you, Father."

She blinked and wiped water out of her eyes, so now she could see the wide-eyed, uh-oh stares of the children.

"Do we still get to help with the picture, Miz Maddie?" one of the kids asked.

The little red-haired imp was peeking out from behind a taller red-haired girl. His sister, Maddie figured. She pulled her soaked shirt away from her body and emptied a puddle of water out of her hat. If this was the first day, what would the rest of this project bring?

"I've never been on the receiving end of a ceremonial christening for a new project. I suppose I should thank our little red-haired friend for a new experience."

As a group, the children exhaled in relief, and their normal level of kinetic energy resumed.

"I'll go find you a dry shirt," a little boy with glasses said. "Jonathan can use my brush to scrub the wall."

"Thank you. And I don't know your name either."

"Keller Ashton." The little boy solemnly held out his hand and Maddie shook it. "I'm sorry Jonathan got you wet. He doesn't have all his manners yet."

"I'm teaching him." The red-haired girl whom Maddie assumed to be Jonathan's sister braced her hands on her slender hips. "He's just precarious."

Maddie frowned for a moment. "Ah. I think you mean precocious."

"That too. Daddy says he'll grow out of it, but I'm not so sure." Concern wrinkled the little girl's brow.

"And what's your name?" Maddie asked.

"Jasmine," the little girl answered. "Like the princess."

"Uh-uh. Your name is Jennifer. Your dad said so," Keller stated.

"I want to be Jasmine."

"You can't just change your name."

"Can too."

"Can not."

"How about if we use both Jennifer and Jasmine, and call you J-J for short?" Maddie suggested.

J-J shot a "so there" look at the little boy, who ignored her and dashed inside. He returned in record time and handed a wadded up shirt—one of his own—to Maddie. "It was the only one I could find."

Maddie held the little boy's shirt up to her full-bosomed body. As snickers started among the children again and Keller's lower lip began to tremble, Maddie tossed the little shirt around her neck and tied the arms in front like a scarf. "Thank you. Now, let's see how clean we can get this wall, shall we?"

By lunchtime, the wall shone white and clean. However, enthusiastic scrubbing with the buckets of water had drenched all the kids. They shivered as the April sunshine disappeared behind clouds rolling across the sky.

Father Jacobs shepherded the children inside, where they faced the challenge of finding a dry change of clothing among their meager wardrobes. "Sorry. The city inspector hasn't approved the plumbing for the laundry room yet."

With a frown, Maddie said, "Well, you'll all need white shirts for painting any way."

"Why is that?"

"It just is," Maddie stated. "I always start a new project with a new white shirt. I need your sizes."

"I want to be a superhero," Jonathan said. "No girl stuff."

"Black's the only cool color for a T-shirt," the teenager stated.

"Father Jacobs, are you up for a shopping trip?" Maddie asked.

"Well, I actually have a lot to do here..."

Maddie focused a laser stare on the man who had blackmailed her into this situation, daring him to come up with an excuse she could shred.

"However, all that can wait." Father Jacobs fixed a smile on his face. "We'll need permission from your parents, and I'll fetch the van."

As the children climbed into the van, Maddie said sotto voce, "Paybacks are hell, eh, Father?"

~ * ~

Maddie drove home much slower than usual that evening— staying close to the posted speed rather than her usual breakneck pace. Her experiences with the children today had tugged at her heart with sadness yet also brought moments of joy. She believed no one should be forced out of their home, especially children. Yet these kids created fun in something as simple as washing a building.

The day made Maddie appreciate her many blessings even more. She smiled as she crossed the bridge leading up to the gray stone castle she and Horace had built when her sister and her two small children came to live with them.

As Madelaine parked the old Woody station wagon in the garage, a hologram of Horace appeared, saying, "Welcome home, my dear. I missed you terribly."

Never mind that he didn't always remember what day or even what year it was. He always knew when Maddie was gone from their home, and his holographic greeting made her smile.

After Maddie changed clothes, she went to the dining room and selected a drink from the espresso machine Horace had modified for them. With a steaming cup of caramel caffe latte in hand, she asked her sister, "How did your interview go today, Daphne?"

Though Daphne no longer wore her hat and gloves, a string of pearls still shone with a lustrous glow above the scooped neckline of a classically form-fitting pink dress. "I don't think they liked me. They thought I didn't see them exchanging eye rolls, but I was just too polite to say anything."

"Well, you're a very smart and attractive woman." Maddie patted her sister's hand. "You'll find the perfect job."

"I think it's easier being crazy. People don't expect as much from you."

An ache for her sister settled in Maddie's chest. After twenty years of living in the shelter of a more innocent era, Daphne was receiving a crash course in the current and sometimes insensitive culture.

As Maddie contemplated a way to ease Daphne's transition back to the "real" world, the perfect solution occurred to her. "Why don't you help me with the mural at the homeless shelter?"

"I'm not an artist."

"Neither are the half dozen children helping me." Maddie told Daphne how Father Jacobs used emotional blackmail to gain her acceptance of helpers, which led to the hose incident and their shopping excursion for shirts to wear while painting.

"I'm not sure how good I am with children." A vee of doubt settled between Daphne's brows. "You and Horace raised Ryan and Rissa."

"Think about it. I'll be leaving about seven tomorrow morning."

~ * ~

Daphne retired to her rooms with Maddie's suggestion replaying over and over in her mind. She had been sheltered all her life. First by her family, then by her husband and, after his death, once again by her family. Being independent scared her. She had never been bold like Maddie. Or driven by a calling, like Horace was to invent mysterious machines.

However, change was all around her, and Daphne was finally questioning how she had lived her life. Her son, Ryan, had traded his playboy lifestyle for an interest in cooking. Her daughter was married and traveled wherever her husband's military assignments took them. Ironically, that led to expanding their household to include Ian's mother, who was adapting to the loss of her own husband.

In addition, one of Maddie's misadventures brought reformed kidnapper, David, to live in the castle.Then there was the elfenchaun, Dorinda, who had been whisked from Ireland of the mid-eighteen-hundreds in Horace's time machine to save her life. If she could adapt her life from over a century and a half ago to modern times, surely Daphne could move forward a few decades.

Sometimes she was tempted to sneak away to the time machine and truly experience the era of poodle skirts and teased hair. However, she hadn't actually lived in that time, so perhaps she would discover it wasn't so innocent after all.

And I would miss my family terribly, Daphne thought. *Linda is right. I need to put away my poodle skirt and join the modern world.*

Daphne took a deep breath. In the morning when Maddie went to paint the mural at the homeless shelter, she would be ready to go.

~ * ~

When Maddie came downstairs the next morning, Daphne was sitting in the kitchen with her hands folded in her lap.

"Am I dressed appropriately?" Daphne indicated her white button-down shirt over a pink T-shirt and Capri slacks. "I wasn't sure..."

Maddie smiled widely. "As long as you don't mind getting paint on what you're wearing."

She hadn't really done anything sisterly with Daphne for almost twenty years. During the time Daphne was caught in her time warp of grieving, Maddie's role was more like a mother or a caretaker. Now she was looking forward to having some fun—and having another adult she could commiserate with about her helpers.

When Maddie and Daphne arrived at the shelter, they gathered with the children next to the scrubbed wall. "Today we're going to paint the entire side of the building with white primer."

Disappointment once again claimed the children's faces, as well as the parents who had gathered to watch the first brush strokes of this project.

"Why aren't we painting pictures today?"

Ah, there's that guilt again. Maddie put a hand over her heart. She sidestepped the question by asking, "Would you like to see the picture we'll be painting?"

The eagerness of the children returned in an instant, and Maddie dug her rough sketch out to show them.

"That's only one house," J-J said. "Daddy said one day we'll have our own house again."

Others chimed in. "We want our own houses too."

There goes my perfect design, Maddie thought. "How about a street with houses and you can each paint your own?"

"I don't want no flowers or picket fences." The teenager crossed his arms and scowled.

"Any flowers," Maddie automatically corrected.

"Whatever."

"Maybe after the primer is done, the children can draw small versions of their houses and color them in so we know what colors of paint to get," Daphne said.

"Excellent suggestion." Maddie smiled at her sister. "Everyone, this is my sister, Daphne, who will be helping us with this project."

"Yeah!" Excitement sparkled in the children's eyes.

And Daphne was worried she wouldn't do well with children, Maddie thought. *She's a natural.*

The teenaged boy regarded Daphne with his usual insolence.

12

"Like the dumb blonde with that cartoon dog?"

Well, except for one young man needing an attitude adjustment. Madelaine bristled. "Young man, this is my sister and you will treat her with respect. Any comments you make to her, I will take personally. Do I make myself clear?"

"Oh, Maddie, he's just being a teenager," Daphne said. "And I need to handle these situations by myself. You've taken care of me far too long. I'm sure we'll get along just fine."

While Daphne smiled at the teenager, Maddie shot a gaze filled with daggers at him over Daphne's shoulder.

"Yes, ma'am."

"There. See?" Daphne's smile broadened. "But I would like to know everyone's name. Maybe we can put those on the T-shirts so I remember?"

The kids smiled and nodded in agreement.

"Devon and I will bring the paint from the Woody." Maddie stared directly at the teenager.

When they walked around the building, Devon said, "I got the message not to give your sister any crap."

"Just making myself clear. Besides, you're stronger than any of the younger kids. Figured you could carry more buckets of paint."

The kid almost grinned. What teenaged boy didn't like to show off his developing muscles? "Take that large bucket, please, while I grab the brushes."

As Maddie bent to gather the brushes, a voice asked, "Whatcha doing?"

"Getting the paint brushes," Maddie repeated, thinking the kid was yanking her chain. But as she straightened and turned around, Devon had already disappeared around the side of the building.

No one else was around, except a black and white Cocker Spaniel with tangled fur that hid his eyes and dusted the ground around his feet.

Chapter Two

"Where did you come from, little fella?"

"The woods a ways down the road. Sometimes the nice man here gives me food."

Maddie stared at the little dog. "Did you just talk to me?"

"I try to talk to a lot of humans. Most of them ignore me. Or kick me."

Maddie frowned.

"I'm pretty fast, though. I usually get out of the way before their boot connects with any ribs."

"Don't you have a family?"

"Nah."

"Ever?" Maddie asked.

"Not for a very long time."

Sadness filled Maddie. "That's not right."

"That's the way it is."

"It's still not right. I could take you to the animal shelter—"

"No way." The little dog backed away from her. "Dogs go there and don't come back."

"Most of the time they find new homes."

"I'll take my chances in the woods." The little dog turned and started to run, but tripped and tumbled.

"Are you alright?" Maddie dropped the paintbrushes on the seat and trotted to the little dog.

"Yeah, all this hair tangles in my feet sometimes, and things are kinda blurry if I don't remember to squint my eyes."

"Why don't you come home with me?"

"Um, thanks, but—"

"Miz Maddie, we're waiting for the paintbrushes." The teenaged boy jogged back around the building. "Hey, I've seen that mutt before."

The dog picked himself up and ran back toward the woods.

"And I hope you're not one of the people who kicks at him." Maddie drew herself up to her full six feet in height and glowered at the teenager.

"Uh, that wouldn't be cool, would it?"

"No, it would not," Maddie stated.

"Is he another one of your relatives?" the kid asked.

"I believe he might become one."

"So don't mess with him either, right?"

"You learn quick," Maddie said.

"Quickly," the boy said.

"Yes." Maddie smiled. "Let's get that wall primed."

~ * ~

Daphne chatted all the way home that evening, excited to be doing something useful and also about meeting an attractive man who seemed interested in her. "J-J and Jonathan's dad is handsome, don't you think?"

"Not in the same league as my Horace, but attractive enough."

The two women laughed.

"He seemed interested in me, didn't he?" Daphne asked.

"The gaping mouth and the way he clung to your hand when he introduced himself seemed to indicate that."

"Do you think I'm too old for him?"

"He looks about the same age. I'm guessing he didn't have J-J and Jonathan until late in life. Do you want me to find out—"

"Oh, no! I don't want him to think I'm too interested." Daphne giggled. "But I hope he doesn't wait too long to ask me out."

As a dreamy look drifted across her sister's face, Maddie's mind returned to the little black and white dog. Devon was right. She had

15

pretty much decided the dog should become part of the family. She would talk to Horace about it later tonight.

After dinner, Maddie ventured down to Horace's workshop.

"You missed dinner." She set a plate of food on a side table that was least cluttered with gadgets.

"Not there," Horace cautioned.

Maddie gasped as the plate disappeared. "What happened?"

"The cloaking device works!" Horace clapped his hands together like a delighted child.

"You're working on a cloaking device? What happened to the jet-pack?"

Horace looked all around the room, then leaned close to Maddie and whispered, "I'll get back to the jet-pack later. More important is hiding my time machine from the military. They want it."

"How do you know this?"

"McGregor of Scotland Yard told me."

Though her niece, Rissa, had been married to Ian McGregor for over a year, Horace still referred to her husband as "McGregor of Scotland Yard." Ian wasn't associated with Scotland Yard, though he was an MP in the military.

"Why don't you just park the time machine in a different year?"

"Too dangerous. You know how many times it's ended up where we didn't intend."

When Maddie's plane had been skyjacked by inept terrorists several months ago, Horace was determined to rescue her before the incident happened. So he and his cousin who worked for NASA had built a time machine out of a fire hydrant-shaped playhouse.

However, the rescue didn't go quite as planned. First the neighbor girl's dog became trapped inside and spun back in time to Ireland. Then two bad faeries snuck inside, accidentally hit the emergency eject button, and were currently cooling their wings in a black hole.

When Horace returned to retrieve the little dog, he encountered an elfenchaun who was being mobbed. He saved Dorinda's life by bringing her back to the future, and she had chosen to stay and live with them.

"I see what you mean," Maddie said. "Perhaps a cloaking device is the best plan. Have you tried it on the time machine yet?"

Horace shook his head. "Only on smaller items. Still needs some tweaking to hide the time machine."

"How do you make things reappear?" Maddie asked. "Your dinner might be cold by now."

Horace flipped a toggle switch and the plate reappeared. "Mmm. I am hungry. Thank you, my dear."

For a while, Maddie simply gazed fondly at her husband as he ate. Then she remembered the other part of her mission in coming to his workshop. "What do you think of having a dog?"

"Whatever you want, Maddie, you know that."

"But I want you to love him too."

"So he's already stolen your heart. Where did you find this dog and what's his name?"

"He was at the homeless shelter, and I forgot to ask his name."

"Was he lost?"

Maddie shook her head. "He said he didn't have a home."

"He talked to you?"

"Well, not like you and I are talking. It was like he sent me his thoughts."

"Fascinating," Horace said. "I've heard of others who communicate with animals. You have such a kind heart, they would trust you instinctively."

"Thank you." Maddie laid a hand on Horace's. "What a nice thing to say."

Horace almost blushed. "So when will our new family member arrive?"

"I'll have to convince him that's what he wants to do."

With a chuckle, Horace said, "That shouldn't take long."

~ * ~

Daphne smiled to herself as she prepared for bed that evening.

Sitting in the chair in front of her vanity, she started to brush her hair, and to remember...

I knew I was going to marry Charlie from the time I was in the first grade.

I showed up at school feeling little and overwhelmed, and drew the attention of the class bully. Charlie told him to leave me alone.

"Who's gonna make me?"

Charlie grabbed the kid by the shirt and lifted him off his feet.

"Hey, it was all in fun. I didn't know she was your girlfriend."

Charlie glanced over at me and said, "Not just my girlfriend. The girl I'm going to marry some day."

And I knew it was true.

Daphne never thought she would meet another man who stirred her like Charlie did. Until today when she met Brenner, J-J and Jonathan's dad.

She laid the brush on the vanity, stood up and took off her robe. Maybe the changes in her life would be positive ones after all.

~ * ~

Both Maddie and Daphne were eager to return to the homeless shelter the next day. Daphne to see what the children had drawn for their houses—and perhaps see the redheads' father—and Maddie to convince the little Cocker Spaniel he wanted to come home to the castle.

However, when they arrived, their eagerness turned to dismay. The wall which had been carefully cleaned and primed with white paint was now covered with splatters of raw egg.

The entire wall would have to be cleaned again and the paint might need to be touched up, which would put them a day or two behind schedule.

"I'm sorry," Father Jacobs said. "We haven't had any mischief for awhile and I've become lax about security."

"I'm sure Horace could come up with some surveillance equipment."

"We don't have the money—"

"I didn't say it would cost anything, did I?"

"You give so much already. I don't expect you meet every need of the shelter."

"I have so much. Why is that, Father?" Maddie asked. "Why do some of us have so much and others have very little?"

"Perhaps that is the experience we choose when we came to this place."

"Sometimes I feel guilty."

"For caring? For giving of your time and talents and resources?"

"But I have a castle while these people have no home at all."

"Being homeless was a very enlightening experience for me," Father Jacobs said. "I learned compassion and gratitude, to say nothing of humbleness. And now I am better able to serve those in a similar situation."

"I feel I should do more."

"How many people live in your castle, Maddie?"

Maddie frowned. "What does that have to do with having much or little?"

"Humor me for a moment."

"Well, Horace and me. My sister and her two adult children—at least until Rissa got married. Then Ian's mother came to stay—we'd be lost without her organizational skills. Then there's David, the reformed kidnapper, and Dorinda from Ireland."

"Did you have to let any of those people live in your house?"

"They're family. Or they needed a place to stay. Besides, they've added so much to our household."

"But did you have to let them stay with you? Not many people open their homes to strangers or to someone who kidnaps them."

"There were extenuating circumstances."

Father Jacobs chuckled. "I'm not trying to make you defensive, Maddie. I'm trying to make you see what wonderful things you've done. You've shared your abundance generously. You don't need to feel guilty for what you have."

A frown flickered over Maddie's brow. "I hadn't thought of it that way."

"Don't let guilt take away the pleasure of what you have. Let others carry some of the burden. It will make them feel better too."

~ * ~

While Miz Maddie was on the phone talking to someone about the mess on the wall, Keller watched Miss Daphne and J-J's dad acting all mushy toward each other. Maybe J-J and Jonathan would have a new mom soon and a house. He used to have two parents and a house. Until his mom got sick and his dad left. Then they had to move out of their house. Now there were just his mom and him. Sometimes they had a place to stay and sometimes they didn't.

If his mom got sick again and went to the hospital, he would probably go to foster care. He didn't like that. What if his mom went to the hospital and didn't come back?

His mom hadn't been feeling good the last few days. She didn't say anything, but Keller could tell by how quiet she was, and how she grimaced with pain when she thought he didn't see.

He didn't want to be jealous of J-J and Jonathan. They were his friends and he wanted them to be happy. But couldn't he be happy too?

So while the others were showing Miss Daphne the drawings of their houses, Keller paused in the chapel room of the shelter. He knelt in front of the altar as he had seen Father Jacobs do and whispered, "Please, God. If I can't have both a dad and a house, can my mom and I at least have a house where Mom can get well. Thank you. Amen."

Then he joined the cluster of children gathered around Miss Daphne to show the pictures of their houses. Miz Maddie had drawn a street on a roll of paper and the children were now placing their houses along the street. Keller considered possible locations for his house. Next to a tree so he could climb up high and see all around? Or close to a hydrant to see fire engines up close? Or maybe beside a park so he could play any time he wanted to?

~ * ~

Again the next day, Maddie hoped to see the little dog at the shelter, but he didn't make an appearance. So while the children and Daphne ate lunch, Maddie set out toward the woods.

"Where are you going, Miz Maddie?" The teenaged boy followed her out of the building.

She considered him for a moment, wondering if he would frighten the little dog farther away. Then decided to give the boy a chance to prove himself. "To look for the little black and white dog."

A odd look crossed Devon's face, then he took the lead on the narrow trail into the woods. "I've seen him sometimes in a tangle of blackberry bushes about a half mile into these trees."

They walked in silence for a time.

"What are you going to do if we find him?" The kid asked.

"**When** we find him, I'm going to convince him he wants to come home with me."

"Lucky dog," Devon muttered.

A short distance later, the kid slowed down. "It's right up ahead. Maybe you should go first so I don't scare him."

Maddie frowned at Devon and he half-shrugged in apology.

"Hey, my doggie friend!" Maddie called. "Will you come out and see me?"

Maddie continued to talk to the dog as she walked slowly around the berry bushes. "I don't see him."

"Wait. I think I do." The kid squatted down. "See? About ten feet into those bushes. There's something black and white. Come on, little fella, growl at me or something."

"Is he moving?" Maddie asked. "What if he's hurt?"

"I'll crawl in and see."

"Be careful."

With a slight smile, Devon got down on his hands and knees and crawled slowly toward the black and white object he had seen.

"Can you see if he's hurt?" Maddie stood on her toes and tried in vain to see the little dog.

"Almost there." The kid's voice sounded muffled as he crawled further into the tangle of bushes.

The silence pulsed worry through Maddie's veins until Devon called out. "He's alive."

"Thank goodness! Can you get him out of there?"

"I'll put him on my jacket and use that as a kind of stretcher to pull him out."

After what seemed like a dog's age, Devon emerged backwards, dragging his coat with its precious cargo.

"He doesn't look good," Devon commented.

Maddie had to agree. The little dog lay so still, emitting an occasional whimper. Dried blood discolored one of his front legs. "I'm going to take him to the vet."

Don't let them put me to sleep!

Maddie touched the little guy's head. "You tell me what you want when we get there."

Devon volunteered to go with Maddie and sit in the back seat beside the little dog.

When they arrived at the clinic, the receptionist began asking questions Maddie had no idea to answer. "What's the dog's name?"

Mr. Razzles.

"Mr. Razzles," Maddie repeated.

"Date of birth?" the receptionist asked.

Maddie relayed what Razzles told her, and did the same with the rest of the questions. Until she asked when his last vaccinations were.

I don't like shots, Razzles said.

"I don't want you to get sick," Maddie responded.

"Pardon me?" the receptionist asked.

Maddie faked a smile. "He's been living on his own and I don't have much information about him."

One of the receptionist's eyebrows lifted. "Do you want to just leave him?"

A horrified look echoed the distress in Maddie's heart at the thought of abandoning the little dog. "I'll be paying his expenses, if that's what you're asking, and he'll be coming home with me."

"Not everyone is as generous and kind as you. Mr. Razzles could have some serious injuries."

"He'll be coming home with me," Maddie repeated.

The receptionist smiled. "He's a lucky dog."

~ * ~

"Six stitches in his right front leg, possible bruised kidneys—probably from being kicked—as well as being dehydrated and malnourished," Maddie announced to her family that evening as they gathered around to meet their newest member. "The vet staff also gave him a hair cut while they checked for injuries."

"He said he's cold." Dorinda brought a blanket for the little dog.

"He talks to you too?" Maddie wasn't sure whether to be delighted or jealous.

"It's not unusual for elfenchauns to communicate with our friends in the animal kingdom." Dorinda smiled shyly. Though she had been in this century a number of months, she still retained a refreshing naiveté about this modern world.

She touched the gash on his leg, then frowned.

"What's wrong?" Ryan asked.

"I was hoping The Touch would return," Dorinda said. "I lost it when I came to this land."

"What's The Touch?" Maddie asked.

"Elfenchauns in old Ireland were able to heal just by touching a wound. I was hoping to help our canine friend."

"I'm sure he's comforted just by your presence," Maddie said.

"You're very kind," Dorinda said. "May I be excused? I think I'll lie down for awhile."

After she left the room, Maddie said, "Her adjustment to this world hasn't always been easy."

"I don't like to see Dorinda sad." Ryan had seemed instantly smitten by the delicate creature when she had arrived with severe injuries from an angry mob in old Ireland. "Perhaps I'll make her a special Irish drink to cheer her homesickness."

Ryan also left the room, leaving Maddie and Horace alone with the dog. "Mr. Razzles also said something about his vision being blurry.

23

He might need glasses. Do you think you could fix up a pair for him?"

"Hmmm." Horace considered the now sleeping dog. "I'll see what I can do."

Chapter Three

After the vandalism at the shelter, Maddie tried to arrive early to be sure all was well before the children came outside to paint. This morning, she found the teenager Devon slumped against the building, snoring softly.

For a while, Maddie watched him sleep. Without the attitude, he seemed younger. Almost innocent. And he didn't smell of smoke and stale beer today.

What was his story? she wondered. *Why was he on the streets?*

Finally, she nudged his foot with a long-handled roller brush. He came awake with a start. His eyes wide with something akin to panic.

"Why don't you go inside to sleep?" Maddie asked.

"I need to keep watch." The boy scowled as he pulled his coat collar closer around his neck.

"It's tough to see anything with your eyes closed. Besides, we have a monitor at my house and can see everything that goes on."

Devon crossed his arms over his chest.

"Why don't you come inside and tell me what you know about the wall incident?"

"I don't want to wake everybody up."

"Father Jacobs is an early riser. We can use his office."

"I don't want him to know what a loser I am."

"So do you want to come to my house and see how the little dog is doing?"

Interest flickered in Devon's eyes, dissolving the scowl on his his face. "Is he gonna be okay?"

"Come and see for yourself."

After a slight hesitation, Devon hoisted himself off the ground and followed Maddie to her car—a red sixties Cadillac this time. Soon they were driving the short distance to her castle.

"Where did you get this old car?"

"Friend of mine needed some cash. It seemed like a good investment."

They rode in silence until the castle came into view. Devon sat up straighter as the turrets became visible against the pale horizon of dawn. "This is your castle?"

"Built it when my niece and nephew were young. They had just lost their dad and we figured they needed something to believe in again."

Devon slid a sideways look at Maddie, staring as they crossed the drawbridge and pulled up in front of the castle. "Wow. It really looks like a castle."

Maddie laughed. "That was the idea. Come on inside. My nephew should have something delicious prepared for breakfast."

Right on cue, Devon's stomach rumbled.

Again, Maddie laughed. She raised the portcullis and led the way inside. As the iron gate clanged shut behind them, Devon jumped a bit.

Their footsteps echoed on the black and white tiled marble floor of the entryway and down the wide hall. A suit of armor stood sentinel on one side and a hologram of Horace flickered on the other.

"Who's the old guy?" Devon asked.

"My husband."

Devon craned his neck to watch the hologram as they walked by. "He kinda looks like Einstein."

"An appropriate description," Maddie said. "Horace invents many wondrous things."

"Ah, smells like breakfast." Maddie sniffed the air appreciatively.

"May I see the dog first?"

When Maddie focused her gaze on him, Devon shrugged. "I want to be sure he's alright."

"Razzles will be in the kitchen with my nephew."

When they entered the kitchen, Razzles braced himself on his unhurt front leg and barked fiercely at Devon.

"Hey, little buddy. I don't blame you for being upset with me. I'm sorry I didn't stop them from hurting you."

Razzles grabbed the slice of bacon Ryan held out to him and subsided to a padded bed with a growl.

"This is Devon, who helps at the homeless shelter. Devon, this is my nephew, Ryan."

Ryan waved a spatula in greeting. "Aunt Mads suckered you into one of her projects, huh? Well, help yourself to breakfast. You'll probably need it."

Hesitantly, Devon took a muffin from a plate on the counter, while Maddie scooped eggs, bacon and several hotcakes onto a plate, along with a couple more muffins. She placed the plate on a tray with two glasses of juice and said, "Come with me."

Maddie led the way to a broad walkway between two turrets of the castle, where a small round table and two chairs sat in an alcove. "We can watch the sunrise from here."

Then she set the plate in front of Devon and sat in the chair opposite. "Now eat and then tell me your story."

Devon stared at the plate of food for a moment. "I don't deserve this."

He stood and walked away a few feet. Then paced back. Stared at Maddie, and walked away again to stand looking out at the sunrise.

"I'm not really homeless," he blurted out.

"So why the charade?" Maddie took a bite of muffin.

"So my mom doesn't find out I'm not a party guy."

Surprise claimed Maddie's face. "Not partying would make most mothers happy."

Devon sat down and nibbled at the bacon. "My mom considers herself the life of the party and wants me to follow in her footsteps. I'd rather hang out at the homeless shelter and help Father Jacobs."

Maddie blinked a couple times as she took this in. More times than she could recall, she sneaked back into her house to avoid being caught after a party. "How do you explain the smell of stale cigarettes and booze?"

"I hang out with a group of kids long enough to smell like that before I go home so Mom will think I've been partying."

"Reversal of a stereotype." Maddie ate more of her muffin. "Are these the kids who egged the mural?"

"Yeah. And I'm pretty sure who kicked the dog, but I didn't see him do it. The damage was done by the time I hitched a ride to the shelter."

"Why did they mess up the mural?

"Some guy came to where we hang out and offered fifty bucks to whoever had the cajones to slow down the project."

"Have you ever seen him before?"

"Nah. He just gave waved a wad of cash and gave the other guys a ride out here."

"What did he look like?"

"Bald, middle-aged white guy with a paunchy gut. Like all the ones who run city hall."

Suspicions tumbled through Maddie. The mayor and city council of Watermark never wanted the homeless shelter built. Didn't even want to admit there were homeless people that might mar the image of the city. "Like the mayor?"

Devon shrugged. "Those guys all look the same."

Darn! There went her idea to draw a picture of the guy while Devon described him. "Could you identify him if you saw him again?"

"You mean like on the cop shows?"

"Yeah." *Why not relate this to something the kid knew?* Maddie thought. "Maybe we should go visit city hall on our way to the shelter this morning."

Devon's eyes sparked with interest.

When they returned to the kitchen, Daphne was eating breakfast. Of course she wanted to be part of their city hall scheme. "I can use my favorite cigarette lighter to take photos. Maybe Horace has other disguised cameras and we can all take pictures."

"We don't want to arouse suspicions," Maddie said. "This should

28

be a casual visit, like to pick up brochures."

"Or leave brochures about the homeless shelter," Daphne said. "Then we could watch reactions."

"I don't think Father Jacobs has brochures," Maddie said. "All the money goes to help the people who are homeless."

"How about to make sure information about the shelter is listed on the city Web site and other places they advertise city services?" Devon asked. "That should really get a reaction from someone who wanted to stop the mural from being painted."

"If that's all they want to stop." Maddie tapped her chin thoughtfully. "Building the new shelter has not gone smoothly. The city has nit-picked plans and inspections from the start of this process. Maybe defacing the mural is only a warning."

"Of what?" Daphne asked.

"That's what we need to find out."

~ * ~

When they arrived at city hall, Daphne slipped out of the Cadillac, turned up the collar of her trench coat, and hurried behind one of the large white stone columns that braced the Greek revival roof two stories overhead.

Maddie simply walked in as if she owned the place, and Devon followed behind her, looking around curiously. They marched up the sweeping staircase with stained cherry wood handrails that ushered visitors to the office of the mayor and city council on the second floor.

"Morning, CatherineLee," Maddie greeted the mayor's receptionist. "Is Mayor Leroy in?"

"Morning, Maddie. Hizzoner doesn't come in until ten at the earliest."

Maddie frowned. The mayor used to be an early riser. "Thought he'd always keep a farmer's schedule."

"Not since he got himself a mistress."

"What? Leroy was afraid of girls until he was almost forty years old."

"I know." CatherineLee signed the mayor's signature to several letters. "I don't think they do anything but play board games pretending to take over the world. But hizzoner decided all really suave men had a mistress, so he got one. Oh, my, my. His mama was mad. I expected her to whip out a willow switch and tan his britches. Now he comes in late and leaves early to go to the country club to be seen with his 'kept woman'. Doesn't much matter. Town this small doesn't need a full-time mayor."

Maddie digested that bit of information a moment, then asked, "Who's updating the city Web site nowadays?"

"That would be Gladys."

"Want to be sure information about the homeless shelter is included in the list of city services."

"Woo-eee. You are twisting Leroy's tail this morning, aren't you, girl?"

Maddie grinned. "Just doing my civic duty to be sure all services are represented equally."

CatherineLee laughed. "I'll be sure to tell hizzoner you came callin'."

With a two-finger salute to her hat brim, Maddie left the mayor's office.

"That didn't get the reaction I expected." Devon hurried to catch up to Maddie. "And I didn't see what the mayor looked like."

"Our visit might produce a delayed reaction," Maddie said. "And the mayor's portrait is in the entryway downstairs. Might be the city council there too. You can see if the man who was handing out money is one of them."

"Don't have to look at pictures. There he is." Devon grasped Maddie's arm and pulled her behind a pillar in the entryway. "That's the guy who paid to have the mural messed up."

The man was tall—almost six and a half feet—with no hair at all on a squarish head that seemed to sit right on the shoulders of his block-shaped body.

Maddie had never seen the man before, and she knew pretty much everyone in Watermark. "You think he looks like every other middle-aged man in city hall?"

Devon shrugged. "Didn't think he was anything special."

"Looks like a gangster in an old movie. Take a picture and let's see if Father Jacobs knows him."

Mr. Square Head scowled as his narrowed gaze surveyed the entryway of city hall. When the mayor skulked in a side door, the man followed him to a private elevator. The doors slid open and they both stepped inside.

"Got a photo of them together too," Devon said.

"Let's find Daphne and get out of here," Maddie said. "I don't like the looks of that man."

~ * ~

When Maddie, Daphne and Devon arrived at the shelter, the children were in a near riot, eager to start painting their houses.

Thanks to the surveillance equipment and Devon sitting by the building, no other damage had been done to the mural.

"Can we paint today?"

"We're going to draw the outline of the houses today," Maddie said. "All of you drew small houses, but we're going to make them bigger. Ready?"

Maddie made a copy of the small street scene onto a transparency, then put that sheet on a projector. When she displayed it against the wall, the scene filled the space nicely.

"Cool!" the kids exclaimed.

"Now, let's work in partners to outline the houses."

At the end of the day, Maddie was quite pleased the children seemed to be taking the project seriously. The red-haired boy was younger and didn't have the attention span required to make much progress, but he was so full of gaiety Maddie didn't have the heart to correct him.

When Maddie and Daphne returned to the castle that evening, Horace had a surprise. He had fashioned corrective lenses for Mr. Razzles from a pair of old driving goggles.

With a great deal of fanfare, Horace fitted the goggles on the little dog's head.

Razzles tipped his head one way and then another, looking at each human in the room. *"Am I supposed to be able to see all this?"*

"All what?" Maddie lifted the goggles off Razzles' head and looked through them at Horace. *He was naked!*

Had he been too engrossed in a project and forgotten to dress? Maddie took off the goggles. *Nope, Horace was fully clothed.*

"You might want to make some adjustments." Maddie handed the goggles to Horace.

When he held them to his face and looked at Maddie, his cheeks flushed. "I see what you mean."

Then he disappeared downstairs to his workroom, muttering to himself.

~ * ~

Maddie was awakened early in the morning by an alarm connected to the security monitors. She stumbled to the bank of monitors and, through bleary eyes, caught sight of several teenagers running away from the shelter. Behind them, graffiti filled the outlines of the houses the children had so carefully drawn.

Immediately, Maddie called Father Jacobs, who had appeared on the monitor surveying the damage. "I just heard the alarm. I'll be there as soon as possible."

As soon as she arrived, she rousted Devon out of one of the bunks at the shelter. "Tell me where to find your 'friends'."

"What?" Devon squinted his sleepy eyes.

Maddie glared at him as he struggled to a sit. "Your friends struck again. Painted all over the mural. Now you are going to show me where your friends hang out. Or I will tell your mother not only do you not party all night, but you're helping a priest with his good work."

With a resigned groan, Devon stumbled to Maddie's car de jour—a nineteen-thirties Studebaker—and slumped into the passenger's seat. "Downtown. Just a few blocks from city hall."

With Devon seated beside her, Maddie punched the gas and fishtailed toward downtown Watermark.

The fastidious brick buildings on Main Street were still closed and locked this early in the morning. But Maddie nudged Devon toward the shuttered glass of the door. "I doubt they're asleep yet since they just returned from vandalizing the mural."

With the look of a man facing the gallows, Devon tapped gently on the glass. "I don't think they're here."

Maddie reached around the teenager and rapped sharply on the door with a paint stirring stick. A scruffy, scowling teenager yanked the door open. "Whaddya want?"

"You been out at the homeless shelter recently?"

A woman with a pierced eyebrow and a tattoo of a kitten on the back of her hand appeared beside him, yawning. "You want your nails done? We don't usually open until ten."

Maddie's gaze flicked to the woman's nails, decorated in leopard and zebra print. "Nice job. But not today. I'm looking for whoever spray-painted graffiti on the mural at the homeless shelter."

The woman's gaze swiveled to the teen beside her. "You trashed a piece of art?"

"No, I just...enhanced it," the kid said.

Recognizing the woman as a fellow artist, Maddie pressed that advantage. "Without the consent of the artists."

"Are you kidding?" the woman said. "You know how I feel about other people messing with my designs. I raised you different than that. Art is sacred. You get your lowbrow carcass into your room. You're grounded."

"Aw, the guy paid me fifty bucks."

The woman braced one hand on her hip and held out the other.

With a scowl, the kid gave her the money, which she handed over to Maddie. "Please tell Father Jacobs that Richard is very, very sorry and will make sure nothing like this ever happens again."

"Thank you."

As Maddie and Devon walked away, she heard the woman continue to bestow her dismay on the kid.

By the time she and Devon arrived back at the shelter, the kids and their parents were awake and surveying the defaced mural.

"That looks like the graffiti on the railroad car we rode to Oregon," Reynaldo said.

Others nodded. Some had a similar experience. "If we draw a box car around the graffiti, we can leave it as part of the mural, and move the houses to a different place on the street."

"Yeah, that will work." Agreement greeted that suggestion. So the mural took on another dimension not in Maddie's original design.

Chapter Four

The next day, the children were finally able to start painting their houses. That is, until mid-morning when the mayor showed up with Mr. Square Head.

"What does he want?" Maddie narrowed her gaze at Leroy Brasman, a bean-pole of a man dressed in a three-piece suit with a watch fob in his pocket.

"Morning, Leroy." Father Jacobs stood with his arms crossed over his chest and his feet spread apart. "What brings you out our way?"

"Why, to see your facility for myself." The mayor held onto a fixed smile as he began to walk around the building. He stopped when he reached the side of the building where the children were painting the mural. "Don't recall a sign permit for this."

"It's not a sign. It's a work of art," Father Jacobs said. "'We obtained the necessary permits and permissions."

"This building is intended as a homeless shelter, and you're depicting homes to promote it. That makes it a sign. You'll have to obtain the necessary permits. In the meantime, all work on this sign must stop. This wall will be repainted in a pleasing shade of white."

With a smug smile, the mayor turned on his heel to leave, with Mr. Square Head following closely behind him.

Until he spotted Razzles, who was feeling well enough to come to work with Maddie that morning.

"Is that a Chihuahua?" Mr Square Head whispered. "I don't like Chihuahuas. They're vicious."

Razzles lifted his lip and growled.

Mr. Square Head edged closer to the mayor. "What did I tell you? Vicious!"

"And they grow. Get as big as bears." The guy nodded to affirm the truth of his statement. "They came after me. A whole mob of them. I wasn't bald before that. Scared me so bad my hair fell out and never came back."

The mayor rolled his eyes. "Never mind about Chihuahuas. We need to stop the grand opening of this shelter. We don't want to bring homeless people to Watermark."

"Don't forget the permits, Father." The mayor called out as he walked briskly toward his luxury sedan. Mr. Square Head followed as closely as a shadow, glancing back over his shoulder numerous times toward Razzles.

Maddie, Father Jacobs and the children watched them drive away.

"What do we do now?"

"Call the Blue-Haired Ladies and lay siege to city hall," Father Jacobs said. "It won't be the first time."

~ * ~

By the time Maddie and Father Jacobs arrived at city hall the next morning, the Blue-Haired Ladies from the local churches were already setting up their chairs and card tables in the lobby. CatherineLee, the mayor's receptionist, and a city police officer were passing out coffee and donuts.

When the mayor arrived at his usual mid-morning time, fury immediately claimed his face. Maddie knew the Blue-Haired Ladies occupied the city hall lobby at least once a month to protest something the mayor had done or not done, and oftentimes she joined them. Sometimes the protest was no more than an excuse to have a monthly card game in a place from which they hadn't been banned. If nothing else, the gathering made for an entertaining afternoon.

"What is it this time?" the mayor demanded through clenched teeth.

"We don't have a place to play—I mean, stay, so we're staying here," one of the ladies declared. The others nodded and voiced their agreement.

"I don't have time for this. I have people coming this afternoon." The mayor turned to the officer. "Arrest them."

"That's my Grandma Gertie," the officer said around a mouthful of donut. "I'm not arresting my grandmother."

"Then give me those handcuffs!" The mayor grabbed the handcuffs from the officer and clicked them closed over Gertie's wrists.

"Rape! Rape!" she yelled.

"I didn't touch you," the mayor said.

Gertie held up her handcuffed wrists. "Looks like kinky sex to me."

"There are laws against certain sexual acts within the city limits," the officer said. "Especially in public and with someone who's not your spouse."

"This is ridiculous!" The mayor blustered.

"As ridiculous as declaring a mural is a sign?" Father Jacobs asked.

The mayor's nostrils flared.

"We simply want to provide services to those who find themselves in dire circumstances," Father Jacobs said. "Surely you can find compassion in your heart for the homeless—"

"There are no homeless in Watermark." The mayor's eyes blazed in denial. "We are well on our way to being the best place to live in the state, then the nation. Perhaps even the world. Having homeless people would blight our reputation. Put a lie to our application for Most Livable City of the Year. We'd have to update our Web site."

"That part is being done," Maddie said. "I talked to Gladys earlier in the week."

"What? I'll put a stop to that."

As the mayor stormed toward the elevator, Gertie slipped out of the handcuffs. "I was kinda looking forward to some action. Been awhile."

The ladies dug out their decks of cards and settled in for a serious game of Nertz, including their fellow protestors—some of the parents from the homeless shelter—in the game.

"Come on, Daphne, you can be at our table." Mabel, who informally organized the ladies, pulled out a chair for Daphne.

"I've never played Nertz before."

"Wipe that smirk off your face, Ethel. You take it easy on newcomers—and young enough to be your daughter too. Would you take advantage of your daughter—never mind. I know you would." Addressing Daphne, she said, "Here's an extra deck I always carry just in case."

After Daphne sat down and shuffled the cards, Mabel continued her instructions. "Now, lay out four cards face up. Next, thirteen go in a pile and put them aside. That's your Nertz pile. You want to get rid of those as fast as possible. When you play the last card in that pile, you yell 'Nertz'."

"Already?" Bertha awakened with a snort.

"No, no. We haven't even started. I'm just telling Daphne how to play." Mabel turned back to Daphne. "Go through the rest of your cards three at a time. The four cards on deck you play like solitaire, alternating red, black, red, black. If you have an ace, it goes in the middle of the table and everyone plays on those, in order by suit from the ace to the king."

"And, before we begin, let's do a fingernail inspection." Mabel spoke louder to be heard over the conversations among the ladies. "Nails must be trimmed short and rounded. No long nails. No sharp edges or points."

"Why is that?" Daphne asked.

"You'll see once the game gets started. Is everyone ready? Go!"

Like the start of an auto race, the three Blue-Haired Ladies at Daphne's table sorted through their cards as quickly as they could. Daphne was amazed that ladies who walked with limps and canes could move through cards so quickly. They tossed aces into the middle of the table, followed by twos, threes and so on up to the kings. Sometimes more than one lady tried to play on the same ace, colliding over the cards. It quickly became obvious why a fingernail inspection was made before the game started, as cards and fingers and nails all collided in the race to play a card before an opponent.

Daphne was soon caught up in the rapid pace of the game, and moaned with the other ladies when one of them quickly dispersed her Nertz pile.

"Okay, count the cards left in your Nertz pile and subtract those from the number you had on the aces," Mabel told Daphne. "That's your score for this hand."

They were several hands into the game when one of the ladies asked Keller's mom. "Hon, are you feeling okay?"

"Probably the intensity of the game." Grandma Gertie continued to sort through her card deck three at a time, tossing an occasional card onto the pile of aces in the middle of the table. "Can be stressful for a newcomer. And the younger generation just doesn't have the constitution for playing cards all afternoon."

"I think it's more than that," Mabel said. "She's tipping out of her chair."

"Oh my tarnation!"

Keller's mom slumped against Bertha. As she startled awake, she bumped the table, collapsing it and sending cards all over the floor.

"I told you not to use that table. Has a weak leg."

"Help me with her. She's not breathing!"

The ladies laid Keller's mom on the floor amid the playing cards, and listened once again for breathing.

"Check to be sure she doesn't have one of those gummy candies Bertha brought caught in her throat."

One of the ladies stuck a finger in the woman's mouth. "Can't find anything and she's still not breathing."

"Well, Ruby Red Francis! Start CPR! Someone else call Fred to get the ambulance here."

While Maddie and another lady teamed up to perform CPR, someone else called 911. The others formed a quiet circle around them, listening intently for the sound of the woman's breathing.

"We've got a breath!" Maddie called triumphantly over the sound of sirens arriving. The ambulance crew hustled in, quickly checked

Keller's mom over and hooked her up to oxygen.

After the ambulance crew took Keller's mom away, Grandma Gertie said, "I think that young man stole my queen of hearts."

"You need to get out more, Gertie. He's too young to be digging his spade in your garden."

"Wonder what's wrong with Keller's mom?"

"Maybe valeria."

"That's not a real disease."

"It says so on the Internet."

"You need to stay away from the computer, Agnes."

"That's where I find my men. Put up a fake photo and have phone sex. Not nearly as messy as doin' it in person."

"Oh, hush up. A woman just went to the hospital in an ambulance. Let's show a little respect for the ill. Besides, you're scaring Daphne."

"Have you ever found a guy on your computer, Daphne?"

Daphne colored slightly. "I don't know how to use a computer."

The ladies standing nearby gasped. "If you thought Nertz was exciting, wait till we show you what you can find online."

The other ladies giggled.

Mabel cleared her throat. "Remember Keller's mom? This can wait until we know she's going to be okay."

"Shall we go to the hospital?" Gertie asked.

"We've been banned from there as a group, remember? We'll have to wait until Father Jacobs calls."

~ * ~

A somber group of kids and adults gathered at the homeless shelter after Keller's mom was rushed to the hospital. The doctors were running tests, but so far couldn't figure out what was wrong.

"Do I have to go to foster care?" Keller remembered other times he had been in foster care when his mom was sick. The lady with bad breath who always wanted to kiss his cheek. The toothless couple who slept as many kids on the floor as possible to get more money. Keller hunched his thin shoulders. At least he hadn't been beaten or abused, as some of the other kids had been.

"You can stay with us until we find out more about your mom," Father Jacobs said. "You know what I used to do when I felt scared and didn't know what was coming next? I'd dress up in a silly costume and pretend I was someone else."

"What kind of costume?" Keller asked.

"I always wanted to fly." A wistful smile stole across Father Jacobs' face. "So I dressed up as a bird. A beautiful hawk with golden wings."

"Could you fly then?" Keller asked.

"No." Father Jacobs shook his head. "But it freed my imagination to think of other things and I forgot I was scared."

So the children made golden wings out of cardboard, then swooped around the shelter in a modified game of hide and seek.

While Father Jacobs and other kids winged their way around the shelter, Keller sat in a quiet corner and watched. Father Jacobs was nice and he tried to make everyone feel better, but Keller was worried about his mom.

The nice lady, Dorinda, looked like she was worried too. She stood in shadows, making it seem as if she had wings. As if she was hovering above the floor!

Keller rubbed his eyes and looked again. How silly. She was just a sad lady standing by the wall talking to Ryan, Miz Maddie's nephew, who brought good things to eat to the shelter.

"Why don't you change into your elfenchaun form more often?" Ryan asked.

What's an elfenchaun? Keller thought. He knew he wasn't supposed to eavesdrop, but how could he move away now without letting them know he could hear every word they said?

"I am far past the age in the Old Country where I should act like a somber adult."

"But you're not in the Old Country," Ryan said.

"True enough."

"If I had the gift of flight, I think I would use it often," Ryan

41

said. "Rarely anyone goes to the wooded area near the castle. You could fly there if you wanted."

"Truly?" Dorinda clasped her hands over her heart in delight. "You wouldn't mind?"

"Why should I?" Ryan was puzzled.

"If I married in the Old Country, I would have to give up my freedom as an elfenchaun."

"I want you to be happy," Ryan said. "You're happy as an elfenchaun, so why would I take that away from you?"

Well, whatever an elfenchaun was, it made Dorinda happy. Keller wondered if he could become an elfenchaun. Then maybe he could be happy until his mom got well.

~ * ~

As Maddie drove home from the hospital, she worried about Keller and his mom. How scary it must be to be ill and not know what was wrong And how frightening for a child to be alone in the world. At least when Daphne had dropped into a fifties time warp, Maddie and Horace had been nearby to help. But Keller and his mom had no one else.

Distracted, she drove up the road to the castle at her usual brisk pace—and didn't realize until she was almost upon it that the bridge over the moat wasn't there!

Maddie slammed on the brakes and slid to a stop against the post of the bridge. Which was once again firmly anchored in place.

She watched the bridge closely as she stepped gingerly out of her car and walked around the vehicle to inspect the rear back panel, now crumpled like the fan-shaped bellows of an accordian.

Cautiously, Maddie put one foot on the bridge. It seemed solid, but she crossed in a hurry—just in case.

Once inside the castle, Maddie set her bag of paint supplies on the hall table—which promptly disappeared.

"Hi, Aunt Maddie." The voice of her nephew came from down the hall, but she didn't see him anywhere.

"Are you throwing your voice for a ventriloquist act?" Maddie asked.

Ryan laughed. "Just helping Uncle Horace to test the cloaking device. He linked it into the electrical system of the castle, and now things are disappearing at random."

"Should make dinner interesting," Maddie said. "Where's your mother?"

"Got tired of waiting for Mr. Perfect to ask her out and went to dinner with someone the Blue-Haired Ladies found on a computer dating service ."

"I'll give her until nine-thirty, then I'm going after her," Maddie muttered.

Chapter Five

"I'll go with you," Ryan said.

"You weren't supposed to hear that."

Ryan was smiling as he reappeared right beside Maddie. "I'll save some dessert for her."

Daphne was home before nine, without even a kiss at the door.

"How did your date go?" Maddie asked cautiously.

"Another frog." Daphne walked down the hallway toward her suite of rooms, carrying her shoes. Maddie followed.

"He thought paying for dinner earned him the right to drive out by the sewage treatment plant and watch the submarine races—his words, not mine."

"You didn't know what that was?"

Daphne shook her head and tossed her broken high heels into the bottom of the closet, where they promptly disappeared.

"What happened to your shoes?" Maddie asked.

"Horace is testing the cloaking device," Daphne stated as if disappearing items were as common as Ryan testing new recipes.

"No, I mean before that. Why were the heels broken?"

"One of them broke when I scraped it down Peter the Plumber's shin. The other came off when I was walking home."

"You walked all the way home?" Maddie clenched her fists, prepared to take a pipe wrench to the plumber's tool.

"No. Devon and his mother gave me a ride home. She seems nice enough. She can't find a guy to suit her either." Daphne stepped out of her pale peach dress and drew a bathrobe around her.

From what Devon said about his mother's partying ways, Maddie figured she wore out men. However, her immediate concern was consoling Daphne. "There must be a man who will appreciate your fine qualities."

"I hope so." Daphne sighed as she settled against the pillows on her bed. "Did the television reappear yet? Or should I read a book?"

Maddie handed her a romance novel and left the room.

~ * ~

Daphne laid in bed with the book open on her lap but not reading. Maybe she should give up dating. She had so hoped Brenner would ask her out, but he did nothing more than look at her with goo-goo eyes. So she thought dinner with a nice man would at least take her mind off Brenner. The Blue-Haired Ladies helped her find a man through a computer dating service, but Peter the Plumber was not a nice man. Her first clue should have been he looked nothing like the picture on the computer. That photo was a handsome man who reminded Daphne of her husband.

If only her Charlie hadn't died...

Charlie was my best friend all through grade school. When we graduated to high school, he gave me his class ring to wear on a chain around my neck and we went steady.

Dates with Charlie were fun! After the football games, we drove to a local restaurant for a burger and fries. Then sometimes we would make out in Charlie's car. But he never pushed me beyond a few kisses and gentle caresses. We had long ago made a pact not to have sex until after we were married, and Charlie was enough of a gentleman to stick to that agreement. He always took me home before my midnight curfew.

I followed Charlie to college. Not to get an education, but because we didn't want to be separated. When Charlie graduated, we married. A fairy tale wedding with Charlie in a tuxedo and me in a beautiful, white lace dress. It was perfect!

We were both virgins on our honeymoon. Eager, but awkward. We weren't sure what to do with arms and legs and other stuff. Like everything else, we approached sex as a team. Bought books in brown paper wrappers and went through the pictures together. Watched movies and tried to imitate what they did. It was pretty funny.

When the twins were born, we were ecstatic. Another dream come true. They were six years old when Charlie was killed in an auto accident. We were supposed to grow old together. Dying wasn't in our plan at all.

The fact Charlie was gone gradually sank in, but I didn't want to face it. I was totally lost. He had been my entire world for so long, and I had no clue how to move forward without him.

So I moved backward—to a time before I was even born—and lived in the nineteen-fifties for twenty years.

Tears leaked out of Daphne's eyes as she remembered the good times with Charlie. Maybe dating wasn't such a good idea after all. Maybe she should just focus on helping Maddie with the mural and finding a career.

~ * ~

When Maddie and Daphne arrived at the homeless shelter the next morning, a crew from the mayor's office was spraying white paint over the mural.

Father Jacobs met Maddie before she could exit the car and vent her fury on the painters. "They have a judge's order."

"That doesn't make it right. At this rate, we'll never have the mural completed in time for the May Day grand opening."

"I'm sure there's a reason for this in the overall plan of the Universe," Father Jacobs said.

"Hmmph." Maddie scowled at the painters.

"You know, I have an idea for an alternate way to finish the mural." Brenner, the father of the two red-haired children, rubbed his chin thoughtfully. "If you paint the mural on pieces of siding, it can be installed on the outside of the building once the issue about being a sign is decided. That means you can also paint inside without being at the mercy of Oregon's rainy weather."

"I like that idea." Maddie nodded slowly. "Father, can you make space inside the shelter for us to paint?"

While painting on the mural progressed—much faster than it would have outside in the unpredictable weather, Father Jacobs called on his connections to lobby the city council to overturn the mayor's edict that the mural fell under the sign ordinance. However, the law was vaguely written with no quick solution in sight.

"If the mayor thinks this is a sign, maybe we should come up with a name for the shelter and incorporate that into the mural," Maddie said. "How much would a sign permit cost?"

"Several hundred dollars," Father Jacobs said. "And I'm not taking any more money from you, Maddie."

"Maybe we could sell cookies to raise money," one of the kids suggested.

"Or paint big pictures for other people."

"That's not a bad idea," Maddie said. "We could auction off our services for another mural, but paint it inside a building so we don't run afoul of any laws."

"I'll ask the church ladies if they will coordinate this effort," Father Jacobs said. "They seemed disappointed our occupation of city hall didn't result in any arrests."

~ * ~

While the Blue-Haired Ladies advertised the auction fundraiser, Keller's mom was still in the hospital, getting worse while doctors continued to be baffled about what was wrong. In one of her nightmares, she thrashed about and called out for her son.

This alerted the hospital social worker and then child welfare to Keller's existence, and triggered an old fear in the boy. "I don't want to go to foster care."

Maddie's soft heart ached for the little guy and she offered to let him stay at the castle, much to Keller's delight. Now they just had to convince the bureaucracy that was the perfect place for him to stay.

On the boy's next visit to the hospital to see his mom, he and

Maddie met with the caseworker. The worker frowned and consulted the case file. "Keller's mom made no mention of your family."

"With her sickness and all, sometimes she forgets."

"I'll have to do an emergency certification and inspect your home."

"Ahh..."

"Is that a problem?" Suddenly the worker seemed suspicious.

"No. No, not at all." Maddie hoped Horace wasn't testing the cloaking device or an invention that blew up parts of the castle. While the worker went to her car, Maddie snuck in a call to her family and warned them they should "act normal"—whatever that was.

~ * ~

When Maddie called to warn the family she would be at the castle soon with a social worker to determine if Keller could continue to stay with them, Daphne saw a chance to prove her worth as a modern woman.

She would fix a gourmet meal to show off her cooking skills and play the gracious hostess.

Daphne tied on an apron and informed her son she would be preparing dinner. Ryan simply shrugged. "I'll be here if you need help."

However, Daphne was determined to do this herself and impress the caseworker with how "normal" she was.

When Maddie and the caseworker arrived, Daphne met them at the door and ushered them inside. A frown flitted across her sister's face when Daphne informed them she was fixing dinner, but Daphne pushed aside the flicker of doubt and kept her smile firmly in place.

While Maddie and the caseworker settled at the small kitchen table to go over paperwork, Daphne began the task of preparing a meal.

Her first challenge was the new stove Ryan had insisted they purchase since he had immersed himself in gourmet cooking. The device had so many more control knobs than the old stove Daphne had used when Linda showed her how to prepare basic food items.

"You'll do fine," Ryan said sotto voce. "Just don't put the turkey in the dishwasher."

"I'm fixing chicken, not turkey," Daphne whispered as she kept a fixed smile on her face.

"I'm teasing you. Relax and you'll do fine." Ryan squeezed her hand and sat at the counter to watch yet another cooking show.

Dismay threatened to overwhelm Daphne as she stared at all the assembled ingredients for her planned meal. Under the influence of one of Ryan's cooking shows, her basic chicken, potatoes and vegetables had quickly turned into a gourmet feast. Well, she didn't have much time to plan since the caseworker wanted to come right away to determine if their home would be a suitable place for Keller to stay.

She would just have to forge ahead and not let second thoughts ruin this placement.

So she mixed together the ingredients for the mushroom dressing and cooked them as directed. All seemed to turn out as the recipe said it should, and she released a sigh of satisfaction.

Except the next step was to stuff the mixture inside the whole chicken.

A whimper escaped from Daphne's throat as she looked at the raw bird. She didn't eat much meat, and only after it had been processed and shaped into something that didn't resemble the animal it came from.

Her noise of distress must have been louder than she thought, because both Maddie and Ryan looked up at her. Daphne tried for a smile that she was sure turned out more of a grimace.

Her son rescued her by coming to stand beside her and discreetly stuffing the mushroom mixture into the chicken and slipping the naked bird into the oven.

Daphne smiled in gratitude and turned her attention to fixing the kale and cauliflower with a creamy sauce. Cooking the vegetables was easy so, filled with confidence, Daphne started the sauce. She whisked butter, flour, milk and cream together over the burner, then turned to chopping bread into cubes while the mixture heated.

After a couple minutes, she began to smell something odd. She turned toward the stove and noticed the sauce was bubbling quickly toward the top of the pan.

"The heat's too high." Ryan's quiet voice once more guided Daphne. "Better take it off the burner for a moment."

As the mixture bubbled over the sides of the pan, Daphne panicked. "Omigosh!"

As soon as she pulled the pan off the burner, pain scorched through her hand. She scrunched her eyes shut and silently berated herself for not using a potholder.

"Quick, put it under cold water." Ryan was beside her in an instant.

Daphne dropped the pan into the sink and turned on the cold water. Steam immediately rose, filling the kitchen with the odor of burned milk.

"I meant your hand." Ryan gently took Daphne's hand and moved it under the still running cold water.

Tears filled her eyes as she looked at her son. Gentle concern filled his eyes, just as it had when he was small and all Daphne could do was grieve for her lost husband. Would she be stuck in that cycle forever? "I should have stuck to the basic food dishes I know how to prepare. I really am inept, aren't I?"

With his thumb, Ryan brushed away a tear running down his mother's cheek. "I don't care if you can cook gourmet meals or not. You're my mom and I love you."

With a hug, he gently led her to a stool at the counter, fetched a cold cloth for her hand, and poured her a glass of wine. "You have most of this done. Let me finish dinner."

Love for her son filled Daphne once more. Then she realized the caseworker had been watching them closely. Dismay filled Daphne. She hoped she hadn't ruined Keller's chances of staying with them until his mother was out of the hospital.

But the caseworker simply made a mark on her form, then said to Maddie, "Now, where will Keller sleep?"

~ * ~

Maddie led the worker to the family's sleeping wing and into a room with thick wooden beams on the ceiling and stone walls framing a media center. Though the room wasn't under the castle, it looked like a cleaned up version of a dungeon.

Keller waited anxiously on a comfy sectional, surrounded by throw pillows shaped like the shields of knights.

When Maddie and the caseworker entered the room, Keller climbed onto a bed that folded down from the outer wall like a drawbridge. Unfortunately, he bumped the button that folded the bed back up and it started to close up like a dragon clamping its mouth over a tasty morsel of prey.

Maddie's quick reflexes caught a strap on the bed and pulled it back down. "We'll get that fixed right away."

Keller quietly climbed down and slumped in a corner of the sectional, hugging one of the pillows to his chest.

"Will Keller have this bedroom to himself?" the worker asked.

Maddie nodded. "We don't have any other children staying here right now."

The caseworker made another checkmark on her form. "How do you plan to provide an education for Keller? I understand Father Jacobs has been giving lessons to the children who stay at the shelter."

"We can continue that until Keller and his mother have a permanent place to stay," Maddie said. "Then we'll help her decide how she wants to meet Keller's schooling needs."

The caseworker asked a few more questions before she nodded and, finally, smiled. "This looks like a child's dream. I'll be checking back with you to see how Keller is doing."

With sighs of relief, Maddie, Daphne, and Keller waved good-bye to the worker.

Then the garages disappeared.

"Oh dear," Maddie said. "I think we'd better get back inside before the castle disappears."

~ * ~

When Keller settled into bed that evening, he asked Maddie,

"Will I really be able to stay in this room?"

"Would you like a different one?" Maddie asked.

"I like this one. It's just..." He frowned. "One of the foster homes where I stayed had a bedroom they showed the worker. After she left, we had to sleep on the floor wherever we could find space."

Disbelief socked Maddie in the belly. Would she never get used to the disgraceful things people did? "That won't happen here."

As Keller snuggled under the blankets, Mr. Razzles hopped up on the bed next to him, turned around three times, and laid down with his furry head on Keller's pillow.

"Can he sleep with me?" the little boy asked.

"Sure." Maddie smiled and kissed both the little boy and the dog. "Good-night now."

When Maddie left the room, Daphne was waiting anxiously outside the door. "I didn't mess up Keller staying here, did I? I mean, I ruined dinner."

"No, you didn't mess anything up." Maddie looked at her sister. Though almost fifty years old, she still seemed an innocent. "Give yourself a break, Daphne. You don't have to rejoin this time period all at once. Take some time and ease back into this different life."

"I just want to be normal."

Maddie laughed. "That could be a challenge in this family."

"Perhaps you're right. I'm going to say good-night to Keller."

As Daphne disappeared inside the little boy's room, Ryan walked down the hall. "I came to say good-night to Keller."

"Your mom's doing that now. By the way, thanks for being so sweet to her and rescuing dinner."

"I enjoy cooking. Rissa said I'd make someone a fine wife someday. Do you think I will? Not be a wife, I mean, but do you think I'll ever get married?"

"Do you want to be married?"

"I don't know. I mean, I like the idea sometimes, but then I'd have to act like a normal grown-up, right?"

"Your uncle Horace and I have been married a lot of years, and neither of us have ever aspired to normal. I think a big part of marrying the right person is finding someone who will accept and love you with all your quirks. And this family has plenty of those."

~ * ~

Keller was drifting off to sleep, warmed inside by the kindness of Miz Maddie and her family, and snuggled on the outside by the dog, Mr. Razzles.

"Please let the angels help my mom get well," he whispered.

Then another visitor appeared in his room, though he didn't hear the door open. He couldn't see her clearly, but she had delicate green wings and a dress to match. "Are you an angel?"

"An elfenchaun."

"What's that?"

"A magical creature who's part elf and part leprechaun."

"What's your name?"

"Dorinda."

"Like the lady at dinner."

Dorinda nodded.

"What kind of magic do you have?" Keller asked.

"Well, I can talk to animals—like Mr. Razzles. And I can do silly things like make butterflies appear in the air." Dorinda waved her hand, and two pink butterfies twirled and dived around Keller's head.

"Can you make my mom well?"

A wistful look crossed the little elfenchaun's face. "Ah, that's a good question. I used to have The Touch that could heal all creatures. But it hasn't worked so well lately."

Keller sighed. "Sometimes I feel that way. I've asked the angels to help my mom get well, but she's still in the hospital. Maybe we need to be with my mom for things to work."

"Maybe," Dorinda said. "Do you want to try?"

With a yawn, Keller nodded. "Can we go to the hospital tomorrow after Father Jacobs' classes?"

~ * ~

Dorinda volunteered to take Keller to the hospital the next day. She didn't drive much, but did quite well with the old motorcycle and sidecar from Maddie's collection of antique vehicles.

Smiling broadly, Keller donned the helmet and old-fashioned goggles reminiscent of a world war flying ace, then settled into the sidecar.

When they arrived at the hospital, Keller led the way to his mom's room.

"You stand by the door and warn me if anyone comes," Dorinda whispered.

She closed her eyes and seemed to concentrate really hard, and Keller thought he saw the shadow of delicate green wings start to materialize behind her.

"Well, hello there, young Mr. Keller." A nurse bustled into the room. "I'm sure your mom appreciates that you come to see her every day."

"But she doesn't always wake up when I'm here."

"That must be disappointing." The nurse checked his mom's pulse, heart rate and respiration while she chatted with Keller. "But keep talking to her. Even though she might not say anything back to you, she knows when you're here and that you love her. Who brought you today?"

"I'm Dorinda." She waved her fingers at the nurse.

"Another of Miz Maddie's family, I presume. You're very lucky. Maddie is a generous woman."

"She definitely changed my life," Dorinda said.

The nurse smiled and changed the IV bag handing from the pole by the bed. "Well, feel free to read to our patient. That can sometimes help people heal."

Keller and Dorinda exchanged a glance. They were here to help his mom heal, but not by reading.

When the nurse left the room, Keller once again stationed himself at the door. "Okay, do it now."

Dorinda closed her eyes and scrunched up her nose, and soon

transformed into her elfenchaun self.

"Oh no," Keller whispered. "Here comes the vampire lady."

A phlebotomist and her rattling cart soon entered the room. "Good afternoon, young man. Who brought you here today?"

He glanced at Dorinda peeking out of the bathroom. "Um, Dorinda, but she had to go to the restroom."

The woman nodded as she drew several vials of blood from the tube in his mom's arm, earning her the nickname "vampire lady." She soon finished her task, wished Keller a nice visit with his mom, and rattled off down the hallway to her next "victim."

Dorinda slowly emerged into the room, her face looking almost as green as her tiny dress. "I thought she was going to take all your mom's blood."

"Naw. Father Jacobs told us the body makes more." Keller took one more look out the door, then closed it securely. "Let's do it now."

Dorinda nodded and swallowed.

"Miss Dorinda, are you okay?"

"Yes. Of course. I just have to concentrate." She drew a deep breath and closed her eyes.

Then the machines near the bed started beeping.

Chapter Six

"What's going on?" Dorinda asked.

"I-I don't know." Keller's body trembled. This didn't seem good.

Several nurses rushed into the room and clustered around his mom. One of them finally seemed to remember him and rushed him out of the room. "Wait in the play area."

For several stunned moments, Keller stared at the closed door of his mom's room, which shut out the frantic voices and hurried actions of the nurses inside. And Dorinda. Maybe she could heal his mom now. He closed his eyes as tightly as possible and prayed to the angels again. Until someone steered him down the hall toward a chair. "Wait here until someone comes to take you home."

But Keller didn't want to go home. He wanted to be with his mom. He wanted her to be well!

As soon as the nurse walked away, he slipped into a darkened room and hid.

Finally the nurses came out of the room, talking quietly among themselves. "Don't know if she'll make it through the night."

"She has a little boy," another nurse said. "So sad."

Keller waited until they passed by and the hall seemed deserted, then sneaked back into his mom's room. Dorinda sat on the pillow, as a white light with sparkles swirled around her and then entered his mother's body.

"Wow," he whispered.

When the light disappeared, his mom seemed to be sleeping peacefully. However, Dorinda's little elfenchaun body was limp and spent, and Keller wondered if she was dead. He touched her shoulder. "Miss Dorinda? Are you alright?"

Gradually, she roused and metamorphed back into human form, looking utterly exhausted.

"Is my mom going to be well now?" Keller asked.

Dorinda drew a deep breath. "Sometimes healing takes a while."

A nurse entered the room and smiled kindly. "Why don't you go home and rest? We'll call if there's any change."

Reluctant to leave his mother, Keller finally took Dorinda's hand and left the hospital.

"How did your visit go?" Maddie asked when they arrived at the castle.

Keller shrugged.

"Well, you can go back tomorrow. Ryan has fixed a special dinner I think you'll like."

"If I can just go to my room, Miz Maddie?"

With a slight frown, Maddie said, "Well, of course. If you're not hungry."

When Maddie turned to talk to Dorinda, she was gone also. Disappeared like one of the objects Horace was testing with his cloaking device.

~ * ~

"Can you come to the hospital right away?" Father Jacobs called in the morning to talk to Maddie. "The nurses asked me to stop by. They didn't think Keller's mother would make it through the night. By the time I arrived, she was sitting up in bed asking for corned beef and cabbage with a pint of Irish ale to wash it down. Do you know anything about this?"

"I don't," Maddie said slowly. *But I'll bet I know who does.*

Maddie went to Dorinda's room and knocked. The young woman opened the door, revealing an airy room decorated in soft greens, with numerous plants on shelves and the window sill. Maddie always felt like she entered a forest when she stepped into Dorinda's room.

"I received a call from Father Jacobs at the hospital."

Dorinda seemed to stop breathing. "How is Keller's mom?"

"Feeling well enough to ask for a pint of Irish ale with corned beef and cabbage."

Dorinda sank onto the bed and drew a deep breath. "Thank the spirits. It worked."

"The Touch?"

Dorinda nodded. "I changed into my elfenchaun form to use it. I didn't have to do that in the Old Country."

"The doctors are talking about releasing her soon if she continues to improve as quickly as she did overnight." Maddie patted Dorinda's hand. "You've given Keller a miracle."

~ * ~

Maddie hoped for another miracle in resolving the disagreement with city hall about the mural at the shelter. While work had continued to progress quickly inside the shelter, agreement on whether or not it was a sign made no progress at all.

To make things worse, Father Jacobs seemed quite disturbed when Maddie, Daphne, Keller and Mr. Razzles arrived.

"What's wrong?" Maddie asked.

"Someone broke into my office last night."

"Oh, no. Is anything missing?"

"Not that's obvious, but I haven't sorted through all the mess yet." The priest closed his eyes briefly. "This is supposed to be a safe haven where people don't have to worry about these kinds of things."

"We need a superhero." Jonathan flexed his muscles and puffed out his four-year-old chest so the superhero picture on his T-shirt appeared to move.

"Maybe Chihuahua man," Maddie said. "Since the mayor's hired muscle is afraid of dogs."

Father Jacobs didn't respond to Maddie's attempt at humor, but continued to frown thoughtfully. "Maybe we can't completely leave our past behind, no matter how much we'd like to believe we've changed."

One of the moms at the shelter was also frowning. "Felicia, something seems to be troubling you."

"I had also hoped to leave the past behind. However, I may have brought danger to others."

"In what way?"

"Mi esposo—my husband has only known gangs his entire life. When Reynaldo was born, he realized this was not a good way of life for a child." Felicia paused, as if the memories were painful. "I didn't want my son to grow up and die as part of a gang. He's bright, sensitive. Can make something better of himself. But gangs do not let go easily. I think they are here for us."

"But they haven't made any move to harm either you or Reynaldo," Father Jacobs said. "Do they want you or something you have?"

Puzzlement settled on Felicia's face. "I'm not sure what you mean."

"Did you bring anything of value with you? Anything the gang could want back?"

"We left with little more than the clothes on our backs. My husband handed us a duffel bag and said—madre de dios! There may be something in the bag."

Reynaldo stood with clenched fists as his mother searched the duffel bag. Tucked away in the bottom was a small statue. "It is all I have left of my father."

"Do you know what's in here, Reynaldo?" Felicia asked.

"Memories," the boy said. "It's an ugly old statue with nothing but memories."

Slowly, Felicia shook her head. "The gang used these to transport drugs. There are probably thousands of dollars of las drogas inside this statue."

Reynaldo's eyes grew round. "But I thought—"

"I'm sure your dad meant it to help," Felicia said gently. "He knew I would realize what was in the statue and what it was worth. His entire life was drugs and gangs. It was his way of supporting us to start a new life."

Reynaldo's face crumpled and he ran out the door.

~ * ~

Mr. Razzles watched Reynaldo run down the road toward the woods. Always before, the boy put on a brave face for his mother. Now that courage had been replaced by pain.

Razzles ran after Reynaldo, but the boy had a head start, and Razzles' legs were shorter than his. "Wait for me!"

Reynaldo stopped and looked over his shoulder. Then all around. Wariness clouded his eyes as darkness rolled across the sky and thunder clapped in the distance.

Razzles caught up to him and sat at his feet, blowing out a breath. "I'm getting out of shape from being spoiled at Maddie's."

Reynaldo looked at Razzles, his tear-filled eyes wide with surprise. "You can talk?"

"If people listen."

"Why haven't you said anything before?"

"Didn't have anything in particular to say."

"Then you heard my dad played me for a fool."

"I heard he tried to help you and your mom in the only way he knew how."

Reynaldo slammed the palm of his hand against a tree trunk. "Why couldn't he be a real dad? Why couldn't he buy us a house and play baseball with me? All he did was fight with my mom and go out with his gang buddies."

"I'll never figure out humans," Razzles said. "Some of them are mean and kick at me. Others let me sleep in their bed and love me."

"You've been homeless too."

"Without a house maybe, but I usually found shelter and nice people like Father Jacobs to give me scraps of food."

"He really cares, doesn't he?"

"Yeah," Razzles said. "And he's going to be worried about us. We should go back."

Reynaldo gazed toward the homeless shelter. "I wish my mom

60

and me had a real home."

"I didn't think I'd ever have a real home. Now I'm at Maddie's castle with Keller. That's pretty cool."

"Maybe some day—"

"Where is it, kid? Where's the statue?"

Reynaldo and Razzles had been so absorbed in their conversation they didn't notice the dark sedan driving slowly down the road until it pulled to a stop beside them.

With the tinted window down, they could see it was Mr. Square Head, with a gun pointed at them.

"Run!" Razzles shouted. With a growl, the dog launched himself as hard and as high as he could and sank his teeth into the man's wrist as it rested on the window ledge to steady the gun. The gun clattered to the pavement and fired.

"Ye-ow! I told you Chihuahuas were vicious!"

"Fool! Go after them!" the driver yelled.

Razzles took off as fast as he could go after Reynaldo into the woods. "This way! I know a place to hide."

Razzles took the lead, dodging tree roots and brambles.

When he reached the blackberry thicket where he had spent most of his time before Maddie took him home, he said to Reynaldo. "You'll have to crawl."

Razzles scrambled into the thick brush with Reynaldo close behind. Soon they huddled in the shadows under a heavy canopy of blackberry bushes.

"They must have gone into these bushes," the stranger's voice shouted. "Go after them."

"I ain't goin' in there," Mr. Square Head protested. "Those bushes are thorny and there's a vicious attack dog just waiting to get me."

"You fool! We wouldn't be chasing that bruja and her kid all over the country if you had done your job."

"How was I to know the kid's father would rat us out for a shorter time in jail? He's always been one of us."

"Yeah. Having a kid can screw up a guy's head sometimes."

"We could just shoot into the bushes and scare the kid out."

"If we kill him, we'll never get that statue. His old lady would go straight to the cops. You'll just have to man up and crawl in there."

Into the silence that settled between the two men came the noise of many feet trampling through the woods and voices calling Reynaldo's name.

"Damn. Sounds like the whole town is coming after the kid. Let's get out of here. We'll come back for the statue."

Reynaldo and Razzles huddled together. "Do you think they're really gone?"

"Let's wait just a while longer to be sure," Razzles said. "Miz Maddie will know where we are."

Soon enough, the sounds of voices and trampling feet were nearby. "Reynaldo! Razzles! Are you in there?"

When they emerged a few moments later, Reynaldo's mother threw her arms around her son. "I'm so glad you're safe! We heard a gunshot and thought..."

"Mr. Square Head wants the statue," Reynaldo said. "It must have drugs in it, just like you said."

"I'm sorry, Reynaldo. I know it means a lot to you because it's from your father, but we have to turn it over to the police."

"Those guys said Dad was in jail. Ratted them out because of me."

"He loves you." Felicia brushed Reynaldo's hair off his forehead. "But once you're in a gang, you rarely get out except when they kill you."

"So what do we do now?" Reynaldo asked. "Mr. Square Head said he would come back for the statue."

"I don't think it's safe for anyone at the shelter right now," Father Jacobs said. "I think we all need to find another place to stay."

"So Mr. Square Head did what the mayor couldn't—shut down the shelter."

"You can stay at my castle until it's safe to come back." Maddie addressed the group. "Even those of us who live there get caught unaware in some of my husband's security inventions."

"I know how you value your privacy—"

Maddie held up a hand to stop Father Jacobs' protest. "You've all become my friends, and taught me I don't always have to be in total control of situations. That it's okay to lean on others for help. You need to know our family is a bit eccentric to say the least, but I'd be honored if you would be my guests until it's safe to return to the shelter."

"Is this a real castle?" Jonathan asked.

"It's so cool there!" Keller's eyes danced with excitement. "Dungeon beds that creak when you lay down on them—"

"Ew!" J-J's nose crinkled. "I suppose there are hands that come out of the walls too."

"Great idea! Do you think Uncle Horace could invent that?" Keller asked.

"We might ask him," Maddie said. "But I have another bedroom I think J-J would prefer. It's fit for a princess and has lots of pink."

"Oh, wow!" J-J's eyes grew round with delight.

"Gather your belongings and let's go to the castle," Maddie said with a smile.

Leading the caravan of kids and parents to her home, Maddie wondered if she had done the right thing. The castle had always been a haven for her family. A place where they could feel free to be their eccentric selves away from the prying eyes of the rest of the world.

However, she couldn't turn her back on the children and parents who had become important to her.

With work on the cloaking device wrapped up and the time machine behind a curtain of invisibility, Horace was back to working on "normal" inventions such as the jet-pack. So she shouldn't have to worry about children being transported to another century.

They just needed to stop Mr. Square Head so they could survive in this time.

Chapter Seven

Keller leaned over the grate that opened into the dungeon below and strained to hear the lowered voices of the adults. With his mom sick so much of the time, he had pretty much always been the one in charge. He didn't like being shut out. When grown-ups decided, he ended up in foster care. He had just gotten settled at Miz Maddie's castle and didn't want to leave.

Now the adults didn't want to talk in front of the kids to keep from scaring them. To Keller, it was scarier not to know what was going on. Thanks to Mr. Razzles' keen nose, the adults couldn't sneak away. The dog and kids had followed the adults around the castle as they sought out private places to talk.

The fake dungeon tucked behind Horace's basement workshop was the site of their latest rendezvous. However, Keller had discovered he could hear sounds from the dungeon through a heating grate above it. So the kids and Razzles gathered around the grate. Thinking they couldn't be heard, the adults huddled amid a rack and a chair of torture in the dungeon and strategized how to best capture Mr. Square Head.

"If we turn the statue over to the police, what's to keep Mr. Square Head from shooting all of us?"

"So we have to keep the statue until we can put Mr. Square Head out of commission, right?

"Or make him think we still have the statue."

"I think we need an expert," Maddie said. *"It's time to call McGregor of Scotland Yard."*

"You know someone from Scotland Yard?"

"That's what Horace calls my niece's husband, which is another story. Ian is actually an MP in the military. Horace didn't want to drag him into the middle of other issues. But lives are at stake, so I think he's the perfect person to call."

"What's a Scotland Yard?" J-J asked.

"Not what. Who," Keller whispered. "They're the best mystery solvers in the world. If you can't figure something out, you call them."

"Wow! Miz Maddie knows Scotland Yard and he's coming here?"

"Quiet! She's calling him now." Keller put a finger to his lips.

"...make copies of the statue in the replicator, then hide the real statue. But where?"

"...in plain sight? It's so ugly I don't want it on my mantel—wait, we can put it in the time machine! The cloaking device made it invisible, so no one can see anything inside."

"...um, yeah. After a few days of things disappearing and reappearing at random, Horace seems to have perfected it. You want to talk to him about that when you get here? I'll let him know. Any other suggestions?"

"... yes, of course! Holograms of security guards inside the castle and on the grounds are a wonderful idea. It will look like we have a small army. Or maybe we should use Chihuahuas. Mr. Square Head is afraid of them. Anything else?"

"...don't do anything foolish until you arrive." After a slight pause, Maddie said, *"That could be more challenging than anything else."*

"Wow! Miz Maddie has a time machine hidden by a cloaking device. Just like in the movies!" Keller said.

"What's a cloak'n'vice?" J-J asked.

"A cloaking device makes things invisible," Reynaldo said.

"Like a superhero!" Jonathan said.

"Maybe we should look for it."

"I don't think so," J-J said. "What if we turn invisible and can't come back?"

"Miz Maddie said things reappeared—after a while."

"This is my fault," Reynaldo said. "If I had told my mom about the statue right away, maybe Mr. Square Head would already be in jail."

"Or maybe he would have taken the statue and shot everyone so we couldn't tell," Keller said. "I'm going to take Mr. Razzles outside."

Reynaldo, J-J and Jonathan followed Keller and Razzles outside.

"What's over there?" Jonathan pointed to the far corner of the castle yard.

"We have to stay in the inner courtyard," Reynaldo said. "Or we won't get to come outside at all. Not until Mr. Square Head is in jail."

J-J took Jonathan's hand and led him back to where Keller was playing with Razzles. However, Jonathan continually wandered over to the stone fence and peeked through the arched openings. "That dog disappeared!"

J-J gave a long-suffering sigh and stalked back over to the fence to fetch her brother.

"Now's he's coming back!" Jonathan pointed to a little white dog who did indeed seem to be appearing a bit at a time from the tip of his pointedly alert ears to the tail curled over his back.

"Oh my!" J-J gasped.

"What are you watching?" Reynaldo asked.

"That little white dog just appeared out of nowhere." J-J pointed through the fence.

"The cloaking device and the time machine," Keller said.

~ * ~

Though there was no sign of Mr. Square Head for several days, the adults kept close watch over the children. So they had no time to sneak away to the far end of the castle yard and further explore the cloaked time machine.

However, with the adults, the kids were allowed in the outer courtyard to play soccer or baseball. They even talked Father Jacobs into wearing his Superhawk costume on occasion.

One day Uncle Horace joined them outside, a rare event to be sure. Keller wished he could visit the older man's basement workshop, but Miz Maddie absolutely refused. Not wanting to upset her, Keller contented himself with fantasies about what mysterious inventions Uncle Horace was working on.

Today, Uncle Horace revealed one of them. He headed straight toward Father Jacobs, who was wearing his Superhawk costume. "Ah, you're here to help me test the jet-pack."

"I'm what?" Father Jacobs seemed baffled.

"You're the test pilot for my jet-pack. You want to fly, don't you?"

Father Jacobs hesitated, glanced at the wings of his costume, then nodded.

"Here you go." Horace handed him what looked like a double diving tank with criss-cross straps that formed a seat and extended over the shoulders. "Step into the seat, then adjust the shoulder straps."

"How do I control it?"

"The buttons on the waist strap. Ignition to start, hover to hover—" Horace grinned. "And jet power gives a burst of speed upward."

"And what button makes it land?"

"Haven't quite figured that out yet..." Horace meandered off, muttering to himself.

The kids were eager to help Father Jacobs put on the jet-pack. After he was securely strapped in, he said, "Okay, back away now."

As the children moved back, the priest pressed the ignition button. The jet-pack rumbled to life, and a grin spread across Father Jacobs' face.

He pressed the hover button, but the device simply hummed. With a slight frown, he briefly closed his eyes and made the sign of the cross, then pushed the jet power button.

The good Father shot upward.

"Spread your wings and fly!" His audience on the ground shouted. In response, Father Jacobs began flailing his arms.

"What's he doing?" Dorinda asked.

"Trying out Uncle Horace's jet-pack," Ryan said. "A victim of his own fantasies, I believe."

She watched him for a moment. "He doesn't seem to fly very well."

"Wait till he gets to the landing part. That should be even more challenging."

"Oh dear." Dorinda slipped away from the group.

While the others were busy watching Father Jacobs in his attempts to soar, Keller noticed a small green-clad figure appear from behind a tree and zoom upward. She soon joined Father Jacobs where he bobbed rather drunkenly in the air.

"Spread your arms." Dorinda demonstrated by reaching her arms wide. "The wind will lift the wings of your costume and help you stay in the air."

"How do I hold the control button with my arms spread?" Father Jacobs shouted back.

Dorinda shrugged.

But the good Father gave it a try, with one arm spread and the other on the hover button of the waist strap. Except he began spinning in a circle rather like a rowboat with one oar.

"Try to land and ask Horace to fix a hand control," Dorinda shouted.

They were all so engrossed in watching Father Jacobs try to fly they didn't notice the dark-suited man sneaking along the fence until he shouted, "I want the statue!"

The group froze for a moment, then turned to stare at Mr. Square Head.

"Bring me the statue or I start shooting."

"I'll go get it," Ryan said. He returned a few moments later and held up an ugly statue. "You mean this one?"

"Yes!"

"Come and get it."

Mr. Square Head made a dive for Ryan, who disappeared into thin air. The man roared and spun around, waving his gun at the others.

"Get the children to the time machine," Maddie whispered to Daphne. "No one will be able to see them." The parents made a protective line between Mr. Square Head and the kids.

"Or maybe it's this one." One of the parents tossed a statue at Mr. Square Head.

When he jerked to catch it, his gun went off, blasting the statue into pieces.

"A fake!" he roared.

"Then try this one." Someone else tossed a statue to one of the other parents, and the group of them tossed it around like a hot potato.

"Enough!" The thug roared and pointed his gun at them.

At least the children were safe, Maddie thought.

And the gunman seemed to realize that at the same time. "Where are those brats? I'm going to shoot 'em all."

"Thought you wanted the statue." Father Jacobs in his costume and the jet pack zoomed past the thug, knocking him off balance. His gun clattered across the ground and one of the parents grabbed at it.

The thug roared again and made a dive for his gun. They clonked heads—hard. But the thug didn't seem to notice. He grabbed the gun and ran after Superhawk, shooting wildly.

"Throw me the statue!" Dorinda flew by in her elfenchaun form.

They tossed the statue back and forth until the thug's gun clicked empty of bullets. But then the jet-pack sputtered before it roared back to full speed. Sputtered again and roared.

"What's happening?" Father Jacobs yelled as he spiraled downward, straight at Mr. Square Head.

The man looked up and his eyes grew as round as the "O" of surprise framing his mouth. The priest crashed into Mr. Square Head and knocked him against the invisible time machine, then tumbled over and over across the lawn until he came to rest against a hedge.

Father Jacobs lay for a moment trying to catch a full breath of air while Dorinda fluttered down beside him. "Are you okay?"

"Just...stunned...for...a...moment..."

Horace hurried over. "I think I've figured out how to land with the jet-pack."

The priest managed a weak smile. "I'm not sure I want to fly any more..."

~ * ~

Maddie added one last brush stroke to the words, "Hawk's Haven," beside an image of Father Jacobs in his Superhawk suit. Nearby, a small green elfenchaun fluttered on the mural, and a painted little dog that looked strikingly like Mr. Razzles sat on the ground watching them through his goggles.

The sign mural that would be attached to the side of the homeless shelter was finished!

The parents and children standing around began to clap and cheer.

Little Jonathan began to clap also—until he spotted the paints, momentarily unwatched while everyone else celebrated. With a mischievous grin, Jonathan dipped his hands into the paint and ran toward Maddie, adding his colorful handprints to the other paint splatters on the shirt that had been white at the start of the project.

Though surprised at first, Maddie quickly began to laugh. Encouraged, Jonathan ran to others, patting his hands on their paint shirts.

When he reached Daphne, she bent down to say something to him and he struck—leaving handprints on her chest.

"Oh!" Startled, Daphne straightened up as Jonathan ran toward his daddy, who had been trying to catch him.

Brenner stared at the handprints on Daphne's breasts. His mouth dropped open. "I—ah..."

Jonathan squirmed in his dad's suddenly loosened grasp and ran across the yard, giggling once again.

In slow motion, Brenner closed the distance between himself and Daphne. "I might as well do something I really need to apologize for."

He dipped his hands in the paint, slipped his arms around her and gripped her derriere, lifting her slightly so his mouth fit perfectly over hers. When he released her to once again chase after his son, the perfect prints of his paint-covered hands branded her backside. And Daphne stood, stunned, her fingertips resting lightly against her lips.

"Jonathan's disappeared again." J-J braced her hands on her

miniature hips in disgust.

"I'll get him this time," Ryan said.

The children watched as Ryan walked through the gate and disappeared. Soon afterward, he emerged as if walking out of a wall, holding Jonathan's hand.

"I was in the fire hydrant house again." Jonathan's eyes glowed huge with excitement.

~ * ~

With Mr. Square Head in jail, Father Jacobs, the children and their parents returned to the homeless shelter. Though Maddie usually loved the privacy of her castle, the silence settled heavily in her heart.

Dinner that evening seemed unnaturally quiet, though Rissa and "McGregor of Scotland Yard" had arrived to visit. After a brief hello to her daughter, Daphne retired to her suite of rooms.

After dinner, Ian McGregor and Horace retreated to the basement workshop to talk about a deal with the military for the technology to both the time machine and cloaking device, as well as a pair of goggles that allowed the wearer to see objects that were cloaked.

While Rissa talked to her brother, Maddie took a plate of food to Daphne. In response to her rap on the door, Daphne responded with a quiet, "Come in."

Maddie set the food on a table and settled on the bed beside Daphne. "We missed you at dinner."

Silently, Daphne nodded.

"Do you want to talk about why you're so upset?" Maddie asked.

After a pause, Daphne said, "I haven't been kissed since my husband died."

"Did you like it?"

"I think so." Daphne touched her lips again.

"That's good then."

"But the kids saw and..." Daphne lifted her tear-filled gaze to look at Maddie. "I'm so embarrassed. I don't think I'll be able to face them again."

Maddie couldn't help it. She laughed. "Of course you will. Just pretend nothing happened."

Daphne stared at Maddie for a long moment. "But it did. Brenner's kiss changed everything."

"Change isn't necessarily a bad thing." Maddie patted Daphne's hand and left the room. "Think about it."

As Maddie was leaving the room, Brenner appeared in the hallway, clutching a fist full of wild flowers.

"Here." He thrust the flowers at Maddie. "Please tell Daphne I'm sorry."

But Maddie didn't take the flowers. "Make your own apology. Face to face."

When Maddie reached the end of the hall, she paused and looked back. Brenner was still standing in front of Daphne's door holding the flowers. Well, it was up to the two of them to work this out.

~ * ~

Think about it. That's all Daphne had done since Brenner kissed her. She never thought she would be interested in another man after her husband died. Yet Brenner occupied her thoughts like the pompoms clinging to her poodle skirt.

For the first time in over twenty years, excitement about a man swirled through her body, awakening hormones and emotions that had long lay dormant.

And panic.

After weeks of waiting for the man to ask her on a date, he had swept her into his arms and kissed her. No warning. No asking permission. Simply awakening her like some fairy tale princess, then...he ran away.

Daphne sighed.

A hesitant knock sounded on her door. Her sister again, Daphne supposed, with a further argument of why she should attend the May Day celebration at the homeless shelter. Well, perhaps she would let Maddie talk her into attending after all. "Come in."

Chapter Eight

After a moment, the door edged open. A fist full of flowers slowly appeared, then a man's arm and his head peeking around the door. Brenner slowly edged into the room, rather like reappearing out of the cloaking device.

He handed Daphne the flowers. "I've come to apologize for Jonathan's behavior with the paint."

"And your behavior?" Daphne asked.

The man hesitated. "I could say I'm sorry, but I'd be lying."

He paced for a while, then stopped and clasped both of Daphne's hands in his. "Things are a little rough for us right now, but they're going to be better. I have a job waiting and a place to stay with my sister. The kids and I—we just stopped here to earn enough money to get us to Las Vegas. This may sound crazy, but..."

Brenner turned away and scrubbed a hand through his hair. "This *is* crazy, but I'm going to ask anyway. Will you come with us?"

Daphne stared at the man. Was this the way modern romance progressed? From nothing to driving into the sunset together? "I've never been away from my family."

"But your kids are grown now and have lives of their own."

Foolish as it seemed, Daphne actually considered the idea. Brenner hadn't become a father until he was in his forties, so he wasn't much younger than she. But what about his children? "I'm not sure I can be a mother. Maddie and Horace raised my children while I was lost in a time warp. What if—what if I mess up your kids?"

"You won't." Brenner grasped her hands again. "I've seen you with the kids. You're a natural mom."

"For a few hours a day. Then I hide away from the real world in my room. I couldn't even get a job."

"If you come with us, you wouldn't need to work. You could be with the kids while I work and they wouldn't have to be with a sitter."

Reality edged away the fantasy that had been building in Daphne's mind. "So I'd just be a nanny for your children?"

"No, of course not. I want to be with you. We'd be a family."

"I haven't heard you mention marriage."

Brenner froze as panic slid through his eyes. "Well, maybe someday...in the future I'll be ready to...do that again."

And there was the bottom line. Sadness drifted through Daphne. She had so hoped... "Your children are beautiful. And your kiss gave me hope I could find love again."

Daphne touched her lips, remembering. "But my values wouldn't allow me to live with a man without benefit of marriage. I just couldn't."

She forced a smile. "If you'll excuse me, I'm going to retire now."

~ * ~

The next morning when Maddie appeared in the kitchen for breakfast, Daphne wasn't there. Ryan just shrugged when she asked about his mother.

Maddie walked down the hallway to Daphne's door and knocked softly. When Daphne bade her come in, Maddie opened the door slowly, not sure what to expect.

Daphne sat at her vanity, wearing a poodle skirt and a cashmere sweater, teasing her hair into a nineteen-fifties hairdo.

"Why are you doing this?" Maddie asked.

"I'm a failure as a modern woman. I figure I might as well go back to an era I can handle."

"Are you going to come to the May Day celebration today?"

"I think not." Daphne considered her freshly polished fingernails. "I don't want to ruin my manicure."

Maddie's feeling the apology from Brenner did not go well was reinforced when she arrived at the shelter for the grand opening celebration. "Where are Jonathan and J-J?"

"Gone," Reynaldo replied. "Went to stay with their aunt."

In spite of the celebration, the children were subdued, perhaps reminded how temporary their lives were by the departure of the two red-haired siblings.

"This is supposed to be a celebration," Maddie said.

"It's not the same without Jonathan and J-J," Keller replied.

Maddie gathered the children around her. "Jonathan and J-J went to live in a new home. Isn't that what you all want? A home of your own?"

"Well, yeah." The children reluctantly agreed. "But wouldn't it be nice to live at your castle so we could all play together?"

The wistfulness in their eyes matched that in Maddie's heart, but she knew their wish wasn't very realistic. "Just because we live in different places doesn't mean we can't still keep in touch and maybe get together once in a while. In fact, after the official ceremony, let's go back to the castle and have our own party. What do you think?"

The suggestion brought smiles and nods of agreement.

"Now let's all wear a smile for Father Jacobs. This is his big day." Maddie pasted a cheesy smile on her face and the kids laughed.

At least they seemed a bit cheered up and gathered around Father Jacobs as he introduced his painting crew.

"I'd like to thank everyone for coming out on this beautiful May Day to help us celebrate the start of a new Chapter in Watermark. That of helping people in dire circumstances make a new beginning. A new job. Friends to support them. A home of their own."

"Over the past few weeks, some very special and creative young people have been working on something that represents these dreams. I'd like to introduce my young painters..."

After Father Jacobs introduced each of the children in turn, he continued, "And now, drum roll, please. I invite everyone to feast your eyes of the magnificent mural these talented painters have created."

As the parents rolled out the pieces of the mural and set them side by side, the mayor jumped up on stage. "No! There are no homeless people in Watermark! We're the most livable city in Oregon. In the entire United States. I'll be grand marshall of parades in every city. I'll be hailed as a model for mayors everywhere. Waterford will be a city without crime. Without pollution. Without homeless people."

The crowd whispered and moved away from the Mayor.

"Leroy, stop that right now. You're making a scene." His mother stomped onto the stage and took his arm, but he shook her off.

"Yes, a scene. And I am the star." He threw back his head, lifted his chin and strutted forward. "I am the emperor. All my minions will do my bidding without question."

"Oh, for pity's sake, Leroy." His mother grabbed him by the ear and dragged him toward his sedan.

Mr. Square Head followed. "Wait a minute. I want my money."

"How did he get out of jail?" Maddie whispered.

Father Jacobs shrugged.

Leroy's gaze swung to Mr. Square Head. "You can help make this dream come true. You can stop the grand opening of the homeless shelter."

"I need that money for my therapy sessions. The doc understands about Chihuahuas. Everyone else just laughs."

"Yes." The mayor seemed to drift off again. "Chihuahuas. Fine animal. Rather like alpacas, aren't they?"

Mr. Square Head grabbed the mayor by both arms and shook him. "Chihuahuas don't have hooves, you fool! They're big, hairy beasts with fangs and claws, and they fly about like giant birds."

"You're crazy." The mayor's mother swatted at Mr. Square Head. "Let go of my boy."

"I need money for therapy."

"You certainly do." The mayor's mother shoved her son into the car and slammed the door. Then she climbed into the driver's seat and sped away, as Mr. Square Head ran after them.

The children giggled, their moods obviously lightened by the mayor's antics. This mood carried over to the celebration at Maddie's castle a short time later.

As soon as they burst over the drawbridge, the celebration began. Once again, Horace came up from his workroom to join in.

"Let's show everyone your new goggles." Horace placed another pair of goggles on Mr. Razzles, then stepped back and smiled.

Razzles tipped his head and took a few tentative steps.

"So what do you think?" Horace beamed proudly.

"He seems a little unsteady," the teenager, Devon, said.

"What's different about these goggles?" Maddie asked.

I don't think things are supposed to be this way, Razzles said to Maddie.

She took the goggles off Razzles' head and looked through them. "Ooh. Everything is upside-down."

"But I thought—drat it all." Horace took the goggles and disappeared down the stairs toward his workshop.

Then Keller looked around and asked, "Where's Miss Daphne?"

"Let's go see if she's in her sitting room," Maddie suggested. She led the children down the hallway like the Piped Piper and knocked on Daphne's door.

Wearing full nineteen-fifties costume, Daphne opened the door.

The children stared at her for a moment, then Maddie said, "Miss Daphne is ready for a costume party. How about the rest of you?"

Once more, Maddie led the children down a hallway to a large room with several trunks of old clothing and hats. Keller found a pirate's hat and spyglass. Reynaldo discovered an old baseball uniform, mitt and autographed ball. Devon found a leather jacket and fake tattoos that made him look like a truly bad party boy. His mother shook her head and smiled. "I love you just the way you really are."

Everyone laughed and acted silly, until Keller uncovered a tiara. "J-J could have been a princess."

Then sadness at missing J-J and Jonathan threatened to overcome them all again.

"Let's draw pictures of each of us in our costumes and send them to J-J and Jonathan," Maddie suggested. "And maybe they'll send us pictures of their new home."

But as they were gathering paper and paints to do that, Razzles began barking. *They're here! They're here!*

"Who's here?" Maddie asked.

Come and see for yourself! Razzles led the children down the hallway and out onto the circular drive in front of the castle, where Jonathan, J-J and their father were getting out of their vehicle.

A stream of cheers and hugs greeted them.

But Daphne paused beneath the archway and waited. Part of her wanted to rush forward and throw her arms around Brenner and his children. Part of her feared being a fool again.

When Brenner spotted her, he hurried over the cobblestones with a spring in his step and a smile on his face. He stopped in front of her and took both of her hands in his. "I couldn't leave you. Let's get married and be a real family."

Daphne stared at him. Was that what she wanted? A whirlwind marriage to a man she barely knew? What if he suddenly decided he didn't want to be married and just drove away again? Then she would be left alone and broken-hearted, without even a poodle skirt to comfort her.

"Perhaps some day we'll both be ready for that." Daphne's comment brought disappointment and bewilderment to Brenner's face. "However, I think I should complete my college degree and find a career that suits me. Then after a proper courtship and suitable period for an engagement, we can decide if we want to be married."

A smile slowly formed on Brenner's face, then took Daphne's hand. "In the meantime, will you save a slow dance for me?"

Amid cheers of the others, Maddie said, "Now come on inside. The party is just beginning."

Epilogue

One year later...

"I now pronounce you husband and wife." The new mayor, CatherineLee, smiled at the couple. She had been elected after the former mayor, Leroy Brasman, was sent to the mental hospital, where he was now sharing a room with his henchman, Mr. Square Head.

Then Father Jacobs added, "You may now kiss the bride."

This time when Brenner kissed Daphne, he didn't run away afterward. He took her hand and walked toward the time machine, now painted with tall trees hanging over a stream edged with flowers.

"Don't forget to drop Reynaldo and his parents off in 1951," Maddie said. "They can enjoy a time before gangs and drugs took over the inner city streets."

"Got my statue too," Reynaldo said. "Ian made sure the police drilled a hole extra careful so they didn't destroy the original when they took out the drugs. And thanks for letting us use the time machine so my dad can be safe from the gang. They're not happy he got out of jail when they went in."

Maddie hugged the boy. "Be sure to ask your mom to take photos of you and your dad playing baseball."

"I will. And thanks—for everything." Reynaldo waved, then climbed into the time machine where his parents were waiting for him.

I'm going to miss him, Mr. Razzles said to Maddie.

"I don't think we've seen the last of Reynaldo and his parents," Maddie said. "By the way, how are you seeing with your new goggles?"

Razzles grinned. *Perfectly! I get to play with Keller every day in our new house Brenner helped build—right next to J-J and Jonathan.*

"And Daphne will be moving in when she and Brenner return from their honeymoon. She finished her counseling degree and planned a wedding in the same month. I think she's arrived as a modern woman."

"Speaking of arriving, Miz Maddie, when do we start our next mural?" Teenager Devon came to stand beside Maddie and blow bubbles at the time machine as Daphne and Brenner spun away.

"Be at the city hall at seven Monday morning. Our new mayor wants to update some walls inside."

Devon flashed a thumbs-up. "By the way, my mom's thinking of giving up her parties to get married. Seems she and Daphne have been talking a lot."

"Are you happy about that?"

"Well, I think I'll still hang out with Father Jacobs at the homeless shelter. He's doing pretty well at flying with the jet-pack. He seems to like being a superhero. By the way, what invention is Uncle Horace working on now?"

A loud boom shook the windows of the castle and Maddie ran toward the house. "I'm not sure, but it seems to be explosive."

The end...for now.

Also by the authors
at
Rogue Phoenix Press

Catching Meara
By Christine Young

Meara Thorton was a feisty, world-class computer hacker—cornered by the FBI and shockingly given the chance to be their newly acquired technical analyst. Brilliant and intuitive, yet aching with the loss of everyone she has cared about, her restless heart led her to discover a love she fought and a world she didn't know could possibly exist.

Jace McKenna was an enigma, a loner, impossibly handsome, sincere and committed. The Apache shapeshifter blood running through his veins burned hotter than the blistering Sierra Madre sun. Jace knew the moment he caught Meara's scent she was his for eternity.

Jokers Wild
By C. L. Kraemer

Four brothers raised in the Northwest.

Two choose to stay and pursue life in Oregon. Two are seduced by the promise of Hollywood.

Life throws the Palmer brothers an ugly curve when two are killed in preventable accidents. Even more upsetting is the lack of justice in the trials of the perpetrators.
The remaining brothers will find justice using a shared passion of all the participants—motorcycle poker runs.

Everlasting Love
Book three in the Forest Ridge Series
By Rosemary Indra

When Miranda Cummins borrows a friend's cabin to finish writing her long overdue book, she's surprised to find the one-room retreat already occupied by Kevin Mathews. Though she feels a spontaneous attraction for Kevin, Miranda has recently escaped a controlling husband and isn't ready for a long-term relationship.

Unsatisfied with his occupation, Kevin is at a crossroads. Miranda understands and encourages him to look at the direction his life is going. Fired up by her encouragement, Kevin returns to Forest Ridge to resume his firefighting career.

When Miranda is threatened by her ex-husband, Kevin realizes he will do anything to protect her. Miranda has shown Kevin a new passion for life. Can he fan the flames of passion into an Everlasting Love?

Shadow of the Legacy
The seventh book in the Legacy Series
By Genie Gabriel

A letter from his dead father and a confession of killing a woman throws a shadow of suspicion over the life of an easy-going cop. When he returns to his hometown to find the truth, he discovers secrets that have held the town hostage for decades, danger that threatens his life, and love with a woman determined to be no more than friends.

Buy these books and check out all the books by these authors at:
http://www.roguephoenixpress.com

www.ingramcontent.com/pod-product-compliance
Lightning Source LLC
Chambersburg PA
CBHW071443170626
46811CB00007B/2470